The Long Shadow

MARK MILLS

**headline
review**

First published in Great Britain in 2013
by HEADLINE REVIEW
An imprint of HEADLINE PUBLISHING GROUP

First published in paperback in Great Britain in 2014
by HEADLINE REVIEW
An imprint of HEADLINE PUBLISHING GROUP

3

Cataloguing in Publication Data is available from the British Library

ISBN 978 0 7553 9234 6

Typeset in Bembo MT Std by Palimpsest Book Production Ltd, Falkirk, Stirlingshire

Printed and bound in Great Britain by Clays Ltd, St Ives plc

Headline's policy is to use papers that are natural, renewable and recyclable products
and made from wood grown in sustainable forests. The logging and manufacturing
processes are expected to conform to the environmental regulations of
the country of origin.

HEADLINE PUBLISHING GROUP
An Hachette UK Company
338 Euston Road
London NW1 3BH

www.headline.co.uk
www.hachette.co.uk

Mark Mills graduated from Cambridge University in 1986. He has lived in both Italy and France, and has written for the screen. His debut novel, *The Whaleboat House*, won the 2004 Crime Writers' Association Award for Best Novel by a debut author. *The Savage Garden* was a Richard and Judy Summer Read and a No. 1 bestseller. *The Information Officer* was shortlisted for the 2009 CWA Ellis Peters Historical Fiction Award. He lives in Oxford with his wife and two children.

The Long Shadow was published in 2013 to critical acclaim:

'Mark Mills has shown that he is a writer of real psychological acuity – but there is one area he has made his own: the untrustworthiness of appearances, and the pitfalls for those who make no attempt to look beneath seductive, attractive surfaces . . . his most richly textured work yet'   *Independent*

'Part psychological thriller, part mystery, this stylish tale . . . [is] extremely readable'   *Sunday Mirror*

'Enthralling . . . The author's gift for an elegantly turned sentence is fully and generously in evidence'   *Daily Express*

Praise for Mark Mills:

'A master storyteller'   *Val McDermid*

'Clever, original, subtle and stylish'   *Observer*

'A compelling, vividly rendered slow burn of a book which culminates in an electrifying climax'   *Guardian*

For Caroline, Gus and Rosie

There are souls more sick of pleasure than you are sick of pain.
G. K. Chesterton

thirty-one years before . . .

SOME MEMORIES TAKE on a dreamlike quality with time: illusory, yet somehow more real than anything the waking world has to offer.

This is one of those memories.

Jacob and I are trudging up the steep pathway that skirts the abandoned chalk pit, the fresh snow squeaking in protest beneath our rubber-booted feet. He is leading the way – it's a point of honour with him – and I am behind, dragging the old sledge my grandfather built me just before he died, almost his last living act. Overhead, through the bony canopy of branches, the sky is cloudless, enamelled, a preposterous blue.

As the path levels off, the trees fall away and we find ourselves at the lip of the chalk pit. (Someone has since put up a chain-link fence; back then, a lone strand of rusted barbed wire was all that prevented unwary ramblers from plunging to their doom.)

We stand there, peering down into this deep scoop out of

the hills, our eyes narrowed against the blinding glare of the low morning sun, our breath rising like steam from our lips. We come here in the summer to hurtle down the scree slope at the head of the quarry in cardboard boxes, but today that same slope is shrouded in a thick white blanket and the chalk cliff rising above it seems strangely dull, almost dirty against the virgin snow which fell so un-expectedly last night.

'Hey, I've got a great idea!' says Jacob.

I know he's lying, making it up as he goes along. It's a control thing. He's always having 'great ideas', playing the Pied Piper, obliging the rest of us to abandon our best-laid plans.

'Oh, yeah? What?'

'Ah, wait and see.'

The sly look doesn't fool me. He's winging it. I don't mind too much. The shallow, open pasture just to the west of where we're standing – the slope we'd planned to sledge – offers few thrills for a couple of twelve-year-old boys. Besides, before long every Tom, Dick and Harry from the village will be there; not forgetting Darren Hodges, who hates us because we go to private school and have 'our fucking thumbs stuck up our posh arses'.

We trudge on, ever upwards, taking the bridleway which branches off and winds through the woods above the chalk pit. I want to challenge Jacob; I know that everything from here on up is unsledgeable, far too steep or treacherous, and he must know it too. I say nothing, though, curious to see how he will talk himself out of the corner. I can see his mind at work, especially when we leave the trees and find ourselves in the open.

His eyes scan the blinding white sweep of hillside above us. It's not vertical, but not far off, and the bridleway is obliged to cut a diagonal path across it, climbing sharply as it goes, forming a sort of raised causeway flanked by a deep ditch on the uphill side and a near-sheer drop on the other. I know from my father, who has heard it from others, that it's an ancient droving trail, possibly Neolithic in origin.

As we approach the top, breathing hard now, Jacob turns suddenly and thrusts an arm back down the bridleway. 'Da-da!'

He announces it as though he's had it in mind all along, when in fact he has simply run out of options.

'Are you mad?'

'Are you scared?'

'No,' I lie. 'But I know something you don't.'

Not only is the bridleway too steep, narrow and uneven to hold a speeding sledge, but the slopes plunging away on either side of it are not nearly as innocent as they appear. The National Trust has recently taken over this section of the Downs, and last autumn a band of volunteers spent more than a month felling and burning the young trees colonising the hillside. I know that beneath the deep snow lie hundreds of slender stumps, like sharpened stakes. If we lose control of the sledge and go off the side—

'But we won't,' interrupts Jacob.

'Well, I definitely won't, because I'm not going to do it.'

'Chicken,' he grins.

It's the ultimate insult, but I don't care, because I'm thinking: now that he's said it he's going to have to go through with the thing. And I'm worried for him, really worried.

'I don't care if you kill yourself,' I say. 'But I'm not going to have you smashing up my grandfather's sledge.'

He doesn't take the bait, the face-saving excuse I've just offered him.

'Chick- chick- chick- chick- CHICKEN!' he clucks, his face inches from mine.

I want to press my palm to the leering mask and push him away. I don't, though; I calmly hand him the orange nylon baler twine attached to the sledge and say, 'Go ahead. Just as long as I can have your watch.'

The watch is a Seiko diver's watch: day, date, rotating bezel, not just water-resistant but waterproof, the works. It's a gift – well, more of a bribe – from his hopeless, absent parents, and Jacob knows I've always coveted it.

He smiles, amused. 'Sure. It's yours. And I promise not to haunt you when I'm dead.'

He decides that sitting astride the sledge is best. Then he changes his mind and lies on his front, his chest flat against the wooden struts. He can use the toes of his wellington boots to guide him and slow his descent.

'What do you think?' he asks, and in the quick glance he throws me over his shoulder I see the first signs of fear in his face.

'I think it's too steep. I think once you're moving nothing's going to slow you down.'

'There's only one way to find out.'

And with that, he pushes off.

My first reaction is to look away, down to my right, where the Sussex Weald rolls off into the far distance, a frosted winter wonderland. But my eyes are drawn swiftly back to the bridleway.

It has only been a matter of moments, but the sledge is already travelling at eye-watering speed, its wide runners enjoying the dry, crisp snow. Surely it can't go any faster? But it does, picking up even more speed.

Jacob is using his feet to hold his line, and he's making a fine fist of it. My God, I realise with a surge of relief, he's going to do it! Just another hundred yards or so before the bridleway levels out at the woods. Yes, he's going to make it, and I am never going to hear the last of it, not that this stops me emitting a triumphant 'Yeehaaa!' on his behalf.

As I do so, the sledge suddenly lurches to the left – the runners must have caught a rut beneath the snow – and although Jacob recovers, he overcompensates. I look on in impotent horror as the sledge slews back across the bridleway and over the edge, into the wide white void.

He seems to hang in the air for an eternity before gravity finally seizes him, claiming him. He drops more than twenty feet in the blink of an eye and is swallowed up by the snow.

He couldn't have lost control at a worse spot. A year ago there was a dense copse of saplings right where he has just landed, and I find myself running like I've never run before.

Twice, my legs fail to keep up with the gradient and I tumble forward into the snow. Twice, when I scrabble to my feet, there is still no sign of Jacob. Only when I reach the spot where the sledge left the track and took to the air do I see him.

He's lying far below me, spreadeagled on his back, as if frozen in the act of performing a star jump. The impact of his fall has disturbed the snow around him and I can see a sapling stump cut off at a cruel angle and pointing heavenwards right beside his neck. I see another one pushing through the snow near his left hip. And two more between his legs, one at the very fork of his thighs.

They're everywhere, and I know instinctively what this means. It's the reason he isn't moving; it's the reason his eyes are closed.

I'm not sobbing as I slide down the slope towards him; it's more of a low moan, a sound I've never made before. Where it comes from, I don't know, don't care. To my shame, I'm already thinking that I'm going to get the blame for this: 'He did it to impress you . . . You must have known what he was like . . . You should never have let him do it . . . Why on earth didn't you stop him?'

With my father's words burning in my ears, I scrabble my way on all fours towards Jacob's body, feeling a path through the dwarf forest of hidden stumps. My bare hands are immune to the cold, but a strange numbness is spreading through my chest. It tells me that the world as I know it has changed forever.

He looks so peaceful lying there that for a fleeting moment I dare to imagine that the God he doesn't believe in has spared him. He could almost be smiling.

My heart lurches.

He *is* smiling.

And now his right eye is open, fixing me with an amused light.

He sits up – not transfixed on a stump – and slowly takes in his good fortune. He's like a knife-thrower's assistant at the end of the act. Death bristles all around him. A few inches either way would have done for him.

'Well, holy shit.'

His father is American, and he has always had an impressive range of expletives to prove it. My personal favourite is 'Fuck me sideways'.

Jacob's wild laughter is ringing off the hillside now.

'No!' I shout in anger, silencing him. 'No!'

I wade through the snow to recover the sledge, which has sunk almost out of sight.

one month to go . . .

EVEN AS HIS fingers groped for his BlackBerry on the
bedside table, Ben knew it was Stella because he'd
assigned her number its own ringtone: 'Ride of the Valkyries'.
It had to be six months since he'd last heard Wagner's stirring
masterpiece blaring from the phone.

'Stella,' he said, rolling on to his back.

'Are you still in bed? I can't believe you're still in bed.'

So much for the spry, I've-been-up-for-hours note he'd
tried to inject into his voice.

'I was working late.'

'Putting the finishing touches to that script you promised
me by Easter?'

'How did you guess?'

'*The Bourne Identity* meets *Rosemary's Baby*.'

'I don't remember describing it that way.'

'No, but I did, to almost every producer in town. And
many of them were . . .' She couldn't find the word.

'Mystified?' suggested Ben.

'Intrigued. Eager to read it.'

'I'm almost there. Another few weeks. A month at the most.' A tired mantra. The truth was, he'd ground to a halt on page seventy-six of the script and was still groping for a third act. For the first time in his career he was well and truly blocked.

'Are you touching yourself?'

Ben wasn't sure if he'd heard her right. 'Excuse me?'

'You sound like you're touching yourself.'

'Well, I'm not!' he lied.

'How's Madeleine?'

He could see the rapid little leaps her mind had made: Ben in bed . . . alone . . . touching himself . . . no sex life, poor thing . . . no *any* life . . . and certainly no wife, because she'd left him.

'She's coping,' said Ben.

Stella gave an amused snort. 'I bet. Still with the banker boyfriend, is she?'

'Last I heard.'

Which had been last night, on a crackling line to St Lucia, where Madeleine and Toby were on holiday at some swanky resort with Lionel and his two kids.

'And Toby?' inquired Stella.

'Toby's good.'

Toby was a sacred subject; he hoped she trod carefully.

'How old is he now?'

'Thirteen.'

'Voice broken?'

'Not yet.'

'Hair down there?'

'Where?'

'Where you're touching yourself.'

'For God's sake, Stella, I am not bloody touching myself, OK?'

'Hey, when did that famous Makepeace sense of humour go south? Relax, or I won't tell you why I called.'

'Let me guess – you're putting up your commission to fifteen per cent.'

'No. Not that fifteen per cent of nothing makes a blind bit of difference.'

'Remind me,' said Ben. 'How did I end up with you as my agent?'

'Because no one else would have you after that stroppy old queen at PDR let you go. And because I'm young, ambitious and bloody good at my job, as you are about to discover.'

'Fire away.'

He tried to sound casual, but these, he knew, were the moments that mattered. A phone call could change everything. Unemployment, penury, boredom, lethargy, all could be banished by a few words.

'I've had a bite,' announced Stella. 'A big bite. *Gangs on an Island.*'

It was the working title of the spec script he'd raced off last summer, and he now wished he'd taken the time to come up with a proper title, one that was a little less, well, self-explanatory.

'Who?'

'You don't know him.'

'Who does he work for?'

'Himself.'

Ben felt his excitement leaking away. An independent producer, probably young, wet behind the ears, and almost certainly with no financial backing of any note. Soho was awash with them right now.

'Don't tell me, he's looking for a free option.'

'I threw twelve thousand at him and he didn't even flinch.'

'Twelve thousand?' In the current market, that was cheeky.

'Plus another eighteen for a polish.'

Eighteen was bloody brazen. Added to twelve, it made thirty: more than the national average wage, even after Stella had siphoned off her commission.

'And a polish means a polish for once, not a rewrite. He thinks the script's in great shape, it just needs the odd tweak here and there.'

'Odd tweak' was a phrase that would usually have set alarm bells ringing, but Ben's thoughts were elsewhere. He was thinking about his ailing motorcycle which needed replacing, and about booking a break somewhere special for him and Toby at the end of August. It was going to be a great summer.

'Ben?'

'I love you.'

'Don't go spending it yet. He wants to meet you first.'

'Just say when and where.'

'Tomorrow afternoon. Oxfordshire.'

'Oxfordshire?'

'Is that a problem?' said Stella, hardening. 'Tell me that's not a problem.'

'No, no.' He gave a little chuckle. 'God, I'll hitch if I have to.'

'That won't be necessary. He's happy to send a car for you.'

They sent cars for actors. They sent cars for directors. No one sent cars for writers.

'He must be new to the game,' observed Ben drily.

'He is. His name's Victor Sheldon. He's an American hedge-fund whizz based over here. He's been sniffing around the film business for a while, looking for the right project to become involved with, and *Gangs on an Island* is one of the scripts he's settled on.'

'One of the scripts?'

'You expect him to put all his eggs in one basket? Name me one producer who does that. Look, our friend could bankroll the movie himself if he wanted to, without a second thought. I've checked him out. We're not talking millions, or even tens of millions. We're past the hundreds, way off the scale. And you, *mon cher* Benjamin, are getting in at the ground floor. For God's sake, for *your* sake, impress him, please him, *work* him. Who knows where this could end? Maybe one day you'll look back at this moment and realise everything that went before now was only a preparation, an apprenticeship . . . yes, a necessary apprenticeship for your break into the big time.'

It was a couple of seconds before Ben spoke.

'God, you're good.'

He meant it. With a few choice lines of complete bullshit she had somehow managed to lend his life more shape and purpose than it had enjoyed in a long while.

'Damn,' said Stella. 'I am, aren't I?'

The house was a four-floored affair in St Leonard's Terrace, just south of the King's Road. Set far enough back from the street to allow parking for two cars (as well as a token patch of lawn), its brick frontage was smothered by an ancient wisteria, like some mutant vine, that trimmed the tall windows with dense green foliage. Ben would have preferred a rendered façade – he was a sucker for white stucco – but that minor misgiving aside, it was exactly the sort of London townhouse he and Madeleine had always dreamed of owning.

It ticked all their boxes: size (large but not ostentatious); location (Chelsea); orientation (south-facing); outlook (a park across the street with mature trees, tennis courts and even a cricket pitch). It seemed inconceivable now that such a house had once lain within their grasp. If only Ben's screenwriting career had fulfilled its early promise; if only both of them had been prepared to mortgage themselves to the hilt, not just Madeleine; if only Ben had agreed to trade in the shares inherited from his grandfather for bricks and mortar. Too many 'if onlys', but not so many that they hadn't almost made the leap north of the river in the 1990s.

Instead, they had stuck with their south London existence, living sensibly, within their means, in a cramped Victorian house which hovered on the fringes of Camberwell. Ben had recently checked the Land Registry records online, and he knew that such caution, *his* caution, had cost them something approaching four million pounds in real terms. This was the difference between the money they'd made on the house in Camberwell at the time of their divorce and the profit they would have made if they'd taken the plunge eighteen years ago and were currently living in a house in St Leonard's Terrace, say.

Four million pounds – more than enough to see out their lives. He could picture their comfortable dotage: a leisurely downsize to an apartment the moment Toby left home, add on a charming bolt-hole in the Cotswolds to ease the strain of city life and stir the creative juices for the plays and novels Ben would be writing by then, and they'd still have close to three million pounds in their back pockets, tax-free, thank you very much.

Given the level at which most people lived, it felt a bit obscene to be thinking in such sums – it *was* obscene – and yet he also felt justified in doing so, because calculations like these lay at the heart of his failed marriage. During their years in Camberwell every newspaper article proclaiming the relentless rise in London property prices had been another rod for Madeleine to beat him with. His prudence had held them back. They'd blown their chance. They should have had the courage to leverage themselves in a rising market. As it was, Ben's common sense had consigned them both, all three of them, to a half-life south of the river.

It was hard to fault Madeleine's line of argument, and not only because she had the silky tongue of a natural-born lawyer. The evidence was in her favour. His one defence, which had seemed entirely plausible at the time, was that he was happy in Camberwell. He loved their ramshackle house; he loved their street with its mad mix of ethnicities; and when Toby came along – finally, their tiny miracle – Ben loved the fact that Sunday morning football in the park meant watching his son stumbling about a pint-sized pitch with kids of every colour and creed. In fairness to Madeleine, she had also appreciated these things, but as a staging post to a more genteel world where people didn't run a key down the side of your car for the hell of it ('It's just a car'), and she could chain up her Piaggio in the front garden without fear of it being stolen by a pack of hoodies with bolt-cutters ('It's just a scooter').

Ben wished no ill on Liz Hurley, but when the actress was robbed at knifepoint in broad daylight in the heart of Kensington by four schoolgirls, he had seized on her misfortune as proof of the perils which lurked in even the smartest districts of London. That was back in 1994, the year they should have taken the plunge and traded up, the year they would have traded up if Ben hadn't been so unadventurous, so bloody set on doing the sensible thing.

There was no denying it, he was a fool to have mistrusted Madeleine's instincts, and as he guided his motorcycle off the street into the flagged forecourt of the house in St Leonard's Terrace, the familiar twinge of envy he always experienced when coming here was swiftly overlaid by an altogether different emotion: magnanimity. He found he was happy for Madeleine that she was finally living in the sort of house she had always dreamed of.

Such heart-warming, self-aggrandising generosity of spirit was not unconnected, he supposed, with the phone call from Stella an hour ago.

Toby had insisted. 'Dad, I just don't trust Basil with anyone else.'

Basil was no name for a rabbit, let alone a female rabbit, but Basil it was. She had yet to be spayed, and as Ben reached inside the hutch to chivvy her out into the run she sank her teeth into the back of his hand.

He yelped, recoiled, the blood already flowing. 'Oooh, you little bitch!'

'Excuse me!' came an outraged Lady Bracknell voice from beyond the brick wall separating the back gardens.

'Not you,' said Ben.

'I should hope not.'

The wall was too high to see over, but he could hear the woman watering her garden with a hose.

'The rabbit bit me,' he explained feebly.

'Good for the rabbit. Three cheers for the rabbit,' came back the disembodied voice. 'That poor thing, cooped up in a cage when it should be running free.'

Bizarre. The voice brought to mind a no-nonsense killer, a woman who'd spent a goodly portion of her life blasting pheasants out of the sky with a twelve-bore.

There was nothing more to say, the conversation had run its awkward course, and Ben made for the house to deal with his hand.

The kitchen was a cold chapel, a shrine to unsparing

minimalism, its travertine worktops free of clutter. There was almost nothing on show: no kettle, no toaster, no chopping board, no unsightly condiments beside the hob. Even the taps at the sink looked like intruders. There was certainly no kitchen roll to be seen. He found it eventually, tucked away in one of the tall sliding cabinets lining the walls, by which time he had stippled the polished-concrete floor with blood.

'Shit.'

He wiped away the alien spots of colour then ran his hand under the tap, watching the blood spiral away down the plughole. The woman next door would have been proud of Basil; the vampire rabbit had done a good job. It looked as if someone had made two neat, deep incisions in the back of his hand with a scalpel. Did Basil have a gap in her front teeth? Was she the Vanessa Paradis of lop-eared rabbits?

He tore off a few sheets of kitchen roll. Pressing them to the wound, he turned and surveyed the room. He had never made it beyond the kitchen. On the two occasions he'd been invited to dinner, drinks had been served in the garden, the meal in the dining room, which flowed effortlessly towards the front of the house from the kitchen, uninterrupted by anything as unsightly as a load-bearing ceiling joist. One cuboid space, perfectly proportioned by some architect or other. Ben struggled to square such a rigid and obvious aesthetic with the man who had commissioned the work.

There was nothing rigid or obvious about Lionel. He was a warm soul with an engaging air of shabbiness about him. He was also ferociously bright, witty and well-read. As Ben had said to Madeleine after first meeting Lionel, while she was walking him to his taxi out front: 'Christ, I'd fuck him myself if he wasn't already taken' (which Madeleine had found very amusing, not realising it was a joke he'd lifted almost verbatim from a Pinter play).

No, he bore Lionel no rancour. Toby liked him, with a few reservations sweetly cobbled together for the benefit of his father. More importantly, Lionel had played no part in the demise of Ben and Madeleine's marriage. That was dead and done for, sealed with divorce papers, before Lionel even showed up on the scene. In his darker moments, though, Ben still fantasised about what he would do if the nameless, faceless Frenchman who had seduced Madeleine in Amiens ever crossed his path. Everything had sprung from that one incident, or rather, from Madeleine's subsequent failure to carry her dirty little secret in silence. Even now, he could feel the bitter, open ache, dulled by time but still there.

It was the legitimate search for a sticking plaster that led him upstairs, permitting him to snoop as he went. The double drawing room on the first floor was a thing of wonder, a tribute to Lionel's love of books, music and art. Lionel's taste was for postwar British painting and sculpture. Was that really a Peter Lanyon canvas hanging above the fireplace? The signature certainly suggested so. He didn't need to check the abstract bronze figure on the Scandinavian sideboard to know it was an early Kenneth Armitage. And that was unmistakably a Peter Kinley oil of a female nude on the wall beside the built-in bookcase.

The place was an Aladdin's cave, and Ben made a slow,

reverential tour of its treasures: Bernard Meadows, Keith Vaughan, Elizabeth Frink, Patrick Heron, Michael Ayrton. No wonder Madeleine had never brought him up here; almost all the artists he most admired were represented. It was good to know she still had his feelings at heart, but irritating to think that she, who had never much cared for his private passion, was the one now living with such gems when the most he had ever been able to stretch to was a bunch of monographs and a Terry Frost screenprint.

A large Ivon Hitchens landscape filled the wall beside the baby grand piano, which stood at an angle near the windows overlooking the back garden. Ben tried to picture Toby seated before the keys, practising for his Grade 4 exam, which he'd recently passed with a Merit. All that came to mind, though, was their tatty old upright, with its chipped veneer and its moth-eaten hammers, jammed up against the panel radiator in the hallway of the house in Camberwell.

On prominent display between the two windows was a large black and white photograph. It showed Lionel and his wife — what was her name again? Sophie? Yes — stretched out on the floor of some photographer's studio with their son and daughter. For all its luminous beauty, it was a sobering image. Ben searched Sophie's face for signs of the rare form of bone cancer that would suddenly carry her off. There was nothing in her large pale eyes or her melting smile that suggested she wasn't long for the world. She exuded a honed and toned vitality. Her face was unlined and her long blond hair had an almost liquid lustre to it. She was — she had been — a beautiful woman.

Ben was taken with a sudden impulse to turn on his heel and leave. It wasn't the artworks taunting him from all quarters; he could cope with those, as well as the other fine trappings of Madeleine's new life. It was finding himself face to face with Lionel's terrible loss that unsettled him. Madeleine's willingness to take on this challenge, to say nothing of the two troubled teenagers thrown into the bargain, suggested a depth of feeling that he struggled to associate with their own relationship.

It suggested he had held Madeleine back in more ways than he cared to think about.

thirty days to go . . .

Ben passed up the offer of a chauffeur-driven car, tempting though it was, choosing instead to make the run out to Oxfordshire on his motorcycle. It served another purpose beyond that of simply transporting him to the meeting.

Gangs on an Island was the sort of film script that could have been written by someone half his age, and probably should have been. He needed to stake a claim for his future involvement in the project, because the moment he banked the option money he would effectively lose control of the script. They would be perfectly entitled to bring in some hot young thing to rework it, obliging him to share the writing credit and thereby give up half of the principal photography payment should the film ever get made. And that's where the real money lay.

Yes, he was the wrong side of forty, but not by much, and certainly not in spirit, he wanted to say. He was the sort of guy who still had his finger on the pulse, his ear to the ground. Hell, he was the sort of guy who would never pass up the chance of a wild thrash up the motorway on his trail bike.

He barely got above 60 mph on the M40, sticking to the slow lane, jammed in with the lorries, riding their slipstreams. He told himself he was in no hurry, but he knew the real truth lay elsewhere. It was a while since he'd hit the open road on the Honda, and he found himself plagued with unnerving thoughts. He knew the engine was burning a bit of oil, but what if it suddenly seized? What if he hadn't retightened the nut properly after adjusting the chain, and even now the spindle was working itself loose, the back wheel about to fall off? And why did the ground rushing by beneath his feet look so close, so granite-hard, so bloody menacing?

He'd once ridden all the way to Sicily and back without any such concerns ever occurring to him. Another time he'd made a month-long loop through France and had never once felt the sharp pain coming at him in waves, lancing his stomach. He hoped it wasn't terminal, the creeping caution that comes with age, the same anxiety that had rendered his parents all but housebound.

He only began to relax once he'd left the motorway at Junction 8 and was wending his way through the countryside east of Oxford. He remembered a couple of the villages from his student days at the university, when he and his friends would strike out from the city in search of pubs with edible food, a far harder thing to come by in the late 1980s than it was now. And as he passed by those same pubs, with their designer graphics and their Farrow & Ball facelifts, he wondered what his younger self would have made of him cruising past on his motorcycle

The story might have caught his fancy: a 43-year-old man desperately in need of the grace and favour of another 43-year-old man who had somehow managed to pull away from the herd, amassing a vast fortune in the process. One of the few things Ben had been able to glean from the internet last night was that he and Victor Sheldon were the same age. That was about the extent of it, though. Sheldon was clearly a private individual who shunned publicity. The only photograph he'd found on the Web was one taken of the back of his head at a charity bash held at the Grosvenor House Hotel, where City types outbid each other for the privilege of having dinner or going skydiving with some 'celebrity' or other. It sounded like a dating service for the movers and shakers of the moment, a pairing of beauty and hard cash. *Plus ça change.* A banker bedding a soap star was no different to an Edwardian aristocrat falling hard for a West End chorus girl. Besides, what did it really matter if many millions of pounds had been raised for good causes, as they had been?

The internet had also furnished a satellite image and several photographs of Stoneham Park, Victor Sheldon's Oxfordshire home. None of them did justice to the stately Palladian pile, which nestled in a low valley on the fringes of a village to the north of Oxford, beyond Woodstock. The Victorian gatehouse was a later addition, its fussy

Gothic stonework a poor herald for the elegant eighteenth-century buildings which stood at the end of the long driveway, beyond gently rolling parkland studded with towering oak trees.

In its simplicity, the main house was much as a child might have drawn a palace. It rose clean and four-square, unencumbered by any wings or pavilions, with a double staircase that climbed one floor to a grand entrance flanked by Ionic columns and topped by a vast pediment that broke the roofline.

At the foot of the staircase was a fleet of large cars. Most were black, with tinted windows, and they brought to mind a clandestine meeting of Mafia dons. Ben guided the motorcycle between a Range Rover Evoque and a Mercedes saloon then cut the engine. He tugged off his helmet and ran his fingers through his hair, scratching life into his tight scalp. Pressing his lips to the petrol tank, he muttered a 'Thank you' – an old ritual borrowed from his mother's wayward brother, Uncle Peter, the man responsible (guilty, his parents would have said) for getting him into motorcycles in the first place.

Directly across from the main house, on the far side of the gravelled forecourt, was another building with an open yard at its heart, entered through a tall archway. It seemed strange that the architect, to say nothing of his client, hadn't chosen to place the stable block out of sight. Why not tuck it behind the stand of chestnuts off to the right, along with the other outbuildings? Presumably because they had felt there was no shame in presenting the machinery of the estate to visitors. It must have been a conscious decision, and that in itself was intriguing.

'Hello.' Ben turned to see a woman hurrying down the main steps towards him. 'You must be Ben.'

'Yes.' He shrugged off his leather jacket in time to shake the strong bony hand she offered him.

'I'm Annabelle, Mr Sheldon's assistant.'

It was hard to judge her age — anywhere between fifty and sixty, he guessed. There was something pinched about her smile which suggested she'd felt the prick of the dermatologist's needle before now. Her straight blond hair, neatly bobbed just above the shoulder, also looked like it might have received a helping hand to rid it of any grey.

'Did you have a good trip?'

'Yes, not bad.'

'Well, it's certainly the day for it.'

Her outfit was a picture of easy elegance: a crisp white cotton poplin shirt worn over a navy blue pleated skirt which wasn't afraid to show off her fine legs. He might have been mistaken, but there was something in her cut-glass accent that hinted at Cheltenham by way of Dagenham.

'Come, you must be parched.' She guided him towards the steps with a light and unexpected touch at his elbow. 'What can I get you? Chef makes his own lemonade.'

'That sounds great.'

'Oh, it's better than great, it's to die for.'

'What an amazing place,' said Ben, following her up the steps.

'Not three years ago. Dry rot, wet rot, rising damp, a

leaking roof . . . you name it, we had it, and in spades. This is our first summer in the house. The builders only left in February.'

The 'we' and the 'our' were telling, possibly intentional, it occurred to Ben. He also wondered if she would have used either word if Mr Sheldon had been present.

'Did you get the message?' Annabelle asked as they breasted the steps.

'Message?'

She stopped and turned to him. 'From Stella. I phoned her to warn you as soon as I knew.'

'I haven't checked my phone since leaving London.'

'Oh dear. You see, I'm afraid Mr Sheldon has been held up, delayed on business.'

'Oh . . .'

He allowed a note of scepticism to creep into his voice. Was this the big brush-off? He'd had them before, the most memorable being one in Los Angeles some years ago. It had been his very first meeting in the City of Dreams, and on that occasion the minion dispatched to deal with him, to offer him a consolation cappuccino before sending him on his way, had been just as charming.

'With any luck he should be wrapping things up right about now, and the plane is ready and waiting at Dinard airport.'

'Dinard? In France?'

She smiled her tight smile. 'It's not as bad as it sounds. The flight time to Oxford airport is under an hour, then another twenty minutes or so to get him here.' She paused. 'He's very keen to see you. I do hope you can hang on.'

Not a brush-off, then. 'Of course.'

'Excellent,' said Annabelle, ushering him inside.

After the glare of the front steps it was a moment before his eyes adjusted to the cool gloom of the entrance hall. It was a vast room with a floor of smooth stone flags and a ceiling of elaborate stuccowork. At the far end, a marble staircase climbed towards a landing, where it divided before turning back on itself. The wall above the landing was filled with what appeared to be an enormous stained-glass window backlit by the sun. It was in fact a monumental butterfly piece by Damien Hirst, its vibrant colours picked out by some unseen spotlight.

Ben must have been staring like an idiot because Annabelle asked, 'You recognise it?'

'An excellent fake.'

She laughed approvingly.

It was one of only three artworks in the room. The other two were almost as large: a pair of Warhol 'Electric Chair' silkcreens which faced each other from the side walls, where they hung against the putty-coloured paintwork above a matching pair of gilt rococo divans upholstered in yellow damask. It shouldn't have worked, this clash of ancient and modern, and yet it was as if the intervening centuries didn't exist.

'Here, let me take your helmet.' She relieved him of it and indicated one of the pedimented doorways on the right. 'Make yourself at home in the saloon. I'll be right back.'

The same counterplay of old and new, then and now, was in evidence in the saloon, although the overall effect was less stark, more homely. The wooden floorboards were wide, irregular and of a deep honey-coloured hue, and there was more clutter on display, even some magazines on the low glass table in front of the yawning fireplace. The library ran off the saloon. He was about to start snooping through the tall bookshelves when Annabelle returned with a tray.

She also had business to attend to – 'Bills to pay, you know, always bills!' – and she suggested that Ben take a stroll around the estate to kill time. 'You can't go wrong. We're ringed by a drystone wall.' He was welcome to go rowing on the lake, but it was best to keep out of the fields fenced off for cattle. The cows had calved recently and were at their most aggressive. Just last week, one of the farm workers had been forced to take refuge up a chestnut tree. 'If he hadn't had his mobile with him he might still be there now,' she chuckled.

The lake was close by, beyond the parterres and flower borders of the formal gardens at the rear of the house, which were reached by a double staircase identical to the one out front. Nothing about the lie of the land suggested that the large body of water should be there, and many backs must have bent themselves three centuries ago to excavating it. Wide and long, its far end was lost to view beyond a wooded promontory. A little way along the shore stood a large stone-built boathouse. It had clearly just been renovated, and would look better once it had weathered down. The same was true of the timber jetty beside it, where a couple of small rowboats were tethered.

Ben clambered warily aboard the smaller of the two,

slipped the oars into the locks and cast off, ignoring the life jackets lying in the bilges. One in the eye for Health and Safety, he mused. Given the way the world had gone, there was probably a European directive from the pencil-necks in Bruxelles empowering the British police to prosecute for such an infringement, but out here he was safe.

He was nearing the middle of the lake when his mobile rang. It was Annabelle, and she had some bad news. Mr Sheldon's business meeting in Dinard had run on.

He had time to weigh his options as he made his way back to the house, but there was really only one course of action open to him.

'I'm afraid I have to get back to London.'

'But he'll definitely be here in time for an early supper,' Annabelle assured him. 'And he says you're more than welcome to stay the night. It'll save you the drive back in the dark.'

'That's very kind, but I have to feed my son's rabbit.'

'Excuse me?'

'He's on holiday and there's no one else to feed her. I really do have to get back.'

He didn't bother to explain that Toby was paranoid about urban foxes, which he was convinced were quite capable of nosing their way beneath Basil's run, which was why she definitely needed to be locked safely away in her hutch by nightfall. Nor did Ben explain that he took a photo of Basil on his phone every evening which he then sent to Toby's phone so that he could gaze upon Basil over lunch in St Lucia.

'Are you sure that's wise?' asked Annabelle.

Ben bristled at the note of warning in her voice. 'I'm not sure "wise" comes into it. It's just the way it is, the way it has to be.' He almost asked her if she had children of her own, but something about her suggested she didn't.

'As you wish,' replied Annabelle curtly.

She didn't accompany him to his motorcycle; she didn't even watch from the top of the steps; she headed back inside the house the moment she'd shaken his hand and wished him a safe journey home. This was no bad thing, because he overdid it on the choke and couldn't get the Honda started. After a few minutes of kicking away like a demented donkey he took time out for a breather, pulling off his helmet and wiping the sweat from his brow with the back of his glove.

'You've flooded it,' came a voice from behind him.

It was a woman, but that was about all he could determine. Dressed in what looked like a parachute jumpsuit, she had some kind of industrial face mask pushed up high on her forehead, and she was coated from top to toe in white powder, as if someone had emptied a sack of flour over her head. A roll-up cigarette smouldered between the fingers of her left hand.

'Yes, I know,' said Ben. 'Thanks.'

'You should let it stand for ten minutes.'

He wasn't good on accents but there was definitely a touch of something northern in there.

'Five usually does it.'

'Time enough for a smoke,' she said, pulling her tobacco pouch from a pocket.

'I've given up.'

'Patches?'

'I'm sorry?'

'Hypnosis? Acupuncture? Alan bloody Carr?'

'No, I just decided to stop.'

'Just like that?'

'Yeah, after I'd chewed off my fingernails and put on a stone.'

A smile flitted across her face. 'Still carrying it, are you?'

'Uh-huh.'

'Must have had one scrawny old arse.'

'Not so old.'

'If you say so, Grandad.' She was enjoying herself now, and so was he, which was why he was a little put out when she carried on her way, up the main steps. 'I hope you get it started.'

'Thanks, I'll try not to pop a hip.'

She gave a little laugh as she climbed towards the entrance.

There were two texts waiting for him on his phone when he got back to London. Both were from Stella. The first read: **A fucking rabbit!** The second was even more concise: **Twat!**

Annabelle must have been in touch with the agency. Somehow he couldn't see Victor Sheldon calling from Dinard, or from thirty thousand feet above the English Channel, or wherever the hell he was.

Ben texted Stella back: **A human being would understand**. A few minutes later he received a reply: **Puh-lease! If I wanted to be one of those why did I become a film agent?**

It brought a smile to his lips. Stella's sense of humour had always redeemed her. Her next communication arrived an hour or so later. Basil had just been photographed and locked away for the night in her hutch with a bowl of nutritious pellets when his BlackBerry pinged: **Dear loser, I just salvaged your career. Lunch with Victor Sheldon at the Wolseley tomorrow. 12.30. Wear a jacket. Don't fuck it up. Archie says you will.**

Archie was Stella's boyfriend, a hulking ex-public school boy who had proudly flunked every exam he'd ever taken, obliging him to fall back on the one attribute no one could deny him: his extraordinary height. He was always pulling you close to drive home the point, or patting you on the head, or talking about the air being 'thin up here'. He had somehow made a small fortune in carbon trading, choosing to mark his success by treating himself to a Range Rover Sport last autumn. The irony of this purchase was entirely lost on poor Archie. Or rather it had been until Ben, foolishly and a little drunkenly, had pointed it out while Archie and Stella were running him home after a London Film Festival bash at the South Bank.

Whatever you thought of Range Rovers, you couldn't fault their braking system. The massive vehicle had stopped on a sixpence, right in front of the most notorious housing estates on the Vauxhall Road, as luck would have it, and once Ben had been ejected from the car, it then tore off into the night as rapidly as a Porsche.

Ben suspected that the only reason he'd lived long enough to flag down a passing taxi was because the pods of young men lurking in the shadows had taken him for some lieutenant being dropped off by his drug lord boss.

twenty-nine days to go . . .

I<small>T WAS A</small> short stroll from the Royal Academy to the Wolseley, and as Ben weaved through the pedestrians on Piccadilly he thought about the other short stroll he would make after lunch – to the London Library in St James's Square, just around the corner from the restaurant. Here he would sleep off the meal in one of the leather chairs in the Reading Room, assuming they weren't already occupied by the usual motley bunch of old boys who snored and snuffled and, on occasion, farted their way through the afternoon.

The Summer Exhibition at the Royal Academy had been a disappointment. The balance this year seemed to have swung even further in favour of good art over bad, a worrying year-on-year trend. The great pleasure to be had from this venerable British institution was viewing the execrable stuff submitted by members of the public and rubber-stamped for exhibition by the committee. Maybe crap artists were a vanishing breed, an endangered species, or maybe the truly atrocious ones were no longer slipping through the net. Either way, it was a concern worth raising with the RA's council.

He was still drafting the letter in his head when he arrived at the Wolseley. He had eaten at the restaurant once before, a dinner with Madeleine when they were still trying to patch up the tattered shroud of their marriage with weekends away at spa hotels and trips to the theatre and other 'bonding treats' (the ghastly phrase employed by their Relate counsellor). The sombre grandeur of the Wolseley, with its black marble columns and its high, vaulted ceilings, had a whiff of Stoneham Park about it, and it wasn't surprising that a man like Victor Sheldon favoured such a setting when it came to breaking bread (or cracking open a lobster).

The moment Ben gave the name of his lunch companion to the string-bean brunette at the front desk, the maître d' hovering nearby sprang into life. 'Don't worry, Melissa, I'll see to it.' He shimmied round the counter. 'Follow me, sir.'

Judging from the number of suits on show, lunch belonged to a wealthy business crowd, the sort of men whose bespoke tailors lay a stone's throw away in Jermyn Street. The country was supposedly in the grip of the worst recession since the 1930s, and yet you wouldn't have known it from the confident hum echoing off the hard surfaces.

The maître d' led him to one of the large tables round to the right. Intended for a large party, it was laid for only two. A smartly dressed man in a charcoal-grey suit and open-necked white shirt was already seated at it, his face buried in an iPad. He looked up and smiled. 'Ben,' he said, rising to his feet and offering his hand.

Ben was speechless. Could it really be?

He wasn't mistaken, because Victor Sheldon now turned to the maître d' and said, 'David, Ben here is an old friend of mine – Ben Makepeace.'

'I'll be sure to remember the name, Mr Sheldon.'

It was a public anointing, reinforced by the left hand which now gripped his shoulder. Ben sensed rather than saw that the spectacle had caught the attention of some other diners nearby.

'Two glasses of champagne, please, David.'

The maître d' nodded. 'Certainly.'

Ben didn't speak until they were alone and seated at the table. 'My God, Jacob, it *is* you.'

Victor Sheldon spread his hands. 'One and the same. Although I'd prefer Victor.' The English accent was gone, though not entirely, replaced by a mid-Atlantic drawl. 'If that's OK with you.'

'Of course, Victor,' said Ben, trying it on for size. 'You look so . . .'

'Different? Twenty-five years can do that to a man.'

So can a clever plastic surgeon, thought Ben. The teeth, the nose, even the ears, they were all different. 'I was going to say "well".' He wasn't lying. The subtle cosmetic refinements had been perfectly judged to smooth away the rough edges of a face which had once been characterful rather than conventionally handsome. A neat back and sides was all that remained of the trademark mop of unruly dark curls.

'You too. Annabelle was quite taken with you. And believe me, that's saying something.'

'She didn't seem so taken with me when I said I was heading back to London.'

Jacob smiled. 'No, she didn't get the rabbit thing. But I did. It told me you hadn't changed, that you were still a man of principle.'

'I fear I'm more Groucho Marx than that.'

'Remind me?'

Ben wagged his hand beside his mouth in a poor imitation of Groucho and his cigar. 'These are my principles. And if you don't like them, I have others.'

Jacob gave a sudden loud laugh. 'That's very good. I didn't know that one.'

The sommelier arrived, and they watched in silence while he opened a bottle of vintage Dom Perignon, filling two slender flutes before retiring.

Jacob raised his glass for Ben to clink. 'It's good to see you again.'

'Yes, it is.'

Jacob took a sip then placed his flute carefully on the tabletop. 'Anyhow, enough of the small talk. Tell me about this film script of yours.'

The sudden change of tone wrong-footed Ben. 'Sure. Right—'

'You ass!' grinned Jacob. 'Tell me about your parents, your sister. God, Emily, how is she? Tell me everything.'

'Tamsin, it's me – Ben.'

'Ben . . .' She sounded surprised.

'Look, I know it's short notice but I wondered if you were free for dinner tonight. I was thinking the Wolseley.'

'Wow, the Wolseley, I'd love to, but I'm sitting outside a bar in Santorini.'

'As in the Greek island?'

'That's the one.'

'Are you there with your sister?'

'Thanks a lot! Actually his name's Paul.'

Paul? They didn't know any Pauls. 'Internet dating?' he speculated.

'So what?' Tamsin replied defensively.

'And is Paul *the one*?'

'No, but he'll do for now.'

'I'm guessing he didn't hear that.'

'He's calling his kids.'

'And where are yours?'

'In Cornwall with Freddie's parents. Look, Ben, this call is costing you a fortune. Why don't you try Imogen? I know for a fact she'd sleep with you.'

'That's not why I phoned.'

'Yes, it is. *Kalí tíhi.*'

'What?'

'It's Greek for "good luck".'

She hung up before he could respond.

He pulled up Imogen's number on his phone, but his thumb hovered over the button, unable to commit. It suddenly seemed so sordid: the pariahs, the outcasts of their close group of friends, the ones whose marriages had collapsed, the ones who had betrayed the cause, now falling into bed with one another, not because they wanted to but because they could. Because, when it came to it, a roll in the hay, however empty of feelings or future prospects, was better than nothing.

God, it was ghastly.

He took a swig of beer then called his parents at home. They were in the garden enjoying their first gin and tonic of the evening.

'And to what do we owe this pleasure?' inquired his father.

He was tempted to give him both barrels there and then, but the last time he'd done that, two years of frosty silence had followed. Ben's sister Emily had finally knocked their heads together and brokered a reconciliation of sorts, but it remained an uneasy truce.

'I'm sorry, Dad. I've been flat out here for the past few weeks.' He silently cursed himself; he'd just handed his father the perfect cue for a snide comment about lying around in bed.

'Fruitfully, I hope.'

'Yeah, I've just sold a film script.'

'Congratulations. Let's hope this one actually gets made.'

You almost had to admire the old bastard; it was such a rare gift.

'I think it stands a pretty good chance. It's low-budget, which is the order of the day.'

'Not so low that there isn't some money up front, I hope.'

'No, and it's good money.'

He couldn't bring himself to say that the good money was coming from Jacob, who was now Victor Sheldon, who was still Jacob. It would have to come out, of course, but right now he couldn't face hearing the sudden lift in his father's voice, the shift in tone from weary scepticism to enthusiastic curiosity. He'd had a bellyful of that sort of thing when he was younger, from the moment Jacob first landed in their lives, like some cuckoo planted in a reed warbler's nest.

thirty-five years before . . .

Though not as attractive as some of its rival boarding prep schools, Dean House compared favourably enough. At its heart sat a large and labyrinthine Edwardian building that had once represented the full footprint of the school but out of which had grown by the late 1970s an unsightly sprawl of jerry-built extensions: a run of new classrooms, impossible to heat in winter, their walls barely thicker than cardboard; a tin-roofed chapel that looked like a barrack hut, as it might well have been in some former life; a dining hall with a flat felt roof that leaked; and a double-storey dormitory block of no architectural merit other than it hadn't fallen down yet.

What Dean House had over other schools, though, was land – more than an acre of good old Sussex woodland for each and every one of the three hundred or so boys in the school. Lost among the ancient chestnuts and beech was a string of lakes, black as polished onyx and linked by an ever-flowing stream. There was even a river, the Ouse, which jumped its banks in winter and whose snaking path marked the eastern frontier of the woods, beyond which lay the forbidden, overgrown pastures of 'someone else's land'.

This was the wild world waiting for them at weekends, a world entirely unknown to them on their first night at the school. It had been hell for Ben. Eight years old, away from home for the first time, and with a ghostly wind woo-hooing down the chimney at the head of his iron bed, he had held his teddy bear tight and stifled his sobs in his pillow. Most of them had done the same, though not all. There was one in their dormitory, Michael Kramer, who seemed to enjoy their weakness, even feed off it, regaling his silent audience with stories of his life in London and his older brother who had seen Bob Marley and the Wailers live in concert.

Jacob wasn't in 'Belfast', Ben's dormitory; he was across the hallway in another capital city of the British Isles, 'Cardiff', whose occupants thought themselves superior because at least they were part of mainland Britain. There were raids and pillow fights, and this is where Ben first got to know Jacob: on the battlefield, as a small but very determined opponent. This determination counted for less in the classroom, where Jacob struggled to the point of needing extra tuition – a weakness which some of the crueller boys were quick to pounce on. 'Thicko' Hogg – a nickname coined by Kramer – fared better on the sports field, although he didn't make the cut for the Under-9s first XI football team. This annoyed him. He thought he was good enough, which he wasn't, and he did himself no favours by harping on about it. Mr Burroughs, the headmaster, finally had to take him aside and give him a talking-to — the first of many ear-bendings, to say nothing of beatings, he was to receive during his time at Dean House.

Ben didn't really have much to do with Jacob until just before half-term. By now, Kramer had taken effective control of 'Belfast', using both his sharp tongue and his extra inches of height to intimidate and coerce. He had also raised up one of their number, Atkinson, to be his second-in-command: a baffling appointment, even for Atkinson, who was a scrawny boy with bottle-bottom glasses which counted against him in a pillow fight. While Ben was still building a shoe rack in Carpentry, Kramer had already finished his project — a small wooden church. He was immensely proud of it and kept it on the mantelpiece in the dormitory. One evening, a Friday evening, as they were changing into their pyjamas, Kramer suddenly hauled Ben's bed away from the chimney, clearing a space before it, before his beloved church.

He ordered them all to get down on their knees and pray to it. When Boswell pointed out that you didn't pray *to* churches, you prayed *in* churches, he received a Chinese burn followed by a half-nelson followed by a dead-arm — one of Kramer's fluid, trademark moves.

'Now get down on your knees, all of you!'

You didn't want to be the first to do it, but neither did you want to be the last, they all knew that.

'Dead-leg for the last one down!'

'Oh, shut up, Kramer.'

It just popped out of Ben's mouth, as if someone, something, had taken possession of him.

'What was that, Makepeace?'

'You heard me,' said Ben. 'Just shut up. We've all had enough of you. Haven't we?' He searched around him for support. What he got was a lot of boys staring at the floor, and Kramer advancing towards him with a cocky grin.

'Shut up or what, Makepeace?'

'I'll . . . I'll punch you in the face.'

'Oh, really? Well, be my guest.' Kramer had stopped walking, but now leaned towards him, pointing at his own nose. 'Hit me right here.'

It wasn't a sucker punch, not technically. Kramer had finished speaking before Ben's fist impacted with his nose, but only just.

Kramer's first mistake was bursting into tears at the sight of the blood. His second was running to Matron, screaming like a baby, because this brought him to the attention of every dormitory between 'Belfast' and Matron's rooms on the far side of the house, which was pretty much half the school.

The nose wasn't broken, and Kramer had asked for it, literally; there were witnesses happy, eager even, to testify to this fact. Matron also weighed in on Ben's side, but the headmaster still felt obliged to take action, not that he put his heart into it, and certainly not his arm. Six token strikes of a gym shoe, not nearly hard enough to leave a lightning mark on Ben's buttocks – the same lightning mark to be found on the sole of a Dunlop Red Flash plimsoll, Burroughs' favoured instrument of punishment ever since the school governors had banned caning.

Ben learned several things over the following few days, chief among them: that it only takes one brief moment to annihilate the authority of a bully. Kramer had gone from ruling his little roost with a rod of iron to being a figure of open contempt and, worst of all for him, ridicule. Ben also learned, as he watched six boys (including Atkinson, who knew which side his bread was buttered) stamp Kramer's precious church to splinters, that the vengeance of the put-upon can be a frightening thing. Less importantly, though not at the time, Ben learned that it felt good to have the senior boys give him a wide berth in the corridors while joking, 'Watch yourselves, lads, here comes Makepeace; and 'Keep your guards high.'

About a week later, as things were dying down, Ben was trudging back from football training when Jacob came hurrying up beside him.

'Great goal.'

Not really, it had been a tap in, and for a moment Ben thought Jacob was back to his old ways, about to start lobbying him about a move up to the first XI. But Jacob glanced over his shoulder, checking they were alone, before blurting out, 'Thank you, Makepeace.'

It was so heartfelt, so unexpected, that Ben almost stopped in his tracks.

'For what?'

'For what you did to Kramer. I just wanted to . . .' His voice petered off into silence.

'What?'

When Jacob looked up at him there was a glint of fire in his dark eyes. 'I hate Kramer.'

'Yeah, he can be a bit of a twit.'

'No,' said Jacob, 'I *really* hate him. And what you did . . . a *double* nosebleed . . .' He paused, frowning, as if unsure how to continue. 'Good job, Makepeace,' he said finally, holding open the swing door to the junior changing rooms. 'Good job.'

Half-term was upon them a week later. It was marked for the new boys and their parents by tea in the big drawing room reserved for special occasions. While the mothers and fathers stood around stiffly, chatting to each other and the masters, the boys were expected to circulate with trays of sandwiches, biscuits and cake. They wore their 'Sunday best': corduroy shorts, flannel blazers and school ties.

Ben's father was away on business – Geneva again, where he seemed to spend half his time – so only his mother attended. Maybe Ben was biased, but it seemed to him that she was the prettiest woman in the room by a mile. Tall and slender and with her dancer's poise, she had pinned back her blond hair, revealing her long neck. She spent most of the time talking to a man who stood out like a sore thumb, a man who made her laugh her high ringing laugh. This turned out to be Jacob Hogg's father.

He was the only man in the room not wearing a jacket or lace-up shoes. In fact, he wasn't wearing shoes at all. Beneath the wide flare of his velvet trousers you could see his bare toes poking out from his leather sandals. His smock-like shirt wasn't tucked into his waistband and his beard was as black as his long hair, which reached almost to his shoulders. To their young eyes he looked a lot like George Best, who was still every boy's favourite footballer, even though he was now playing for Fulham.

The most distinctive thing about him, though, was his accent. Had anyone known that Jacob Hogg's father was American? Ben certainly hadn't.

'Hey, Hogg,' said Harris as they were topping up their trays at the serving table (the 'Thicko' preface had been dropped since Kramer's crashing fall from favour). 'Is your dad a Yank?'

'Yes.'

'Why didn't you say?'

'Don't know,' shrugged Jacob.

But he did know, as they all did: in a place like Dean House, 'different' was just another reason to be worried.

Ben discovered more about Mr Hogg once he was in the car with his mother and heading for home. They had barely left through the school gates when she reached across and squeezed his bony knee.

'I'm so proud of you, my darling.' She smiled at his confusion. 'Mr Hogg told me what you did to that bully who was making Jacob's life hell.'

'But Mum, I didn't do it for Jacob.' He didn't know why he had done it – he wasn't a violent boy by nature – but he was pretty sure that Jacob Hogg hadn't been in his mind when he let fly with his fist.

'And modest with it,' said his mother, ruffling his hair. 'I'm very proud of you, and your father will be too.'

That was enough to secure his silence, to make him take

the credit and be done with it. Besides, his mother was still talking. 'He's an interesting man.'

'He looks like George Best.'

'Yes, I suppose he does a bit. He teaches at Sussex University. I imagine he's a leftie. Most of them are, there. But then why is he educating his son privately? That doesn't make sense. Maybe she insists – his wife, I mean. She's also an academic at Sussex. Anthropology, I think, or was it sociology?'

Most of it went straight over Ben's head, and anyway, she seemed almost to be talking to herself. He found his attention drifting towards the world passing by outside, the kaleidoscope of russets, yellows and ochres staining the autumn hedgerows.

'They're moving to America at Christmas.'

'The Hoggs?' That was news to bring him back.

'Yes, Boston. But only for a year. Jacob's going to stay on at Dean House. They don't want to disrupt his education.' Ben was still trying to figure out how that would work when his mother continued, 'They'll fly him to America for the holidays, but exeats and half-terms are out of the question. I offered to help out.'

Help out? What did she mean? He must have been frowning because she glanced over at him and added, 'You know, have him to stay with us. He seems like such a sweet boy.' When Ben said nothing, she asked, 'He is, isn't he?'

'Yes.'

What else could he say? That Jacob was OK? That he could be quite irritating? That they were hardly best friends?

'You don't mind, do you, darling?'

'Of course not, Mum.'

With any luck his father would put his foot down, kill off the idea. His father was good at that sort of thing.

twenty-four days to go . . .

BEN HAD NEVER known a deal to go through so quickly. Within ten days of the first call from Stella, a little over £18,000 had landed in his bank account, courtesy of Tortoise Pictures. The name was Jacob's wry nod to the notoriously slow process of getting film projects off the ground. Ben found this strangely comforting. He had brushed with enough dilettantes who talked a big game to know that most of them faded from the scene long before they ever got to tread the red carpets of their dreams.

The money cleared on a Friday, two days before Madeleine, Toby and the others were set to return from St Lucia. They would be landing on Sunday morning, tired and jet-lagged after a night flight, and Madeleine had texted to suggest that Ben wait until the Monday to see Toby. This fitted perfectly with his plans. Before leaving on a whistle-stop tour of the Far East, Jacob had invited him to Sunday lunch up at Stoneham Park, proposing that he also stay the night so that they could go through the film script in detail once the other guests had left.

Unsurprisingly, *Gangs on an Island* hadn't been the chief topic of discussion during their long and pleasingly liquid lunch at the Wolseley; there had been more than a quarter of a century of other news to catch up on. Nonetheless, Jacob's enthusiasm for the script had still shone through. He knew the story inside out, and his considered comments were couched in the reassuring language of a seasoned film producer. He spoke in terms of 'three-act structures' and 'character arcs' and 'dramatic beats'. Ben wondered at first if he wasn't simply parroting the opinions of the woman he'd recently appointed to head up Tortoise Pictures, but these cynical whispers were soon drowned out by the clamour of Jacob's undoubted passion for film. His terms of reference were extraordinary. He knew his stuff – he *really* knew his stuff – from the latest, yet-to-be-released Hollywood fare right through to obscure period films by eastern European directors. ('You haven't seen *Ashes and Diamonds*? You have to see *Ashes and Diamonds*'.)

Jacob had been keen to point out that his foray into film production was more than just a hobby for him. He was in it for the long haul. 'Which probably makes me a fool. I've looked hard at the business, I've even had one of my best people model it, and film is a mug's game, no two ways about it. But the first real money I ever made came from betting against the research. Not that I'm in it for the money. The most I'm hoping for is that Tortoise pays its way. That'll do me just fine. If I was in it for the money I'd stick to what I know, what I do already.'

'And what exactly do you do?' Ben asked.

'I make rich people richer.'

'That simple?'

'I wish. It's a whole lot easier to make them poorer.'

The reply was typical of him: wry and self-effacing. Victor Sheldon was a quite different creature from the Jacob Hogg of Ben's youth. The burning need to assert himself was gone. He seemed almost embarrassed by what he had achieved. He certainly appeared uncomfortable discussing it, ascribing his success to lucky timing and the vision of two colleagues who had lured him away from the merchant bank in New York where they had all worked and into the hedge fund business.

'I was a company man at heart, happy to draw my salary and bank my bonus every year. I thought they were reckless. I only went with them because I heard I was about to be fired. Turned out later it was a rumour they'd whipped up to force my hand.'

'They must have seen something in you.'

'Sure, someone to do the heavy lifting, the nuts-and-bolts stuff, the number-crunching. It's very mathematical. In fact, we just took on the top maths and philosophy graduate from Oxford this year. Personality of a three-toed sloth but, boy, has she got a brain on her. We weren't the only outfit fighting to get her, but we won the auction. You know what clinched it for us? We bought her parents the bungalow of their dreams in Worthing.'

'You're kidding.'

'It was cheap at the price, maybe one-tenth of what she'll earn in her first year with us. But she appreciated the gesture.'

'I bet she did.'

'She even cried. Her parents had worked their fingers to the bone to give her the kind of education they never got, and she paid them back in a moment, not even twenty-two years old, just like that.' He clicked his fingers. 'Imagine how that must have felt, for all of them.'

'You old sentimentalist.'

'Maybe,' shrugged Jacob. 'But also a pragmatist. I knew her family story from her tutor at Balliol, and I used it to get her.'

There was nothing self-congratulatory in his tone, just a take-it-or-leave-it honesty which permitted Ben to ask, 'And what did her tutor get for his troubles?'

'A very fine meal at Le Manoir aux Quat'Saisons. Oh, and some funding for a "research project".'

Their laughter was quickly forgotten the moment Ben inquired about Jacob's own family. 'And your parents? How are they? Where are they? Still in the States? Still teaching?'

'That's a story for another time.' The catch in his voice and the dark look in his eye suggested more than just a token resistance to Ben's curiosity. The subject was evidently off limits, for now at least.

Unlike the wild divergence of their career choices, their private lives shared an uncanny number of similarities: both divorced, both currently single, both fathers to one child – boys of a similar age. Marcio was a touch older than Toby. He lived in Paris with his Brazilian mother, Luciana, an ex-model whom Jacob had married after a shotgun romance during New York Fashion Week in 1994.

'We had five wild years before Marcio came along . . . the best of my life by far. The next five were the worst. Not Luciana's fault. She's a great woman. Always was. And still so beautiful. You can't imagine how beautiful. I really screwed up.'

Jacob's willingness to detail his failings as a husband, to shoulder the blame for the slow souring of the relationship, not only surprised Ben, it drew a similar candour from him.

He couldn't help thinking that it must have been an unedifying spectacle – two middle-aged men licking their wounds in between mouthfuls – but there was no denying that it also felt good unburdening himself. It felt like a purging, like a new beginning, as though he were standing on the threshold of some grand adventure. This pleasing sensation, helped along by two excellent bottles of wine, took a knock over the coffees and calvados when their talk turned to Stoneham Park and to Victor's great passion – contemporary art.

Ben remarked that he'd been unsettled by the works in the entrance hall: the two sobering images of electric chairs by Andy Warhol which greeted you as you stepped inside in the house, and the ironic religiosity of Damien Hirst's giant stained-glass window piece above the staircase, a shimmering cemetery of dead butterflies.

'When you boil it back to the bones, what else is there?' said Jacob intently. 'Just death, and the foolish hope we can somehow cheat it.'

'What about life?'

'Noise . . . to drown out the rattle of death.' Jacob's quick glance took in the clamour rising around them. 'Animals howling at the moon. That's all we are.'

It was a brief flash of the shadowy, brooding boy he had known all those years ago.

Ben's last act before leaving London on Sunday morning was to stop by St Leonard's Terrace. He let Basil out of her hutch and pinned a piece of A4 to the run: WHERE THE HELL HAVE YOU BEEN? It was signed with his best approximation of a rabbit's paw print.

He locked the front door, posted the keys back then pulled on his new helmet – one of many items from yesterday's shopping spree. The shirts, trousers, shorts and shoes he'd also splashed out on were in the bag lashed to the back of the motorcycle.

He wasn't usually up and about at this hour on a Sunday morning and the city was pleasingly deserted, still shaking itself awake. He wormed his way through South Kensington and across the park, where the joggers, roller-bladers and dog-walkers offered the first real signs of any life. Before joining the Westway, he stopped briefly to plug his iPod into the helmet speakers he'd fitted last night.

Nick Cave and the Bad Seeds carried him most of the way to Stoneham Park, although, appropriately, 'Country Boy' by Johnny Cash was filling his head when he turned past the gate house into the estate.

There were maybe ten of them in total. Most were still seated beneath the sunshade at the big teak table on the back terrace, the detritus of brunch spread about them. Those not perusing the Sunday papers were talking in subdued tones, and from the look on their faces it had been a heavy night. Only Jacob – Victor, it had to be Victor from now on, he had been very clear about that – looked like he might have abstained from the revelries.

They were a mixed bag, everything from a pale young Irish girl to a paunchy sixty-something gentleman who looked like he might be of Middle Eastern origin, but they all gave off the slightly jaded air of the affluent. The sunglasses on display would have set the average person back a week's wages.

Ben forgot their names the moment Victor introduced them, possibly because they showed almost no interest in the new arrival. They only perked up when a handsome sandy-haired fellow remarked knowingly, 'Ah, Ben, yes . . . the friend.'

A ripple of laughter ran around the table, but it was a large woman in a loud summer frock lying on the grass who spoke. 'Don't be offended.' Her voice had a husky quality to it, as if bruised by years of excess. 'It's just that we've never heard Victor refer to anyone as a friend before.'

Victor turned his amused gaze on her. 'Martha, you're my friend.'

'No, Victor, I'm your publicist. It's not the same thing.'

'God, the things you must know about him,' came a female voice from the end of the table.

'Disappointingly, Victor's as pure as the proverbial driven,' replied Martha.

'Darling, you're not at work now,' chipped in a fey man with a Germanic accent from beneath a Panama hat.

The sandy-haired fellow leaned forward in his chair. 'If anyone's got the dirt on Victor, it's got to be Ben.'

All eyes turned towards him.

'I can't,' he said, apologetically. 'I swore I wouldn't mention the sheep or the tub of margarine ever again.'

It went down well, helped along by Victor's cry of mock outrage. 'Traitor!'

'I knew they'd take to you,' said Victor as he accompanied Ben upstairs. 'But don't feel you have to reciprocate. Most of them aren't worth the time of day.'

It was a corner room dominated by a monumental Jacobean four-poster bed. The en-suite bathroom was large enough to accommodate a free-standing Victorian tub, twin sinks, an open shower and a seating area centred on a low table.

'You'll sleep like a king in that bed. There's even a rumour it belonged to one.'

'Really?'

Victor gave a wry smile. 'Well, that's what the dealer in Florida told me.'

'A well-travelled bed, if not a royal one.'

'Right. And she's definitely English.' Victor ran his hand down one of the carved columns of dark oak. 'It felt good bringing her home.' He looked up and smiled. 'She's happier here.'

Yesterday had been a day of outings to Oxford and Blenheim Palace and Winston's Churchill's grave in the churchyard at Bladon. Today was to be a day of rest and relaxation, of tennis and croquet and sailing on the lake (if the wind picked up, as forecast).

'After which, with any luck most of them will bugger off to beat the traffic back into London. Did you bring your tennis gear like I said?'

'Yeah. No racquet, though.'

'We have racquets.'

'Something told me you might.'

'Do you still play? Of course you do.'

'Not as much as I'd like to,' Ben replied.

'Great, I might actually beat you for once. Revenge for the semi-final.' Ben frowned, trying to remember. 'Our last year at Dean House . . .' prompted Victor. 'The Apsley Cup . . .'

'Oh, God, the Apsley Cup.'

'Two years on the trot you walked off with it.'

'Did I?'

Victor scrutinised him closely. 'I'm searching for false modesty, but you don't remember, do you?'

Ben shrugged.

'The first time, you beat Glen Stringer from the year above in the final. Poor Stringer was in tears. You won the first set seven-six on a tie-break, and you broke his serve late in the second to take it six-four.'

It was coming back now, but not in any meaningful way.

'The curse of numbers,' Victor went on. 'They stay with me. They always have.'

He turned at the door as he was leaving. 'Oh, Massoud,

the Iranian, although he prefers "Persian" . . . he may well ask what I was like when I was younger. You can tell him I had a wild streak, dangerous even. We both know you won't be lying.'

And with that he was gone, leaving Ben to wonder just who Massoud was, and where exactly he fitted in Victor's life.

'Victor,' he said quietly. It would take him time but he'd get there in the end. In fact, the name was already beginning to suit him. It had a no-nonsense ring to it. Jacob was just too, well, biblical.

Ben hadn't spotted the swimming pool on his last visit. It lay a discreet distance from the main house, beyond the walled vegetable garden, with its long lean-to greenhouse and its fruit cages and its ordered rows of vegetables.

A large wooden building with a pitched shingle roof served as the pool house. Beside it stood a vine-threaded pergola where a couple of members of staff were already laying a long table for lunch in the mottled shade.

Only one of the guests, the Irish girl, was in evidence. She lay stretched out, pale and slender, on a sunlounger beside the pool. She removed her earphones as Ben settled himself down beside her.

'Where are the others?' he asked.

'Getting changed, I think.' She wiped a smear of sunscreen from her forearm. 'There's talk of tennis and sailing and other things I don't do, so I'm just going to lie here and listen to Radiohead.'

'Which album?'

'I'm not very good with names.'

He placed his palm against his chest. 'Ben.'

'Lorna,' she replied with a smile, mimicking his gesture, her palm coming to rest just above her breasts, which were small, pert, and barely covered by a scrap of a bikini top.

Ben tugged off his T-shirt and lay back on the lounger. 'How do you know Victor?'

'Oh, I don't, really. I'm Martha's girlfriend.'

Martha, the large lady in the loud print dress. 'Victor's publicist?'

'I know what you're thinking – she's old enough to be my mother.'

'That's not what I'm thinking.'

Lorna tilted her head at him and asked in her soft Irish brogue, 'Are you flirting with me, Ben?'

'I wouldn't know how to, Lorna.'

'Well, if you are, don't stop. I'm enjoying it.'

'Really?'

'I'm bi-sexual, not a lesbian.'

He was out of his depth now, casting desperately about for a response. She spared him having to come up with one.

'Why are you so brown?'

'Battersea Park. I go and lie there whenever work's not going well, which is most of the time right now.'

He didn't intend his reply to sound so self-pitying, not that it mattered, because Lorna ignored it. 'I don't know why I bother.' She ran a hand over the pale pillow of her midriff. 'I never go brown, just different shades of red. I could never go your colour. Do you have foreign blood? You look like you do.'

'My mother's half-Italian.'

'But you have blond hair.'

'So has my mother. Her father was from the north, near Turin. They have their fair share of blonds up there.'

'Martha's got a villa in Umbria. We were there last month. Again. With the same people. Again.' She looked at him intently. 'I'm too young to spend my time sitting by a pool with people twice my age.'

She seemed to have no idea of what she'd just said until he replied, 'I feel the same way about swimming pools and people half my age.'

The realisation broke across her face. 'Oh God, I didn't mean you. Anyhow, you're not twice my age.'

'Not far off.'

'Far enough.' She leaned over and pulled her phone from her handbag. 'What's your number?' He told her and she punched it in. 'What am I going to call you? Brown Ben, I think. Yes.' She tapped away some more before dropping the phone back in her handbag. 'There, I just texted you.'

'I left my phone in my room.'

'Then you'll just have to wait and see what it says, won't you?'

'Give me a clue.'

'Where's the fun in that?' she pouted.

He would have pushed her further if at that moment Victor, Martha and a couple of the others hadn't appeared from the direction of the main house.

Only Ben and Victor were up for tennis, and Victor was too well-mannered to abandon his guests. It was a pity; there were two courts, one grass, one hard, both beautifully sculpted into the slope beyond the pool house. The consensus swung in favour of dinghy sailing on the lake.

The boathouse was home to three Lasers, rigged and ready to go. There was also a rack of windsurfing boards, an old wooden motor launch, and a gleaming white jet ski tied with a giant blue ribbon.

'It's a birthday present for Marcio,' Victor explained. 'So don't go getting any ideas.'

He paired them off according to their experience, levelling the crews for a race. By now there was a brisk summer breeze cat's-pawing the surface of the lake.

'What's in it for the winners?' demanded Hugh, the sandy-haired man, who didn't look overly pleased about having Martha in his boat.

'Bragging rights over lunch,' replied Victor.

'Bugger that! I need a proper incentive.'

Victor thought on it. 'OK, how about two bottles of Château Petrus nineteen sixty-one?'

'You don't . . .' came Hugh's incredulous reply.

'Incentive enough?'

Clarissa, Ben's crewmate for the race, suggested, 'Whoever wins should have to share them with the rest of us at lunch.'

This didn't say much for her faith in Ben's ability to bring them to victory.

Hugh looked aghast. 'You can't just open a Petrus sixty-one. It needs time to breathe.'

'For God's sake, Clarissa,' spat Norbert, the Austrian, in his flawless but accented English. 'Don't you know *anything*?'

Clarissa had never sailed before, but Ben was quite happy to concede the helm to her. He really didn't care whether they won or not, which was fortunate, because they were distant spectators to the neck-and-neck battle for first place, Hugh and Martha losing out by half a boat's length to Massoud and Norbert. Victor was playing race umpire from the motor launch, and Hugh immediately raised an objection with him that the others had committed an infringement, stealing his wind as the two boats had rounded the last buoy together.

'It's their duty to stay well clear of the leeward boat,' he blustered.

Victor decided against disqualification. Yes, it had been a 'muscular manoeuvre' by Massoud, but not an illegal one.

Hugh's reaction to this verdict was so preposterous that Ben assumed he must be joking. He only realised his error when he called out across the water in a parody of John McEnroe contesting a line call: 'You CANNOT be serious!'

'Oh dear . . .' muttered Clarissa beside him, and in that same moment Hugh spun round and transfixed Ben with a venomous glare.

'He's joking, right?' muttered Ben, for Clarissa's ears only.

'Speaking as his wife of fifteen years . . .'

'You're married?' Victor hadn't introduced them as a couple, and nothing he had observed suggested they were anything more than the vaguest of acquaintances.

'I must have sinned in a former life.'

She delivered the line with a look of such sodden dismay that Ben had to fight not to slip a consoling arm around her shoulder.

Hugh recovered quickly, apologising for his behaviour. 'Can't help it, I'm afraid, it's in my DNA.'

'Being an arsehole?' asked Norbert innocently.

'Competitiveness,' bristled Hugh. 'I don't seem to know any other way.'

They had tied up the boats at the jetty and were making their way back towards the pool.

'Maybe it's the adversarial nature of your job,' suggested Victor. 'Hugh's a barrister,' he explained to Ben.

'Oh, so's my wife . . . well, ex-wife.'

'Which chambers?'

When Ben told him, Hugh made a poor fist of trying to sound interested. 'Family law, right?'

'Yes.'

'Not good for the divorce,' observed Massoud.

'Actually, it didn't come to that – lawyers, I mean.'

'How very grown-up of you,' drawled Norbert.

'I'm a criminal barrister,' said Hugh before the conversation drifted too far from his favourite subject.

'Which is to say his fees are criminal.'

'My dear Victor, I can take most things, but a lecture on fees from a hedge fund manager, well, that's pushing it.'

Victor gave a hearty laugh. '*Touché*.'

Hugh wanted retribution on the croquet lawn but everyone else was for frittering away the half-hour before lunch beside the pool. Ben wasn't going anywhere later, certainly not driving, and when approached by one of the staff he opted for a cocktail. The caipirinha arrived promptly, mixed to perfection by the barman in the pool house. He savoured several large sips, tuning in and out of the conversations unfolding around him, intrigued yet alienated by the topics on offer: the ever-spiralling cost of beachfront property in Sardinia . . . the worrying dictatorial drift in the former communist countries of central Europe . . . the quality of the salt-beef sandwiches served up on the ground floor in Selfridges.

He polished off the caipirinha then slipped away from the dreary, soul-sapping chatter into the water, swimming a few lazy lengths before wrestling himself on to a lilo. He lay on his back like a corpse in its coffin, drifting to and fro on the eddies, lulled almost to sleep by the booze and the low rhythmic hum of the pool's filtration system. He found his thoughts transporting him to Morocco, to the swimming pool at La Gazelle d'Or in Taroudant, the finest hotel he'd ever stayed in. The three days and nights that he and Madeleine had spent there at the end of their honeymoon had been a wedding gift from her parents, an oasis of peace and luxuriant inactivity after a week of barrelling about the Atlas Mountains in their crappy hire car.

It wasn't the oversized pool that stirred these memories, or the crushing brilliance of the sun, or the smell of seared lamb now wafting over from the barbecue; it was, he realised, the cloying perfection of the place. Just like that hotel on another continent, there were no false notes, no rough edges.

Nothing had been left to chance; every detail had been thought through, carefully judged to satisfy the needs and aesthetic sensibilities of the privileged classes. Even the casual summer uniform of the staff at Stoneham Park – khaki shorts, Converses and washed-out black T-shirts – had, presumably, been decided upon by someone.

Such impeccable taste required a clear vision and a firm guiding hand. Did Victor trouble himself with such matters? Was there any truth in his story of a Florida furniture dealer spinning him a yarn about the royal heritage of an antique Jacobean four-poster, or had he heard it second-hand from some interior decorator? Had he sat in a saleroom at Christie's or Sotheby's and bid in person for the two Warhols now hanging in the entrance hall, or had some gallerist turned a fat profit flogging them on to him (along with the nihilistic claptrap Ben had been subjected to at the Wolseley)?

He couldn't help thinking that the flawless refinement of Stoneham Park owed more to teams of architects, interior designers, garden designers and art consultants than it did to the man who had employed their services, even if that same man had shown a delicacy of touch in the reshaping of his own face.

He pulled himself up short. Why such disloyalty? There was no call for such meanness of spirit. Victor's behaviour hardly warranted it. Something his father had once told him blew into his mind: 'Don't fall for that nonsense about money not buying happiness. It's a myth peddled by the rich to keep poor people poor.'

Maybe that was it. He wanted to believe that Victor's

remarkable metamorphosis from neglected child of self-absorbed academics to master of his own enchanted universe had come at a price, at some dire personal cost. But the truth was, Victor Sheldon seemed far happier in his skin than Jacob Hogg ever had been.

Eavesdropping once more on the poolside conversation, on the one-up-on-you wisdoms being bandied about, Ben could hear Victor contributing, but gently, from the wings, whereas in the past he would have fought his friends for centre stage. Not that they were his friends; he had pretty much dismissed them all out of hand earlier on. No, 'friend' was the tag he had reserved for Ben (to Hugh's malicious amusement), and although Ben had been touched to hear it at the time, it had also puzzled him. If that was how Victor really thought of him then why hadn't he made contact before now? After all, he'd been living in the country for more than five years.

He shrugged the question aside and rolled off the lilo into the water, allowing himself to sink to the bottom of the pool before twisting and kicking out for the shallow end.

He was making his way up the demilune of steps when he saw her approaching across the grass. He only recognised her as she drew closer, and only then because she was smoking a roll-up. Gone were the overalls, the bulky boots, the industrial face mask and the liberal dusting of white powder. She was now wearing the simplest of summer dresses, a loose pea-green number cinched at the waist with a narrow leather belt. Her auburn hair was tied back in a ponytail, and her eyes — green with a whisper of grey, if he remembered correctly — were hidden behind a pair of black bug-eye sunglasses.

'Well, well, well . . . look who's finally here.'

'The beautiful Molly Mo.'

'Sleep well, did we, Mo?' Victor added to the chorus.

'Some of us were up with the lark,' she replied. 'Some of us have been working, not slobbing by the pool.'

'I'll have you know we've been racing dinghies on the lake,' countered Hugh.

'Hugh lost,' said Massoud.

'I did *not* lose, I was cheated of victory. Anyway, Ben and Clarissa lost by about fifty boat lengths.'

Victor made the introductions. 'Mo, this is Ben.'

'Ah, yes, motorcycle man,' she said.

'Good to see you again.'

Victor frowned. 'You two have already met?'

To which Mo replied, 'You mean he didn't ask after me?'

'Don't be insulted,' said Ben. 'You weren't exactly looking your best.'

'I was in my gear,' she explained to Victor.

It turned out that she was a sculptor who worked out of the stable block.

'Never call her a sculptress,' boomed Hugh. 'As I learned to my cost yesterday.'

'Hugh, the day you start calling your female colleagues barresteresses you can call me a sculptress. How's that for a deal?'

'Done,' chortled Hugh appreciatively.

It was interesting to observe Mo's effect on the group.

There was an immediate shift in tone, the tired banter giving way to something lighter, more playful, more irreverent. Ben wondered what her status was exactly. Victor's friend? Some artist he'd commissioned? His lover? It was no clearer to him by the time they took their seats for lunch, but he hoped it wasn't the latter. He managed to plant himself at Mo's end of the table. Annoyingly, so did Hugh, who seemed set on monopolising her, showing scant regard for his wife's feelings. He only broke off from his devotions when he was ready to broaden his audience, holding forth on the subject of the high-profile trial he'd been involved with earlier that year. In fairness to him, he sparked a lively debate around the table.

Hugh had been vilified with impunity by the press following his vigorous defence of a man accused of abducting, sexually violating and then murdering a twelve-year-old boy. Only when the jury handed down a unanimous guilty verdict had it emerged that the defendant was already serving time for two prior convictions on similar charges.

This begged the question: how could Hugh have defended a man whom he must surely have suspected of being guilty of the most heinous crime? Hugh retaliated that it wasn't for him to speculate on the guilt or innocence of his clients. His job was to defend his client fearlessly and to the best of his ability, however unpopular the cause in the eyes of others. He cared nothing for the roasting he'd received in the media.

'It's true,' confirmed Clarissa. 'Hugh doesn't care if people hate him. In fact, he rather enjoys it when they do.'

'My darling,' Hugh replied, managing to strip the word of all affection, 'do you really expect me to lose sleep because I'm pilloried by a bunch of idiots who know almost nothing of what they're talking about?'

Ben remembered the case, remembered the criticism that had been levelled against the defence barrister for his ruthless cross-examination of the victim's family. He decided to let the matter lie, though, not wishing to go head to head with a man so certain of his position, so determined to defend it, and so adept with words.

Mo had no such qualms. Undaunted by Hugh's thunderous eloquence, she asked if he drew any satisfaction from flummoxing honest witnesses in the stand.

'Satisfaction doesn't come into it. It's my duty to test the prosecution case, to put all relevant matters before the jury.'

'Even if they prove to be irrelevant? Even if they cause terrible harm and upset along the way?'

Hugh shifted in his chair. 'It's for the judge to police his court, to rein me in if he feels I'm overstepping the mark. He chose not to.'

'But another judge might of?'

'Might have – yes,' said Hugh, correcting her English.

'Which suggests the law's a movable feast, depending on which judge is presiding.'

'The law, my dear, is the law,' replied Hugh with the benign tolerance of an adult addressing a small child.

Mo ignored the condescension. 'But how can that be when we're always hearing about appeal court judges who can't agree with each other?'

Ben had to smile. She was sniping, winding Hugh up under the guise of genuine curiosity. 'I'm not trying to hold your feet to the fire,' she said at one point, in all apparent innocence. Her tenacity gave others the courage to weigh in. Was there no one Hugh wouldn't represent, however repugnant? Did he court controversy or did he always take the cases he was offered, however pedestrian?

Hugh responses grew increasingly pompous. Before long he was holding forth about the constitutional importance of lawyers. Advocates like him played a vital role in the proper functioning of society. Yes, it could be tough and dirty work at times, but it wasn't the primary consideration of a lawyer to question the morality of what he or she did. There were far higher principles at stake.

'I couldn't do what you do,' said Mo.

'And I,' replied Hugh, 'couldn't carve a human head from a block of marble without it looking like the back end of a donkey.'

Mo deftly rounded off the game. 'I know a number of critics who'd say that's exactly what my heads look like.'

Ben caught the look of cool devotion in Victor's eye during the laughter that followed. It suggested that he and Mo were indeed a couple, and the realisation stung.

'You do heads?' asked Ben.

'Mostly. I can show you later if you want.'

'And you do films, apparently,' cut in Martha from the far end of the table.

'Yes, although there's not much to show, I'm afraid. Probably nothing you've ever heard of.'

He was wrong. A couple of them had seen *Inside Out*, the American comedy he'd been involved with back in the late nineties. It was an early script of his which had been snapped up by an American studio and then ritually sacrificed on the altar of low humour by a dizzying number of other screenwriters. The film had performed rather well, and for a brief moment Hollywood had been keen to know if Ben had any more kooky comedy ideas up his sleeve which they could massacre. He had then committed the cardinal sin of wanting to be taken seriously as a writer, only pitching worthy storylines that stood a shot at an award. By the time he'd wised up and figured out that they wanted him for one thing alone, it was too late; even the offers of lucrative comedy rewrites had dried up by then.

His moment had passed. He'd blown it. A door had opened and he'd pulled it shut in his own face. Years on, mention of *Inside Out* might still be relied upon to raise a dim glimmer of recognition amongst people of a certain age, but even they couldn't mask the unspoken question in their eyes: why nothing of any note since then?

He saw that same look now around the table as he trotted out the standard speech: nature of the beast . . . cruel profession . . . most of what you write never sees the light of day . . . get paid anyway . . . best things I've ever written still out there somewhere, lost in development hell . . . maybe one day they'll resurface . . . God only knows in what form, though . . . ha ha.

He knew it was coming, and it was Hugh who finally

asked, 'Tell us about this script of yours that's going to make a mint for Victor and turn him into a movie mogul.'

'It's called *The Bet*.'

'Since when?' asked Victor.

'It's a working title. It can change.'

'That bodes well,' said Mo mischievously. 'The producer and the writer can't agree on the title.'

The subject matter suddenly seemed so trivial – maybe it *was* trivial – but he gave it his best shot. It was the story of two rival inner-city gangs with a violent history who find themselves abducted and transported to a remote island. Here they are provided with food, water, alcohol, drugs, as well as all the means necessary to annihilate each other. Their abductors, a corps of hardened commando types, even instruct them in the use of the weapons on offer. It's to be a no-holds-barred fight to the death, and the whole thing has been set up for a group of nameless, faceless high-rollers who, it later turns out, are present on the island to witness the unfolding mayhem. Vast sums of money are at stake, sums so large that underhand efforts are made to determine the outcome. By this time, though, the two gangs have realised that if they're to stand any chance of getting off the island alive they're going to have to bury the hatchet and learn to work together.

'It's a take on society's attitude to our disenfranchised, criminalised youth,' said Ben, feeling a touch disingenuous. 'No one really cares as long as it's each other they're killing.'

'It's more than that,' insisted Victor. 'It's a morality tale.'

'A morality tale?' scoffed Hugh.

Victor eyes burned with a quiet fire. 'I wouldn't expect you to understand, Hugh, you for whom personal morality must always play second fiddle to the law.'

The silence around the table was telling. Best not to ruffle the feathers of our genial host too much, it said.

'Well, there's no law on this island,' Victor went on. 'It's utterly lawless. That's the point. It's a Hobbesian state of nature. It's like Golding's *Lord of the Flies* with the heat turned up under it. It's also stuffed with great characters, great humanity, and humour. Hard to believe, but you're wincing and laughing almost in the same moment.'

Hugh was still bridling after his public dressing-down. 'I still can't see it scooping the Oscar.'

'Not every novel is written with one eye on the Pulitzer or the Man Booker.'

Lorna broke in. 'Well, it sounds right up my street. I'm definitely going to see it when it comes out.'

'Me too,' declared Massoud.

'I think I'll wait for the DVD,' said Mo, to a burr of laughter, during which she caught Ben's eye and mouthed the word, 'Joke.'

He tilted his head in acknowledgement.

Most of them were gone by five o'clock, nudged on their way by Victor, who claimed he had some work to do. While the others packed, Ben took himself upstairs to the stately perfection of his bedroom. He flopped on to the bed and fired up his BlackBerry. Nothing prepared him for the candour of the text Lorna had sent him earlier: **If you want to fuck call me. Lorna x**

He stared at the display, trying to recall the last time someone had made such a brazen pass at him. When that failed, he tried to recall the last time someone had made any kind of pass at him. And when that failed, he forwarded the text to his old friend, Edwin, along with a covering message: **Just received this from a bisexual Irish girl who's in a lesbian relationship. Help! What do I do? B**

Like Ben, Edwin was divorced. Unlike Ben, Edwin hadn't fought to save his marriage. Separation had been a welcome deliverance from a loveless and sexless relationship. Longer on personality than looks, and loaded to the gunwales with cash from his job in corporate finance, Edwin hadn't had to work too hard to find a string of young women happy to help him bury the memories of what he now referred to as 'the tunnel years'.

It didn't feel quite right calling Toby on the back of sending such a text, but he was eager to hear his son's voice.

'Hi, this is Toby. I can't take your call right now but leave a message and, who knows, I might even call you back.'

'Hi, Tobes, Dad here. I hope you had fun. And hey, who knows, maybe you'll call me back some time.'

He hung up then immediately tried Madeleine's mobile. She answered after a couple of rings.

'Ben.' She sounded strangely pleased to hear from him.

'Hey, Mads. How are you?'

'You know me. Pleased to be home.' She had never much

enjoyed holidays abroad. She preferred familiarity, her own roof over her head, her own creature comforts.

'Next time I'll go in your place. How about that?'

She laughed her polite laugh. 'Mustn't grumble, right?'

He wanted to say that he rather missed her grumbles. It was true. He did. 'No, grumble away. I hear St Lucia's not all it's cracked up to be.'

'It was amazing,' she cooed. 'Pure paradise. And Toby made a whole load of new friends. One of them, her name's Alice . . . Oh Ben, she's the most beautiful little thing you've ever seen, and she only lives five minutes away, just the other side of Sloane Square. How weird is that?'

Possibly not quite as weird as Madeleine imagined. 'Amazing.'

'They've made plans to see each other again, but don't for God's sake tell him I told you.'

'How is he? I just tried his phone.'

Toby hadn't slept on the plane, not a wink, and had taken himself off to bed. It was probably best if Ben tried again in the morning. He said he'd call as soon as he got back to town.

'You're away?'

'Yeah, out near Oxford.'

'Anyone I know?'

He could hear the slight tightening in her voice. 'I doubt it. He's called Victor Sheldon.'

'Victor Sheldon . . .?' She repeated the name as if it rang a bell, at which point he heard Lionel's muffled voice in the background: 'Victor Sheldon? What about him?' 'Ben's staying with him,' explained Madeleine. 'With Victor bloody Sheldon?'

Madeleine came back on the line. 'Lionel's looking rather impressed, so I suppose I should be too.'

'Don't be. He's just an old friend I lost touch with years ago. See you tomorrow.'

But she wasn't finished with him yet. 'You're not going to pick Toby up on the motorbike, are you?'

'Since when is that a problem?'

'You've really got to get yourself a car.'

'I told you, I intend to.'

'You've been saying that for months.'

'I know, but it's going to happen.'

'Listen, I've talked it through with Lionel and he's happy to lend you the money. It doesn't have to be anything special – a VW Polo, maybe, or a Toyota Yaros.'

Madeleine knew next to nothing about cars, which meant she'd been doing her research, and not very well.

'Toyota Yaris,' he corrected her.

'Whatever, a second-hand one in good condition shouldn't cost more than a few thousand.'

'Tell Lionel I'm touched by the offer,' he said sourly, 'but it won't be necessary. I've just got a job.'

'A writing job?' Her tone hovered somewhere between surprise, relief, and concern that he might be talking about a whole new line of work: trainee barista at Starbucks, possibly.

'Yes, Mads, a writing job.'

He drew a certain cheap satisfaction from hearing Lionel quizzing her further in the background.

'Does the Victor Sheldon you're staying with have anything to do with hedge funds?' she asked.

'Yep, that's the one.'

The moment he hung up, his BlackBerry PING-ed with a new text message. It was from Edwin: **You old dog! Happy to help out with Lorna but only if she brings her friend along too. Woof woof!**

You wouldn't be barking if you could see her friend, thought Ben.

Lorna and Martha were the first to leave, though only after they'd bickered about who was going to drive the Audi, and whether they should put the roof up now or just before they hit the motorway. Ben sought some deeper meaning in the parting kiss Lorna planted on his cheek, but if it was there it was well hidden. One cursory peck was all he received, no hand on the arm, no stolen glance, nothing that acknowledged the text she'd sent him.

In the general descent of bags and the searches for misplaced iPads, phones and the like, Ben found himself alone in the saloon with Massoud, who wished him well with the film project. It would definitely get made, he said, because when Victor put his mind to something it invariably came to pass. 'But you don't need me to tell you that, you've known him longer than anyone.'

No chance encounter, then; Massoud was fishing, as Victor had warned him he might.

'Longer than most.'

'And has he changed?'

'He's got a bit more cash in his back pocket.'

Massoud laughed, but Ben could see him searching for a way to keep the conversation alive. He helped him out, sticking to Victor's brief. 'I couldn't really say if he's changed, but he's definitely more settled.'

'Settled?'

'Yeah, he had a wild streak in him when we were younger . . . reckless . . . unpredictable. I don't see it now, but I guess that doesn't mean it's not there.'

When they'd shaken hands and Massoud had left, Ben dropped into the leather sofa. 'And the Oscar for male actor in a supporting role goes to Ben Makepeace.'

'The first sign of madness,' came a voice from behind him. 'Talking to yourself.' Mo was standing in the doorway.

'Well, you don't need to worry because I'm not talking to myself, I'm talking to Gerald – my imaginary friend.' He indicated the empty armchair opposite.

Mo approached it and jerked her thumb over her shoulder. 'Fuck off, Gerald.' She took a seat, scrutinising Ben with a beady eye. 'You need help.'

'You think?'

'That film idea of yours . . .'

'What about it?'

'It's sick, that's what.'

'A little, I grant you.'

'Where did it come from?'

'God knows. South London, where I live . . . *Lord of the Flies* . . . crap TV. Toss it all in the pot and stir thoroughly.'

'My, that's *some* art.'

'I defer to you real artists,' he replied with a respectful tilt of the head. 'I'm just a storyteller.'

Victor really did have some work to do, and once the last guests had disappeared down the driveway he placed Ben in Mo's care. The prospect of being alone with her had helped him through the afternoon, and it soon transpired he wasn't the only one who had found the company a tad trying.

'Sad to see them go?' asked Mo, leading him towards the stable block.

'Devastated.'

'Hard to believe, but they weren't as God awful as the last bunch.'

The stable yard was a cobbled affair with a stone well-head at its heart and brick buildings that rose two storeys on all sides. Mo's studio lay on the far side of the yard, beyond a pair of enormous double wooden doors reaching almost to the eaves. She hesitated before tugging them open. 'I warn you, it's a mess.'

She wasn't lying. The double-height space looked like a mechanic's workshop after a blizzard had ripped through it. Pieces of equipment were scattered about the place – generators, extraction units, stepladders, drills, angle-grinders, mallets, chisels – all seemingly bound together by a spaghetti junction of electric cables and hoses and snaking steel ducts, and all coated in a layer of white dust.

'I was going to give it a clean this morning but couldn't face it.'

Ben didn't reply, his attention drawn to the heavy wooden pallet in the middle of the studio, on which stood an enormous rectangular block of pale stone. Laced through with dark veins, it was some eight feet across and maybe six feet high.

'Can you make out the face?' asked Mo.

At first sight, the stone didn't appear to have been worked on. Ben squinted, searching the abstraction of its rough-hewn surfaces for signs, features.

'Honestly? No,' he finally replied with a note of apology.

Mo's lips curled into a smile. 'That's because it's on the other side.'

The contrast was extraordinary. It wasn't just the polished contours that Mo had drawn from the crude mass; it was the colour beneath this new skin. The stone seemed to glow, lit from within by some alien fire.

It was the head of a young man, carved on the horizontal, as though he were lying on his side. There was a distinct classical look to his handsome features: the unbroken line of the angled brow and the long nose, the heavy-lidded almond eyes, and the bow of the full lips, which were slightly pursed.

Ben found himself stepping forward and running his hand across the glassy surfaces, up along the brow, then across the gentle rise and fall of the cheekbone towards the ear which, like the hair that curled around it, had been blocked out but not yet finished off.

It brought to mind a fallen statue, some monumental figure from another age that had shattered into pieces when it had come crashing down. It could have been the head of the famed Colossus which had once stood astride the harbour entrance at Rhodes. Intriguingly, there was something in the noble set of his features that also seemed to acknowledge this downfall, a touch of melancholy around the eyes and the corners of the mouth.

Ben said all this to Mo. When she didn't reply, he turned to find her staring at him with an expression that was hard to fathom.

'What?' he asked, concerned that he'd offended her in some way.

She shook her head. 'Nothing. I'm glad you see those things.'

He wanted to say more, that he was in awe of what she had created, spellbound by the otherworldly creature she had brought into being from a hunk of rock.

'It's Persian onyx,' she said. 'Tough as anything to work, but it won't weather down.'

'Where's it going to go?'

'I'll show you if you want.'

'Sure.'

'Let me grab my camera first.' She disappeared through a door in the corner of the studio, calling over her shoulder as she went, 'Come on up.'

A wooden staircase climbed steeply, giving way to a large living room tucked under the roof. It was a place of exposed beams, stripped floorboards and Scandinavian designer furniture. There was a lot of leather and brushed steel on show, as well as a fair amount of paper. Charcoal sketches on sheets of A5 were taped to the walls and spread across the floor. Most of them were so abstract as to defy any interpretation.

'There's juice in the fridge,' called Mo, disappearing down a corridor.

'You want one?'

'Yeah, cranberry.'

The galley kitchen was separated from the rest of the room by a breakfast bar, and he was pleased to find the fridge well stocked. It suggested this was where she lived, rather than a dust-free work space that had been placed at her disposal. The dirty pans stacked beside the sink implied the same.

Mo reappeared with a camera.

'You live here?'

'Yeah. Why?'

'I assumed you and Victor . . .'

'Were an item?' She sounded amused by the idea. 'What makes you say that?'

He handed her a glass of cranberry juice. 'I don't know – the way he looks at you.'

'I think he likes me, but I'm hardly his type. Maybe if I had legs up to my larynx, pneumatic breasts and a volcanic temper.' She paused. 'Actually, I can do the temper if pushed.'

'Is that really his type?'

'You obviously haven't met his ex-wife.'

'Luciana? No. But he told me about her.'

'I don't like to speak ill of a sister, but that woman is a Class A bitch.'

'That's not what *I* heard.'

'No?'

'Victor didn't have a bad word to say about her. In fact, he took all the blame for the bust-up.'

'Then he's changed his tune. I got a whole different story from him, and it fitted with the woman I met a few months back. She's toxic. Beautiful, yes, but ugly as all sin to anyone with half a brain.'

Odd that Victor had painted such a different picture for him. 'I wouldn't bank on the average man having half a brain when it comes to beautiful women.'

Mo gave an amused snort. 'That's the truth.'

He heard more of her story as they strolled through the grounds of the estate, skirting the farm buildings and making for the lake.

Victor had discovered Mo's work a couple of years ago at a group show of stone sculptors held at an Oxfordshire manor house near Burford. He had bought both of the pieces she'd exhibited, and although they hadn't met at the time, a month later he had shown up at her studio in Yorkshire and bought a third which she was still working on. All were for his house in the south of France – just one of his many foreign homes, apparently. She was able to describe the villa on the Cap d'Antibes in detail because she'd travelled there several times at Victor's request, initially to help him decide on the place-ment of the three sculptures, then later to oversee their installation.

She had been wary at first, suspicious of his intentions, but they had proved to be entirely honourable. She was the artist and he wanted her to be happy. He had also insisted on paying her a hefty fee for the extra time and effort, which, given that she'd only recently struck out on her own after years of working for others, had been very welcome.

'He was my first real client. And he's still my best client by a mile. You wouldn't believe how some of them haggle over money, especially the wealthy ones. Not Victor. He's like my patron. I'm very lucky. I owe him a lot.'

She certainly did. Earlier in the year, when she'd lost her studio up near Leeds, Victor had offered her the space in the stable yard, along with the apartment. Both were rent-free for as long as she was working on his commission. Better still, if she wanted to stay on afterwards then they were hers for the having at a peppercorn rent. She said she was seriously tempted to take him up on the offer.

'Really?' asked Ben. 'I mean, you must have strong ties up north.'

'Family, of course. And friends.' She hesitated. 'Maybe even a boyfriend.'

Not what he wanted to hear, but he took it in his stride, even producing a convincing chuckle. 'You're not sure?'

'*He's* not sure. He's making up his mind.'

His name was Connor and he was an architect attached to York Minster. They had met while Mo was apprenticing as a mason at the cathedral stoneyard. Connor didn't like the idea of a long-distance relationship, although Mo suspected there were other factors at play. 'We're at that age.'

'Which age is that?'

'Both in our early thirties, been together a while . . .'

'Ah, the big M or bust.'

'You've got it.'

They walked on a little way in silence, the light from the westering sun glancing off the lake and making them squint.

'It's not the only choice,' suggested Ben. 'You could always do what we did.'

'What's that?'

'Get married and then bust up.'

Mo's laughter caught in the branches of the trees. 'Thanks for the hot tip.'

'Don't mention it. There's more where that one came from.'

Later, while showering before dinner, he thought back on their time alone, retracing their footsteps to the copse of trees beside the lake that was to be the final resting place of her gargantuan stone head. Victor's instinct had been to place the sculpture closer to the main house, where it could be more readily appreciated, but Mo had won him round to her thinking. Better that it be lost in the land-scape, discarded like some true relic. It would turn the copse into a place of pilgrimage, of quiet contemplation. A number of trees had already been felled to make space for it, and a concrete base had been sunk into the soil in readiness.

Standing beneath the high-pressure jet, head bowed, the water pummelling his shoulders to an itch, he also thought about the easy familiarity that had sprung up between them right from their very first exchange, when he had flooded the motorcycle and she had stopped to tease him. He wasn't imagining it. There was definitely something there, something all the more precious for being inexplicable.

A wiser voice reminded him of the ten-year age difference, to say nothing of the long-term boyfriend, and he felt the sweet frisson of the past hour begin to wash away, draining down the plughole at his feet. He needed to hold himself in check. He knew what he could be like. There was a reason why Edwin had dubbed him 'Headlong' at university – several reasons, in fact. Most of the girls had let him down gently; others had been less kind. The memory of one particular moment still had the power to bring a warm flush of embarrassment to his cheeks. Georgia was now a bigwig in science and nature programmes at the BBC. At the time, she'd been a second year modern languages undergraduate at Brasenose College, slim as a reed, painfully beautiful, and with a boyfriend in London. Their tentative dalliance had come to an abrupt conclusion one evening when Ben had produced a copy of Hemingway's *The Old Man and the Sea*. He had marked in pencil several short passages relating to the fisherman's failed quest to bring home his monster catch, and he had foolishly insisted on reading them aloud.

He could still picture Georgia seated on the beanbag in his colleage rooms, the glow from the gas fire lighting the look of polite bewilderment on her face. For him, Hemingway's words resonated with bittersweet parallels of his own predicament, his own heroic struggle to land Georgia. For her, they were downright baffling, and certainly not warranted by one drunken snog in a darkened stairwell after a hockey club disco.

Years later, he had gone on to make the same mistake with Madeleine, falling too hard for her, and too quickly. She had felt oppressed by the certainty of his convictions, which he had called 'love' and she had called 'slightly creepy'. Edwin had advised him to 'stop fucking stalking the poor girl'. Backing off had been the right thing to do then, and it was the right thing to do now.

He raised his head so that the water hammered against his skull, beating some sense into it.

The second Mo materialised from the gloom shrouding the back terrace Ben felt his resolve falter. She had exchanged the green dress for jeans, a white T-shirt and a tight black cardigan which showed off her narrow waist. Her hair was pinned up in a messy chignon, possibly not quite as artless as it would have you believe, and she had applied a little make-up, just a touch of eyeliner.

'I do love a man who stands when a woman appears.'

'Our prep school might have been a sanctuary for sadists and paedophiles,' said Victor, 'but they were sticklers when it came to manners. Right, Ben?'

'Absolutely. Manners maketh man. Matron was always saying it.'

Mo took her seat at the head of the table, flanked by her two consorts. 'And was Matron a sadist, a paedophile, or both?'

Victor poured her a glass of white Burgundy. 'Neither. Miss Beaumont is best described as a "reluctant witness". It's no coincidence she ended up getting engaged to another "reluctant witness" before they both high-tailed it.'

'That's right! I'd forgotten. She got engaged, didn't she? Who to?'

'*To whom*, Makepeace, *to whom*. Have you learned nothing, boy?' Victor abandoned the outraged stentorian tones for his own voice. 'Mr Turnbull, of course.'

'God, Mr Turnbull . . .' A forgotten face coalesced in his mind's eye. A helmet of long wavy hair damped down with Brylcreem and parted at the side. Mr Turnbull, young and friendly, though not in the come-hither-sit-on-my-knee sort of way favoured by some of the masters. He taught geography rather badly and was always rigging up zip-wires around the place so they could fly through the trees. He was also a dab hand at building camp fires, skinning rabbits and making jamjar bombs of bicarbonate of soda mixed with vinegar. No doubt the Mr Turnbulls of the world were an extinct breed, long since killed off by Health and Safety.

'I can see this is going to be a bundle of laughs,' said Mo.

'Wait till you hear about the time Ben beat me at marbles.'

Mo looked up from the cigarette she was rolling. 'Paedophiles *and* marbles. You boys had a seriously weird childhood.'

It was a light supper of home-cured gravadlax and salad from the garden. As ever, it was served up by someone else.

The conversation soon turned into a post-mortem of the weekend guests. For all his bombast and lolling superiority, Hugh the barrister was known to Victor because they were both trustees of a charity for victims of domestic abuse, just one of several charities Hugh was involved with, apparently. 'But a little of him still goes a long way,' Victor conceded.

Lorna was the next corpse to be loaded on to the slab.

'Did she hit on you?' Victor asked him.

'Hit on me?'

Mo caught Victor's eye. 'Yep, she hit on him.'

'Don't be too flattered,' said Victor. 'She hits on everyone.'

Apparently it was all part of a sick game Lorna liked to play with Martha. If Ben had responded to her text, she would have shoved his reply under Martha's nose as evidence that she was desired by someone else, that she didn't need to hang around if she didn't want to. A fierce argument would then have flared, followed by a passionate reconciliation. Whatever you thought of it, this curious cycle was the glue that held the two women together.

Mo asked to see the text. Ben pulled it up and handed her his phone.

'That's much saucier than the one I got.'

'You too?' he asked.

'Excuse me! I'll have you know I'm very popular with lesbians.'

Ben turned inquiringly to Victor, who said, 'Nah, still waiting for my text.'

'We can sort that out in a jiffy,' announced Mo, tapping away at Ben's phone. '"Seriously tempted but don't want to tread on Victor's toes. He carries a big torch for you."'

'So to speak,' said Ben.

'Very good, I like that.' Mo tapped some more. '"So to speak."'

'I wouldn't send that if I were you,' deadpanned Victor.

'What's the worst that could happen?'

'Let me see. Oh yeah, I could fire you, kick you out on the street, and then I could destroy your sculpture.'

'*Your* sculpture,' she corrected him. 'You've already paid for it.'

'It'll hurt you a hell of a lot more than it hurts me.'

Ben was unnerved by the sudden turn the conversation had taken. It wasn't so much the calm menace of Victor's words, it was the look in his eyes. Many years had passed since he'd witnessed that flat, stony glare, but it was no less chilling now than it had always been.

Mo seemed completely unfazed by it. She raised the phone and fired off the text with her thumb.

A slow smile broke across Victor's face. 'Damn you. That was my best poker face.'

'And it wasn't bad. But your nostrils flare when you're lying.'

'My nostrils?'

'Only slightly.'

They had hardly finished eating when Mo announced she was turning in early. It was an unexpected disappointment made worse by the news that Ben wouldn't be seeing her in the morning. She was setting off first thing for a meeting at her gallery in London.

'Good luck with the script. Maybe I'll see you again some time. Maybe at the party.'

'The party?'

'I haven't decided if I'm inviting him yet,' joked Victor.

They watched Mo vanish into the night. Victor was the one to break the silence. 'Pretty special, huh?'

'If you're into that sort of thing.'

'And what sort of thing is that?'

'Beauty, brains, talent, humour . . .'

Victor laughed. 'Don't be fooled. She can be a real handful.'

Ben would have liked to sit there and chat all night about Mo. He would have liked to know when the party was so he could work out how long he'd have to wait before seeing her again. But Victor was also leaving early in the morning, another business trip abroad, and he wanted to talk about the script. This, after all, was the reason he'd invited Ben out to Stoneham Park.

'I've had an idea, a story idea. I'm not sure you're going to thank me for it.'

'Major or minor?'

Victor leaned across to top up his wine glass. OK, major, thought Ben. He wasn't wrong.

'I've been thinking that one of the gangs should be Asian.'

He had been here before, many times, but it didn't make it any easier to handle. He could see characters and relationships dissolving into the ether, taking vast swathes of dialogue with them. He could see the whole lovingly constructed house of cards collapsing before his eyes.

'Asian?'

Did Victor mean it in the British sense of the word, which, for all its current political correctness, was a ridiculous catch-all term for pretty much every ethnicity between India and

Taiwan. Surely he couldn't be talking about Chinese Triads. He wasn't. It was far worse than that.

'Pakistanis. British Pakistanis. Although I don't think one has to be specific. It's film. The racial thing speaks for itself, you know, visually.'

Ben nodded, taking it in. 'Can I be perfectly honest?'

'Sure.'

'Race is a can of worms. No, worse, it's Pandora's box.'

'Not if you ignore it, play away from it.'

'So why bother tossing it into the mix at all?'

Victor hesitated before replying. 'Did you consider it? When you first had the idea, I mean?'

'I can't remember. Maybe. Just long enough to reject it out of hand.'

'I'm surprised. What's the racial profile of the gangs around where you live? Exclusively white? I doubt it. Not even predominantly white, I'll bet. We have to confront the reality, we have to tackle it. Not head on, like I say, but with the same light touch that's already in the script.' He hesitated. 'It would be irresponsible not to.'

Ben stared at the hand gripping his wine glass. It seemed to belong to someone else.

'All I'm asking is that you think about it.'

Not true, thought Ben. He's made up his mind, and he's the paymaster. A token polish had just become a page one rewrite.

'Take a couple of days to let it percolate. I can see you're not convinced. Nor was I when it first occurred to me.'

'Sure, sure . . .' said Ben distractedly.

'Ben, look at me.' Victor waited for him to comply. 'I meet a lot of unsavoury types in my line of work, people who put personal gain before everything else, even other human lives. Conflict is big business, and there are some out there who'll do whatever it takes to stir it up, keep it bubbling away. Believe me, I've met these people. Religion and race are just two of the tools they use to further their own ends. It's a game for them, just as it is for the high-rollers in our story – *your* story. I don't want to labour the parallels, and I don't think you should either. They should sit there in the background, a metaphor for what's really going on in the world right now.'

It was quite a speech, intense and heartfelt. A contemporary allegory. A modern parable for a modern age. Maybe it wasn't such a bad idea after all. It might just elevate the story into something he could be genuinely proud of.

'I know it means a lot more work but you'll be paid for it, of course. I was thinking another twenty thousand – on top of the fee for the polish.'

'It's way too much,' blurted out Ben.

'You really need to go on a negotiation course.'

'I'll have to run it past my agent first, and they don't call her Rottweiler for nothing.'

Victor laughed. 'That's more like it.'

A flood of well-being carried Ben through to coffee and a glass of the finest single malt whisky he had ever tasted. He even permitted himself a cigar.

A warm summer's night; a faultless setting; an old

friendship rekindled; a writing fee that harked back to the glory days of his early career; and finally, finally, the ache of certain desire for a woman who wasn't Madeleine. Strange stirrings of things both familiar and forgotten. The low buzz of alcohol in his bloodstream and a fat Cuban jammed between his fingers.

He wanted to bask in these sensations, to stretch the night out, but Victor was thinking of his dawn departure and the batch of papers he had to go through before bed. He tamped out his cigar in the ashtray and got to his feet.

'Stay. Finish your cigar. Polish off the whisky.' He tilted the bottle to gauge how much was left. 'Well, maybe not all of it if you want to see straight in the morning.'

They hugged farewell, as they had after lunch at the Wolseley, and when they drew apart Victor asked, 'Do you think you could work here?'

'Work here?'

'Your bedroom . . . the library . . . the pool house. There's even space in the stable block, although I wouldn't recommend it. Mo makes one hell of a racket when she's on the job.'

Mo hard at it in the stable block while he tapped away at his laptop in the library. He could see it.

'I only ask because I know how precious you writers can be about where you work.'

'Yeah, I'm really attached to my rathole of a flat.'

'So move in, come and stay. Or not. Come and go as you please. Whatever you want. You decide.'

'You mean it?'

'Christ, Ben, how much hospitality did you show me when we were kids? Of course I mean it. I've even run it past the boss and she's signed off on it.'

'The boss' was his nickname for Annabelle, the blonde woman whom Ben had encountered on his first foray out to Stoneham Park. She was on holiday in France but would be back on Wednesday. 'Any time after that's OK. It's your call.' Victor gripped his shoulder. 'I hope you do. It would be great to have you around.'

Victor was making his way up the double staircase when Ben called after him. 'I forgot to say, you were right about Massoud. He asked me about you.'

'What did you tell him?'

'Exactly what you said.'

Victor offered a salute. '*Gracias, amigo.*'

When Victor disappeared inside the house, any lingering doubts Ben had about the proposed script changes went with him. Not just a month at a stately home in the country but a ludicrous fee to go with it. He would have to set some of the money aside to pay last year's tax bill in January, but given how little he'd earned he'd still be well in the black.

A clear view of the road ahead, at long last. The money would buy him the time to finally sit down and write the play he'd been toying with for the past year. Yes. There could be no excuses now.

He flattened another sip of the smoky nectar against the roof of his mouth. God, it was damned good whisky. He'd never heard of the distillery, and a thought occurred to him. Pulling up the internet on his phone, he tapped in the details of the label and clicked through to a specialist whisky website.

'Jesus Christ . . .' he muttered.

It was a two-thousand-pound bottle and they'd just put away a good third of it!

He sucked on the cigar and raised the chunky glass tumbler to the house, to Victor, as much in admiration as in gratitude. Victor had played him beautifully, appealing to his vanity (a parable for a modern age), his desire (Mo), and his greed (a writing fee only a fool would have turned down) in order to swing the argument.

There was no doubt about it, Victor Sheldon was a man accustomed to getting his own way, and he would do whatever it took to carry the day.

Jacob Hogg had come of age.

three weeks to go . . .

T OBY WAS TANNED to a light mahogany, and although his face split with delight on seeing Ben, there was something hesitant in his hug when Ben scooped him up and blew a wet kiss into his neck.

'Dad . . .' he groaned, feet dangling, wriggling like a fish on a hook to free himself.

'Ben, he's beyond that sort of thing.'

Ben glanced at Madeleine and let Toby slither to the ground. 'Sorry, Tobes, I couldn't help it.'

'No, I'm not,' said Toby to Madeleine.

Madeleine shot Toby a less than motherly look. 'Go and get your things together.'

'I've already packed.'

'Is it the small bag that fits in the top box?'

'Yes, Mum.' The facetious note in Toby's voice flirted with danger.

'Well, go and check you haven't forgotten anything. I need to speak to your father.'

*

Ben knew something was up when Lionel followed them out into the garden. In fact, why wasn't Lionel at work on a Monday? He'd had a whole day to recover from the flight. Only when they were seated at the tin table on the terrace and Madeleine was pouring the coffee did Ben see what was coming.

It was a showy ring, big on diamonds.

It winked at him and then landed a punch in his gut.

'You're getting married . . .' Not quite a statement, not quite a question.

'Lionel proposed in St Lucia.' Madeleine reached for Lionel's hand.

'Congratulations.' Ben knew he had spoken – he had felt his jaw move – but it was as if the word had been uttered by another. 'Really. Congratulations.' This time he made a conscious effort to look each of them squarely and meaning-fully in the eye.

There was a misting of embarrassment in Lionel's gaze, or maybe it was pity. 'Thank you.'

'When?'

'We haven't settled on a date,' replied Lionel. 'Some time in the autumn, though.'

'Does Toby know?'

'They all know,' said Madeleine. 'Hugo and Lucinda too. There's no reason for them not to.'

Lionel shot Madeleine a wary glance. 'Toby's taken it OK. No more than OK.'

'Oh, for goodness sake, he's fine with it.' Madeleine quickly realised that this bald assertion made her look foolish. 'OK, there were a few tears, but that's only to be expected. Your opinion will make a big difference to him.'

'My opinion?'

'Come on, Ben, he worships you, you know he does.' He wanted to tell her that he knew no such thing but he didn't get a chance to. 'It's your job too to help him through this. There's only so much we can do.'

How gratifyingly grown-up. They were all in this together.

'Don't worry,' he said. 'I'll do my bit.'

'Do you think you could sound a little less, well, grudging?'

'Yes, Madeleine. Just give me a little more, well, time to get my head round it.'

Lionel could have taken the easy path and kept his distance, but he even contrived to snatch a private moment alone with Ben. It happened out the front of the house, while Ben was loading Toby's bag into the Honda's top box.

'This can't be easy for you, I know.'

Ben pushed the hair out of his eyes. 'I'd be feeling a whole lot worse if it was anyone other than you.'

He meant it, and when he offered his hand, Lionel gripped it firmly.

'He's your son. I'll never take him away from you.'

In the movies, Madeleine and Toby would have appeared from the house on the back of this touching exchange. They didn't, though, and Lionel filled the awkward silence with a question.

'So, you know Victor Sheldon?'

'Yeah, from years ago.'

'I hear it's some place he's got out there in Oxfordshire.'

'It certainly is.' He didn't say that it was going to be his home for the next month or so. 'Have you had any dealings with him?'

'I wish! No, he's way out of my league. He made a fortune anticipating the crash . . . shorted the subprime mortgage market. He's got great radar, a sixth sense.'

'He puts it down to hard graft and mathematical models.'

'He's lying. That stuff can only carry you so far.'

'I'll tell him he has an admirer.'

'Better still, ask him what he thinks about the current market capitalisation of BP.'

It was accompanied by a little chuckle, but Ben sensed Lionel was only half-joking.

As soon as Toby realised they were heading away from Chelsea Bridge, their usual route back to Ben's flat, he raised his helmet visor and shouted, 'Where are we going?'

'The Wolseley.'

'What's that?'

'An art gallery.'

'Dad . . .' The pain was evident in his voice.

'Two weeks on a beach . . . you need a bit of culture, young man.'

They were treated like royalty from the moment they crossed the threshold.

'Ah, Mr Makepeace,' said David, the maître d', swooping on them. 'And this must be Toby. A pleasure to meet you, Toby.'

David relieved them of their helmets, which he handed to one of his subordinates before leading them through to the dining area. It was a prime table at the heart of the restaurant, and as soon as they were seated Toby found his napkin cracked like a whip and laid on his lap.

'Your mother must be a very beautiful woman,' said David, leaning conspiratorially close, 'because you don't get your looks from your father.' A little wink and he spun on his heel, summoning a waiter as he disappeared.

'Dad . . .' said Toby.

'Tobes . . .?' said Ben.

'What are we doing here?'

'Having lunch, of course.'

'Do they know who you really are?'

'What, you think they've mistaken me for Brad Pitt?'

'In your dreams.'

The waiter handed them their menus. 'Can I get you something to drink?'

'A Coke, please,' said Toby, half-expecting the request to be vetoed. Ben returned the wine list. 'And a bottle of Badoit. Thank you.'

Toby scanned the menu, wide-eyed.

'Have whatever you want,' said Ben. 'This one's on me.'

It sat there between them, brooding like a witch's curse, but they both knew this wasn't the moment to discuss it. The lively buzz in the air demanded a different kind of conversation, and there were plenty of far cheerier things to catch up on.

Ben received a blow-by-blow account of the holiday in St

Lucia, of the hotel's three swimming pools and its private beach and the small villa set among the palms that Toby had shared with Lionel's children, Hugo and Lucinda. The tales of windsurfing and para-sailing and deep-sea fishing were accompanied by a slide show of photos which Toby pulled up on the old iPhone he'd inherited from Hugo, his soon-to-be stepbrother.

They had even gone hiking in a rainforest. This sequence of snaps contained the one that stung the most. Taken by someone else, it showed all five of them standing beside a waterfall, toothy smiles and arms draped around each other. It was everything he and Madeleine had privately dreamed of – three kids, two boys and a girl, ideally – but Ben had somehow been photoshopped out of the image, replaced by a short and greying stranger.

The rainforest was followed by more shots of the beach which Toby seemed in a hurry to get through.

'Hey, hold your horses. Who's that?'

'Oh, just some girl.'

'Enlarge, please.'

Toby stretched the image out. She was pretty as a picture, with large blue eyes set in an elfin face, and straight blond hair that shimmered like silk.

'Does she have a name?'

'Alice. But she says "Aleece".'

'She's got a speech impediment?'

'She's French.'

'That's a pity.'

'Why?'

'Well, she's gorgeous but she lives in another country.'

'No, she goes to the French Lycée in South Kensington.'

'You're joking!'

Toby eyed him suspiciously. 'Mum told you, didn't she?'

Ben laid his hand on his heart. 'I swear on the streetlight on the corner shoving back the shadows.'

Toby frowned, trying to place the words. 'Joni Mitchell.'

'You listened to it?'

'It's rubbish music, Dad.'

'You mean *so* rubbish that you remember the lyrics?'

'I mean *so* rubbish I can't forget the rubbish lyrics. Swearing on a streetlight doesn't mean anything. It's not like swearing on, I don't know, the Bible.'

Ben raised an eyebrow. He had never hidden from Toby that he wasn't a believer.

'OK, your mother's life, then. Grandma's life.'

Toby had him over a barrel, and he raised his hands in a gesture of surrender. 'OK, OK, Mum might have mentioned something. But she never said *Aleece was a leetle French cupcake.*'

'Dad . . .'

'Tobes . . .?'

'Put a sock in it.'

Stoneham Park might not have been the Coral Cove Resort in St Lucia, but it offered enough in the way of amenities to stir Toby's interest.

'Can I come and stay with you?'

'Sure, of course. I'll be working, but it doesn't mean we can't have some fun. It's a better place to be than my flat.'

'Dad, can I tell you something? I never liked your flat.'

'Me neither.'

'So why did you buy it?'

Be shrugged. 'Don't know.'

'Was it cheap?'

'Not particularly.' He could remember the mix of delight and bewilderment in the estate agent's voice when he'd made the offer on the place. That should have been a sign. 'I guess I wasn't thinking straight at the time.'

'Maybe you should sell it.'

'I'd lose money on it.'

'So?'

'That's the trouble with you Chelsea types, you don't know how the other half lives.'

Toby appeared flummoxed, embarrassed. He avoided Ben's eye.

'Hey, I was joking.'

'I know, Dad.'

What thoughts were swirling through his young head? Not good ones, for sure, and Ben swiftly turned the talk to holidays. They had to decide what they were going to do with their week together at the end of August.

It had been cleared with Madeleine, blocked out, booked in and they spent much of the rest of the meal travelling the world, exploring their options.

It was too hot to traipse the streets of the West End, so on leaving the restaurant they headed south, making for St James's Park.

The recent heat wave had dulled the grass to a drab tan, and the leaves seemed to hang limp on the plane trees and the oaks. Passing the bandstand, they took the narrow bridge spanning the turbid lake and bore left.

'Do you think they'll still be there?' asked Toby.

'I don't see why not.'

It was a good couple of years since they'd come here to gawp at the pelicans, and Ben had never seen such a crowd gathered. This might have had something to do with the video that had gone viral on the internet since their last visit, the one showing a pelican snaffling up a live pigeon and swallowing it whole. If so, then those hoping for a repeat of the gruesome spectacle would have been disappointed. Most of the pelicans were resting near the water's edge, and those few that were up and about appeared listless, bored.

When one of the birds hopped on to a park bench and began preening itself, you sensed that it had one black and beady eye on the closing throng, already anticipating the scraps of food which would come its way as reward for the tired performance.

It was a depressing spectacle, and an unwelcome harbinger of what they both knew was coming.

Ben waited until they had taken refuge from the sun in the shade of a mulberry tree.

'Mum told me . . . about Lionel and her.'

Toby was lying on his back, staring up at the spreading boughs. 'Oh.'

He wasn't going to give his feelings away cheaply; Ben would have to work for them.

'What are you thinking?'

Toby closed his eyes and a small frown corrugated his brow. Ben waited, and when nothing more was forthcoming he plucked some blades of grass and tossed them at Toby. The first batch missed completely; the second landed on his face. Toby wiped them away. Only now did he turn and look at Ben with pained eyes.

'It doesn't change anything, Tobes.'

'That's what Mum said, but it does. It means things can't ever be like before.'

'That was true already.'

'But people divorce and get back together. Adam Pritchard's mum and dad did.'

'Who's Adam Pritchard?'

'I don't really know him. He's in the year above.'

It was upsetting to think of Toby drawing any kind of hope from the experiences of someone he hardly knew.

'Don't you love Mum any more?' His voice shook on the brink of a sob.

'How could I not love someone who grew you inside her?'

'So stop it. Stop them.'

'I can't, Tobes.'

Toby's eyes searched his face. 'No,' he said quietly, with resignation. The tears came now.

'Hey, come here.' He lay down beside Toby and slipped an arm around him, drawing him close. Toby twisted, burying his face in Ben's shirt, clinging to him.

'I'm not going anywhere. I'm never going anywhere. I'll always be here. Always.'

They were the only words of comfort he could offer. Anything more would have been lies. He couldn't promise to make things better or to take the pain away. Even the passage of time couldn't be relied upon to do that, although it would probably oblige.

Theirs wasn't an extraordinary story – fractured families were almost the norm nowadays rather than the exception – but this was no consolation to Toby. And with his son's tears dampening his shirt, Ben also failed to draw any solace from it.

He felt a stab of shame, and then anger, at both himself and Madeleine for what they'd done to their beautiful boy. First the separation, then the divorce, then the imposition of a new family, and now this: the grim finality of it all.

He dredged his own past for parallels, but his childhood had been a relatively happy affair. Yes, there had been tensions at home. His mother had always resented the amount of time his father spent abroad on business (almost as much as she had disliked his authoritarian posturing whenever he was around). By and large, though, his parents had got on well – well enough to make each other laugh and to curl up on the sofa together in front of an old black-and-white movie on a Saturday afternoon, and even, on occasions, to hold hands in public (a cause of crippling embarrassment to Ben and his sister Emily).

He might not have been exactly smothered with love when

younger but neither had his parents inflicted any deep emotional wounds on him of the kind now tormenting Toby. In fact, he could think of only one thing, but that hadn't been a wound so much as a running sore, and he had learned to live with the irritation of it easily enough.

thirty-five years before . . .

'MY GOODNESS, YOU'RE a well-travelled young fellow, aren't you?' said Ben's father.

'Not really, sir,' replied Jacob. For some reason he had gone all coy and cute, and Ben wanted to tell him to be normal. Well, maybe not normal, because 'normal' for Jacob was pretty weird and irritating. Something else, though, something in between.

'Please, call me Lawrence.'

'Are you sure that's all right, sir?'

Ben's father pointed a finger at Jacob. 'Ah! There you go again! No more "sirs", Jacob.'

'No more sirs, sir.'

It was a joke, and not a very good one, but his father was practically choking on his food, snatching up his napkin from his lap to cover his mouth.

'Lawrence,' scolded his mother.

His father waved aside her reprimand. 'Very good,' he said, when he had swallowed and was able to draw a proper breath. 'Very good indeed.' He threw back a big slug of red wine.

Ben glanced at his mother and saw that she was looking at him with something like sadness in her eyes. But it couldn't be that, he thought.

It was Jacob's first night in their house and he had already passed his first test, the only test that really mattered. Ben's father approved; he wouldn't be putting up any resistance. Ben knew this before he went to bed, because as he wandered down the corridor to the bathroom to have a pee and brush his teeth he heard his parents' voices drifting up the back staircase from the kitchen and he stopped to listen.

'Eight years old and a rapier wit,' said his father.

'Ben too,' replied his mother. 'He can be very funny.'

'Yes, yes, of course,' said his father.

Ben heard the clatter of crockery. Someone was doing the dishes, possibly his father, because for all his general hopelessness about the place he didn't mind washing up. Ben knew it was his mother at the sink when he heard the sound of a cigarette being lit and someone exhaling hard, as his father always did, like a whale blowing. 'I'm more than happy to help the little chap out if you are.'

'I'm not against it.'

Ben could tell that his mother's words carried another message, so why couldn't his father?

'Excellent. And it's only for a year, you say?'

'Just exeats and half-terms,' replied his mother. 'And it's not as if you're going to be around for most of those.'

'Oh, that's nice. Thank you for that.'

'Well, it's true, isn't it?'

Ben didn't hang around. He knew what was coming. He knew the arguments for and against. They were equally convincing, although on balance he thought his father had the better deal. 'Bringing home the bacon' didn't sound like much fun, but it sounded a whole lot better than 'being shackled to a hot stove'.

Because it was Jacob's first night, he was sleeping in Ben's bedroom on the old canvas camp bed. Or rather, he was supposed to be, but he decided to sleep on the floor instead. He said it reminded him of Brazil and Bolivia and Indonesia. These were the places he had lived with his parents, the countries which had so impressed his father over dinner. Not forgetting America, of course, where Jacob's mother had just been given a job at a university for a year, and where he had spent the Christmas holidays. His new home was a town called Cambridge, which was near Boston.

They weren't in the same dormitories at school, so it was the first time they'd lain on their backs in the darkness and talked themselves to sleep. Ben had never heard Jacob's stories before, but he was surprised he hadn't heard about them from the boys in Jacob's dormitory. They were that good.

Indonesia was a country near Australia – well, not a country like we thought of a country, but loads of islands all jumbled up together. There were jungles everywhere, and paddy fields for growing rice that climbed the mountains like mirrored staircases. There were also lots of tigers and volcanoes. Jacob had actually seen a volcano blowing its top. And in the olden days, near where they used to live, there was once a volcano out at sea that made a wave so big that afterwards an anchor from a boat was found five miles inland.

The stories were so good that Ben wondered if Jacob was making them up. He didn't say anything, though, in case they stopped.

Tigers sneaked into houses at night, sniffed people lying in their beds and then left. Other tigers came hurtling out of the jungle and decapitated people with one swipe of their paw. Jacob had never seen a tiger in the wild, but he had seen men who could put meat skewers through their cheeks and their arms without feeling any pain or even bleeding when they pulled them out.

And that was just Indonesia.

The next morning, Jacob said, 'Please don't tell anyone else. They're my stories, but I don't mind sharing them with you.'

That's how it began, although it really began the moment Ben's fist made contact with Michael Kramer's nose. Everything went back to that split second of blind violence, which Jacob had chosen to interpret as a personal favour.

There were times when Ben wished he hadn't punched Kramer on the nose. He couldn't turn the clock back, though. Jacob was now part of his life. Everybody at school knew it, because Jacob told anyone who would listen, even the teachers, that Ben's parents were now his 'guardians'. He acted as if this made him one of Ben's best friends. But Ben's best friends didn't cheat in tests, and they weren't rude to the senior boys, and they didn't steal sweets from the tuck shop when Mrs Spurdle wasn't looking (although she was half-blind anyway).

Jacob didn't seem to care what people thought of him, although he was always on his best behaviour with Ben's parents. This was one of the reasons Ben liked him more when they were at home. It was also good to have another boy to play with. Emily was only five, too young still to stick in goal and fire footballs at. Ben had tried it at Christmas and it had ended in tears and a telling-off.

Jacob, on the other hand, was just like Ben: mad on sports and far happier outdoors than in. Climbing and leaping and throwing and running were their thing. Even when the weather was rotten they would both much rather be messing around in the wet and the cold than making Airfix models or playing Monopoly. There was more than enough to keep them occupied and entertained. There was a large garden with several lawns and a tarmac tennis court and big cedar trees for climbing. There was also a paddock with an empty stable which made a perfect camp. On the north side of the house lay a tangled copse which used to be a clay quarry. Dry in the summer, for much of the year it was dangerously deep in water, and there was an old rowboat which they were allowed to use (but only if a grown-up was around). Best of all, though, the house sat at the foot of the South Downs, with their wild woods and their steep slopes which were perfect for sliding down on old fertiliser sacks they nicked from the farm next door.

They had only lived in Sussex for two years, and Ben still had clear memories of the house they'd left behind in London: the leafy square out front, his small bedroom on the top floor, reached by endless flights of stairs. It had been his father's idea to move to the countryside, even though he now had to spend more than two hours a day on the train going to and from work in London. Ben's mother was less keen than his father on life in the country. His father loved it. He loved dressing up in country clothes and shooting pheasants and going to the pub in the village where the owner called him 'squire' and served him beer in his own pewter tankard. He also loved cricket, and he opened the batting for the village team with a bald man called Kenneth who was a dentist in Brighton.

There was no denying it, life was more fun for Ben with Jacob around during school exeats and half-terms. This became clear when Jacob flew off to America for the Easter holidays and Ben spent four weeks practising his bowling against some stumps he'd chalked on to the garage wall.

He wasn't the only one to feel Jacob's absence. His father mentioned it several times. So did Emily. She missed being hurled on to the sofa and tickled until she almost weed herself. When Ben offered to fill in, she played along for a bit then said it wasn't the same with him.

'Here, let me have a go,' said his father, swooping on

Emily, who twisted and kicked and rolled around, giggling and gasping for breath.

'You see, Ben?' he said. 'This is how it's done. This is how me and Jacob do it.'

nineteen days to go . . .

TRUE TO FORM, Madeleine had made a stack of plans to keep Toby occupied for the rest of the summer holidays. There was a tennis camp in Battersea Park and a drama course in Fulham, and she was thinking of signing him up for a week of sailing on a reservoir out near Hampton Court.

'*Mens sana in corpore sano*,' said Ben.

'And what's wrong with that?' bristled Madeleine.

'Nothing. Don't be so defensive.'

'You make me defensive.'

'Well, I don't mean to. I'm just trying to find some time when he can come out to Oxfordshire with me.'

'Stay on the line, I'll grab my diary.'

That pleased him: old school through and through, a deep-dyed pen-and-paper girl, still fighting the good fight against the dark arts of electronica.

'Sorry,' said Madeleine. 'My iPad's out of juice. I'll have to call you back.'

The best she could offer him was five days at the

beginning of August, Monday to Friday. Ben didn't complain. It suited his own plans, allowing him a couple of weeks to settle in at Stoneham Park and make a sizeable dent in the rewrite. He reckoned he was looking at about a month in total. That's what he had told Lucinda, the bright and bookish young woman whom Victor had lured away from the British Film Institute to run Tortoise Pictures.

Tortoise's offices on Wardour Street were extremely smart and way too large for its skeleton staff of two. 'Believe me,' Lucinda had said, 'we're going to need every inch of space when *The Bet* goes into production.' Such rosy optimism was always welcome, even if he'd brushed with it too many times before to take it seriously. Lucinda was up on the new title, and she was up on the changes that Victor had suggested. She didn't just approve of them, she was eager to talk through the nuts-and-bolts implications for the script.

'They're not as radical as I first thought.'

'I agree.'

'Am I dreaming? I can't remember the last time a writer agreed with me.'

They decided that the love story at the heart of script would naturally take on a greater significance, given the new cross-racial nature of the relationship. This would require some subtle enhancements. The rest of the plot, however, was pretty much race-proof. Ben's biggest challenge would be bringing to life a cast of credible new Asian characters.

'I know you can do it. I mean, you can't have much first-hand knowledge of young white gang members, and yet they're all completely believable. Their dialogue is, well, very convincing.' For a middle-class, middle-aged man, added her eyes.

He didn't let on that he'd spent many hours on buses – usually upstairs, where the school kids liked to hang out – eavesdropping and surreptitiously scribbling away. A line like 'I isn't even lying to you, blood. So much of me wants to suck her inside out' wasn't dredged from the darker reaches of his imagination, it was copied down verbatim on the top deck of the No. 39 as it crawled round the Wandsworth one-way system at four o'clock in the afternoon.

It had been a fruitful discussion, and Ben had emerged into the clammy heat of Wardour Steet afterwards with a definite spring in his step. He had been impressed by Lucinda, and flattered rather than threatened when she had handed him a script as he was leaving. 'We've just optioned it. I'd love to know what you think.'

Tortoise Pictures was an outfit with big plans and high hopes; she had left him in no doubt of that.

Victor was thrilled to hear that Ben would be decamping to Stoneham Park for the duration of the rewrite. 'Thrilled' was the word he used in his email from São Paolo, where he was about to go deep-sea fishing with a senior cabinet minister who was, he strongly suspected, the grandson of a Nazi fugitive. **Which just goes to show something or other,** probably that Paul was wrong about the unjust not inheriting the kingdom.

Ben was to make himself at home and to remember to pay homage at the altar of Annabelle. **She thinks of it as her place, which I'm cool with. It wouldn't be what it is without her, so please play along. And don't take any nonsense from Mo. If you get the spineless shandy-drinking southerner lecture – yawn – chuck it right back at her, but not too hard, she's a delicate Yorkshire flower beneath the body armour.**

This last bit surprised him. Over the past few days he had imagined any number of scenarios with Mo, but none of them had involved her berating him for being a spineless shandy-drinking southerner. And as for the body armour, yes, she was direct, plain-spoken, but he had also found her warm, open and very amusing. Or maybe he had only glimpsed the best of her in the half-day he had known her. When looked at with an honest eye, one lunch, a short stroll and a snatched dinner weren't much to go on.

She must have heard by now that he was coming to stay up at Stoneham Park, and he wondered how she'd taken the news. With the same quiver of anticipation? Unlikely. But he allowed himself to think that the prospect of his company didn't leave her entirely cold.

'Fuck off,' said Mo.

Ben paused in the entrance to her studio. 'Really?'

'Yes, really. Fuck off.'

'OK.'

'Goodbye,' she said curtly.

He made to leave but turned back. 'Bad day?'

Mo glared at him. She had pushed the mask up on to her forehead when she saw him enter; she now pulled it off altogether and dropped it at her feet. 'Bad week. Bad hangover. Bad period pains. But you wouldn't know anything about those,' she added, as though he might be personally to blame.

'You're wrong. I know a girl who swears by pomegranate juice. But then again, she's mad as a wet hen.'

'A wet hen?'

'Oooh, is someone smiling?'

'Against her better judgement. When did you get here?'

'About a minute ago. I heard the drill.'

'It's not a drill, it's a pneumatic chisel.'

He noted it was hanging from her left hand. 'Are you left-handed?'

'Why? You too?'

'A bit of both,' he replied.

'How does that work?'

'I write, throw, do most things with my left. But when it comes to cricket and golf I'm right-handed.' He swung at an imaginary golf ball to demonstrate the point.

'Are you any good at cricket?' she asked.

'That was golf. This is cricket.' He swung again, his best cover drive, keeping the elbow nice and high.

'From the look of that, you'd be perfect for the local village team.'

'You think?'

'Definitely. I've seen them play and they're shit. I also know they're short of players.'

He ignored the insult. 'I'm only here for a month.'

'Annabelle said.'

'What else did she say?'

'Not much. That your son might be coming too.'

'Toby.'

'Or not Toby.'

'That's good.'

'No, it isn't.'

'Can I see how it's coming on?' He took a couple of steps towards her but stopped, raising his hands as she levelled the pneumatic drill at him like a gun. 'You know what they say, don't point it unless you're prepared to use it.'

'Oh, I am. I'll see you at seven thirty.'

'Seven thirty?'

'Mrs Danvers has a welcome dinner planned for you. I cleared my diary especially.'

'Well, I hope you're in a better mood by then.'

'Don't bank on it.'

It was an unfair slight. Annabelle had little in common with the plain, bitter and vengeful housekeeper in Daphne du Maurier's *Rebecca*. In fact, Mo in her current state would have fitted a casting director's brief far more accurately.

Annabelle, looking ridiculously healthy after her holiday in France, welcomed Ben warmly and accompanied him upstairs to his room. A large desk had been installed between the windows since his last visit. 'In case you want to work up here.' There was wi-fi throughout the house. Annabelle scribbled down the network key then talked him through the touch-screen tablet which ran the lighting, music, TV, even the electric curtains. Every room in the place had its own independent media system that drew off the mainframes down in the basement, but you could also connect your own device if you wanted to. If you switched to intelligent mode then a system of sensors could track you as you moved between the bedroom and the bathroom, turning on the lights for you, and automatically transferring your music or the film you were watching.

'That's a bit too Big Brother for me.'

'Me too,' said Annabelle. 'But Mr Sheldon loves his gadgets.'

The ground-floor alarm was always set at night by the last person to head upstairs, and she showed him how to arm and deactivate it from the panel set in the wall at the top of the staircase. 'I won't actually do it because Chef's in the kitchen and he'll set it off.'

That's where they found him, fiddling around with some crayfish on the giant table in the middle of his stone and stainless-steel kingdom. His name was Gregoire, and Ben had met him briefly before, just long enough to compliment him on the chargrilled lamb he'd served up for Sunday lunch. He was a Frenchman of a certain age, nudging sixty, Ben guessed, but still with a full head of long silver hair which he wore pushed back off his craggily handsome face. Happy to hear that Ben would eat anything put in front of him, Gregoire was positively delighted when Ben said he generally made do with a banana and a cup of coffee for breakfast, because this meant he wouldn't have to get up early and lay on a spread.

'But he might want someone to peel the banana for him,' observed Annabelle drily.

'Then I give him a lesson,' growled Gregoire. He took a banana from the fruit bowl and tossed it to Ben.

'It's OK, I think I've mastered it.'

'You think, but maybe you are wrong. Show me.'

Ben made to peel it.

'Ah no!' declared Gregoire, triumphantly. '*Les singes . . .* how do you say?'

'Monkeys.'

'Yes, monkeys, they open from the other end, the bottom. It is easier.'

Ben gave it a go, amazed to discover it was true. 'I had no idea . . .'

Gregoire laughed. '*Tu vois, ils sont pas des idiots, les singes.*'

Their next port of call was the walled vegetable garden, where Gregoire's wife, Camille, was hard at work in the lean-to greenhouse, as long as two train carriages strung together. They found her down the far end, beyond a cohort of tomato plants, tending to a colourful array of potted aubergines and peppers. She was an attractive woman with the same easy air about her as Gregoire. Her greying hair was tied back in a messy ponytail, and her long fingers were cruelly blighted by arthritis, Ben noted.

Moving on, Annabelle explained that Victor had lured

Gregoire and Camille to England after their restaurant near Nice had gone bust. 'He thought about bailing them out, but their standards are far too high to make a viable business of it.' They had been happy to give England a try because the move abroad had actually brought them closer to their two grown-up daughters, both of whom now lived in Paris. 'They're going to give it a year and see how they feel, but I already have a hunch they'll stay on with us.'

When Ben set eyes on the old stone house that was now their home, he could understand why. Draped in wisteria and ringed by a garden dripping in roses, it was one of two picture-postcard houses that stood just beyond the farm buildings, at the head of a gravel track leading to a long run of cottages. The other house was occupied by the farm manager and his family, the cottages by farm workers and gardeners, all of whom were out and about on the estate at this hour.

Victor's chauffeur was at home, and he was the reason for their visit. Lance lived in the end cottage, where the track gave way to a five-bar gate and rolling pasture. They found him in the back garden making the most of his boss's absence, enjoying the afternoon sunshine with his wife, Cheryl, and their young daughter, who was splashing around in a pink paddling pool.

Lance was a short, squat, bulldog of a man. Any shorter and you might have wondered how on earth he managed to reach the pedals. His hair was cropped close to his skull, and his accent was unmistakably working-class London.

The West Ham football shirt narrowed it down still further, the claret and blue clashing horribly with the yellow and black patterned surf shorts which reached well below his knees.

Annabelle made the introductions before announcing, 'I spoke to Mr Sheldon earlier and I'm sorry to say he's had to extend his trip.'

'That's too bad,' grinned Lance.

'He also said that Ben's to have free use of all the cars in his absence.'

'Even the classics?' asked Lance.

'No, not those.'

Lance's dark pebble eyes roamed over Ben. 'Got a clean licence, do you?'

'Three points.'

'Speeding?'

'Faulty brake light on my motorbike.'

'Harsh.'

'Tell me about it.'

Sitting on Ben's desk at home was a quotation he'd printed out and placed in a photo frame some years ago. It was from Jerome K. Jerome's *Three Men in a Boat* and it read: *I like work. It fascinates me. I can sit and stare at it for hours.*

This had always annoyed the hell out of Madeleine, who had taken it as proof positive (if such a thing were needed) of his feckless irresponsibility when it came to work. It was true that he had never allowed professional matters to jeopardise the serious business of living well, but even Madeleine would have been proud of him for the way he applied himself on his first afternoon at Stoneham Park.

Firing up his laptop, he launched straight into the rewrite, achieving far more than he could ever have imagined in the three hours he was seated at the desk in his room. He broke off only once, to make himself another coffee in the kitchen. Just where this burst of inspiration came from, he had no idea, but such moments were rare, transitory, to be respected whenever you were fortunate enough to find yourself in step with one of them.

Invigorated, he took himself off to the pool for a swim before dinner, pushing himself hard, to his limit, which proved to be a rather sobering twenty lengths.

Christ, he was out of shape. It seemed that giving up the cigarettes had done nothing for his stamina. The creeping hand of old Father Time, no doubt. What better opportunity than this to loosen its grip and turn back the clock? He could picture the regime: a month of work and healthy eating punctuated by regular exercise. He might even take up running again. Yes. Why not? The beauty of the surrounding countryside cried out for it.

He marked this new resolution with two knee-buckling gin and tonics on the back terrace before dinner. Mo mixed them both, and the first one came with an apology.

'I'm sorry about before.'

'Forget it.'

'I was in a bit of a grump.'

'Hey, it happens.'

She looked at him askance. 'Are you always so bloody reasonable?'

'Sure I am. Ask my ex-wife, she'll tell you.'

She had a great laugh, one that bubbled up from deep in her gut, but it was the way her eyes locked on to his when they clinked glasses that pleased him most.

She offered no explanation for her behaviour earlier, so he told her about his afternoon and the introductory tour of the estate which Annabelle had taken him on.

'So, you met Lance and lived to tell the tale?'

'Er, yes . . .' he replied uncertainly.

'He can kill a person with one punch to the throat. That's what he told me once.'

'Then he needs to work on his small talk.'

She smiled. 'Didn't Annabelle say? He's ex-army.'

'Isn't he a bit short for that sort of thing?'

'Maybe it means he can go places other men can't. Hey, you could write a film about him.'

'You know, it's not a bad idea.' He put on a gravelly American film-trailer voice: 'Dwarf Commando. Just when you thought it was safe to open the fridge.'

She liked that a lot. 'You've got to do it. That's a film I have to see.'

When Annabelle eventually joined them, she arrived on a cloud of scent. 'Oh God,' she said, flapping at the air around her. 'I've overdone the Chanel, haven't I? I'm sorry, I was in a rush. Victor called. It's why I'm late.'

Her arrival killed off the playful, gin-fuelled nonsense that had sprung up between Ben and Mo. Suddenly they were acquaintances again, school children in the presence of a teacher.

Gregoire and Camille made up the numbers, which was entirely appropriate given the amazing spread they'd prepared. The starter of warm shellfish was a revelation, and all the more remarkable for the fact that Stoneham Park lay about as far from the sea as any place in the British Isles. It was easy to forget that money had a way of ironing out such inconveniences; the whelks and razor clams had arrived by special delivery direct from Cornwall that same afternoon. The crayfish, on the other hand, were local – from Gregoire's own traps which he'd laid in the River Cherwell.

As dusk surrendered to dark they raised a toast to their absent host/friend/employer for the bounty he'd provided but would never share in. Gregoire was eager to know more about Ben and Victor's history, and Ben told it pretty much as it had been: that Victor (he almost called him Jacob) had figured large in his life during the five years they'd spent together at a boarding prep school in the south of England. It had been a different age back then – no Facebook, no email, no internet at all – and from the age of fourteen they'd gradually lost touch following Victor's move to the States, where his parents had finally decided to settle after years of uncertainty.

Gregoire asked if the signs had always been there that Victor would one day make such a success of himself. Ben chose his words carefully, aware that Annabelle was observing him closely.

'No more so than many others.' (Absolutely not.) 'Although he always had an eye for an opportunity.' (He was unscrupulous.) 'And he knew what he wanted.' (He could be a pushy pain-in-the-arse.)

Camille was of the opinion that true success came in many forms, and that money was one of its least reliable indicators. This was a view heartily endorsed by Mo but challenged by Annabelle. 'Mr Sheldon is wise enough to know there will always be people who hate him for what he has achieved. But he is so far ahead of the rest of us. That's his gift. He sees things early. Money is just a by-product of that vision.'

It was a warning shot – don't you dare bite the hand that feeds you – and it drew the discussion politely yet firmly to a close.

Later, lying dwarfed in his four-poster bed, trying to read, Ben knew that Mo was the reason his eyes kept skimming over the words, barely registering them. She had told him she was a night owl, and he could picture her padding about her apartment in bare feet, having kicked off the new shoes which had been giving her grief during dinner. He could see the shoes, a pair of emerald-green leather slingback wedges which would have had Madeleine salivating in envy, not because she couldn't afford several hundred pounds of hippy chic designed by someone with an unpronounceable name, but because she wouldn't have been able to carry them off.

Mo could, even when she paired them with a grey taffeta

dress that was formal to the point of geekiness. Somehow, it worked as a combination. Somehow, everything about her worked.

Not for the first time, he doubled back and started the chapter afresh.

eighteen days to go . . .

BEN WAS WOKEN by the silence, his subconscious brain demanding to know what mishap had befallen Trisha in the flat below. Where was the dull but persistent beat of her huffing and bumping her way through her favoured exercise DVD? How come he couldn't picture fifteen stone of pale Glaswegian flesh lurching around the living room to the wildly optimistic strains of 'It's Raining Men'?

Trisha hated him. He stood for everything she despised: he was middle-class, privately educated and English. He couldn't fault her facts, but she seemed to take them as irrefutable proof that some toffee-nosed forebear of his had butchered untold numbers of noble Jacobite boys at the Battle of Culloden. Recently he had found himself drawing a certain masochistic pleasure from her thinly veiled contempt, from the frosty exchanges about ground rent, common parts and wheelie bins. It was almost as if he'd come to regard her as some kind of penance to be paid for the failures in his personal life and his career.

Perverse, he thought to himself, throwing back the duvet

and swinging his legs out of bed. How could he have allowed himself to sink so low? He was already breathing hard by the time he reached the gatehouse at the end of the driveway. He kept on running, though, bearing right along the road. After a hundred yards or so the drystone wall that ringed the estate gave way to a stretch of overgrown hedgerow and then the first straggle of houses. A black cat streaked across his path, and he tried to remember if that meant good luck or bad.

Stoneham proved to be a deceptively large village, much of it tucked away, well back from the high street, beyond the village green with its giant oak tree and its pond bristling with reeds. There was a pub and a church – the bare essentials for sinning and then seeking absolution – as well as a shop which had yet to open at this early hour. Behind the church a narrow lane led to the village playing field. It was a tranquil spot, leafy and secluded, fringed with towering chestnuts that screened it off from the surrounding fields.

He set himself the challenge of running five times round the cricket boundary before heading for home. He barely managed two circuits before pressing his palms to the wall of the wooden clubhouse and stretching out his tight calf muscles. Best not to overdo it on the first day of his new fitness regime, he told himself. Besides, he had to keep something in reserve for the swim.

Any slower and the jog back to Stoneham Park might have qualified as a brisk walk.

★

Annabelle was happy for him to set up shop in the library. It occupied the north-east corner of the building which meant that it was awash with morning sunlight, and the morning was the time of the day when he did his best work.

The room was a pure eighteenth-century gem, the only space in the house that hadn't felt the touch of later ages, or so it appeared. The tall bookcases lining the walls were in fact a recent addition, the originals having been sold off more than a century ago when the owners had fallen on hard times. No one knew what had become of them, but Annabelle was immensely proud of their replacements, because it was she who had turned detective, hunting down the clues. An early Victorian watercolour of the library, now languishing in the collection of the Metropolitan Museum of Art in New York, had been her greatest coup, enabling them to run off a set of near-perfect replicas. She had also sourced the marble portrait busts of long-dead writers and thinkers who surveyed the room from atop the bookcases: Socrates, Plutarch, Dante, Bacon, Descartes, Spinoza, Hobbes . . . They weren't identifiable from the watercolour in the Met, Annabelle explained, but she had turned up their names in the papers of Horace Walpole, who had visited Stoneham Park in the 1740s.

It amused Ben to think of himself working away in the presence of such intellectual giants. Between their world-changing scholarship and the trivial sensationalism of *The Bet* lay a great unbridgeable gulf.

He said as much to Annabelle, who laughed. 'Oh, I'm

sure they won't mind. They might even be amused. Look, I think Spinoza might be smiling.'

If they did mind, their disapproval had no impact on his capacity to work. He picked up where he'd left off the previous day and powered ahead. At some point he would hit a wall – he always did – but for now the new characters were springing effortlessly to life, and he was enjoying their company. He almost felt bad knowing what horrors lay in store for them, knowing which of them would survive and which would die. He was open to pleas of clemency. It had happened before: a minor character barging their way into the story, demanding to be heard, spared.

He had just decided to work through lunch when Mo appeared in the library. As luck would have it, he was also sitting back in his chair and laughing at a line of dialogue he'd just tapped into his laptop.

'Do you always find yourself so amusing?' she asked.

'Not me – a young chap called Ali. He's becoming quite the wag. I might have to let him live.'

'Playing God as well as laughing at your own jokes?'

'Two of the few pleasures of being a writer.'

She smiled weakly, taking a seat next to him. There was something wan and washed out about her, as if she'd slept badly, or not at all.

'How's it going?'

'It isn't,' she replied.

'Want to talk about it?'

'No, let's talk about your glasses.'

The small wire-framed reading glasses were perched on

the end of his nose. 'These? They cost me a fiver from a petrol station.'

'I'm almost inclined to take you seriously.'

'My son says they turn me into an old man.'

'Then Toby's being polite. You're already an old man.' It pleased him that she'd remembered Toby's name. 'Do you have a photo of him on there?'

'Sure.' He pulled up a shot of Toby at his school sports day.

'Look, it's a mini you.'

'Most people think he's got more of Madeleine in him.'

'Come on, let's see her.'

It was a photo he'd taken of Madeleine standing with Toby in the Chapter House at Wells Cathedral.

'My God, she's beautiful.'

'You reckon?'

'Come on, she's stunning.'

'I guess. That was taken right at the end.'

The painful memory was soon forgotten when Mo invited him to dinner later. Thursday was Gregoire's night off, and Annabelle was heading into Oxford to see a play with some friends.

'You might want to eat before,' she warned him. 'I'm the world's worst cook.'

'What's on the menu?'

'Whatever grabs my fancy at the butcher in Woodstock. Last time it was lamb kidneys wrapped in bacon.'

'OK, now I'm worried.'

'What do you suggest?'

'That I come with you.'

'Mission accomplished,' she grinned. 'I was fishing for company.'

They arranged to leave at four. He was usually written out by then, his eyelids heavy, his thoughts turning to the sweet prospect of forty winks to set him up for the evening. There was to be no power nap today, though.

Annabelle didn't have a problem with him taking the Maserati, although she did ask him to be especially careful. It was Victor's baby, his private runaround; pranging it wasn't an option. Ben headed out front ten minutes early – time enough to familiarise himself with the Maserati's many bells and whistles, he figured.

He had never sat at the wheel of such an exquisite vehicle before. From the gentle give of the tan calfskin seats to the walnut trim of the dashboard and the liquid resonance of the sound system, the car exuded a discreet and nonchalant class. He tapped WOODSTOCK into the touch-screen satnav. The voice was that of a well-spoken woman, and she wasn't happy that the long driveway of Stoneham Park didn't figure in her database.

'Proceed to the highlighted route,' she demanded haughtily. He killed the power then pulled out his phone.

Sitting in a Maserati GranTurismo and wishing you were here x

Toby's reply was almost instantaneous: **No way!!**

Way!!

OMG! V jelus

Promise not to take it above 100 till you get here

Cant wait!
Miss you. Speak later x

He had just fired off the text when he was startled by a rapping on the passenger side window. It was Mo. She tugged open the door. 'Are you kidding? I'm not going in this.'

'Why not?'

'You don't mind people thinking you're a total prick? Let's take my Golf.'

'Come on, indulge me, just this once.'

She grunted then folded herself into the seat. 'You boys and your toys.'

'Endearing, isn't it?'

'Pathetic is what it is.' Dropping her bag at her feet, she attached the seatbelt then pulled the hem of her short summer dress towards her knees. 'Victor once drove me into Oxford in this thing and he beamed like a well-fed baby all the way.'

'I won't.'

He turned the key and the engine came to life with a throaty purr.

'You're doing it already.'

'First and last time, I promise.'

He chose Previous Destinations on the satnav's menu. WOODSTOCK appeared at the top of the list. He was about to select it when something caught his eye.

Further down the list, almost at the bottom, was a postcode. It was his own postcode in London.

He struggled to make sense of it.

'You don't need that,' said Mo. 'I know the way.'

He turned off the satnav and slipped the gearstick into Drive.

The Maserati was loaded with power and it handled like a dream, but the discovery of his postcode took the edge off the driving experience and disengaged him from the conversation with Mo.

What was it doing there, sandwiched between ALDEBURGH and another postcode? And when exactly had Victor gone to Aldeburgh? Since their first meeting? It seemed unlikely. He had spent most of his time abroad on business following their lunch at the Wolseley. Then again, it was possible that others had used the car in the meantime – Lance, perhaps, or even Annabelle. Also, the fact that his postcode was stored in the system didn't necessarily mean that the car had actually made the journey to his street. Maybe someone had simply been curious to see where he lived. But that in itself was pretty odd, and surely they would have turned first to the internet for an answer.

Fortunately, Woodstock offered a degree of distraction from these hydra-headed thoughts. He hadn't visited the old market town since his time at university, and he'd forgotten just how beautiful it was. There was a quiet grandeur to the place, which no doubt owed something to the imposing arched entranceway to Blenheim Palace which loomed at the western end of the high street.

The queue in the butcher's bought them time to weigh their options before settling on fillet steak for their dinner.

Mo had a prescription to pick up from the chemist down the road. There was no queue here, just a large woman behind the counter who greeted them with a gruff and ill-mannered, 'Yes?'

'I'm picking up a prescription,' said Mo.

'Name?'

'Mo Channing.'

The woman searched the trays of prepared prescriptions. 'I have one for a Molly Channing.'

'Mo's short for Molly.'

'Is it now? Address?'

Ben could almost hear Mo's sinews beginning to stiffen. 'Stoneham Park.'

'And would that be Number 2, The Stables?'

The subtext was clear: don't get ideas above your station, young lady; you live where the horses used to live.

'Yes, it would be.'

'Anything else?'

'Let me see . . .' Mo's eyes scanned the tall wooden unit behind the counter. 'Yes, some of that cotton wool, please.' It just so happened to live on the very top shelf, obliging the woman to manoeuvre her considerable bulk up some wooden steps in order to reach a packet of the stuff. Descending, she affected the look of someone who has just stumbled into base camp after a successful assault on the summit of Everest. 'Will that be all?' she asked tightly and a little breathlessly.

Mo gave her the sweetest of smiles. 'Yes, thank you.' Then after a beautifully engineered pause, 'Come to think of it . . .

better safe than sorry . . . I'll have another packet of the cotton wool.'

'Something tells me you have a problem with authority,' chuckled Ben as they left the shop.

'First up, that's not authority, it's a fat lass with attitude. And don't tell me you don't. Everyone who works for themself has a problem with authority.'

They walked on a little way. 'It's strange, I never used to.'

'I know. Victor told me. You were the golden boy. Captain of this, head of that.'

'You don't want to believe everything you hear.'

'You weren't head boy?'

'OK, I might have been.'

'So what went wrong?'

She was joking; his father hadn't been when he'd asked almost exactly the same question back in 1985.

'I don't know. I hit sixteen and suddenly all that stuff didn't matter any more. I'd had enough of playing the game, toeing the line.'

'You rebel. And two years later you got into Oxford.'

He didn't mind her teasing him; in fact, he rather relished it. 'I had a great English teacher, Mrs Phipps. And I've always read books, lots of books. It helped in the interview. You could blag it back then, slip in under the radar. I wouldn't stand a chance now. I was off the rails.'

'At sixteen I was doing things with boys I haven't done since.'

'Look at us, two total fuck-ups. Now where the hell did we park the damned Maserati?'

Victor had spent the past couple of months teaching Mo to play tennis, and his student did him proud. She had all the shots. She also had something you couldn't teach: a great natural touch – 'good hands', as the Aussie pro at Battersea Park would have said. Maybe this wasn't so surprising, given that she made her living with her hands.

They played barefoot on the grass court, no games, just scuttling about and hitting the ball back and forth, working themselves into a lather. The building humidity suggested there was truth in the rumour of impending and much-needed rain, as did the cumulus clouds twisting themselves into ominous shapes high overhead.

It was Mo's suggestion that they take a dip in the pool afterwards to cool down. She had a fine body, lean and taut, hardened by the physical nature of her work. Her breasts were larger than he'd imagined, although that could have had something to do with the clever cut of her bikini top.

She was obviously at home in the water, cutting through it with no apparent effort, even when she was idling up and down the pool beside him.

'You've done this before, haven't you?'

'You're looking at the runner-up in the Yorkshire County Under-Thirteen Girls Fifty-Metre Butterfly.'

'Butterfly? Respect. I don't think I've swum fifty metres of butterfly in the whole of my life.'

When he demanded a demonstration, Mo swam two elegant lengths of the stroke.

'I'm seriously impressed.'

'It's not as hard as it looks.'

This was a lie. It was considerably harder than it looked. Even after Mo had offered him some pointers – 'It's all in the second kick that drives the shoulders and arms out of the water' – he continued to thrash around like a fish in its final death throes, barely making any headway and swallowing a bunch of water into the bargain.

'Don't stop, don't stop,' he heard Mo call. 'You've almost got it!'

Foolishly, he believed her. Only when he had latched on to the side of the pool and had finished coughing did he see her standing in the shallows, laughing wildly at his abortive efforts.

They grabbed some salad and tomatoes from the greenhouse then raided the wine cellar. It lay off a long corridor of storage rooms sunk beneath the main house. Mo knew exactly which wines she was allowed to help herself to and which were off limits. 'Although Victor bungs me something special from time to time. He's very generous like that.'

The room next to the wine cellar was sealed by a steel door with a ventilation grille set in it, and in the darkness beyond, Ben could see lights winking and dancing on a run of tall computer stacks. It seemed like a lot of activity for a house that was silent as a church, deserted but for two people poking around in the basement.

'God, it's a good life,' he said as they made their way back upstairs, Mo cluthcing two fine-looking bottles of red wine.

'Don't get too attached to it. It's not real, and it's not forever.'

'It's real enough for Victor.'

'You think? Empty houses all over the world? Surreal, more like.'

Annabelle had left for Oxford while they were playing tennis, so they closed up the house before making for the stable block. The only way to reach Mo's apartment was through the studio, which meant passing right by her sculpture.

'I won't look if you don't want me to,' he offered.

'No, it's OK.'

Since his last visit she had finished off the left ear and carved a couple of curls around it, but that was about the extent of the progress. 'I don't get it. You've hardly touched it.'

'That's the point. I can't. The fear's got a hold of me.'

Apparently, it had only happened to her once before. She described it as the sculptor's equivalent of writer's block. But at least as a writer you could afford to experiment, to try out something new, knowing that you'd saved the original and could always return to it. Stone-carving was a reductive process, irreversible. Once you'd removed material, you could never put it back.

'But it's beautiful,' said Ben. 'Just keep doing what you've been doing.'

'But what if I don't want to? Michelangelo described it as freeing a figure from a block of stone, like it's trapped inside, fully formed, waiting to be revealed. I've always seen it the same way. But I don't like what's being revealed. I want to . . .' She made a couple of abrupt, sweeping gestures with her hand, 'I don't know, hack into it. Or something. I can't decide.'

'Maybe it's like a Russian doll. Maybe there's another one hiding inside.'

'Interesting,' she said. 'But not *that* interesting. Let's go find a corkscrew.'

They ate on a tin table in the yard: fillet steak, sautéed potatoes and a mixed salad. Ben ended up doing the cooking, from necessity rather than choice – Mo showing few signs of getting round to feeding them. Fortunately, the simple menu fell within his limited abilities, and while he fiddled around at the cooker, Mo took charge of the music and the wine and the conversation. She was in a voluble mood, her struggles with the sculpture downstairs apparently forgotten.

She was leaving in the morning to drive up to Yorkshire for the weekend. A friend of hers was having a thirtieth birthday bash at a nightclub in Wakefield.

'What did you do for yours?' she asked.

It surprised him that he had to think about it. 'We threw a party at our house in Camberwell.'

'Did you dance?'

'Of course.'

The neighbours hadn't complained about the music, because the neighbours had crashed the party, as had the neighbours' friends. It was coming back in detail now, not all of it welcome. He saw Beth, draped in a bottle-green sequin dress that clung to her hourglass figure like a jewelled snakeskin, letting rip to James Brown in the drawing room. His best friend Beth, five years dead now, taken early by ovarian cancer.

Mo must have detected something in his expression. 'What?'

'Nothing. Thirteen years is a long time.'

'You're forty-three?' Mo exclaimed.

'Uh-huh.'

'My God, you don't look a day over forty-two.'

'Tee hee.'

It was dark enough for candles by the time they ferried the food downstairs to the table. A distant rumble of thunder greeted their arrival and a weird wind was stirring the still heat in the yard. Mo confidently predicted that the rain would pass them by. She was wrong. Half an hour later it began to fall in drops as big as grapes. The tin tabletop was soon ringing like a dinner gong and they were rushing to take refuge back in her apartment.

It was the first rain in weeks, and they threw open the windows, enjoying the sound of it, the smell of it, its cooling scent. Armed with coffees and another bottle of wine, they dropped on to the leather sofas that faced each other across the low glass coffee table.

Mo set about rolling a joint. 'You don't mind, do you?'

'I'm so outraged I might even join you.'

It was grass and she had bought it off a bloke in Stoneham called Mikey. 'You should meet him.'

'Why?'

'Because he's very funny. He's also captain of the cricket team, the one that's short of players.'

'Mo, it's not going to happen.'

'Come on, it'll be fun.'

'More fun than I can handle.'

She laughed. 'Live a little. They're a good bunch of boys.'

He saw a way to change the subject. 'Doesn't Victor mind you consorting with the local drug dealer?'

'God, no. I'm his spy in the community, his eyes and ears, although I never tell him what they really think of him.'

When she didn't elaborate he demanded, 'Come on, out with it.'

'He made one big mistake. He didn't use enough local labour when he was doing up this place. He brought in his own people.'

'If it wasn't that, it would be something else. It's the English way. We don't like those who live on the sunny side of the fence.'

'True.'

'Plus he's a foreigner, an American who's made his fortune in finance. The poor guy doesn't stand a chance. They probably think he's personally responsible for bringing the British economy to its knees.'

'Maybe he played a part. He made a mint from the crash.'

'Yeah, he shorted the subprime mortgage market. I don't

know what it means either. I heard it from my wife's boyfriend . . . sorry, fiancé.'

'Fiancé?'

'Last week's little surprise.'

She hesitated. 'That must be tough.'

'It's OK, I'm fine with it.'

'Good for you. A toast to the happy couple.' She raised her glass, knowing full well he wouldn't join her. She slid the joint and the lighter across the coffee table. 'Here, this'll help.'

She was right; it did. But so did being with someone who took his upset as understood. He'd spent so much of the past week worrying about Toby's state of mind that he hadn't found time to explore his own feelings. Mo seemed to sense this, and she was happy to leave him be.

She was more demanding when the subject turned to Victor. 'Last night at dinner when Gregoire was quizzing you about him I got the feeling you were holding back.'

'Holding back?'

'It was just a feeling.'

'It was a long time ago. It's hard to remember.'

'He remembers,' she said pointedly.

'Oh?'

'He told me he was jealous of you . . . of your family . . . the love you got from your parents.'

Ben handed over the joint. 'His own parents weren't so bad, just a bit hopeless.'

'Bad enough for him to cut them out of his life completely.'

This was news to him, although Victor had hinted at problems during their lunch at the Wolseley. 'Yeah, well, he was always very good at bearing grudges.'

'Ah, so you *do* remember.'

'Am I paying for this session?'

'Better owt than een, Mr Makepeace.' He raised an eyebrow at the bizarre accent she'd adopted. 'My Austrian psychoanalyst voice,' she explained. 'I do other impressions too.'

'None as convincing as that, I'll bet.'

She smiled. 'Don't think you can deflect me with sarcasm.'

Ben found himself rising to the challenge. Yes, everybody had a story to tell, a history they were entitled to, but that didn't mean they were all equally deserving of our sympathy. Ben's next-door neighbour in London was an unmarried single mother with a drug problem and three children of varying colours fathered by three different men, all of whom had vanished into the ether. The eldest child, a thirteen-year-old daughter called Tanya, kept the show on the road. It was she who got her younger siblings up every morning and gave them their breakfast and got them dressed and delivered them to school. And it was Tanya who cooked them their tea and put them to bed at night.

'There's so much negative stuff in the press about the "youth of today", but the remarkable thing about kids today is that so many of them are just like Tanya. They get on with it. They make the best of the crap hand they've been dealt. They don't let it defeat them. That's the real story, but for whatever reason it's not newsworthy.'

Mo was looking at him in a strange fashion.

'I'm sorry,' he said. 'I tend to get a bit strident when I'm stoned.'

'A bit?'

'I'll shut up.'

'No, no, I couldn't agree more. I'm just wondering what your point is.'

'My point . . .' he replied, groping about for the trailing line of his argument. 'My point is this . . . yes . . . that the Tanyas of the world have a real story to tell about hardship and suffering. Some middle-class type bleating on about not being hugged enough as a child doesn't really cut it in comparison.'

'You mean Victor?'

'I know he felt his parents let him down, left him to rot in an English boarding school. But the truth is they thought they were coming back from the States after a year and they didn't want to disrupt his schooling.'

'That's not how he tells it.'

'Well, that's the way it was. Yes, one year became two, then three, more, but only because his mother's contract at Harvard kept being extended. And they always flew him back to Boston during the holidays.'

This wasn't quite true. On a couple of occasions Jacob had spent the Easter break with Ben and his family.

'Anyway, things weren't so bad for him. He had a whole other family to see him through it. He got a lot of love from my parents, especially my father, who treated him like a second son.'

'Zo, ve are finally beginnink to get somevere.'

He tried not laugh. 'I'm sorry, I'm getting Nazi torturer, I'm getting Blofeld in the Bond movies, I'm just not getting Freud or Jung.'

He was rewarded with a cushion hurled straight at his head. He parried it away with his arm. 'Why are you so interested in me and Victor?'

'I don't know, I think it was watching the two of you together the other day. I've never seen him so relaxed, or so nervous. It's weird. You unsettle him.' She paused thoughtfully. 'I suppose I'd never looked on him as vulnerable before. I mean, I've heard him express vulnerability – for a private man, he's surprisingly open – but they're just words, and we're all good at telling people what we think they want to hear. It's not the same thing as seeing it with your own eyes, though.' She broke off suddenly, glancing at what remained of the joint between her fingers. 'Oh, God, I'm talking shit, aren't I?'

'No, it's fascinating. Well, something. Actually, "shit" is a pretty good description.'

As they worked their way through the bottle of wine, the rain outside began to ease off and the talk turned to lighter matters: to films they had seen, books they had read, to their favourite American TV shows and the relative merits of Harold Lloyd, Buster Keaton and Charlie Chaplin as silent comedians.

There wasn't much they agreed on, and when it came

to music, even less. A three-month trip through America in her early twenties had left Mo with a love of country and western music, which happened to be one of Ben's bêtes noires. He couldn't stand the plodding melodies and the mawkish lyrics.

'I'll die happy if I never have to listen to "Achy Breaky Heart" ever again.'

'OK, Billy Ray Cyrus has a lot to answer for, but that's not real country. I'm talking about Johnny Cash and Willie Nelson and Kenny Rogers.'

Worryingly, she levered herself off the sofa and crossed to the music system.

'Don't feel you have to,' he said. 'All they sing about is booze and breaking up and, I don't know, Jesus.'

'You are so wrong.' She selected a track then turned to face him. 'A classic by Jimmy Buffet. Don't fight it.'

The song was called 'My Head Hurts, My Feet Stink, And I Don't Love Jesus.'

'You've got be joking!'

She was, of course, and she wasn't done playing DJ quite yet. Next up was 'I Don't Know Whether to Kill Myself or Go Bowling'. It was followed by 'My Wife Ran Off with my Best Friend and I Sure Do Miss Him'. She had the bit between her teeth, skipping through her collection, playing just enough of each song to reduce them both to hopeless hysterics: 'You're the Reason Our Kids Are So Ugly' . . . 'I'd Rather Pass a Kidney Stone than Another Night with You' . . .

She saved the best till last: 'I Still Miss You, Baby, but My Aim Is Getting Better'.

'OK, OK,' he gasped, 'I take it all back, I've seen the light.'

When Mo came and sat back down she dumped herself at the end of Ben's sofa. 'Last one, then bed.' She reached for her tobacco and papers. 'I've got a long drive tomorrow.' When she was done she held the cigarette up between her thumb and her forefinger, offering it to him.

'I don't smoke.'

'But you just did.'

'That was different.'

'I won't tell anyone.'

'Temptress.'

'Wimp.'

'Do you want to kill me?'

'No,' she replied, 'I want to kiss you.'

'Hussy.'

'Spoilsport.'

'I'm not the one with a boyfriend.'

'Glad to hear it. Girlfriend?'

'No.'

She looked at him with an expression of puzzled inquiry. 'You haven't thought about it?'

'No more than twenty times tonight.'

'So?'

'I don't want you to do anything you might regret.'

'Well, I won't know unless I try, will I?'

'Good point,' he said. 'Can't argue with that.'

She crawled along the sofa towards him like a beast closing in on its prey, her eyes never leaving his. She reached out a hand and ran her fingers through his hair, down his neck and along the line of his jaw. It was a tender and unexpected gesture, and the kiss, when it finally came, was long, languorous, unhurried.

Mo buried her face in his neck. 'Shit,' she muttered softly.

'Feeling guilty?'

She shook her head and purred into his ear, 'I've wanted to do that since the first time I saw you.'

'Really?'

She sat up and looked at him searchingly. 'Do you have any idea how attractive you are, Mr Makepeace?'

'No, tell me, Ms Channing.'

'You're a bright lad – figure it out for yourself.' She rose suddenly to her feet. 'I'm jiggered, and I've got an early start.'

'Are you kicking me out?'

'Yes.'

He heaved himself up off the sofa. 'Thanks, that's the most fun I've had in a long time. Especially the bit at the end.'

'Remind me?' she asked innocently.

This time there was something more urgent about their kiss, and their hands were more daring.

Ben picked his way carefully across the stable yard, still feeling the effects of the joint, the uneven cobbles slick beneath his feet. The wind had fallen to a whisper and overhead the moon had freed itself from the bank of departing rain clouds, lighting his way home.

He could still feel the pressure at the base of his back where Mo had slid a hand beneath his shirt and pulled him close against her. 'Bloody Victor, throwing you in my path': words he had let go unchallenged but which held out hope of more than a couple of lingering kisses.

He passed beneath the archway and the house loomed into view. He saw that Annabelle had yet to return from Oxford; her Range Rover wasn't parked out front.

The Maserati was.

It stood there, silent, brooding, his postcode stored away in its satnav.

He had managed to put the matter from his mind for much of the evening, and he told himself to walk on by. The one false note in a perfect day. Don't indulge it. He was halfway up the front steps when he turned back, pulling the car key from his pocket.

It was still there, as he knew it would be: number eight in the list of Previous Destinations, just below ALDEBURGH. Ignoring WOODSTOCK in the number one slot, was it really feasible that Victor had entered six other destinations during the few days he'd spent in the country since their lunch at the Wolseley? Possibly, if the postcodes had started with an OX – for Oxford and its surroundings. But they didn't. There were a couple of north London codes, a TW– (Twickenham?) and a TN– (?) and an SL– (?).

It should be easy enough to check them out on the internet and make a judgement of sorts. There was no pen or paper to hand so he pulled up the Note feature on his BlackBerry and tapped in the postcodes. Having started, he carried on past his own, entering all the others on the list along with any places names that appeared.

It felt like snooping, but he consoled himself with the thought that he wasn't the one who'd started it.

seventeen days to go . . .

THE TEXT WAS waiting for him when he returned from his run:

Morning Makepeace. Just wanted you to know I haven't been thinking about you

Weird. Me neither. Where are you?

Leicester Forest East services on the M1. Stoneham Park it ain't

Where's Leicester?

Southern twat. What u doing?

Sweating. Just back from run

Mmmmm

About to have shower

MMMMM

Then morning dump

Git! Gotta go

Speak later?

Bad idea

OK. See you Sunday

Can't wait x

Me too. Over and out x

Only three days to wait, but he was already feeling the sting of separation. He didn't know for sure if Mo would be shacking up with Connor while up north – there had been no talk of him the previous evening – but 'Bad idea' said it all.

Best not to think about it. Best to think about something else, like the flirtatious tone of the exchange.

He tried to lose himself in the script, which went well enough to begin with, until another thought folded itself into the mix. Saving the changes, he went online.

He worked his way methodically through the postcodes he'd tapped into his phone last night. First up was what appeared to be a privately owned house set in large grounds just north of Tunbridge Wells. Next came Petersham Nurseries, a restaurant down by the river in Richmond. SL5 9RR proved to be Sunningdale Golf Club, which was out to the west of London, near Ascot. There were then a couple of North London postcodes: one a residential street in Highgate, which the satellite option on Google Maps showed to be stuffed with mansions; the other in Kilburn, which was either the Tricycle Theatre or a pub called the Good Ship. Last on the list before his own postcode was Aldeburgh.

Ben had been there a couple of times to stay with friends who'd rented a cottage near Saxmundham as a weekend bolt-hole. Aldeburgh was an attractive town on the Suffolk coast, known for its shingle beach and its fish and chips and its summer music festival. The Web revealed that the festival had run from 8 to 24 June this year. If Victor had visited for the festival, this meant, at the very least, that Ben's post-code had been entered two weeks before their lunch at the Wolseley.

But Victor could easily have travelled to Aldeburgh for other reasons, and at a later date. According to the internet, the seaside town was also home to a fine old golf club with an eighteen-hole championship course ranked fifty-third in England by *Golf World*: maritime heathland . . . gorse-lined fairways . . . far-reaching views of the River Alde and the North Sea . . .

Then again, would Victor really have driven almost a hundred miles to play a course ranked fifty-third by Golf World, when the same outfit rated Sunningdale, so much closer to home, third in the country?

Where was the hard evidence on timings? There wasn't any. It was all wild conjecture.

He needed to think like Detective Constable Leon Grosse, a personal favourite amongst his many offspring who'd never made it from the page to the screen. Grosse looked doomed to see out his days on the yellowing pages of a series proposal for television, although one of the many executives who had turned the idea down had done so on the grounds that the central character was too far ahead of the times, but he sincerely hoped the times would catch up with him before too long.

Others had been less kind, variously describing Grosse as 'utterly devoid of all endearing characteristics' (which was the point) . . . 'a vile, narcissistic misanthrope' (finally, someone who understood him!) . . . and, best of all, 'like the disturbed love child of Colombo and Lucrezia Borgia' (a genius description which had earned that particular rejection letter pride of place on his fridge door).

Though well into his forties, Grosse had doggedly resisted all efforts to promote him beyond the rank of detective constable. He favoured the dirty, nuts-and-bolts business of police investigation over the politics of ambition. This also meant he was better placed to indulge his other great interest: playing God. Grosse always got his man (or his woman) but depending on his mood would sometimes choose to keep the evidence he unearthed from his superiors, allowing the perpetrator of the crime to walk free. He might, for example, decide that a murder victim was so unpleasant that they weren't deserving of posthumous justice. Other times, he might be so admiring of the subtlety and sophistication of a criminal's plan that he couldn't bring himself to expose it. Favours would often come his way from those he had spared, but Grosse never demanded them. The money, and sometimes the sex, were never ends in themselves.

Despite his dubious morality, or maybe because of it, Grosse was touched with a rare genius for sniffing out malefactors. He saw things his colleagues missed. He knew that the big answers lay buried in the smallest details.

Ben closed his eyes and inhaled, sucking Grosse inside him – calm, meticulous, methodical Grosse, who lived in his dead mother's house with his loopy sister and a dog he despised (although not quite as much as the dog despised him). Opening his eyes, he re-examined the list: a grand house near Tunbridge Wells, a fashionable but low-key restaurant in Richmond, Sunningdale Golf Club . . .

And there it suddenly was: the answer. Well, possibly. It all depended on whether Victor was a member of Sunningdale or not.

The boot room lay just beyond the pantry, at the far end of the flagged corridor running off the kitchen. It was the obvious place to search first. There were racks of wellington boots and walking boots and, above them, coats and hats of all styles and sizes hanging from wooden pegs. Leather cartridge belts and cartridge bags dangled from another rail beside a locked steel gun cabinet. There was also a long oak countertop with two butler's sinks set into it. A tall wicker basket bristling with walking sticks and umbrellas stood beside a wooden chest containing croquet mallets and balls. There was no sign of any golf clubs.

He found them eventually in the pool house, tucked away in a small room off the well-equipped gym. They were Callaways, the same make his father had always favoured. Simple coincidence? Probably. There was no plastic membership badge for Sunningdale attached to the bag, but there was a green fee tag for the same golf club, which all guests were required to display when out on the course. It was dated Tuesday, 29 May – almost two months ago.

Sunningdale Golf Club figured third on the list of previous destinations in the Maserati's satnav, which drove back the probable date on which his own postcode had been entered far deeper into the past than he'd imagined. Nothing was proven, but even an inveterate sceptic like DC Leon Grosse would have found his interest piqued by such a discovery. He would also have challenged the evidence, testing it from all angles, punishing it, torturing out the truth.

Ben grabbed a mallet and a ball from the boot room and headed outside for some solo croquet on the back lawn. He did his best thinking when on his feet, moving about, but he'd hardly got going before Annabelle appeared, hurrying down the steps towards him with her phone.

'It's Mr Sheldon. He wants a word.'

'Are you winning?' quipped Victor.

He was in Brasilia and he sounded remarkably chirpy given that it was six o'clock in the morning for him. Something had come up; he had a big favour to ask of Ben.

'I'll cut to the chase. I need you to go to Italy and buy a boat for me.'

'A boat?'

'Not just any old boat.'

It was a Riva speedboat, and it had been in the same family since 1966, when it was built. Such a pure heritage was almost unheard of, and by all accounts the boat was in original and near-perfect condition. 'I've got someone driving up from Genoa to Lake Como today to check it over, but it's a formality. Negotiating a price won't be. The owner's asking for seven hundred and fifty thousand euros, which is more than I want to pay.'

'Seven hundred and fifty thousand euros for a speedboat?'

'A work of art – the finest Super Aquarama to hit the market in years. I've been given a small window to make a pre-emptive offer before they go wider with it. It has to happen this weekend.'

'I'm hardly the man for the job,' said Ben.

'I'd send Annabelle, but between you and me she lacks the necessary charm when it comes to this sort of thing. They're parting with a family heirloom. It requires subtlety.' Victor paused briefly then added with feeling, 'I can't tell you how frustrated I am to be stuck here. This boat is a dream of mine. I've known about it for a while, but I never thought I'd get a shot at it.'

What else could he say? Besides, a weekend in Italy was hardly a grim prospect, and it would certainly help take his mind off Mo and Connor and whatever they were up to.

There were practical considerations, not least of all that his passport was sitting in his desk drawer in London. Victor dismissed them as details. Annabelle would sort everything out. 'She's very good like that. You won't have to worry about a thing.'

'Except that I know bugger all about boats.'

'Hey, I've spent half my life operating from a position of almost complete ignorance.'

'Yeah, right,' replied Ben sceptically.

'I'll email you some stuff, how's that?'

Better than nothing, he thought. But not by much.

Unsurprisingly, the rest of the day was a write-off on the work front, although a neat exchange of dialogue came to mind while he was heading into Oxford. He knew better than to entrust the lines to memory, and the moment he had parked in the motorcycle bay on Broad Street he scribbled them down in the small notebook he always carried with him.

The shoe shop recommended by Victor was a short walk away in Turl Street. Ben remembered it from his time at the university, and the window display seemed hardly to have changed in twenty years. It was a shop that sold shoes for life, hand-stitched and with thick leather soles, the sort of shoes you could only dream of owning when on a student budget. The dress-code brief from Victor was smart/casual, and he opted for a pair of suede chukka boots with an eye-watering price tag just shy of £250. He didn't have to hand over a penny. Annabelle had phoned ahead; the shoes were simply added to Victor's account.

The city centre was clogged with droves of weary tourists wilting in the heat, and Ben limited himself to the shortest of loops: along the alleyway leading from Turl Street to the Radcliffe Camera, then through the courtyard of the Bodleian Library, before skirting the Sheldonian Theatre and popping out on to Broad Street. By the time he had finally persuaded the surly young porter in the lodge at Trinity that he was a bona fide graduate, he had lost all desire to make a tour of his old college.

'You know what, I think I'll come back another day.'

'As you wish, sir,' came the porter's reply, dripping with a false courtesy that said: *Yeah, fuck right off*.

Annabelle had clearly been on the case during his absence. A printout of his itinerary was waiting for him when he returned to Stoneham Park. He was booked on a nine o'clock flight to Milan, which meant a dawn departure. Lance would drive him to London City Airport, making a detour to pick up his passport from his flat. Another driver would be waiting for him in Milan, ready to whisk him straight off to his hotel on Lake Como, the Villa d'Este – 'No rooms left, I'm afraid, so you'll have to slum it in a suite.' He would have just enough time to check in and freshen up before three o'clock, when Signore Viani, the boat's owner, would pick him up from the hotel's landing stage in the Riva. Signore Viani had suggested a spin down the lake to his villa before dropping Ben back at the hotel. Just when or where business was discussed was open to Ben's discretion, but he had almost twenty-four hours to secure the deal. A car would pick him up from the Villa d'Este at 2 p.m. the following day and drive him back to Milan for a 4.30 p.m. flight.

On the page, abstracted in black and white, it all seemed straightforward enough. The reality would be quite different. He was expected to summon up a mysterious charm ascribed to him by Victor in order to buy a Riva speedboat for less money than the owner was asking for.

Three hours at his laptop, trawling the internet, helped stem his building alarm. He approached the research methodically, recording salient facts and figures in a notebook: variations in hull length and engine size throughout the production cycle of the Aquarama, past auction records, current prices being demanded by boat dealers around the world, and the like. When the information Victor had promised to send through finally landed in his email inbox, it came in the form of three links to websites he had already filleted thoroughly, which made him feel better.

He shut down his computer knowing that there wasn't much more he could do in the way of investigation. He also knew from the many testimonies and videos littering the Web that, at the very least, tomorrow afternoon he would be skimming across the waters of Lake Como in one of the very finest motorised vessels ever built by man. As for the rest, all he could do was wing it and hope for the best.

Victor called as Ben and Annabelle were about to sit down for dinner. He was still in the Brazilian capital and had slipped out of a meeting at some government ministry or other, so he couldn't talk for long. He had heard back from his man in Italy and the Riva was in tip-top condition, although its twin Crusader engines would need an overhaul some time soon. He had set his heart on the boat and would be happy to pay the asking price, but happier still if he didn't have to. Moreover, Ben could keep twenty per cent of everything he knocked off the price. Ben turned the offer down. He had checked out the website of the Villa d'Este. An all-expenses-paid weekend away at one of Europe's most luxurious hotels was reward enough.

Annabelle had overheard the conversation. 'He told me you wouldn't accept.'

'And what did *you* think?'

'I'm used to people taking everything they can get from Mr Sheldon.'

'Maybe I'll regret it.'

'Maybe you will, because even if you save him a small

fortune you won't see a penny of it now. I know how he works. He made you an offer in good faith and you rejected it.'

'You think I've offended him?'

Annabelle seemed amused by the idea. 'He's a businessman. He'll be delighted with the outcome.' She paused momentarily. 'Although he might be slightly concerned too.'

'About what?'

'The lack of incentive. I mean, why would you bother to drive a hard bargain when there's nothing in it for you?'

Ben had to smile. 'Annabelle, do you never stop looking after his interests?'

'It's what he pays me for.'

'Well, you don't have to worry. I'll still give it my best shot.'

Ben had detected nothing in Annabelle's behaviour that suggested she was in any way threatened by his sudden appearance on the scene, and any suspicions he still harboured were dispelled over dinner. Her guard dropped; the air of efficiency and cold kindness deserted her. She even went out of her way to say just how pleased she was to have him around.

'Mo tends to keep herself to herself, and life can be pretty lonely around here when Mr Sheldon is away.'

She was incapable of referring to Victor as anything other than 'Mr Sheldon' (or sometimes 'Mr S'). It was a habit she'd tried and failed to shake, she explained when Ben pulled her up on it. 'Even Mr Sheldon finds it strange, but I spent too long working as his personal assistant to change my ways now.'

'You were his PA?'

'From when he first set up on his own here in England. There were only five of us back then. Now there are more than twenty in the Berkeley Square offices. It's been quite a journey.' Victor had hired her knowing she was in a bad place, knowing she needed a break. She had just come out of a failed marriage, a childless marriage. 'And I was hardly a spring chicken, even then. Most people would have taken on someone half my age. He gave me a chance . . . another chance at life.'

The last thing Ben had expected from Annabelle was such a raw and ready confession. Yes, they'd sunk a bottle of wine between them, but he sensed that something else lay behind such frankness, a sort of veiled complicity.

You of all people should know what I mean, she seemed to be saying.

sixteen days to go . . .

B EN'S ALARM WENT at five, and at five thirty Lance was already waiting out front at the wheel of the Mercedes. He wasn't upset about having to get up at such an ungodly hour.

'I got me a pink ticket from the wife, says I can stay on in town, seeing as I got to be back tomorrow to pick you up.' London City Airport lay just south of his old stomping ground in the East End. 'Going to drop by my old ma then catch up with some mates. Nah, don't worry about me – I'm laughing.' Once they were on the road, he asked, 'So where we going then? Where's your gaff?'

Ben was tempted to lie, to see if it drew a reaction, anything that indicated Lance already knew the answer. It would have been tough to talk his way out of it, though, and he made do with nudging the conversation towards the subject of cars, first the Mercedes they were in, then the Maserati. He rhapsodised about his jaunt to Woodstock a couple of days ago.

Lance thought the Maserati was an OK ride, although he'd

only driven it a few of times 'to fill her up for the old man'. This seemed to confirm what Annabelle had said: that the Maserati was a vehicle reserved by Victor for his own personal use.

When he asked Lance about his time in the army he got little more than name, rank, and serial number in return. Lance had served with 1st Battalion The Princess of Wales's Royal Regiment, and had done two tours in Iraq.

'Saw some stuff over there I wish I hadn't. Did some stuff too. You bozos got no idea.'

As to how Lance came to be Victor's chauffeur: 'I know a bloke knows a bloke knows him.'

He was much more talkative when the topic turned to football. Given where Ben lived in London, Lance feared he might be a Chelsea supporter.

'No, I'm a Millwall fan.'

Lance shot him an acid look in the rear-view mirror and growled, 'You're havin' a laugh.'

'No one likes us, no one likes us . . .' Ben chanted to the tune of Rod Stewart's 'We Are Sailing'.

'Too bloody right, mate.'

Ben grinned. 'Don't worry, I saw your West Ham shirt the other day.'

The rivalry between the two clubs reached back more than a century (and was probably best described as a profound mutual hatred).

'I tell you, if you really was a Millwall fan you'd be walking the rest of the way.'

Fortunately, there was no danger of bumping into Trisha

at this early hour of a Saturday morning. Ben slipped upstairs to his flat, grabbed his passport from his desk drawer, and little more than half an hour later Lance dropped him off at London City Airport in the Docklands. It was the first time he'd flown from the airport, and it had almost nothing in common with the cattle markets of Heathrow and Gatwick. There were no packed seating areas, no hordes staggering around the place like souls in limbo. In fact, the airport was almost deserted. He could have dumped himself at any number of tables in the French café where he downed a faultless coffee and a croissant, and when his flight was called it took him all of a minute to walk to the gate. It was a small plane with lots of engines: two deeply pleasing details for a person who hated flying, for whom the damned physics of the thing had never added up.

It didn't stop him throttling the armrests of his business-class seat as the plane hurtled down the runway.

Milan Malpensa Airport was hardly the most attractive gateway to Italy, but it felt good to be back in the country, a feeling almost at once of senses quickened. Ben's driver was a gaunt, stick-insect of a man holding a piece of card on which was scribbled: MAKEPISS. He didn't speak a word of English and Ben was forced to bring his limited Italian into play. Their conversation had dried up long before they'd joined the autostrada and were hammering north towards the mountains in the oversized Audi 4X4.

The Villa d'Este stood proud and palatial on the north

shore of Lake Como, trapped between the water's edge and the hills rising sharply around the lake, hemming it in on all sides. The setting was far more dramatic than the photos on the hotel's website had suggested, but after the discreet grandeur of Stoneham Park there was something oppressive about the fussy opulence of the hotel's interior, with its marble hallways and its dripping chandeliers and its generous sprinkling of gilded antique furniture. Not that he complained when he was shown upstairs to his suite.

The bedroom was almost as large as the spacious living room, and both had French windows giving on to a long balcony, shaded by an awning, that offered a panoramic view of the lake. It was the perfect spot to snatch some lunch and run through his notes. Time was tight, so he ordered a club sandwich and a beer from room service before going to shower in the marble bathroom.

He headed downstairs with ten minutes to spare and took a stroll along the lakefront towards the hotel's small marina. He passed the swimming pool on the way, an unusual affair that protruded into the lake on a huge floating pontoon connected to the shore by two gangways. Its wide wooden decks were loaded with loungers, although only the hardiest sun-worshippers were cooking themselves at this hour.

He heard the Riva before he saw it, the deep growl of its engines heralding its approach. A few moments later it shot into view around the headland, slowing as it carved a lazy turn. Ben arrived at the landing stage beneath the main terrace as a hotel dockman, struggling to contain his excitement, was tying up the Riva. It really was a thing of beauty, sleek and sinuous, its mahogany hull and decking glowing warm in the sunlight.

Signore Viani greeted Ben with a firm handshake and an open smile. He was a tall man, almost as tall as Ben, and surprisingly trim for his seventy-odd years. He was accompanied by his son and his young grandson, both of whom he introduced in impeccable English.

'Three generations of Vianis,' observed Ben.

'Indeed. And one day, maybe four.' Signore Viani laid a hand on his grandson's shoulder. 'If Arturo here gets his skates on.'

Ben laughed, as much at the older man's use of the English idiom as anything. He knew already that he was going to like Signore Viani, which was annoying. It wouldn't make his job any easier.

It was an exhilarating fifteen-minute run up the lake to the villa, Signore Viani at the wheel, the boat at full throttle for much of the way. You didn't need to be an expert to appreciate the Riva's power and poise. It levelled off the light chop, smoothing out the ride to the point that at times it almost felt as though they were airborne. At speed, conversation was out of the question, and Ben sat back on the bench seat, taking in the view and turning every so often to look at the ridiculously long wake left by the boat.

Signore Viani's villa was a neoclassical building set on a

slight rise some distance back from the water's edge. Stone steps climbed from the landing stage to a wide lawn fringed with cypress trees, where a pack of boys and girls was playing football. Arturo hurried to join the mêlée. '*Attenti!*' he cried. '*Messi arriva!*'

The three men carried on past to the villa. Arturo's father, Iacopo, headed inside while Signore Viani and Ben installed themselves on the flagged terrace. Signore Viani apologised for the chaos and the noise. The whole clan was in residence: Iacopo and his two sisters, along with their respective families.

'My wife passed away last year and they are worried about me. They don't understand that trying to remember the names of all my grandchildren is the thing that will be the death of me.' Ben laughed. 'Do you have children?'

'A son. Toby. He's Arturo's age.'

'You didn't want more?'

'It wasn't possible.'

'I'm sorry,' said Signore Viani. 'That was an indiscreet question.'

'It's fine.'

'Then maybe I can ask you another one. Why did Mr Sheldon send you as his representative?'

'I've been asking myself the same thing.'

'Do you know much about the Riva Super Aquarama?'

'Considerably more than I did twenty-four hours ago.'

Signore Viani smiled. 'You're very honest.'

'I don't have anything to hide. Victor's an old friend of mine. I'm staying with him at the moment. He would be here himself if he could, but he's in Brazil.'

'A favour for an old friend, then. There's nothing in it for you?'

Ben hesitated before opting to tell the truth. 'He offered me a percentage of everything I knocked off the asking price. I turned him down.'

It was his way of letting Signore Viani know that he intended to haggle.

'And you really get nothing for your efforts?'

'No. Actually, that's a lie.' He extended a leg. 'He bought me these.'

'A pair of boots?'

'Not just any old boots, I think you'll agree.'

Signore Viani gave a sudden loud laugh. 'Yes, very fine boots indeed.'

Tea and a selection of cakes arrived on two trays, one carried by Iacopo, the other by his blonde and nervy wife, who promptly retired. She left them to some gentle horse-trading. The Vianis pressed their case first, laying out the pedigree of the Riva, which they referred to by its name, *Chloe* (presumably to lend the impression that they were parting with a member of the family rather than a boat). *Chloe* had been bought off the plans by Signore Viani's father – a middle-aged man's gift to himself following the sale of his first business. Printing was the Vianis' thing, and it had obviously treated them well. The villa on Lake Como had been bought the following year, 1967, as a summer bolt-hole from Milan.

Chloe had been lovingly cared for right from the first – always dry-docked in Como during the winter months, and regularly revarnished to the same obsessive standards set by Riva's own craftsmen. All of her mahogany was original, as were her two Crusader engines. In fact, there probably wasn't a Super Aquarama like her anywhere in the world.

What could Ben say? They knew what they were selling. It would have been churlish to counter with the one reservation raised by Victor's expert: that the engines would need to be overhauled at some point.

'We're all agreed, she's an exceptional boat,' Ben conceded. 'So why are you selling her?'

It was almost nothing, the merest flicker of movement in Signore Viani's eyes in the direction of his son. What did it mean? Was the money required for Iacopo? Debts, possibly? A business venture gone sour? Was *Chloe* being sold out of necessity?

'I am an old man,' said Signore Viani. 'Too old to be racing around the lake. A boat like *Chloe* needs to be used, to be loved. And cars are more Iacopo's thing,' he added with a slight barb.

'Look, I have to be honest with you,' said Ben. 'To someone like me it seems like an obscene amount of money to spend on a boat. But if Mr Sheldon is happy to hand over six hundred thousand euros, who am I to question him?'

The fact that the figure he'd just mentioned was 150,000 euros shy of what they were asking wasn't lost on Iacopo, who addressed his father in rapid-fire Italian, clearly distressed, even angry.

Signore Viani silenced his son with a calming gesture of his hand before turning to Ben. 'It's not enough.'

'Are you saying that if I put a suitcase containing six hundred thousand euros in cash on the table here you would reject it?'

'I don't see a suitcase,' countered Signore Viani.

Ben hesitated. 'We both know what your father paid for *Chloe* in real terms back in nineteen sixty-six. If she goes to auction, there will be paperwork – profits to account for, taxes to pay.'

'You underestimate my accountant.'

'With respect, any accountant would advise you to accept the offer.'

Signore Viani pondered his words. 'Clean, you say?'

Iacopo had fallen silent, no doubt running the numbers in his head, but now blurted out in Italian, '*Papa, non è ancora abbastanza.*'

'*Non è mai abbastanza, Iacopo,*' fired back Signore Viani.

'Give us ten minutes, please,' he asked courteously of Ben before rising to his feet and gesturing for Iacopo to follow him inside.

Ben strolled to the edge of the terrace, taking in the view. Signore Viani was definitely bailing his son out. *Father, it's still not enough*, to which Signore Viani had snapped, *It's never enough, Iacopo.*

Iacopo was right; the offer was on the low side, even if the money didn't need to be declared. Victor hadn't instructed Ben to make a cash offer, but he couldn't see it being a problem, not for a man of Victor's experience in moving money about the planet.

He wandered down on to the lawn to watch the kids' football match. The sides were uneven, four versus three, and when Arturo spotted him, Ben found himself signed up to the weaker team. '*Lui è inglese*,' explained Arturo, which raised a chorus of, '*David Beckham!*'

Ben didn't want to try too hard, although he upped his game when it became clear that a couple of Arturo's cousins were quite capable of running rings around him. It made you despair of English football. Even the girls liked having the ball at their feet and running at the opposition.

At a certain point, his back to the goal and under assault from marauding imps, Ben hoofed the ball down the other end of the lawn. They all stopped and stared at him, even his own teammates, as if baffled by such a cowardly act. 'Route one!' he called, gesticulating down the lawn.

'Route one!' they cried, disappearing en masse.

Ben was beginning to build up a healthy sweat when Signore Viani rescued him. He was alone, no sign of Iacopo. 'Come, I'll take you back to the Villa d'Este.'

As he was untying the Riva, Signore Viani asked, 'Do you know the story of Chloe?'

'Chloe?'

'Daphnis and Chloe.'

'Yes, it's Greek, set on the island of Lesbos.'

Signore Viani pushed off and climbed aboard. 'I'm impressed. Have you read it?'

'Years ago.'

It was coming back now. He'd read it at Oxford, an early Greek novel by Longus about two babies abandoned in the wild, one discovered and reared by a goatherd, the other by a shepherd. Daphnis and Chloe's youthful friendship develops into love, a love that confuses them and which can't be consummated until they have undergone all kinds of terrible torments and trials.

Signore Viani fired up the Riva's engines. 'It was my father's favourite book. He believed in its message of fate.'

Ben had a sudden inkling of what Signore Viani was driving at. 'Let me tell you a bit more about Mr Sheldon,' he said.

'Yes, do that.'

While they idled along, sticking close the shore, Ben sold Victor hard but honestly, painting him as a worthy partner for *Chloe* – an alternative destiny. When he had finished, Signore Viani relinqished the wheel to him.

'Don't be afraid of her,' he said. 'She likes to be pushed.'

They parted company on the landing stage at the Villa d'Este. Signore Viani passed up the offer of a drink on the hotel terrace, and for a moment Ben feared he had blown the deal. He was convinced of it when the Italian then said, 'Iacopo thinks we can get more from someone else.'

'I couldn't say. Maybe he's right.'

'Iacopo is not often right,' came the terse reply. 'Six hundred. Cash. But it must be quick, please.' Signore Viani extended his hand.

Ben took it, sealing the deal. 'It's been a pleasure.'

'Yes, it has. And I see now why Mr Sheldon sent you.'

It was a great result. Ben wasn't the only one to think so. Annabelle's reply to his text read: **Good boy!!!**

He received it as he was heading for the swimming pool, having just made a reservation for dinner downstairs later. He picked a sunlounger down the far end of the pontoon, and when swooped on by one of the pool attendants he ordered an orange juice. It had only just gone five o'clock – still too early for a celebratory glass of champagne.

The juice was waiting for him when he heaved himself from the pool. He lay back on the lounger, enjoying the gentle prickle of the water drying on his skin, basking in the heat and the satisfaction of a job well done. He found himself replaying the events of the past couple of hours in his head. Why hadn't Signore Viani haggled over the money? He must have known he could have squeezed a bit more out of Ben, and yet he hadn't even tried. The only explanation seemed to be that he didn't care. He didn't care, because whatever he raised from the sale of the boat was going to his son anyway. And why should he fight to fill the coffers of Iacopo if it was Iacopo's recklessness that had obliged him to sell the Riva in the first place? No, Signore Viani had needed to know that *Chloe* was going to a good home, the right home. An extra fifty thousand euros here or there in his son's pocket was a secondary consideration.

A tall and rather beautiful woman installed herself two loungers along from him. She slipped off her chiffon robe to reveal a slender, fine-boned figure tanned to the colour of teak, and a bikini as black as her long straight hair.

Pleasingly distracting, thought Ben, stealing glances at her under the pretence of reaching for his orange juice on the slatted side table. She ordered a green tea from the pool attendant, her flawless accent suggesting she was Italian. Or maybe she was simply one of those multi-cultural, multi-lingual Euro types: Spanish mother, Greek father, boarding school in Switzerland, degree from the Sorbonne, doomed by her looks to a life of yet more privilege and plenty. Whatever her history, there was an ease about her, a loose-limbed grace that quietly proclaimed she was entirely at home in such surroundings. She seemed to occupy the space she had selected on the pontoon as if it were hers by right.

What, he wondered, did she make of him? Had she even registered his presence? Did she know an interloper when she saw one? Could she spot a fraud at five paces? It was curious to think that this was exactly the lifestyle he had once pictured for himself. His father had helped nurture the vision, nudging him towards it: a well-paid job in the City, foreign travel, a foreign wife (half-Italian in his father's case). In short, wealth coupled with a whiff of the exotic to lay to rest the dreary British parochialism which had blighted the Makepeace name for generations.

By jumping off the path ordained for him, Ben had betrayed this dream; his father had left him in no doubt of that. Maybe if he'd had more success as a screenwriter he would have been forgiven. A house in the Hollywood hills with an Oscar on the mantelpiece and an actress for a wife might have proved to be an acceptable alternative.

He saw it now, a parallel existence minutely removed by a few cruel twists of fate from the divorced man living alone in a shoebox flat in Battersea: a studio executive getting fired just as she's about to green-light your script; a director pulling out at the eleventh hour, the lead actors fading from view at the news, the project propelled into deathly turnaround. The slow, torturous loss of reputation and self-belief.

And yet, here he was, sunning himself beside the pool of a five-star hotel in Italy. His two destinies seemed somehow to have intersected momentarily, and he was almost tempted to ask the woman to trap the moment with a photo taken on his phone. It would certainly be a way of striking up conversation: 'It's for my miserable fucker of a father.'

It wasn't required.

'A beautiful boat,' she said unexpectedly, with a nod towards the landing stage. 'The Riva. I saw you arrive.'

'Oh. Yes.'

'Is it yours?'

'No. Sadly. A friend of mine's thinking of buying it. In fact, he just has.'

An hour later, they were still talking and Ben had shunted on to the sunlounger previously separating them. Her name was Chiara and she worked in the silk business, sourcing fibres for the many factories which made Como the capital of Italy's silk manufacturing industry. She spent much of her time travelling for work, mainly to China, which she loved almost as much as her native Tuscany. Originally from

Florence, she now lived in an old farmhouse in the hills just north of Lucca. 'About the only one you English haven't bought,' she half-joked. Maybe she lived there with someone. If she did, it wasn't her husband because she wasn't wearing a wedding ring.

As the lengthening shadows crept across the pontoon towards them, Ben ordered two glasses of champagne and they toasted the successful purchase of the Riva.

'He must be very rich, your friend.'

'He is. Would you like to meet him?'

'What, you also buy his women for him?'

Chiara had been in meetings most of the day and was flying out to the Far East tomorrow evening. It was her suggestion that they have dinner together, though not in the hotel restaurant which she said could be a bit formal. She'd already booked at a place she knew in Cernobbio, just down the road, and Ben was welcome to join her.

Only a madman would have said no.

Back in his suite, he showered then checked his emails. There was one from Victor: **Racing to catch a plane. Just heard the news from Annabelle. God knows how you did it! Bargain at that price, even for cash. Vintage bubbly on me, I insist. Just sorry you don't have anyone to share it with. Thank you, thank you. Victor**

Ben lay on his bed, naked, reading his book and sipping a cold beer from the mini-bar. Through the open French windows the lowering sun had turned the lake to a sheet of burnished gold. Feeling himself beginning to drift off, he set the alarm on his phone to wake him in half an hour. He was brought back from the brink of sleep a few minutes later by a text arriving. It was from Mo.

About to hit the bright lights of Wakefield

No bright lights here, just the sun going down on Lake Como

Lake Como!? Wtf!?

Running an errand for Victor. Will explain all tomorrow

Monday now for me. God I miss you

He knew he would have responded in kind if he wasn't about to go out to dinner with Chiara.

I bet you say that to all the boys

Fuck off x

X

Chiara was already waiting for him in the lobby when he headed downstairs at eight o'clock. She was wearing a sleeveless chiffon dress with a deep V-neck and a graduated hem which climbed above her knees at the front.

Ben greeted her with a kiss on both cheeks. 'You look amazing.'

'Thank you.'

'Silk, by any chance?' He meant the dress.

'How did you guess?'

She had arranged for a hotel car to drive them to the restaurant.

'I thought you said it was a walk.'

'In these shoes?'

She flashed him a smile and one of her black leather stiletto sandals. Could ankles so slender really bear her weight without snapping?

It was called Harry's Bar, a lively place on the small piazza right by the harbour in Cernobbio. She had reserved one of the tables on the terrace out front, and as soon as they were seated Ben announced, 'Let's get one thing straight – this is on me.'

'Oh? Not your friend Victor?'

'Maybe if you'd allowed us to eat in the hotel, damn you.'

She laughed. 'Don't worry, I won't order the lobster.'

She was great company. There was a kind of stately ease about her, but it was coupled with a playful irreverence that kept tipping over into teasing. She had their poor waiter eating out of her hand before they'd even ordered their cocktails. Though quite happy to speak about herself, often with a disarming honesty, she somehow made you feel that you sat at the centre of her world. She rarely asked anything as obvious as a question; she didn't need to.

A couple of ex-boyfriends popped up in their conversation, but there was no mention of a current one. While they were tucking into their main courses – they both had the grilled Lavarello, some kind of lake fish recommended by the lovestruck waiter – Ben came straight out with it and asked if she was in a relationship. She wasn't.

'Why do I find that hard to believe?'

'Maybe because you think it is what all women want.'

He had meant it as a compliment. 'No, no . . .'

'I like to travel. Every man I have been with wants me to stop. Men are jealous animals. They do not like the idea of their woman alone. Look at us here. What man would say to me, "Oh, darling, have a wonderful dinner with the stranger you have just met at the hotel"? I would have to lie to him, and I don't want to lie to the man I love just because he cannot accept our dinner here is completely innocent.'

OK, thought Ben. Message received.

'Would you want the woman you love to lie to you?' she asked.

'That depends.'

Chiara already knew he was divorced; he now told her about Madeleine's momentary infidelity at a legal conference in France, and how it would have been better for all concerned if she'd kept it to herself. She hadn't been able to, though; she had needed absolution from him, and once the genie was out of the bottle . . .

'When was this?' asked Chiara.

'Two or three years ago.'

'Hmmmm.' A pensive grunt. 'And do you still love her?'

'She's the mother of my child.'

Chiara reached across the table and gently took his hand. 'Maybe it is your son you love, not his mother.'

It seemed to happen of its own accord, their hands shifting so that their fingers intertwined. He felt the electrifying charge of her thumb stroking the tender underside of his wrist, and her large eyes held his in their dark embrace.

OK, thought Ben, message possibly misinterpreted first time round.

'You see my point?' She glanced down at their hands. 'If I had a boyfriend he would never believe this is completely innocent.'

'You're right. We men just don't get it.'

Her laughter turned a few heads at nearby tables.

Neither of them wanted desserts so they went straight for coffees and a couple of glasses of grappa. Chiara disappeared off to the ladies' room with her clutch bag while they waited for the drinks to arrive. Ben caught the attention of the waiter and asked for the bill. He returned almost immediately to say that '*La Signora*' had just settled it, his tone caught between terminal infatuation for *La Signora* and contempt for the cheapskate who had allowed her to pick up the tab.

'That's not fair,' said Ben as Chiara dropped back into her chair. 'I told you it was on me.'

'I was passing the desk.' She raised her glass of grappa, obliging him to clink. 'You can pay next time.'

The few words they exchanged in the back of the car on the short trip back to the Villa d'Este were said for the benefit of the driver. The real conversation took place silently between their two thighs, which were pressed together in the darkness.

They retrieved their respective room keys from the hotel reception desk and made for the lift. Ben pressed the button.

'I lied,' said Chiara. 'There isn't going to be a next time.'

He hardly knew her, and yet the words bit strangely deep.
The lift doors slid open and he followed her inside.

'What's your room like?' she asked.

'It's a suite.'

'Good,' she said. 'Lots of space to play.'

fifteen days to go . . .

B EN WAS DIMLY aware of Chiara disentangling herself from
him, and of it being morning now, daylight bleeding
around the edge of the curtains.

The next thing he knew she was perched on the edge of
the mattress in her blue silk dress, smiling down at him and
running her fingers through his hair, pushing it back off his
face.

'I have to send some emails.'

She bent and kissed him, her tongue forcing its way
between his lips. The fingers of her right hand traced a slow
course down his stomach, beneath the sheet, reaching for
him.

'Oh, you're awake too,' she said. 'And how are you this
morning?'

'Sore,' he replied.

'*Poverino . . .*' she pouted. Pushing back the sheet, she
planted several soothing kisses before taking him in her
mouth, so gently that he wasn't sure at first if she had or
not.

Christ, how could he be so hard again? Had she slipped him a magic pill during the meal?

Chiara looked up at him and smiled. 'Later. When I'm back. I won't be long.'

The next time he woke it was just after ten o'clock, not that this meant anything. For all he knew, she'd only been gone five minutes.

He wandered through to the living room. They hadn't closed any of the curtains the night before, and in the harsh light of the new day the field of battle looked entirely different. At a certain point they had both discarded their clothes. Ben's shirt and trousers now lay neatly draped across the back of the sofa, where Chiara had presumably placed them when she'd got dressed. There was a sweet tang in the air: fumes from the two glasses of cognac he had poured them but which they hadn't got round to drinking.

He flopped into an armchair. He felt surprisingly clear-headed, given how little he'd slept. He hadn't wanted to sleep, not after the first time, when Chiara had removed her knickers but not her dress. He stared at the sofa. It appeared so innocent, with its patterned green fabric and its tasselled trim, but what he saw were the many uses they'd put it to that first time. He'd never known anything like it, never known a woman to twist herself into so many different shapes.

He carried the cognac glasses through to the bathroom and emptied their contents down the sink. He showered quickly, one ear out for a knock at the door.

Half an hour later there was still no sign of Chiara so he

called her room, 117. He'd logged it last night when they'd asked for their keys at the front desk. The phone rang then went to message.

Room 117 wasn't a cheap room; it had a lake view. Ben knew this because he could see the lake through the open door from the corridor outside, where the maid's trolley was parked. There were two of them, changing the sheets on the bed. Ben left them to it. What would they know?

Downstairs, he was informed by the receptionist that Signora Bonetti had checked out. She hadn't left him a message. There was no question of the hotel releasing her contact details, although they would be happy to forward a message to her. He let it go.

What kind of woman woke you with a tender kiss, took you in her mouth, promised to return in a short while and then vanished into thin air? Answer: the sort of woman who'd given you fair warning that there wasn't going to be a next time. Chiara had clearly wanted to avoid any awkward farewells.

On Victor's advice Ben had packed his tennis gear, and with a few hours to kill before his two o'clock departure he went in search of a game. There were eight courts, most of them clay, set high on the slope behind the hotel. One of the hotel's pros was happy to have a knock for an hour (and for a cheeky fee). By the end of the session Ben was feeling considerably better.

Chalk it up to experience. You've just had the wildest sex of your life with the most beautiful woman you've ever slept with. Stop feeling so bloody sorry for yourself.

Sound advice from the voice of reason in his head. Streaming with fierce sweat, he wandered back down the hill to the hotel, disconsolate but resigned.

He swam then had a light lunch by the pool, enjoying a last blast of the Italian sun. He had arranged for a late checkout, and while he was running through the paperwork at the desk the receptionist handed him a telephone message: '*Chi va piano* . . . Chiara XX'.

It had been left for him an hour ago, and he could picture her dictating it, right down to the two kisses, which made him smile. As for the Italian, he could look it up when he was back in England.

Lance was far from his usual garrulous self during the trip back to Oxfordshire from London City Airport. Despite having had most of the day to recover, he was still feeling the effects of his night out with his mates. He had woken up at one in the morning under a pool table in some bloke's garage near Chingford. 'And then we went out.'

'It doesn't show in your eyes,' said Ben.

'Very funny,' replied Lance from behind his very dark sunglasses.

He drove most of the way in silence and with the aircon at full blast, fired at his face to keep him alert.

Ben was greeted like a returning hero on the front steps of Stoneham Park by Annabelle.

'We were told he definitely wouldn't budge on price.'

'Oh, so that's why Victor offered me a percentage.'

Annabelle smiled. 'Maybe it was a test.'

'A test?'

'It's not for me to say,' she replied enigmatically.

Even with twenty-five years of European travel under his belt, it still struck him as extraordinary that you could have lunch in one country and dinner in an entirely different one: different climate, different people, different language. He had also come to realise over time that returning home, even when he'd had his fill of being away, left him feeling vaguely melancholic. It had nothing to do with the bills waiting on the doormat and the dirty washing to be dealt with; it was more elusive than that, an unaccountable dip in his spirits which never lasted more than one evening.

This time it was compounded by a mix of conflicting emotions. There was exhilaration – the shameless depravity of his night with Chiara would be a memory for life, as would the still fragrance of her brown body and the sucking bite of her lips – but it was tempered by an anxiety, bordering on alarm, that he might never travel to that bewitched place ever again, not with Chiara, for sure, but not with anyone else either.

And then there was the icy hand of guilt. He told himself that he'd only just met Mo, that she was in a long-standing relationship, that he wasn't beholden to her feelings; and yet she'd made those same feelings pretty plain to him in her texts over the past couple of days. If *he* felt that he had betrayed her in some way, could he really expect her to feel any differently? Of course not. Which was why he would lie to her. He knew that already.

These thoughts came at him from all quarters as he was strolling by the lake at dusk. The sun had only just slipped below the hills and Stoneham Park seemed to tremble in the eerie purple light – a strange, restless, betwixt-and-between place, suspended in time. A vapour trail chalked across the heavens offered the only clue that this wasn't the eighteenth century. Come to think of it, the huge oak trees now towering about the place would have been dwarfed by the main house three hundred years ago. It occurred to him that Victor hadn't only bought a country estate, he had bought a dead man's vision of how that estate would one day look, long after he was gone, his body stripped back to bones in the soil of Stoneham churchyard.

That's where William Burnett was buried, according to Annabelle, together with his son and his grandchildren and a smattering of other relatives. A meagre three generations of Burnetts before the bloodline had run dry and the dream had fallen into another's hands. Burnett had made his money from sugar, liquidating his plantations in Barbados and returning home to play at being a gentleman. So many of the country's stately homes owed their existence to the eagerness of men like Burnett to distance themselves from their commercial origins. It was the English curse: trade was a dirty word. Even during the Victorian age, the moment you'd made a fortune in coal or wool or steel you sold up and went in search of a new kind of status, possibly acquiring a title in the process and easing yourself into the ranks of the aristocracy.

Victor and his kind – the Russian oligarchs, hedge-fund

billionaires and technology moguls – were the natural heirs to this tradition. They were the new aristocrats, men who had pulled themselves up by their boot straps, accumulating fortunes so vast that even the industrialists of past ages seemed like paupers by comparison. But like those men whose homes they now lived in, they wanted more than just money; they wanted social standing, a new kind of recognition for themselves and their progeny. In short, they wished to become part of the establishment.

Ben didn't begrudge Victor his wealth, but he was annoyed with himself for passing up the chance to place his hands on a small slice of it. He had done the calculation on his phone while waiting at Malpensa Airport to fly home. Twenty per cent of the 150,000 euros he had saved Victor on the purchase of the Riva converted to a cool £24,304.59 (at the rate being offered by the bureau de change in the airport). That hurt, even more than it had last night, when Chiara had admonished him over dinner for his folly in turning down the percentage.

'You worked for it. You earned it. You saved your friend a lot of money.'

'Can we change the subject, please?'

'No, I want to hear you say you have learned a lesson.'

'Jesus . . .'

'Say it.'

'OK, OK, I've learned a lesson.'

'An expensive lesson.'

'You're enjoying this, aren't you?'

'In Italian we say "*A caval donato non si guarda in bocca*".'

'Good for you.'

Never look a gift horse in the mouth. It wasn't the only proverb Chiara had tossed his way. She had signed off their brief encounter with the first few words of another: *Chi va piano* . . . He had looked it up on the Web not an hour ago in the privacy of his room: '*Chi va piano va sano e va lontano*', which roughly translated as 'He who goes slowly goes safely and far'.

He would have preferred a nod to the fleeting ecstasy of their time together in his suite, not a piece of prudent advice that ran entirely counter to the experience. In fact, it was so at odds with the delicious abandon of those hours that he wondered for a moment if she'd meant it as a warning of some kind. This, of course, was ridiculous. It was obviously intended as a joke, heavy with an irony that only he would understand.

two weeks to go . . .

T HERE WAS ONE major drawback to tackling the rewrite at Stoneham Park that Ben hadn't reckoned on before leaping at Victor's offer. At best, his working routine could be described as idiosyncratic. This was fine when he was at home, where he could potter about, lose himself in a book, go for a walk, or – holy of holies – snatch an afternoon snooze whenever the mood took him.

At Stoneham Park there was almost no avoiding the hawk-eyed scrutiny of Annabelle, who was forever bustling about the place with her lists and her bundles of paper – 'Keeping the caravan rolling,' as she liked to say. It wasn't an issue when the words were flowing, but the moment the well ran dry he needed to be up and about, on the move. Displacement activity was good for inspiration, even if to others it looked like shirking.

Things started well enough on his first day back from Italy. The two rival gangs had been cleverly abducted, drugged and transported to the island. Some of them were still labouring under the illusion that this was a new kind of reality show, that they were going to become household names, media celebrities, showered with fame and fortune. In the previous draft, the wiser among them had made the others see sense — a wordy exchange, low on visual drama, which had always bugged Ben. He now stole a moment from his time in Italy and folded it into the story: the football match between Signore Viani's grandchildren, which he'd only been drawn into because the teams were unevenly numbered. He gave the Asian gang an extra member then had one of their abductors casually execute him with a head shot, levelling the teams. Point made. No need for discussion. Revulsion coupled with the instant understanding that this wasn't a reality TV show.

He was happy with the changes, but he soon found himself meditating bleakly on the script as a whole. Was this really how he earned his living? He spent most of his waking hours in a parallel universe of his own creation, a violent fantasy world where people shot other people in the head. It wasn't natural. It certainly wasn't healthy. He was forty-three years old, for God's sake, halfway through his life. Did he intend to devote the remainder of his precious time on the planet to trotting out stuff like this? He had a vision of himself, bald and bent by age, his nose pressed to the screen, his arthritic fingers fumbling at the keys, turning into words the juvenile imaginings of his addled brain.

Such thoughts would catch him in their undertow from time to time, and he'd learned how best to handle them: don't swim against the current, go with it, allow it to carry you out to sea, conserve your energy for the long haul back to shore once it had dissipated of its own accord. Work, meanwhile, was out of the question. Mo would have provided the perfect diversion, but she'd texted him earlier to say she wouldn't be back from Yorkshire until very late, possibly around midnight.

He found Annabelle in Victor's study, which was about the only room in the house he hadn't yet seen because it was generally kept locked. She was seated at a vast glass and stainless-steel desk, talking to someone on a telephone headset. She signalled to him from behind a bank of wafer-thin monitors that she wouldn't be long.

In terms of its footprint, the room was a perfect mirror of the library on the opposite side of the house. It took Ben a few moments to register this, though, because in every other respect the two spaces couldn't have been more different. Whereas the library paid literal homage to the house's eighteenth-century origins, Victor's study was a stark tribute to the modern age, stripped back to a few essentials and some high-tech trappings. The long conference table down the other end of the room was less a piece of furniture than a piece of sculpture: a single monolithic form moulded from white plastic, with three organic, fin-like legs supporting an asymmetrical tabletop the colour of a South Seas lagoon. Filling the wall beyond it was an enormous photograph, maybe two metres by three, which Ben recognised but couldn't quite place. It was a panoramic shot looking down on the packed trading floor of a stock exchange, a frozen moment in the frenzied lives of the hundreds of traders jammed together in their colourful jackets.

'Andreas Gursky,' announced Annabelle from the far end of the room, her call over.

'Ah, Gursky, yes.'

She came and stood beside him. 'They always make me think of worker bees in a hive. It looks like chaos but you know there's method in the madness. There has to be.'

'It's beautiful.'

'It's where Victor started, you know? Well, not there – that's Chicago.'

'When's he back?'

'Friday, all going well.'

'And is it?'

'I suspect he'll have made enough to pay for the Riva.' Several times over, judging by her thin smile.

'Annabelle, don't you find it weird? The sums of money, I mean.'

'At the beginning, maybe, but you soon get used to the extra noughts. In the end, it's the same life.'

'No, it isn't.'

'OK,' she conceded. 'The good things are better. But the bad things are just as bad.'

'What are the bad things?'

A fleeting expression, hard to decipher, touched then vanished from her face. She produced a surgical smile. 'You might have to give me a few minutes to think about it.'

He was tempted to press her further, but something in the set of her jaw warned him not to bother. Instead, he came clean with her: he was stuck, he needed distraction, he thought he might take a drive through the countryside. 'It beats playing croquet by myself.'

She surprised him by saying that she didn't give two hoots about how he chose to spend his time. She knew what writers were like. A friend of hers in Oxford was a novelist. 'She seems to spend half her time watching talk shows on TV, but it works for her. She's even scooped a couple of literary prizes. I know I come across as a bit of a busybody but I'm really not. What you do is a mystery to me. How you do it is your own business.'

She dug out a map of the surrounding area and suggested a looping circuit through the Cotswolds which took in her favourite pub, in case he wanted to stop off for a bite of lunch.

It was the perfect chance to get to proper grips with the Maserati. The short hop to Woodstock with Mo had been like trotting around a paddock on a racehorse. He didn't need the satnav – he had the map with Annabelle's meandering route marked on it in felt-tip pen – so he let the screen lie blank, revelling in the ride. Motorcycles had been a feature of his life since he was seventeen, and from then until now he had never driven a car to make him think he might one day give them up. The experience was that good. Whether simply cruising along or threading the coupé through a sequence of corners in Sport mode he drove with the windows down to better enjoy the resonant bark of the engine bouncing off the hedgerows.

The intoxicating mix of power, precise handling and good

looks released a memory of flying across Lake Como at the wheel of the Riva. That had been another experience to stir the soul. He wondered if familiarity could ever blunt such sensations. How long – for a man in Victor's position, say – before they became commonplace? When you could have anything you wanted, was it possible to be satisfied with what you already had, or were you condemned to a never-ending quest for more sensations to trump the last: more power, more poise, more beauty?

The curse of the filthy rich, he reflected as he nosed the Maserati through the stone gateposts of the pub car park. Poor things! Your heart had to go out to them.

He killed the power but hesitated before removing the key. He told himself not to bother – what was the point in looking at it again? – but his hand still twisted the key, bringing the dashboard back to life.

It wasn't there. Not a single one of the previous destinations stored in the satnav was there. They had all been deleted.

Maybe it was an electronic glitch. He turned the power off then on again. Same thing: a blank screen staring back at him. He reached across for the manual in the glove compartment. It spelled out in a few easy steps how to clear the history.

Who had sat where he was sitting and stared at the same page? Not Victor, that much was certain. Lance? Possibly. But when? He had spent the weekend in London after dropping Ben off at London City Airport, which narrowed it down to sometime last night, or earlier that day. Annabelle, on the other hand, could have done it at any time over the past few days. Who else? Gregoire? Camille? It seemed unlikely.

The real question, though, was why? He found himself reaching for an innocent explanation that had nothing to do with his own postcode. Maybe Annabelle had used the Maserati at the weekend but didn't want Victor to know she had. But if that was the case she could simply have deleted any destinations she'd entered. According to the manual, there was an option to remove individual locations. And if Victor didn't have a problem with him using the Maserati then Annabelle surely had free use of the car; there was no need for her to cover her tracks.

The Swan was a riverside pub with a leafy garden out back. He opted for the grilled trout. The menu was keen to point out that it was a local fish, caught on a rod and line, which went some way towards justifying the hefty price. Even before he'd picked the trout bare he'd exhausted all the other possible explanations, following them through until hard logic stopped him in his tracks. He didn't like what he was left with.

Whoever had cleaned out the satnav's history must have known it wouldn't go unnoticed by Victor on his return. Therefore, the instruction had come from Victor himself.

It wasn't watertight, but at least it had the merit of not leaking like a sieve. Was he overreacting? Was his mind playing him dirty tricks? He seemed incapable of judging any more.

There was a whole host of friends he could have called on

for advice, men and women who had risen to the top of their chosen fields: lawyers, management consultants, journalists, academics, even the odd politician. They were people with big brains and a firm grip on the world, so why he phoned Edwin was anyone's guess.

'*Oye como va, compadre?*'

'Let me take a wild guess,' said Ben. 'You've met a Spanish girl.'

'Pueerrrto Rican.'

'And does she have a name?'

'Cassandra,' replied Edwin, still trowelling on the Spanish accent.

'Ah, a prophetess.'

'Actually, she works in a sandwich bar near Moorgate tube. But, boy, does she know how to cha-cha-cha.'

'I thought the cha-cha-cha was Cuban.'

'Jesus, Ben, you're such a fucking swot. Sometimes you've just got to go with it, feel it . . .' Worryingly, Edwin began to sing: '*Oye como va mi ritmo . . . Bueno pa' gozar mulata . . .*'

'Do you want to lose your job?' Ben interjected.

'Relax, I don't do open-plan any more, I'm too fucking important. The idiot Swiss have given me my own office.'

As Edwin had moved between merchant banks over the years his employers had gone from being the 'idiot Yanks' to the 'idiot Krauts', and now the 'idiot Swiss'.

'So, did you bang that lesbian?'

'No, Edwin, I didn't *bang* her.'

'Oh, holier-than-thou. You were the one who texted me all overheated, remember?'

Ben didn't bother to explain the twisted purpose behind Lorna's text, and when Edwin suggested they get together next week and check out the bar at a new hotel making waves in Soho, he kept it suitably vague: he was out of town, holed up in the countryside, head down on a new script.

For all his skittish exuberance, Edwin was a well brought up fellow. When he asked about the script, Ben explained that it was a story about two guys who hadn't seen each other in decades, not since they were kids together at boarding school. Then one day they meet again – a chance encounter, or so it appears, until one of them finds his postcode stored in the other guy's satnav, and it's obviously been there for months.

'Nice,' said Edwin. 'I like it already.'

'I don't know, I'm not sure the whole satnav thing really works. I mean, so what?'

'So what? One of them has obviously been spying on the other one. It's plain fucking creepy whichever way you slice it.'

'That's good to hear,' lied Ben.

'Let me guess, they had their issues when they were younger.'

'No, not really.'

Edwin seemed not to hear him. 'Yeah, I like it. The long shadow of history and all that. Sasha will love it.' Sasha was

Edwin's ex-wife, mother to his two daughters. 'She was always saying men are basically little boys with body hair and bigger dicks.'

'Yeah? And what did you say?'

'I told her she was talking out of her stinky bum hole, of course.'

thirty-two years before . . .

'MUM, WHAT ARE you doing?'
But he could see what she was doing. She was on
her hands and knees in the hallway, rummaging through
Jacob's battered brown suitcase.

'Oh, Benjamin!' she gasped. She only ever called him
Benjamin when she was angry with him, but this time she
wasn't angry, she was startled, her hand going to her heart.
'You gave me the fright of my life.'

There was a scatter of items near her right knee: a pair of
pliers with red plastic handles (which he recognised from the
toolbox in the garage), two golf balls, a small clay mouse
with a leather tail (one of many which inhabited the shelf
on the Welsh dresser in the breakfast room), a miniature glass
bottle of Schweppes tonic water . . .

'Where's Jacob?' she asked.

'Showing Dad the newts we found at the lake.'

'Well, go and check the coast is clear.'

She returned to her search, pulling a large glass marble
from the tangle of unfolded clothes. She made to replace it.

'That's mine,' he said.

'Are you sure?'

'Yes, it's mine.'

'Oh, let him have it, it's just a marble.'

But it wasn't just a marble – well, not *any* old marble – and he was about to protest when—

'Please, Benjamin, just go and check they're not coming.' This time she *was* angry. 'And don't for heaven's sake tell your father about this. I mean it. Not ever.'

Ben dreaded the drive back to school on Sunday evenings. He had learned to hate the meandering route his father always took, sullenly counting down the minutes, the miles, the markers. The level crossing on Spatham Lane was exactly halfway, he had once calculated.

This time, though, he barely registered the trip, his mind on other matters. His mother had offered no explanation of what she'd been doing in the hallway, not that one was needed. It was pretty obvious she'd been rifling through Jacob's stuff, removing bits and pieces he'd pilfered from their house over the weekend. Ben wondered how long it had been going on. Had she spent the past three years sneakily searching Jacob's suitcase every time they were about to return to school? Had she even confronted Jacob? Maybe it was a sort of game they played, with Jacob knowing she was on to him (how could he not know?) but still chancing his luck every time he came to stay. But stealing wasn't a game. His father held strong views on the subject.

Slowly, and with increasing anger, he recalled the

possessions of his which had mysteriously disappeared over the past year or so: the penknife he'd bought with his pocket money in Minehead, the leather baseball last seen in the potting shed, the Rolls-Royce Dinky toy, the catapult Uncle Peter had given him two Christmases ago . . .

The list kept growing. Things went astray, of course, they got mislaid or they slipped out of pockets unnoticed and you learned to live with the loss. That's the way he had always seen it. It had never once occurred to him that Jacob might be behind the disappearances.

The marble proved beyond doubt what Jacob was capable of. Ben knew exactly where it had been, where it had always been: in an old cigar box tucked away at the back of the bottom drawer of the desk in his bedroom. How could his mother have made him give it up without a fight? It wasn't fair. It wasn't right. She probably would have made him do it even if he'd told her the story behind the marble, he thought sourly.

It was a 'shooter', a one-and-a-half-inch cat's eye with six purple, green and black vanes at its centre, and he'd won it off Jacob back in the autumn term, fair and square. Any number of witnesses could testify to this, because the epic battle had drawn a large crowd.

It had started as a bit of a joke for Ben: taking on a 32-er, a pretty serious rating in marble terms, with a measly little 4-er. The maths was straightforward, a simple case of division (or multiplication, if you preferred). Ben had to hit Jacob's marble eight times in order for it to become his, whereas Jacob only had to hit him once.

As far as Ben was concerned, the outcome was a foregone conclusion. There was almost nothing to divide them when it came to skill at marbles. If anything, Jacob had the edge over him. But on that cold clear day in late October, with the low autumn sun casting its slanting rays across the ugly concrete quad at the heart of the school, the gods decided to get behind Ben, guiding his arm.

There was a noticeable change in Jacob after the third of three audacious long-range shots by Ben miraculously found its mark. He grew grumpy, even angry: the sun was in his eyes, the crowd was making too much noise. After the fifth strike on his prized marble, two of the senior boys who had set themselves up as umpires told him to shut up and get on with it, at which point his technique went completely to pot. It was all over just seconds before the bell rang for the end of break.

To his mother it was just a marble; for Ben it was a trophy of battle, hard-won, a memento of a special day when his eye had been in and he could do no wrong. OK, so Jacob was annoyed that Ben had never allowed him a shot at winning it back, but that was no excuse for stealing it back. That one act made a nonsense of their friendship, of all the good times they'd had together, and there'd been many over the past few years. Trust was like a mirror: it could only be broken once. He'd read that somewhere; now he knew what it meant.

He didn't sense the usual lump in his throat when his father dropped them off at school just in time for Sunday evensong; he was burning with too much indignation still. The school's new chapel, recently completed, was an octagonal brick affair topped by a copper spire which was already turning green. With its huge glass windows, modern lighting and comfortable seats, it didn't feel like a particularly holy place to Ben, but he tried his best to think holy thoughts, like compassion and forgiveness.

It wasn't easy with Jacob standing beside him belting out 'The King of Love My Shepherd Is'. When the whole school launched into the third verse — 'Perverse and foolish oft I strayed . . .' he glanced at Jacob, but the saintly expression on his face didn't falter one bit.

He wondered how that same face would look later when it realised the suitcase had been stripped of its stolen treasures. The marble would be a consolation. Where would he hide it? He must have somewhere he stashed the stuff, somewhere no one else knew about.

When it came time for prayers, Ben unhooked the hassock from the back of the chair in front and knelt with his head bowed. They were always given a minute or so for their own private prayers. He didn't waste this period of silence, although what he came up with was less of a prayer than a pledge, a vow to himself: that come what may he would find Jacob's secret hiding place.

It took him almost two weeks, and in the end he only struck gold because he was hit hard on the hip by a cricket ball one afternoon during batting practice in the nets.

Jacob ran with a slightly different pack at school, and Ben soon discovered that sticking close to him wasn't easy without arousing suspicion or putting his own friends' noses out of joint. It was a fine balancing act and nothing came of it. Jacob never seemed to sneak off anywhere. Choosing his moments carefully, Ben also made thorough searches of Jacob's chest of drawers in the dormitory they now shared, his sports locker in the basement, and even his tuck box. This required picking the padlock with a compass. The only item of interest he turned up was a page torn from a porn mag. At first glance, and before realising his error, he assumed the woman was giving birth to a cucumber. Annoyingly, the other side of the page was taken up with adverts.

The ball was bowled by Pendleton, one of the 1st XI's pace men. It was a vicious in-swinger that put Ben back on his heels. He tried to steer it down the leg side, missed, and there was an audible CRACK as the ball made contact with his hip bone. He crumpled to the ground, biting back the tears. It was an honour to be invited to practise with the senior boys; he wasn't going to ruin it by blubbing.

He thought at first that his hip might be broken. He couldn't put any weight on his left leg and he had to be helped to the sanatorium, where Matron prescribed an aspirin and some Vicks VapoRub: the same trusty combination she had administered to Zahid Faruki when he had returned from his native Pakistan with what turned out to be malaria. The school's lone pair of crutches was already in use, so Ben had to make do with a walking stick borrowed from Headmaster Burroughs to help him hop about the place.

When it came to ensuring that an ill or injured boy got a good night's sleep, Matron liked to administer eight spoonfuls of Benylin cough mixture at bedtime. Ben slept like a bear in hibernation that first night, then floated through breakfast and morning classes in a daydream. His hip was still sore as hell at the end of the day, but he was the one who suggested to Matron that she lower the dose of Benylin, not sure that he wanted to feel like a zombie two days on the trot.

He nodded off immediately, but whenever he shifted in his sleep he would be woken by a shooting pain in his hip. He knew that this happened about every hour or so because his watch had a luminous dial and hands.

He was awake and his watch was reading a quarter to eleven when he heard the creak of bedsprings followed by the light pad of feet on floorboards. A shadowy figure passed by the end of his bed and slipped from the room. He reached for his torch and fired it at the far end of the dormitory. Jacob appeared to be in his bed, but Ben could tell immediately that a pillow had been stuffed down it to create the illusion.

He knew he had to move fast. Wincing against the pain, he eased out of bed and hobbled towards the door. 'It's not true!' came an indignant voice from the darkness, but it was only Briggs talking in his sleep again.

'Copenhagen', their dormitory, was one of three that gave directly on to the broad landing at the top of the main staircase. He knew instinctively that Jacob hadn't headed downstairs because downstairs lay certain doom: the headmaster's study and the teachers' common room. Even at this late hour, he could hear the dim hum of voices down there in the darkness, and the faint odour of cigarette smoke rose up to meet his nostrils.

A noise . . . off to his left . . . down the long corridor that led to the linen room and the toilets. Maybe Jacob was simply going for a pee. No. Who stuffed a pillow down their bed when they went for a pee?

Sure enough, the toilets were deserted, and the linen room was locked, which only left the narrow staircase that climbed to the very top floor, where the servants used to live in the old days, before the house became a school.

It was a labyrinth of narrow corridors and locked rooms which the boys only ever glimpsed at the beginning and end of every term because their empty trunks were stored in a big boarded space under the roof. For the rest of the time, the top floor was strictly out of bounds. The school had even installed a gatekeeper in the form of Mr Jobson, a burly man, hairy as a baboon. Everyone knew this because he was head of swimming and was always strutting around the pool in his tiny red Speedos. They called him Kong behind his back. He taught history and had a bit of his own to go along with it. Rumour said he was divorced and that somewhere there was a son. It wasn't rumour that he had fought the Mau Maus in Kenya. The boys took this to mean that he had killed people, although they could never get him to admit to it. Mr Jobson's rooms sat directly above 'Oslo', Ben's dormitory in the second year, and late at night they had often heard him clomping about and playing classical music loudly.

He wasn't playing music now, though, he was typing. Ben could hear the telltale clickety-clack as he slipped silently past Mr Jobson's door. Everyone said that the top floor was haunted by the ghost of a dead maid who had thrown herself from a window. Ben's father thought ghosts were a load of nonsense, and although Ben didn't believe in them he still felt a wave of fear prickle his scalp as he groped his way along the pitch-black corridor.

In the end it was the darkness that guided him to Jacob, to the faint strip of torchlight bleeding beneath the door of the attic room where the trunks were kept. His instinct was to burst in and catch Jacob in the act, but he quickly figured there was a more satisfying way of dealing with the situation. He even smiled at the thought of what he would do.

Mr Jobson was still typing away in his room, but as Ben passed by the door the sound suddenly stopped. He froze, gripped by panic. A voice – one word, spoken softly with an inquiring tone. Relief swept through him a few seconds later when the typing started again. Exhaling silently, he continued on his way.

Only when he was safely back in his bed did he replay the moment of terror in his mind. He couldn't swear by it – the blood had been beating so loudly in his ears – but he was pretty sure that Mr Jobson had said, 'Jacob?'

It was a simple case of play-acting, of dragging out the injury to his hip until Sunday afternoon, when he knew the school would be deserted.

This wasn't without its sacrifices. It meant not captaining the Colts 1st XI on Saturday afternoon against Ashdown House. Jacob was moved up from the 2nd XI to take his place. It was a home game, and Ben watched from a deckchair on the boundary as Jacob played out of his skin, taking two wickets, a great diving catch at extra cover, as well as knocking up 31 runs just when the opposition looked to be gaining the upper hand. As ever, Jacob was bowled out while trying to slog a near-perfect ball for six over square leg. It didn't matter; Mr Deakins still awarded him man of the match. In spite of everything, Ben was happy for Jacob, happy to see the look of coy pride on his face as he fielded the pats on the back from his teammates.

Ben waited till they were heading for tea in the pavilion before making his move. 'Well done. You played a blinder.'

'I was lucky,' shrugged Jacob. 'First slip dropped me when I was on three.'

'There was nothing lucky about that catch.'

'No.' Jacob glanced around to check no masters were in earshot. 'That was one motherfucker of a catch, wasn't it?'

Ben had to laugh. 'We'll re-enact it for Dad next time we're home.'

They did that sort of thing a lot, re-creating their moments of sporting excellence in the garden for his father's benefit.

Jacob stopped suddenly and turned to him. 'Thanks, Ben.'

'For what?'

'For being so big about it. That should have been you out there today, not me.'

Don't talk like that, thought Ben, or I won't be able to see it through.

He did, though, exaggerating his limp to and from Sunday morning chapel. It was usual for the whole school to disappear into the woods after lunch. There were streams to dam, lakes to raft on, ropes to swing from and cliffs of soft sandstone to climb. It was the one moment when they were allowed to run riot, to run truly free. Yes, there were teachers present, but even they understood that different rules applied in the woods. They were only there to ensure that the boys didn't kill themselves or each other.

During the week, a dirt-stained shirt might earn you a reprimand or even a punishment, but on Sundays you could return from the woods caked in mud like a caveman and no one gave a hoot. This was part of Headmaster Burroughs' philosophy that, as with all caged animals, boys at boarding school needed be let loose from time to time if they weren't to grow mad or depressed. Nothing embodied this thinking more than Q Day.

No one seemed to know what the 'Q' stood for, but they all knew what it meant: the top year of the school – split into eight 'tribes' – took to the woods for a night and a day of war games, challenges, and other general mayhem. Wednesday and Sunday afternoons during the summer term were given over to constructing the giant camps which each tribe would have to sleep in (and defend). Young trees needed to be cut down and lashed together to form the framework, perimeters needed to be built, firepits and mantraps dug. It was time-consuming work, and on Sunday afternoons the lower years of the school were expected to help out. They did this willingly, eager to rub shoulders with the senior boys, offering their services to the tribes they supported.

This was why Ben found himself with pretty much free run of the school that Sunday afternoon, having been excused duties because of his injured hip. Most importantly, there was no danger of running into Mr Jobson on the top floor; with his army background, he was always in the thick of it when it came to Q Day preparations.

It was a strange and slightly creepy sensation, finding himself alone in the deserted school. The noise was the thing he noticed most, or rather the lack of it. Sounds which were usually drowned out by the general hubbub were suddenly amplified: the squeak of a door, the ticking of a wall clock, the draught from an open window rustling pieces of paper on a noticeboard.

He had to be careful. Every sound he made would also be magnified, and there were still a couple of teachers around. Matron was his biggest threat; she was always pottering about upstairs. He decided to tackle the problem head on, going in search of her, calling out her name. If he had found her he would have asked for another aspirin, but she seemed to have vanished. Grabbing his torch from the dormitory, he hurried for the top floor.

The empty trunks in the huge L-shaped attic room were stacked three or four high, creating a maze of narrow passage-ways lit from above by a couple of bare electric bulbs. Ben didn't search aimlessly; he tried to put himself in Jacob's shoes. He decided he could ignore the trunks on the grounds that they didn't offer a permanent hiding place. Fortunately for him, almost nowhere did, which was why a few minutes later he found himself on his hands and knees peering beneath the two giant water tanks raised on chunky wooden joists.

A couple of the floorboards felt loose to his touch, although not so loose that he could prise them up by hand. He was forced to abandon the search and head back downstairs. First stop was his classroom, and the steel ruler he kept in his desk drawer. He then went to his sports locker and grabbed the cotton bag for his games kit.

Nothing prepared him for the sheer amount of gear he found jammed between the floor joists once he'd levered up the boards beneath the water tanks. His torch revealed a mini Aladdin's cave. The first item he registered was his catapult, which had gone missing a year ago. On seeing it lying there he felt a weird mix of elation and anger, recalling the many hours Jacob had spent helping him search for it. The marble was there too, as was his penknife, along with other bits and pieces which had disappeared. There were even some things he hadn't missed until now, like a packet of Top Trumps cards (easily overlooked because it was only Tanks) and a pencil sharpener shaped like a small camera which he'd got in his Christmas stocking. All this stuff, he realised, had been stolen from him relatively recently, within the past year or so.

It soon became clear that he wasn't the only victim of Jacob's light fingers. As he scooped out the stolen gear into his games kitbag, he came across a brown leather wallet which he would have been able to identify even if it hadn't been embossed with Rory Pullen's initials: R.W.P. Poor Rory had had to go without pocket money for a whole term, that's how annoyed his parents had been on hearing he'd lost the wallet.

He quickly realised he was going to have to make some changes to his plan, which hadn't developed beyond getting his own stuff back and then disposing of anything else, possibly by burying it. But that wouldn't be fair. The Rorys of the world had a right to have their things returned to them.

A new plan began to take shape in his mind. He would pile everything into a bin bag and leave it in the headmaster's study. Burroughs would quickly figure out what the items were and assume that the thief had had a change of heart. The items would then be made available for the boys to reclaim.

No, it didn't work. Ben would have to include his own things in the bin bag or Jacob would immediately guess that he was the one behind the raid on his stash, and he could never allow that to happen. But if he included his things – stuff that had been stolen from his home – then Jacob would know that he was on to him.

He was about to reject Plan B when he began to see its appeal. So what if Jacob was aware that he knew his dirty little secret? It would give him a hold over Jacob. It might even make Jacob mend his ways. Do it again, to me or anyone else, and I'll spill the beans on you.

Annoyingly, this power would come at a cost. He could never claim back his catapult or his penknife because both were banned by the school. He would have to let them go forever, and he wondered if it was a price worth paying.

He didn't have to decide immediately. Right now, there were others things to worry about, like not getting caught with a bag full of stolen goods. That was a situation he would never be able to talk his way out of.

thirteen days to go . . .

MO WAS BACK. Ben found her Golf parked out front when he set off on his morning run. She must have pulled in very late, because he'd worked in his room until well after midnight – the window open, hoping to hear her return – before finally turning in.

The Golf was crammed to the gills with gear, which could mean something but probably didn't, he decided, jogging on by and down the driveway. There was no accounting for it. Some days, he reflected, you were gasping for breath after a couple of minutes, joints and muscles screaming in protest; other times, you skipped merrily along, barely breaking a sweat. By the time he reached the village green in Stoneham he was even toying with the idea of signing up for a marathon. He swiftly rejected it as too much of a cliché.

Hardly a week went by when he didn't receive a begging email from a friend looking to be sponsored for some feat of endurance or other. What was it about hitting forty that turned committed couch potatoes into triathletes and mountaineers? In the old days, a charity parachute jump had been enough, but now everyone he knew seemed determined to compete in an Ironman or climb Mont Blanc or cycle from Land's End to John O'Groats – always for some worthy cause.

The charity angle was deeply suspicious: *Dear All. In September I shall be going white-water rafting in Costa Rica for charity . . .*

Yeah, right. Why don't you pay for you own bloody holiday to Central America?

Come to think of it, it might be worth a shot.

Dear All. Next spring I shall be travelling to the west coast of France where I plan to surf every named wave between Brest and the Spanish border – for charity. Help the Aged are eager to draw attention to the body/mind benefits of long-boarding for senior citizens etcetera . . .

It wasn't just the running. He clocked up fifty effortless lengths on his return. Only the boredom of ploughing up and down the pool eventually drove him from the water. Soaking in a hot bath back in his room, he wondered whether this new-found stamina had something to do with the prospect of seeing Mo again. Maybe the thought of it was enough to release a cocktail of invigorating endorphins into his system.

He didn't have to wait too long before setting eyes on her. When he headed downstairs for his morning coffee he found Mo and Annabelle having breakfast on the back terrace.

It wasn't the reunion he had imagined. Mo mumbled a greeting, and as he drew closer he saw that she'd been crying.

Annabelle's sharp look left him in no doubt that he was intruding. He retreated, making a feeble excuse about the coffee machine coming to the boil back in the kitchen.

He tried not to speculate about the signs – the tears, the car filled to bursting with her possessions – but everything pointed to Connor finally making up his mind about their future together. What a complete and utter berk. Ben could have hugged him.

He knew he was getting ahead of himself. You couldn't just draw a line under an eight-year relationship. Mo had said it herself: they were at that point, all or nothing, which, he now remembered, often meant a bit of nothing to scare the other person into all.

Madeleine had never resorted to such theatrics, although she'd come close on a couple of occasions, threatening to move out of their microscopic flat in Islington because Ben was so violently opposed to the idea of a relationship that required the rubber stamp of the state to validate it (i.e. marriage). Friends of theirs had gone the whole hog, though, hiring Transit vans, putting their stuff in storage and crashing on other people's sofa beds . . . until the whole stupid charade was swept aside by tearful reconciliations, the wrenching sobs soon drowned out by the merry pealing of wedding bells.

So it goes, he thought. The endless round.

Such weary cynicism shamed him. Mo's red-rimmed eyes were real. She was hurting – real hurt – the kind that made you want to curl up in a ball on a bed. She had looked so desperately depleted sitting there at the table: the slumped shoulders, the hang of her head. If Annabelle hadn't been present he would have taken her in his arms and held her close. He wanted to do it now, to tell her that it would all work out, that Connor would see sense, because that's generally what men did in the end.

He was in the process of composing a text to her when she appeared at the library door.

'I was just texting you.'

'Saying?'

'Oh, you know – pull yourself together, that sort of thing.' She smiled weakly. 'Is it Connor?'

'Henceforth known as "the Antichrist".'

'Want to talk about it?'

'Maybe later. Right now I need a strong man to help me with some boxes of books.'

They emptied the Golf together, carrying everything across the stable yard and up to her apartment, where they heaped it in a corner of her bedroom.

A tiny white silk chemise lay tantalisingly discarded on the unmade bed next to an ancient teddy bear, its velvet paws and feet worn down to the nap.

'What's his name?' asked Ben.

'Have a guess.'

'I don't know – Lucky?'

'Creep.'

She offered him coffee and they drank it outside in the sunshine, at the tin table in the yard. Mo had heard about Ben's trip to Lake Como from Annabelle, but only the bare bones of it. He filled in a few of the gaps.

'And did you fall into bed with an Italian beauty?'

The question came out of nowhere. So did his reply. 'Of course not. We did it on the sofa.'

Her face split in a smile. 'Don't make me laugh, I'm trying really hard to feel sorry for myself.'

He reached across the table and took her hand. 'Want to share it with someone who's a lot happier than he's letting on?'

Mo frowned. 'You mean that?'

'Yes, I do.'

It was as he'd suspected. Connor had sat her down on Sunday night and told her he thought their relationship had run its course.

'And his reasons for making such a monumental mistake?'

'There were a few. But only one that really counts.' She seemed reluctant to elaborate.

'You don't have to say.'

'I probably shouldn't. You'll run a mile.'

'Try me. You might be surprised.'

He thought Aids; he thought Hepatitis B (or was C the one you really didn't want?). He thought a lot of things very quickly, and he was wrong on all counts.

'He wants to have kids.'

'And you don't?'

He read the answer in her eyes a split second before she replied.

'I can't.'

She fought and failed to hold back the tears. He slipped off his chair, rounding the table to kneel beside her. 'Hey . . .' he soothed, slipping an arm around her shoulders. He held her while she sobbed, her cheek wet against his neck.

She eventually pulled away, dragging her forearm across her eyes. 'It's nice to be held.'

'Any time.'

She placed her palm against his cheek, as she had a few nights ago, but there was no kiss now. 'Thank you.'

He couldn't bring himself to say that having kids wasn't all it was cracked up to be, because it wasn't true. He had watched, mesmerised, while eight and a bit pounds of writhing baby boy had worked their way out of Madeleine's body. There had been blood and shit and God knows how many other secretions and excretions, and he had stared in rapt wonderment at the spectacle of it all as though it was the most natural thing in the world, which of course it was. The initial resistance of the umbilical cord to the surgical scissors in his hand was a sensation he'd carry with him to his grave.

Some people said that a man who'd witnessed his wife giving birth could never look on her again as a sexual creature, the thinking being that she would always be relegated in his mind to some sort of biological entity. That hadn't been Ben's experience. If anything, he had desired Madeleine more than ever following Toby's birth. She was the one who had begun to lose interest in him, fixated with the little bundle they'd struggled so hard to create.

The best he could offer Mo was to tell her about the hoops they'd had to jump through before Madeleine finally fell pregnant. She thanked him kindly and said that unfortunately

IVF offered little hope for someone with her condition. A number of doctors had been very clear about that.

'What pisses me off, what *really* pisses me off, is I've wasted the last two years in a relationship that was going nowhere. Connor always swore it wasn't an issue for him, but it was. I know that now. I even got him to admit it. The fact is he's spent two years looking for other ways to bring us down because he was too weak to face up to the real reason. I was too absorbed in my work, I was away too much, I'd changed, I'd lost interest in his career.' She paused. 'God, I feel so . . . STUPID.'

He was back in his chair by now. 'You must have sensed something was wrong.'

'What do you mean?' she asked, almost aggressively.

'Well, if that's the sort of thing he was saying then why take Victor up on his offer of moving down here? Maybe you knew in your heart what he was really about. Maybe you were testing him, forcing his hand.'

'Damn you.'

'I'm not saying I'm right.'

'I mean damn you for seeing right through it.'

'Two wasted years could have been more. Think of it that way. You're still young.'

'Youngish,' she countered. 'And barren.'

What a horrid word that was. It even had a hollow ring to it when spoken, like some desolate echo.

'Ah, but not wholly unattractive.'

'Even looking like this?'

'You'll scrub up OK.'

'Gee, thanks, you charmer.'

'Anything to see you smile,' he said. 'I love your smile.'

Mo pinched the remaining moisture from her eyes. 'Yours isn't too bad, either.'

It was as far as they got because at that moment Annabelle appeared in the yard with a young man in blue overalls. This was Phil the plumber. He had a pierced eyebrow and a tattoo on his neck of a flaming skull (so badly done that Ben took it at first to be of an old lady with red hair, possibly Phil's grandmother). Phil had come to install a water softener. The groundwater pumped out of the aquifer beneath Stoneham Park was so hard that it had furred up the heat exchanger in Mo's boiler, reducing her shower to a tepid trickle.

The job was going to take up the best part of the day – six hours to be precise, which Phil could be, seeing as this was the ninth water softener he'd had to install on the estate. Deciding where to stick the thing was half the challenge, and Ben left them to it, poking around in the studio for a suitable location.

Mo followed him outside into the yard. 'Tuesday night is Aunt Sally night at the Bull.'

'I have no idea what you're talking about.'

'Then just say yes.'

'Yes.'

'We can walk it. I'll pick you up at six.'

'Six is when I speak to Toby. Six thirty to be safe.'

'Bring your throwing arm. You're going to need it.'

The Bull was a fine old village pub which, refreshingly, had been spared the generic gastropubification of recent times. There were hunting prints on the walls, lurid carpets on the floor, and you could hardly see the low oak beams for all the horse brasses that were hammered into them. There was even a glass jar of pickled eggs sitting on the bar. Only the inclusion of Thai Curry (just below Scampi in a Basket) on the menu blackboard told you this wasn't the 1970s.

Barry the publican was as bald as the two coots in the Victorian waterfowl diorama screwed to the wall behind him. He pulled Mo and Ben a couple of pints of a local beer and announced he'd be joining them outside later for a few legs of Aunt Sally.

The back garden was drenched in evening sunshine and teeming with people.

'Yo, Mo,' boomed a voice. 'And with a beau.'

The man got a big laugh as he came to greet them. He was black-bearded and broad-shouldered like a medieval baron.

'RDN,' he said, sizing Mo up.

'RDN?'

'Ridiculously distracting neckline.'

'ROT,' replied Mo. 'Ridiculously offensive T-shirt.'

The man's T-shirt, pulled taut over his domed paunch, was emblazoned with the legend: *I MAY NOT BE A GYNAECOLOGIST BUT I'M HAPPY TO TAKE A LOOK.*

This was the Mikey whom Mo had mentioned before: captain of the cricket team, supplier of marijuana. He took Ben's hand in his meaty paw, eyeing him with ill-disguised hostility before turning his attention back to Mo and steering her off into the throng.

Others were far more welcoming. A debonair old boy wearing an open-necked shirt and a paisley cravat introduced himself as Cedric, although Ben soon discovered that everyone referred to him as 'the Colonel'. He had a pencil moustache and an unashamedly upper-class accent in which he proceeded to deliver Ben a lesson in the history and rules of Aunt Sally.

The game was peculiar to Oxford and its surrounding areas, with roots reaching back to the English Civil War, when Charles I had set up court in the city. Finding themselves under siege from the Parliamentarian army, the Royalist soldiers had invented the game to while away the hours. They must have had limited resources at their disposal because as far as Ben could tell, Aunt Sally involved throwing pieces of wood at, well, another piece of wood.

It soon became clear that the game was treated with almost sacred reverence by those who played it, which included the Colonel. It was also harder than it looked. The stumpy little skittle thing (the 'doll') sitting on the bendy metal arm thing (the 'swivel') sticking out of the pole in the ground had to be knocked off its perch with a direct hit from one of the thick wooden baton things ('sticks') thrown underarm by the contestants for it to count as a strike (a 'doll').

The pub team played their league matches on Wednesday evenings. This was just an open practice session for team members and anyone else who wanted to have a go. It was also an excuse to raise money for the church appeal while drinking large quantities of beer. Players were charged a £1 fee for each leg of six sticks thrown, and the pub chipped in fifty pence for every pint drunk. Ben was happy to observe, but the Colonel, fresh from 'clanging off' an impressive five dolls in his first leg, was having none of it.

'My dear boy, live a little. And don't worry, all of us here have blobbed at one time or another.'

'Blobbed?'

The Colonel formed a circle with his thumb and finger. 'The big zero. The dreaded nought. The circle of shame.'

'Now I'm definitely sitting it out.'

'What do you do by way of a living?' inquired the Colonel.

'I'm a writer.'

'Ahhh, an observer, a chronicler of other men's follies and foibles.' He gripped Ben's arm. 'We all have to feel the heat of our brothers' mockery to know that we belong.'

Ben felt the heat before he'd even thrown his first stick.

'Backs to the wall, boys,' bellowed Mikey. 'We got us a leftie.'

There was laughter and a few catcalls. Ben caught sight of the Colonel in the crowd. The old devil formed a circle with his thumb and forefinger, which could have meant, 'Don't worry, you'll be OK,' but most probably was a taunt.

There were no groans or jeers when Ben missed completely with his first two sticks; those came when he scored a doll with the third, the crowd denied the spectacle of a novice blobbing. He was safe. He relaxed, scoring one more doll with his last throw.

'Bravo,' declared the Colonel. 'A most respectable score for a virgin.'

Mo was next to play, with Mikey providing the commentary. 'Annnnddd from the fair county of Yorkshire . . .'

'Where's that?' someone called.

'Fuck knows. Up north. Who cares?' Mikey let the laughter subside before continuing in his presenter's voice. 'As I was saying . . . from the fair county of Yorkshire we have the beautiful . . .' Mo gave a theatrical little flick of her hair in response to the whistles, 'the sexy . . .' Mo wiggled her arse, 'the oh so naughty . . .' Mo placed her forefinger to her pouting lips in a parody of girlish innocence, 'Mo-ooooo Cha-aaaanning . . .' Ben joined the chorus of applause, letting rip a couple of piercing wolf whistles.

Mo clanged off a confident four, and when she was done she didn't rejoin Mikey and his mates, she sought out Ben and the Colonel.

'Colonel, thank you for looking after my friend.'

'It's been the most terrible ordeal, my dear.'

'Worse than Korea?'

'The Battle of Imjin River was a walk in the park by comparison.'

'Oi, Colonel, tell us one of your stories,' called a lanky young fellow within earshot.

The Colonel turned. 'I'd love nothing more, Richard, but sadly my throat is a little parched.'

'My round,' said Ben, relieving the Colonel of his empty beer glass.

'Well, if you insist, dear boy.'

It wasn't the last round Ben bought, nor was it the last leg of Aunt Sally he played. For all its simplicity, the game was stupidly addictive and Ben was determined to improve on his score, which turned out to be a very good thing for the church appeal.

Mo didn't exactly ignore him; she appeared and disappeared over the course of the evening, happy to leave him in the Colonel's care. He didn't mind. He knew he'd have her to himself later, and the Colonel kept him entertained with a steady stream of conversation and further introductions.

Night had fallen and Ben was leaning a little drunkenly at the bar waiting to be served when Mikey appeared at his side.

'What do you want?'

'Nah, don't worry,' said Mikey, 'I'm getting a bunch in for the boys.' He drummed his fingers on the counter then turned suddenly and asked, 'So, you boffing her or what?'

'Mo? No. I'm a leftie, remember?'

Mikey's eyes narrowed briefly then he let out a booming laugh and slapped Ben on the back. 'You're all right, my friend.' Strange that those few words of endorsement should matter to him. 'So, how many dolls you bag yourself, then?'

'My best is four, but I'm not done yet.'

'Let's hope you score more on Sunday.'

'Sunday?'

'Didn't Mo say? She's signed you up for the cricket. Bit of a demon with the bat, I hear.'

'She's never seen me play. No one's seen me play, not for twenty years.'

'She got it from his lordship, and his word's good enough for me.'

'Mikey, listen—'

Mikey silenced him with a raised hand. 'Tssk, tssk, tssk, it's a done deal, my friend – move on.' He leaned a little closer. 'And relax. Between you and me, we're total shite.'

'Yeah, Mo said.'

Mikey laughed his booming laugh again. 'Yep, you're all right.'

If Ben was feeling pleasantly sloshed, the Colonel was sailing a good three sheets to the wind by now. Ben found him leaning purposefully against a tree when he returned outside with the drinks. 'Good boy,' said the Colonel, taking his pint. 'One for the short stagger home.'

'Where do you live?'

'On the other side of the green. But there's a pond between here and there, as I once discovered to my cost. Soaked myself silly and lost a shoe. Still there, I suppose, stuck in the mud, if you're ever in need of a suede loafer from Lobb's.'

They installed themselves on the low wall by the yew hedge.

'Were you really in Korea?' Ben asked.

'Yes, with the Glosters. I was a second lieutenant in fifty-one, still wet behind the ears, just turned twenty-one. Bloody debacle. Shouldn't even have been there. Ring a bell? Bloody UN. Confederacy of dunces. Hung us out to dry.' He took a slug of beer. 'Maybe we slowed down the Chinese advance by a few days. Best that can be said.' The Colonel cut him a quick glance. 'I'll wager you've never even heard of the Imjin River.'

'No.'

'Why should you? A world away from this, I can tell you – playing Aunt Sally with an arthritic elbow . . . tending my roses . . . walking the dog . . . talking to a headstone once a day.'

His wife, Felicity, had died last year, suddenly and in her sleep. She now lay buried in the churchyard. 'Life's a queer thing. One day you're laughing with the woman you love, the next she's rotting in the ground just across the way. I'll join her there soon enough. I'm almost ready. Not quite.' He paused, pensively. '"How sour sweet music is when time is broke and no proportion kept. So is it in the music of men's lives."'

'Shakespeare?'

'Was there nothing he didn't know? Felicity loved her Shakespeare.'

They'd had two sons. The first had died of AIDS in the late 1980s, and the Colonel was estranged from the youngest, who now lived in western Australia with his wife and three children. 'Can't really blame him for choosing to put himself on the other side of the planet. I was a brute of a father. Wish I could say it was the military life that made me that way, or combat. Not sure I can, though. Truth is, I learned my lessons too late in life. A slow learner. Always was. I don't like to think of the damage I've done, but maybe it's less than some.'

Mo wandered up. 'How's it going?'

'Swimmingly,' replied the Colonel. 'But does your friend ever stop talking about himself?'

Mo was ready to leave; she just had a couple of goodbyes to say first. They watched her sidle off through the shadows toward the pub.

'She's one of the good people,' observed the Colonel. 'Ravishing too. Don't mess it up.'

'We're just friends.'

'I know, dear boy. And every night the Pope prays to Allah.'

The sky was clear, and the high moon cast their shadows at their feet as they strolled back along the road to Stoneham Park, Mo's flip-flops slapping the tarmac like the smack of wet lips.

'Seems I'm playing cricket on Sunday.'

'Yeah, sorry about that.'

'Are you going to watch?'

'What, waste a good afternoon?' She smiled. 'Yeah, I'll be there. Mikey's got me on tea duty. I have to make sandwiches for thirty.'

After the fun and bonhomie of the past few hours there was something mildly disconcerting about the brooding silence of Stoneham Park. They might just as well have been returning to a sleeping monastery.

It was Mo's idea that they abandon the driveway for the path that cut across the park.

'When do they sleep?'

He meant the cows, which were on their feet, grazing.

'Are they following us?' Mo asked.

'I don't think so. Actually, I think they might be.'

They were. Not the full-grown ones – the curious young-sters, the adolescents, the hoodies of the bovine world, big enough to do damage.

'Scare them off,' ordered Mo.

'*You* scare them off.'

'Run at them. They don't like that. They'll scatter.'

'Don't tell me – I wave my arms and say "shoo" at the same time?'

'Exactly.'

In the wash of moonlight flooding the park, Ben saw more of them trotting over to join the ranks of the trailing pack.

'I've got a better idea,' he said. 'On the count of three we make a break for it.'

'I'm wearing flip-flops.'

'So take them off.' Mo managed awkwardly to remove them while walking. 'Give them to me.'

But she turned and hurled the flip-flops at the calves. They didn't even flinch. 'One, two, three,' she blurted, breaking into a sprint before she'd even finished.

'Hey!'

He took after her. Damn, she was quick. And so were the calves. He could hear the beat of their hooves and their heavy breathing closing from behind.

The finishing line came in the form of a kissing gate at the edge of a fenced-off copse of trees. Mo was through it in a flash, Ben following a few seconds later, their fear-fuelled laughter ringing off the trees. They turned to survey the herd of calves gathered on the other side of the iron fence. They looked so wide-eyed, so innocent, which they probably were.

'My hero,' said Mo, just before she kissed him, her tongue darting between his lips.

Ben pulled away. 'Hey, you left me for dead.'

'I'm trying to make it up to you.'

'I don't know, I've just seen a whole other side of you.'

But he didn't resist when she pulled him close and kissed him again. This time she took his hand and placed it on her breast, her nipple hardening beneath the cotton.

'God, I'm feeling horny,' she gasped. 'Must be the brush with death.'

'What's that smell?'

'I think I trod in some cow shit.'

They sat shoulder to shoulder at the end of the jetty, Mo dangling her feet in the lake to clean them. It was one of those rare nights when the temperature barely drops with the going down of the sun, when a T-shirt's enough to see you through till dawn.

'I told my friend Chloe about you.'

'Oh?'

'She doesn't like southern men. She thinks you're arrogant, full of yourselves.'

'Damn, a thumbs-down from the bigot.'

'She liked the look of you though.'

'The look of me?'

'That Sunday, after lunch, when I showed you where the sculpture was going . . .' He remembered; Mo had taken her camera with her. 'I might have fired off a couple of extra shots when you weren't looking.' Then, in an exaggerated Yorkshire brogue, 'Aye, she thought thee was reight cumly.'

'Then you can tell her all is forgiven. You can also tell her I'm from Yorkshire originally.'

'Give over!'

'It's true. Well, going back a bit.'

'What, the Ice Age?'

'Not quite that far.'

Ben knew the history intimately because it had been drummed into him from an early age by his father's mother. Mo insisted on hearing it, even though he warned her it was a load of nonsense. Grandma Makepeace was an old snob who had sniffed out the most illustrious lineage in her family tree, skipping between the male and female lines whenever it suited her purposes, studiously avoiding the bastards and other undesirables as she worked back through the generations, laying her golden thread.

This dubious scholarship had led her to Joshua Claybourn, a mill owner in Knaresborough, Yorkshire, in the late eighteenth century, whose second son – William, an engineer – went south and made an even larger fortune in the new railways. His greatest coup was the sale of his stake in the Richmond-Staines-Uxbridge line to South Western Railways, which allowed him to set himself up in a country estate on the hill between Dulwich and Camberwell. Unfortunately, he then turned his sights abroad, becoming involved in a project for a main line between Florence, Rome and Naples. The outbreak of revolutions across Europe in 1848 effectively scuppered the scheme, although William's considerable investment (much of it spent on bribes to officials in the Tuscan, Papal and Neapolitan courts) might not have been lost if Pope Pius IX hadn't then banned railways as somehow symbolic of the dangerous liberalism which had recently flared into violence across his territories.

Within a year William was dead of an apoplectic fit, and his sons were soon forced to sell off large parts of the Grove Park estate to developers, who set about carpeting the hillside with townhouses for the burgeoning middle class. The family's decline was ungracious and rapid. Three generations on, Grandma Makepeace was born to a Surrey haberdasher, the youngest of three daughters.

Bright and ambitious, she was also determined to recover something of the lost glory of her family's past. Her looks helped her to marry above herself: a lanky insurance clerk from Guildford who, frustratingly, turned out to be not quite as go-getting as she'd hoped. Money was tight, but she scrimped and saved and worked at night as a seamstress in order to provide her only child with the sort of education that would offer him a passport to the top.

Ben's father knew what was expected of him and he'd delivered the goods, gaining an academic scholarship to Charterhouse School then an exhibition to Worcester

College, Oxford, before landing a job with Cazenove, one of the oldest stockbroking firms in the City.

'I once heard her say she'd only cried twice in her life – the first when she was a young girl and her dog was killed by a car in front of her eyes, the second when she heard my father had been elected a member of White's, the gentlemen's club in St James's.'

'I know what White's is.'

'Dad only made one mistake in her eyes, he fell in love with a Catholic girl of Italian extraction. You see, she's never quite forgiven Pope Pius IX for destroying the family fortune.'

Mo's reply came with an incredulous little laugh. 'She sounds like an old cow. No offence.'

'None taken. She is. And worse than ever at ninety-five.'

'She must love *you*,' said Mo with sarcasm.

'How'd you guess? I'm the traitor who's undone all her good work.'

Before he knew it, he was on his back and Mo was strad-dling him.

'Well, you're *my* hero,' she said, pinioning his hands to the boards and lowering her head to kiss him. He felt himself hardening under the soft, searching pressure of her hips. 'It takes courage . . .' she whispered before kissing him again, 'to do what you've done . . .' another kiss, 'to say no.'

Lying there beneath her, it suddenly struck him why he hadn't yet told his parents about Victor. It wasn't his father's reaction he feared, so much as his grandmother's. The Jacob she had known as a grimy, scab-kneed, rough-and-ready young boy had gone on to achieve everything she could ever have hoped for from her own grandson: the untold wealth, the country estate, the social standing. The Restoration would have been complete. She could have died happy.

He sought comfort from this sour realisation in Mo's body, freeing his hands and taking her by the waist.

She broke off from their kiss, sitting upright. 'It's going to happen. You know that, don't you? But not tonight.'

'Oh?'

'A part of me would be doing it out of revenge and that's not fair on you.'

'Don't worry about me – avenge thyself.'

Mo laughed. 'Connor never made me laugh the way you do.' Then after a brief pause, 'You see, I'm thinking about him.'

She shifted as if to dismount but he held her in place by the hips.

'At least let me—' He stopped himself just in time.

'What?'

'No, I can't say.'

'You have to now.'

'Out of the question.'

'What if you whisper it?'

'OK.'

She leaned down, placed her neat little ear next to his lips. The moment she heard what he had to say she recoiled.

'No!'

'Just quickly.'

'What sort of girl do you take me for?'

'I'll let you know afterwards.' This time he didn't prevent her pulling free and rising to her feet, he just smiled up at her. 'It was worth a shot.'

'And if you'd said please I might have said yes.'

He lunged for her leg but she was too quick for him, slipping his grip and darting off down the jetty.

twelve days to go . . .

B EN FOUND THE grave easily enough. It was in the overflow to the main churchyard: a neat square plot reclaimed from the woods on the other side of the track. Tall trees pressed in on the drystone wall that enclosed the peaceful resting place.

The headstone read:

And So To Sleep
FELICITY MARY ARMITAGE
1929–2011
Beloved Wife of Cedric

Beautifully judged, thought Ben: the epitaph lifted from Shakespeare's *Hamlet*, the soft pale stone which would allow the words to weather slowly into oblivion . . .

There was a single white rose in a fluted glass vase, no doubt snipped from a bush which Felicity had once fed and pruned. The narrow patch of turf to the right of the grave was vacant – reserved, Ben knew, for the Colonel, who had confessed last night that it was the main reason he had put himself forward as treasurer of the church appeal. He had described himself to Ben as a 'Christian atheist'.

'It's a load of old mumbo-jumbo, of course, but I love the theatre of the thing on Sunday mornings – the nervous young priest in his ill-fitting robes, the choristers who can't sing, the organist who can't play, the hymns full of blind hope, the church warden who reads the lesson as if he's listing those fallen in battle. It's wonderful stuff. Priceless. Wouldn't miss it for the world. Felicity was a wicked old girl. She used to catch my eye and try and make me laugh.'

The wicked old girl now lay at Ben's feet, rotting in the ground, as the Colonel had so graphically put it. Ben also recalled the lines of Shakespeare the Colonel had quoted: 'How sour sweet music is when time is broke and no proportion kept. So is it in the music of men's lives.' He had looked them up late last night in the privacy of his bedroom. They were from *Richard II* – not a play he knew – part of a soliloquy delivered by King Richard while contemplating his imprisonment. The Colonel seemed to be saying that the sweet harmony of life could be destroyed in a moment.

This sentiment had touched something in Ben, and he had read on, intrigued by the confessional note of the speech, in which King Richard accepted a degree of responsibility for the errors he'd made and which ultimately had brought him down. One line in particular had lodged itself in Ben's head.

Long after he had gone to bed it was still there, tolling like a bell, preventing from sleeping.

'I wasted time, and now doth time waste me.'

Twenty years of toil in the same profession and what did he really have to show for it? A couple of film credits, a broken marriage and an empty bank account. These weren't unfamiliar thoughts, but with nine simple little words bloody Shakespeare had somehow lent them new life, new vigour. Bloody Shakespeare, four hundred years dead, had shoved a mirror in his face and said: take a long hard look, mate, and tell me what you really see.

It wasn't a pretty sight.

He saw a man with a contrary streak who had kicked half-heartedly at the privilege of his upbringing, speaking of art but secretly dreaming of money and acclaim, until all three had eluded him. He saw a husband who had privately sneered at his wife's drive and ambition while enjoying the benefits her hard-won salary had brought them both. Most painful of all, he saw a father who had set a poor example to his son: here, my boy, this is the way to do it – cynicism tempered with a dash of lazy self-centredness should see you through life well enough.

I wasted time, and now doth time waste me.

A hard truth, but he had faced it squarely last night and had found himself feeling better almost immediately. He wasn't King Richard locked up in a castle, or even the Colonel mourning the cruel loss of his wife in the twilight years of his life. He had his freedom, and time was still on his side. Professionally, he was in a better place than he'd been for years. The same was true of his finances. And as for romance, he stood tantalisingly on the brink of a new relationship; Mo had left him in no doubt about that. His mother had always said that nobody finds happiness by searching for it. She was right. It had been handed to him. Victor had burst back on to the scene and catapulted him towards a new, far brighter future. Perversely, he had been kicking against this reversal, unwilling to shrug off the cloak of self-pity he'd been shuffling about in for the past couple of years.

He had made a number of resolutions before finally falling asleep. He would learn to look outward again rather than inward. He would put the nagging misery of introspection behind him. He would throw himself into the script and make it as good as he possibly could, accepting it for what it was. He would work hard, play hard and earn well. In short, he would do all the things he should have done a long time ago.

Standing there at the foot of Felicity Armitage's grave, surrounded by the dead and done for – and almost with their tacit approval, it seemed to him – he renewed those same vows to himself.

He pulled the wooden gate shut behind him and was about to jog on down the track when he spotted the temperature board beside the lych gate. It recorded the progress of the church appeal in red, like mercury rising in a thermometer. The target was £110,000, of which £60,000 had been raised so far. Would the Colonel be out later, he wondered, with his brush and his pot of red paint to log last night's takings at the pub? It seemed unlikely for a few hundred quid at most.

He had once spotted footmarks in the glaze of early morning dew, but his laps of the playing field had always been made in private.

Not today.

There was a man seated on the bench near the score hut. He was smartly dressed in chinos and a light summer jacket and was fiddling with his phone, tapping away at the screen.

'Morning,' said Ben as he made his first pass.

'Good morning, Mr Makepeace.'

Ben drew to a halt, turning back and searching the man's handsome face. Someone from the pub? The strong jaw and deepset blue eyes rang no bells. 'I'm sorry, did we meet last night?'

'We've never met.'

'I don't understand.'

The man held up his phone. 'Angry Birds. Do you play?'

'No.'

'Don't start or you'll never stop.' He patted the space beside him on the bench. 'Have a seat, Ben.'

Ben didn't budge. 'Who are you?'

'My name's Patrick Fedden.'

He produced a business card from the breast pocket of his jacket and held it out. It identified him as a Senior Investigator at the Serious Fraud Office.

Ben's first thought was of the last set of accounts he'd

submitted to the Inland Revenue, of the holiday in France he'd put through the books as a 'research trip'.

Fedden must have read his expression. 'Don't worry, I'm not here for you. At least I don't think I am.' He patted the bench again. 'Take the weight off your feet.'

This time, Ben did as instructed, handing back the business card.

'Keep it. You're going to need it.'

'I'm very confused.'

'Of course you are.' Fedden's phone rang. 'Excuse me,' he said, answering it. 'Fedden . . . I'm with him now, sir . . . Absolutely . . . Of course . . . It goes without saying.' Fedden hung up. 'Let me turn this off.' He killed the phone and turned to Ben. 'Victor Sheldon.'

'What about him?'

'Formerly known as Jacob Oliver Hogg. Hedge fund supremo. Multi-millionaire. Multi-*multi*-millionaire.' Fedden paused. 'Balzac once said that behind every great fortune lies a great crime. In my experience, he was wrong. A number of crimes tend to lie behind every great fortune.'

'I don't see what this has got to do with me.'

'No? What were you doing in Italy last weekend? We already know you didn't pay for the flights and the hotel yourself, and I believe the young lady picked up the tab at the restaurant.'

That didn't just shock Ben, it scared him into silence.

'Well?' insisted Fedden.

'I went there to check out a boat for Mr Sheldon.'

'A boat?'

'A speedboat.'

Fedden looked impressed. 'A man of many talents. From what we've been able to learn about you you're a scriptwriter.'

'I am.'

'And an expert in speedboats too? That's not in the file.'

Again, Ben was flummoxed, unable to respond.

Fedden smiled. 'Relax, I'm just rattling your cage. The job requires it. It doesn't give me much pleasure.'

A patent lie, thought Ben. Fedden was enjoying himself enormously.

'Massoud Rostami. Does that name mean anything to you?'

'No.'

A pained expression furrowed Fedden's brow. 'Now why would you do that? Why would you want to lie to me? We know you were here the same weekend Rostami was staying.' He paused. 'I tell you what, I'll chalk that one up to unthinking loyalty towards an old friend, but I'd advise a policy of honesty from now on. You're either with us on this or you're against us.'

'I don't even know what "this" is.'

'Oh, I'm sorry.' Fedden's tone had shifted from cocksure to cocksure with an edge of facetiousness. 'Victor Sheldon is the subject of an investigation.'

'By the Serious Fraud Office?'

'The SFO and the FSA – the Financial Services Authority. They thought we should be the ones to approach you.'

'Why me? What do you want from me?'

Fedden's broad smile revealed him to be a fan of dental bleaching.

'I thought you'd never ask.'

Ben jogged back through the village, but only to keep up appearances. The moment he reached Stoneham Park he slowed to a walk.

Life had turned once more on a sixpence, the life he had just resolved to embrace, to throw himself into. Bloody Shakespeare. *So is it in the music of men's lives.* Patrick Fedden had destroyed the harmony in a moment, reducing it to a jangling cacophony.

They were after Victor, and they wanted Ben's help. 'A bit of cloak-and-dagger. Nothing too serious. You'll get the details once we know you're on side.'

They couldn't force him to do anything, and he had until the end of the week to decide. Fedden had scribbled down his mobile number on the business card he'd given Ben. 'In case I'm out of the office. And don't even think about mentioning this conversation to Sheldon. We'll know if you have.'

He could believe it. Christ, what didn't they know? They were up to speed on everything: the history of his relationship with Victor, the film project that had brought them back together again, the exact timing of his visits to Stoneham Park, the trip to Lake Como . . .

That had been one of the more shocking revelations. If they knew he hadn't paid for the Italian trip then they obviously had access to his bank and credit card transactions.

Was that even legal? Weren't there laws against such things? Didn't a judge have to sign off on such powers? He had always thought of the Serious Fraud Office as a toothless organisation. *Private Eye* was probably to blame for this; the satirical magazine dubbed the SFO the 'Serious Farce Office' for its supine efforts to police the City and follow through on prosecutions. Apparently they were wrong. The SFO clearly had significant resources at its disposal, and it wasn't afraid to use them in order to shape a case against Victor.

Would they succeed? Maybe not. A man of Victor's means would build himself the best possible defence with the help of the most expensive lawyers, lobbyists and PR consultants. History showed that the wealthy had a great knack for slipping the noose.

He left the driveway, taking the same path across the park as he'd done with Mo. The calves showed none of last night's boisterous curiosity. In fact, they barely glanced at him as he trudged through their territory, almost as if they sensed there was something unclean about him now.

He found her in her studio, sitting in a chair, gazing intently at her sculpture. She spotted the flip-flops in his hand.

'What a gent. Did you get chased again?'

'No, must have been you they took such offence to.'

He dropped the flip-flops on the floor in front of her, sending up a puff of dust. She slipped her bare feet into them, reaching for his hand. 'Good morning.' She rested her head against his hip.

Ben nodded at the sculpture. 'Feeling better about it?'

'Not much. I don't know what to do next.'

'Then do nothing. I've been thinking about it. Leave it unfinished. If it was good enough for Michelangelo . . .'

Mo looked up at him. 'You mean the four prisoners? You've seen them?'

'Years ago,' he replied.

'Go on.'

'What's to say? They blew me away.'

The prisoners were part-carved figures which looked as though they were fighting to escape from their giant rough-hewn blocks of marble, torsos twisting, muscled arm and legs thrusting to break free. Like the majority of tourists who made the pilgrimage to the Accademia gallery in Florence, Ben had queued round the block in order to see Michelangelo's David. But it was the four prisoners lining the approach to the monumental masterpiece who had stayed with him over the years.

It was hard to say why exactly. It was more than the stark contrast between the finished parts, polished smooth as glass, and the crudely chiselled mass from which these liquid surfaces emerged. Those four figures somehow enshrined Man's foolish quest, his eternal struggle to rise above the base matter from which he was made, to set himself apart, to deny himself his oneness with the whole.

Ben tried to explain this to Mo, and not very well judging from the silence that followed.

'Come with me,' she said eventually, rising to her feet. 'I want to show you something.'

He followed her upstairs to her apartment, expecting to be shown a photo in a book, or possibly one of her own sketches. He wasn't expecting to be taken by the hand and drawn silently down the corridor to her bedroom.

She pulled the door shut behind them. 'Curtains closed or open?'

'Open.'

'Right answer.'

They undressed each other slowly before dropping on to her bed, sinking into the deep duvet, skin on skin.

'Reggie,' she said.

'Reggie?'

She tipped her chin towards her teddy bear, who was surveying them from his perch on the pillows. 'Reggie the teddy.'

'He's giving me the eye.'

'No, he isn't. He likes you. Don't you, Reggie?'

'Actually, it's quite creepy. Do you mind?' He stuffed Reggie under one of the pillows.

'Don't, he'll suffocate!'

That was even creepier. Fortunately, she was only joking.

'Don't move. Just lie there.' She knelt naked beside him and ran her hands over his body, exploring it. 'You have very soft skin for a man.'

'Do I?'

'Hasn't anyone ever told you?'

'No.'

Not true. Chiara had said the same thing, but this definitely wasn't the time to bring it up.

Mo's hand closed gently, tentatively, around him. 'I'm a bit nervous. Connor's the only man I've slept with in eight years.'

'Do you mind if we don't talk about him? It's distracting.'

Mo smiled down at him. 'You're bigger than him.'

'OK, keep talking.'

Madeleine had been a strangely silent lover, almost as if she feared words would break her concentration. Even when she came, which she was never able to do with him inside her, she barely made a noise. Mo wasn't afraid of the sound of her own voice, whether she was being coyly coquettish or downright demanding.

She could have been anything she wanted to be with him, such was his hunger to feel her, hold her, taste her, enter her. She came twice before he was even close, the first time with his tongue deep inside her and her fingers woven through his hair, the second with her face buried in a pillow and her hands gripping the rails of the headboard so tightly that her knuckles showed white. The third time she came, so did he, face to face, eyes locked, falling, falling together . . .

'Don't move,' she whispered. 'Stay inside me.'

They lay welded together, damp from their exertions. Only when the strain of bearing his weight on his elbows proved too much did they slowly separate. Mo reached for him immediately and held on. They lay on their sides, gazing at each other.

Mo seemed puzzled, almost troubled. 'Tell me that's not normal for you.'

'Why?'

'Is it?'

'No.'

'Good, because I'm not sure I can go there again.'

They laughed exhaustedly then kissed.

'We're a good fit.' She smiled and stroked his face. 'Don't worry, I'm talking mechanics not marriage.'

'I know.'

She took his hand and placed it between her legs, clamping it there with her thighs. 'Don't be insulted if I nod off.'

'You just stole my line.'

When he woke he found himself alone in the bed. There was a note beside him on the mattress.

He held it at arm's length, adjusting his focus to the spidery scrawl: 'I need to speak to Mo urgently. Please call me when you wake up. Annabelle'

He fell for it, but only for a heart-stopping second or two.

She was downstairs in the studio, kitted up for work, fiddling with some equipment.

Ben waggled the note at her.

'Sorry, I couldn't resist it.'

Seeing her standing there, it struck him that he would never be able to look at her in the same way again. He knew every corner, crease, rise and fold of the lithe body hidden by the baggy overalls. The curiosity, the nagging desire and the anticipation were gone forever, washed away on a flood of all-seeing, all-knowing intimacy. He still held the taste of her in his mouth. Even now, their molecules were mingling.

'You were right,' she chimed. 'About Michelangelo's prisoners. You've opened my eyes. It's not a head, it's a face. No, not even. It's a mask.'

'Man is least himself when he speaks in his own person, but give him a mask and he'll show you his true self.'

'That's good. I like that. Who said that?'

'I don't know. Probably Oscar Wilde, along with everything else. You can stick it in the catalogue blurb.'

She tilted her head at him. 'What's the matter?'

'Nothing.'

She slipped her arms around his waist and peered up at him with bedroom eyes. 'Sweet gentle Ben with the big beautiful penis that fits so perfectly . . . what's the matter?'

He tried not to smile. 'Was that my reward?'

'That was for us.' She nodded over her shoulder. 'This is just a lump of stone.'

He sighed. 'Christ, what a fucking cliché. I'm already coming between you and your art.'

'No, you're not. But I *do* have to work now. It's the way I am, the way I've always been.' She hesitated. 'It's one of the reasons Connor dumped me.'

'The guy's an idiot.'

'That's what I told him, but did he listen?' She smiled then kissed him on the lips. 'I don't care any more. Really, I don't. You've set me free, Mr Makepeace. Worry about that instead.'

He didn't worry about it. He loved the idea of the promise it held.

Mo was right, the sex had been special, tender and fierce by turns, with none of the usual awkwardness of the first time. There was no accounting for that kind of connection, although he suspected he owed Chiara a small debt of gratitude for releasing something in him.

Back in the main house, back at work, the post-coital cloud began to darken then dissipate. How much happier would he be feeling if Patrick Fedden hadn't barged into his life a few hours ago? He tried to dismiss the question but there was no ignoring it. Fedden had redrawn the map of his future in an instant, sounding a death knell for him and Mo at the same time.

When it came out that he had been collaborating with the Serious Fraud Office – as it surely would at some point – would Mo sympathise with his predicament? Would she stand by him and risk the wrath of Victor? He drew up a mental balance sheet on her behalf. She would lose her studio, her home, her patron, the main source of her income, and in return she would get Ben: spy, traitor, screenwriter (no longer gainfully employed).

It was a no-brainer. He knew which side he would cast his lot if he were her.

Recovering Fedden's business card from its hiding place in the side pocket of his washbag, he headed down to the swimming pool for some privacy. He ignored the mobile number Fedden had scribbled on the back of the card and dialled the main number for the SFO.

'The Serious Fraud Office,' said a female voice.

'Yes, can I have extension number . . .' He hesitated. 'Actually, Patrick Fedden, please.'

'Who shall I say is calling?'

'Ben Makepeace.'

When Fedden finally picked up he didn't bother with any niceties. 'I didn't expect to hear from you so soon.'

'I just wanted to check you were for real.'

'I'm afraid I am. Have you decided what you're going to do?'

'Not yet.'

'I meant what I said. You're either with us or you're against us. And you really don't want to be against us.'

'I haven't done anything,' said Ben indignantly.

'Really? Is Mr Sheldon going to buy the boat you looked at for him in Italy?'

'Yes, I think so.'

'Then that makes you a party to the transaction, which I'm sure will be totally above board – no cash payments, nothing dodgy that could be held against you.'

'I'm sure too.'

'You don't sound very sure, Mr Makepeace.' There was a brief silence. 'By Friday at the latest, please.'

Ben hung up. He deleted the number from the phone's memory. Whatever you thought of Fedden – and Ben was beginning to find his smug and sardonic air intensely irritating – you also had to admire the man. He wasn't just good at his job, he seemed to have the gift of second sight.

Presumably Fedden had been winging it, because there

was no way he could possibly have found out about the cash payment for the Riva which Ben had negotiated. Surely the SFO's reach didn't extend that far. And yet he could swear there'd been something archly knowing in Fedden's voice. How could that be?

Time to summon up the spirit of Detective Constable Leon Grosse. What would Grosse do? He would ask himself the simple questions, the questions which others ignored as being too trivial or obvious to trouble themselves with. Grosse would ask: who knows about the cash payment on the Riva? There were four names. Ben was able to dismiss the first three almost instantly: Signore Viani, his son Iacopo, and Victor. The fourth name was less easy to shake off.

Annabelle.

It didn't make sense, not at first, but the harder he punished the hypothesis the more it fitted.

At the playing field Fedden had warned him not to mention their conversation to Victor – 'We'll know if you have'. Ben had accepted this statement unquestioningly, overwhelmed by the scope of Fedden's knowledge. But there was nothing in the information Fedden had vaunted that he couldn't have got from Annabelle: Ben's history with Victor, the film project, the details of the Italian trip. This would also explain why Fedden had known exactly where to find him. Annabelle was aware that he jogged to Stoneham every morning; he'd even told her he ran round the playing field.

Annabelle was Fedden's source, probably his one and only source.

It made a lot more sense than the alternative scenario, that he'd been the target of a sophisticated surveillance operation which included the monitoring of his bank account and credit cards. That now seemed plainly absurd to him.

There were still questions, though, questions that even DC Leon Grosse was unable to answer. Why, for example, if Annabelle had already been signed up by the Serious Fraud Office, did they also require Ben's services? Maybe they were simply covering as many bases as possible. Or maybe they imagined he could gain access to information that was beyond Annabelle's reach. Either way, it suggested the SFO was having difficulties with its investigation, and that cast things in a whole new light.

Strolling back towards the house, he found himself wondering whether his postcode in the Maserati's satnav wasn't in some way connected. It certainly now seemed likely that Annabelle was the one who had deleted it.

Gregoire informed him that Annabelle was in Oxford, running some errands. This was probably no bad thing. He was so fired up he might have been tempted to confront her right then and there. By the time she returned at about six o'clock he'd had a chance to cool off and figure out a strategy.

Fedden had overplayed his own hand and revealed it in the process. He wasn't going to make the same mistake. No, he would sit tight, carry on as normal. Only when Victor returned would he make his decision.

The curls of hair were gone, trimmed back with the pneumatic chisel, reduced to dust and flakes of stone. Mo had even removed one part of the left ear.

She seemed to be having doubts.

'I hope you're bloody right.'

Ben held up his hands. 'Hey, don't hold me to account, it was just a suggestion.'

'What do you think?'

'I think it's better already. Less fussy. More enigmatic.'

'Enigmatic's good. We like enigmatic, don't we, Gerald?'

'Gerald?'

'I've decided to name him after your imaginary friend.'

'You remember?'

'Of course. And after that we came in here and you saw it for the first time. Do you remember what you did?'

Ben thought back to that Sunday, after Victor's guests had left. What had he done? 'I told you it looked like the head of the same giant classical sculpture toppled by an earthquake.'

'Before that, before you said anything. I'll tell you. You reached out and ran your hand over the stone, like this. You started here, at the corner of the eye . . . then across the cheekbone and down towards the lips.' She turned back to him. 'That's when I realised.'

'What?'

'That you were a sensualist.'

'I've been called many things ending in -ist, but never that.'

'What things?'

'I don't know – sexist, idealist . . . egoist.'

'Then you've been hanging out with the wrong people.' Mo moved a little closer, a ghostly figure in her powdered overalls, and kissed him.

'You taste of dust.'

'It gets everywhere, even with the overalls. It's why I never wear anything underneath.'

'You're naked under that?'

'Uh-huh.'

'I don't believe you.'

'Stay there. Don't move. I'll show you my routine at the end of the day.' She made for the wooden pegs on the back wall. 'I come over here and I hang my mask up. Then I kick my boots off like this. Then I undo the zip and slip off my overalls, stepping out of them, like this. I then give them a little shake before hanging them up.'

She stood there naked, completely unabashed, like some nymph in a cave. A breathless surge of desire drove Ben towards her, but she darted off. 'Then I go and have a shower.'

She was through the door to her apartment in a flash, pulling it shut in his face. He tried the handle but she'd slipped the catch on the lock.

'Dinner's in half an hour and I have to get ready,' came her voice from the other side.

'That's not fair.'

'Life's not fair. As my grandpa says: man is born to 'ardship as surely as sparks fly up from a fire.' The line was delivered in broad Yorkshire.

'Well, *he* sounds like a miserable old git.'

There was a startled intake of breath then the door swung open. Mo stood perfectly naked before him once more. 'Are you insulting Grampy Shorrock?'

'Forgive me. How can I make it up to you?'

'Oh, I'm sure I'll think of something,' she said, drawing him inside.

Gregoire had prepared herb-crusted rack of lamb with tabbouleh and salad. He loved cooking, but serving the food and dealing with the dirty dishes he left to Steph, the girl-friend of one of the gardeners. She fulfilled a number of roles around the place, always with a smile and an uncom-plaining courtesy. She was studying part-time to become a dog trainer, and her own dog – Mika, a Siberian husky with ice-blue eyes – was always to be found at her heel, except in the kitchen. Gregoire didn't tolerate animals in his kitchen, not unless they were dead.

Over dinner, Annabelle broke the news that Victor would be back tomorrow morning, two days earlier than planned. He had decided to skip out the New York leg of his trip and fly straight home from Brazil. She and Mo began speculating about what terrible pieces of tourist tat he would bring them. He always returned from his travels bearing gifts, the kitscher the better. It had been fake grass hula skirts from Hawaii, Chairman Mao cigarette lighters that played 'The East is Red' from China, and he'd returned from Australia with kangaroo scrotum bottle openers.

Ben tried to make contact with Mo under the table, but every time his foot advanced, hers withdrew. She took the opportunity of Annabelle filling their wine glasses to fire him a sharp look of reprimand. Lay off, it said, and I'm not joking.

He couldn't complain; she'd been very clear with him in the shower earlier: she didn't want Annabelle to know about them. 'One day I'm crying on her shoulder and the next I'm rolling around with you. How's that going to look?'

'Do you care?'

'Yes, I do.'

She had cared enough to fire up her hairdryer after the shower so that he wouldn't be spotted returning to the main house with wet hair.

'I know what Annabelle's like. She'll feel excluded and then she'll sulk, and she's only just come out of the last one I sent her into.'

'What did you do?'

'I forgot her birthday.'

Spending the night together was out of the question unless Annabelle was away. They would just have to pick their moments carefully.

At the time, the prospect of this had seemed bearable, even appealing – the subterfuge would add an illicit tang – but the reality of having to keep his hands off her in company proved much harder to deal with.

Mo played her role to irritating perfection, right through to the friendly but chaste goodnight kiss in the kitchen after the three of them had loaded the dishwasher and tidied up.

Alone with Annabelle, sipping their mint teas at the kitchen table, Ben was sorely tempted to bring up Patrick Fedden's name. If he didn't it was only because another scenario had occurred to him over dinner.

What if Fedden had approached him because he suspected Annabelle was an unreliable informant – a double agent, so to speak?

It required more thought, it required a lot more thought, and this was enough to make him hold his fire for now.

eleven days to go . . .

VICTOR BLEW BACK into their lives with a fanfare – literally – announcing his return with a series of staccato blasts on a Brazilian samba whistle which filled the entrance hall with the sound of carnival.

The distribution of the bounty took place over coffee on the back terrace. There were wooden samba whistles for all of them, and Havaianas flip-flops and Brazilian flag beach towels.

'Remarkably tasteful,' observed Annabelle. 'Even useful.'

'Yeah, sorry,' apologised Victor. 'I wasn't on my game.' He clicked his fingers. 'Oh, I almost forgot . . .'

Delving back into the big canvas bag at his feet he pulled out some packages sealed in bubble wrap. 'Don't worry, Chef, there's one for you too.' He handed a package to Gregoire. 'Be careful, they're fragile, kind of precious.'

Mo was the first to release hers from the bubble wrap. 'Oh God, what is it?'

'What do you think?'

'It can't be!' laughed Ben.

But it was, they all were: painted porcelain studies of a doctor seated in a chair performing a rectal examination of a man leaning against a desk, his jeans around his ankles.

'You'll notice that each of them is unique, handmade, hand-painted.'

'*C'est magnifique!*' declared Gregoire.

Annabelle looked horrified. 'This has got to be the most disgusting gift I've ever received.'

Victor accepted the compliment with a nod. 'Thank you. The guy also did a fine line in autopsies and amputations but they weren't a patch on these.'

It was interesting to observe Victor's impact. There was a palpable shift in atmosphere as he took possession of the place once more. The slightly listless mood of the past week was swept aside by his energy and quiet command. The master had returned and everyone perked up a touch, like foot soldiers suddenly finding themselves in the presence of an officer.

He was looking well, more than well – tanned, healthy, rested. 'I spent a couple of days at the beach in between meetings. I'm telling you, I was tempted to buy a place there. I still am. God, what a country. Have you ever been?'

'No.'

'Then we'll go there. How are you set next February?'

'February?'

'Carnival in Rio. My treat. We'll take the jet.'

'Count me in,' said Ben.

The others were gone by now, and Victor had had enough

of talking about himself. 'So how's life been? Are you happy here? Are you working well?'

'Very happy. And ripping through the rewrite.'

'I can't wait to read it. I can't wait to *make* it. Tortoise's first film . . .'

'You really think it's going to happen?'

'You don't?'

Ben shrugged. 'Maybe I've spent too long in this business.'

'Listen, I'll finance it myself if I have to.' Victor leaned forward in his chair to drive home the point. 'It's going to happen, and it won't be the last film we do together, I'm sure of that, too.'

Lucinda at Tortoise Films had emailed Victor Ben's notes on *Adrift*, a thriller script they'd also optioned. 'I thought your points were spot on, very astute. We both did. We also thought you might want to have a shot at a rewrite after you're done with *The Bet*.'

Ben hesitated. 'I don't know, I'd feel bad. It's the other guy's idea and he's done a great job.'

'Trouble is, he thinks he's done a perfect job. He's dug his heels in, won't budge on the changes Lucinda's asking for.' He shrugged. 'Don't worry about it for now. The offer's there. You've got plenty of time to think about it.'

Ben generally took a couple of days to recover from a long-haul flight. Not Victor. He was raring to go.

'Let me freshen up then I'm taking you out to lunch in Oxford – a thank you for your good work in Italy.'

Ben didn't have a choice in it, not that he minded being

sucked along in Victor's slipstream. He had felt like a man under house arrest ever since Patrick Fedden had come knocking. It would do him good to get out of the place.

They took the Maserati, Victor at the wheel, Ben intensely aware of him tapping away at the satnav screen as they cruised down the driveway.

Victor pulled the car to a halt by the gatehouse. 'That's weird – someone's deleted the history.'

'What history?'

Victor slipped the car back into Drive. 'It doesn't matter.'

But it did. It changed everything. It removed the black sack of suspicion Ben had been humping around for the past week or so. Victor was innocent. He hadn't ordered the history to be deleted, because he didn't have anything to hide.

Ben let this pleasing thought germinate, put down roots. They were south of Woodstock and well on their way to Oxford when he saw for certain what he would do.

'There's something I've got to tell you.'

Victor glanced across at him. 'Sounds serious.'

'It is.'

'Then sit on it, I'm not in the mood for serious.'

'It's important.'

'Save it for now. You'll see why soon enough.'

A few minutes later Victor pulled the Maserati off a round-about on the fringes of the city. He seemed to be heading for a BP garage, but he bore left into the BMW dealership beside the petrol station. He drove past the main entrance and pulled up in front of the motorcycle showroom.

'You're thinking about buying a bike?'

'I've already bought one,' said Victor. 'That's it.'

A beast of a machine filled the next-door bay: BMW's monster GS 1200 trail bike, fully fitted with aluminium panniers and top box.

'That's one serious piece of kit,' said Ben.

'You like it?'

'What's not to like?'

'I'm glad you approve, because it's yours.'

Ben stared at him, speechless.

'You turned down my offer of a commission on the Riva. Think of it as a consolation prize.'

'I can't accept it.'

'Listen, we both know how much money you saved me. This didn't even cost a tenth of that.'

'It's too much.'

'Too late is what it is – it's already registered in your name. Now shut the hell up and go and pick yourself a helmet.'

Ben was still dazed. 'A helmet?'

'How else are you going to get it home?'

Ben chose a helmet then sat with a salesman and signed some paperwork with a shaky hand. He didn't ride the bike away. It made more sense to pick it up on their way back out of town after lunch.

Victor had booked at the Cherwell Boat House. A waitress showed them to their table on the raised wooden terrace overlooking the river and the long row of punts which could be rented by the hour.

Although they'd both be driving later, Victor felt they could still permit themselves a glass of champagne.

Ben raised his flute. 'Thank you.'

'It's my pleasure. Again.'

'I'll shut up now.'

'No, tell me what's bothering you. You said it was important.'

A rowdy party of eight was generating a fair amount of noise at a nearby table but Ben still lowered his voice before replying.

'I was approached the other day by someone from the Serious Fraud Office.'

Victor grew very still. 'Go on.'

'A man called Patrick Fedden.'

The name obviously didn't ring any bells with Victor. 'Start at the beginning,' he said. 'And tell me everything.'

Ben described the encounter in forensic detail, right down the fact that Fedden was a fan of Angry Birds. He broke off only once, when the waitress returned to take their order and Victor sent her on her way, requesting a bit more time.

'Have you told anyone else?' he asked.

'No, of course not. I've been going half-mad trying to make sense of it. I can't help thinking Fedden was holding something back.'

'Oh?'

'I'm probably wrong.'

'Run it up the flagpole anyway,' deadpanned Victor.

'It was what he said when I called him back . . . well, more the way he said it . . . about hoping the deal on the Riva was totally kosher or I'd be implicated. I just got this feeling he knew way more than he was letting on.'

'Maybe he does.'

'But how? He can't have got it from the Vianis or from you.'

'What are you saying?'

Ben couldn't bring himself to actually utter her name. The most he could muster was an awkward look.

'Ah . . . Annabelle,' said Victor knowingly.

'Like I say, I'm probably wrong.'

A smile played at the corners of Victor's mouth. 'Yes, you are, but not by much.' He removed his sunglasses and laid them carefully on the table. 'I owe you an apology. His name's not Patrick Fedden. It's Dominic Blythe. He's my head of security.'

'Your head of security works for the Serious Fraud Office?'

Victor gave a husky chuckle. 'That would be something. No. The number you called on the card he gave you isn't the number for the Serious Fraud Office, it's a line to Dom's office.'

'I don't understand . . .'

'I needed to know I could trust you.'

It was at that moment that the waitress returned once again to take their order. Victor glanced at Ben. 'If we don't do this now we might never.' He picked a starter and a main course off the set lunch menu.

Ben wasn't in any state to choose. 'I'll have the same, thanks.'

They sat in strained silence for a moment after the waitress had retreated, Ben caught between indignation and the sweet relief that he and Mo were safe.

'It was a test?' he asked coldly.

'I'm a cautious man. I've learned to be.'

'Do you have any idea what I've been through?'

'You're angry. I understand. It's my fault, and I'm sorry, but hear me out—'

'What's to say?' Ben broke in. 'You thought I was the sort of person who'd sell you out.'

'You're wrong, I didn't.'

'So why bother with the whole fucking charade?'

Victor seemed almost amused by his outrage. 'Jesus, Ben, calm down, OK? Just listen to what I have to say.'

'It better be good.'

'Oh, I think you'll find it is.'

Victor spelled it out clearly and with an honesty that wavered uncertainly between self-congratulation and self-criticism.

He felt he had reached a critical juncture in his life. He had single-mindedly devoted the past two decades to the accumulation of wealth, and good luck had favoured him in this ignoble quest. He had moved from trading stocks on Wall Street to trading bonds at just the right time. Any earlier, and he would have been too entrenched in the bond markets to see the wood for the trees. He would have been too 'corporatised', too anaesthetised by the heady remuneration package Deutsche Bank was offering, to question the absurdity of what Wall Street was getting itself into.

With hindsight, it was so glaringly obvious that even those who'd been annihilated by the crash now claimed to have seen it coming. In reality, only a small handful of people had appreciated the destructive potential of the ticking bomb that was the subprime mortgage bond market. Parcelling up lower middle-class America's home loans and selling them off to investors made sense in a rising property market – everyone was getting rich trading the debt – but if house prices stalled or, God forbid, began to fall . . .

An even smaller number of people had figured out a way to bet against the subprime mortgage market, effectively buying insurance against any future downturn in the form of credit default swaps. What Victor and his two colleagues at the hedge fund hadn't counted on was the eagerness of the very investment banks packaging subprime mortgage bonds to take their bets that the whole thing would go belly up before long.

'My job was to find the crappiest triple-B rated slices to bet against. Mortgage default rates only had to climb a few percentage points for us to cash in. It was a no-brainer. We were basically being offered eight-to-one odds on what we figured was a two-to-one bet.'

'How much did you make?'

'Much more than I'll ever need.'

'Go on, give me a figure, I can take it.'

Victor hesitated. 'Somewhere between one and two.'

'One and two?'

'It begins with a "b".'

'Jesus Christ,' hissed Ben. 'Personally?'

Victor gave the merest of nods.

'That's . . .' But he couldn't find the word.

'Obscene?' suggested Victor.

'I was searching for something more polite.'

'No, it *is* obscene. I never saw it that way, not back then, or if I did, it was no more obscene than the people taking our bets. These were guys I'd dealt with for years, guys I knew, some of them well. I'd even been a guest of a couple of them out in the Hamptons at the weekend, chatting with their wives, body-surfing with their kids, shucking littleneck clams together.' Unsavoury memories, if his expression was anything to go by.

'We were just "dumb money" in their eyes. Never a word of warning, never a "Hey, Victor, old buddy, are you sure you know what you're doing?" No, they figured we were going straight to hell and they were more than happy to sell us the tickets. Anything to boost their bonuses.'

Victor appeared to stall, mired in the mud of reminiscence. Ben gave him a nudge. 'You see things differently now?'

'Yes, I do. Subprime mortgage bonds were peddled to the world as a social movement. Everyone could be a homeowner. Why? Because lenders could keep their rates low by selling on their risk. Bullshit. What they were really doing was sucking in Joe Schmo from Idaho with teaser rates they knew they were going to hike in a couple of years. Joe might be screwed, unable to meet his new payments, but what did it matter to them? By then they'd already pocketed their fees and flogged off their downside to the markets.' He paused thoughtfully. 'It was always about screwing the poor. That's where it all started. And that, in the end – in the beginning – is why I'm rich as Croesus.'

Ben couldn't quite see where Victor was heading with this. 'You've developed a conscience?'

'More a sense of duty. I plan on giving it back.'

'Giving it back?'

'Uh-huh.'

'All of it?'

'Most of it. How much does one man need?'

'I don't know.'

'Come on, you must have thought about it,' said Victor.

'No.'

'Liar. Everyone dreams.'

Ben smiled weakly. 'OK, Madeleine used to say that four million would just about cover it till we died.'

Victor's reply was immediate. 'I'll pay you twice that if you help me.'

'Help you?'

'Give it away. I want to set up a charitable foundation. I'd like you to head it up. What do you think?'

Ben took a moment to stitch together a reply. 'I think you shouldn't joke about giving people eight million pounds.'

'If all you want is four then you can give the other half away. It's up to you.'

The waitress appeared with their scallops, which were accompanied on the plate by an artistic drizzle of carrot-coloured jus.

'Well?' said Victor, when they were alone once more.

'I'm sorry, I can't get my head round that figure.'

'Think of it as a Picasso painting, and not even a very good one, something the old guy knocked off in a couple of hours after a boozy lunch. For the same price I'm asking for ten years of your life. A precious decade.'

Victor proposed a salary of £500,000 a year, along with a large apartment in South Kensington which would be signed over to Ben at the end of the ten years. 'It's worth a bit over three million now, probably more by then.'

'I have to ask,' said Ben. 'Why me?'

'Because you're the right man for the job. Como proved that. You charmed the socks off old man Viani. I know, because he told me. You want to hear what clinched it? You knew the story of Daphnis and Chloe, which I sure as hell didn't till I looked it up. That's right. That's why he was happy to drop his price.' Victor leaned forward in his chair. 'Listen, Ben, you're not just smart, you have a winning way about you. It's a rare combination and it's what I'm looking for.'

Ben poked at a scallop. 'I'm a writer. It's what I do. It's all I've ever done.'

'And I wouldn't expect you to stop. In fact, I'd be disappointed if you did. There's no reason you couldn't juggle your writing with the charitable work, no reason at all.'

It didn't make sense. He had just been offered financial security for life, so why wasn't he feeling better?

The question niggled at him as he guided the BMW

through the country lanes west of Witney. It had been Victor's suggestion that he take a circuitous route back to Stoneham Park after their lunch, a chance to get to know the motorcycle. Well, he'd only put twenty miles on the clock but he already knew what he thought. It was perfect in almost every department – grunty, torquey, great balance for a big machine – but it just wasn't him. It would never be him. It was too bold, too brash, too bloody flash. It was the motorcycling equivalent of driving a Range Rover Sport.

He wondered how long the bike would last parked in his crime-ridden street in Battersea, but then he remembered that he would no longer be living in Battersea, not if he took Victor up on his offer. He tried to picture himself knocking around a three million-pound apartment in South Kensington, but the images he conjured up stubbornly refused to fall into focus.

He was in shock. Was it any surprise? It had been a roller coaster of a day. He'd woken that morning staring into the abyss, caught between an old friend and an investigation by the Serious Fraud Office. It had turned out to be a test of loyalty, a stepping stone to the big prize, a job at the heart of Victor's organisation, but the recollection of what they'd put him through still smarted. He'd spent twenty-four hours skewered on the horns of a terrible dilemma. It would take a while for the puncture wounds to heal.

Victor's head of security, the oleaginous Dominic, had worked a real number on him, right down to the fake call from his supposed boss, and all with Victor's approval and collusion. It had been cruel behaviour, almost sadistic. And what if he had failed the test? What then? Would they have strung him along for a while longer? To what end? No, he would have been out on his ear. That's how close he had come to losing everything.

These were unsettling thoughts, and they refused to be silenced by the memory of Victor's token apology over lunch. But there was also something else bothering him, tugging at his sleeve, something important that had been said but which he couldn't locate precisely . . .

Where was DC Leon Grosse when he needed him?

Mo's reaction only compounded his confusion.

'Are you for sale?' she asked, when he sought her out in her studio and broke the news to her.

'I don't know. It's a big commitment. Victor says I should take some time to think about it.'

He told her only that the proposed salary was good, not that it was ludicrously generous. He certainly didn't say what he was really thinking: that it was enough for them to see out their lives together in complete comfort.

'There's no shame in being bought by him,' said Mo with a wry smile. 'Take it from me.'

'Is that what he's doing?'

'Of course it is. He likes having you around, and Victor gets what he wants. People with his kind of money always do. I'm just surprised.'

'Surprised?'

'Well, one minute you're helping him buy a vintage speed-boat and the next he's talking about giving his money away.'

'Not all of it – most of it.'

'If you say so.'

'Cynic,' said Ben.

'Maybe.'

Later, lying spliced together in her bed, he almost told her how close he'd come to losing her, how the thought of it had left him feeling as hollow as a rotten tree.

'Connor called earlier, while you were out.'

'What did he want?'

'Me. He was in tears.'

Ben felt a cold hand close around his heart. 'Well, he can't have you.'

'It's weird, I felt nothing, not even anger, just . . . nothing.' She twisted to face him. 'Tell me this is the real thing. I need to hear you say it.'

He kissed her softly on the lips. 'It's the real thing.'

'Even if he owns us both it'll still be ours, won't it?'

'Why do you say that?'

'I don't know,' she replied with a ghost of a frown.

He pushed a stray strand of hair out of her eyes. 'Of course it will.'

But he knew what she meant.

thirty-two years before . . .

H EADMASTER BURROUGHS BROKE the news to the whole
school at the end of morning chapel. It made a change
from the usual round of petty announcements.

'There is a thief among us.' Burroughs raised his hand to
silence the murmur rippling through the chapel. 'A penitent
thief. And if Jesus himself was ready to grant eternal life to
a penitent thief, who are we to pass judgement?'

Ben had suspected this might be coming. The Crucifixion
was a strange subject for the reading, Easter long gone, a dim
memory.

'As we have just heard,' Burroughs went on in his high
nasal voice, 'Jesus turned to the thief on the cross beside him
and said, "Truly I tell you, today you will be with me in
paradise."'

As ever, the senior members of staff were ranged behind
Burroughs on chairs, grim-faced courtiers to their lanky
king.

'A bin liner containing a large number of objects was left
at the door of my study. It has already been established that

they are stolen goods. Whoever you are . . .' Burroughs paused to survey the faces tilted up at him, 'I salute you for your change of heart.'

Ben kept his eyes locked on the stage. He didn't dare glance at Jacob, who was seated just three chairs along from him.

'From lunchtime today, the items will be on display in my study, where they can be reclaimed by their rightful owners.'

When Jacob approached him during break and asked for a word in private, he went along unquestioningly to the changing rooms.

It wasn't the first time he had seen Jacob cry, but he'd never known him quite so upset, so desperate.

'It's me,' he choked. 'I'm the one.'

'Why are you telling me?'

'You'll know it's me. There's stuff in there that's yours.'

'What stuff?'

'Stuff from home.'

That annoyed him – it wasn't Jacob's home, it was *his* home. 'What stuff?'

Jacob listed the bits and pieces.

'Well, that's the end of my catapult and penknife. You know I can't ask for them back.'

'I'll get you new ones, I promise. Please don't say anything, Ben. I'm really sorry. I'll never steal anything ever again. Please, Ben.'

It was a strange encounter, both of them acting: Jacob

playing the thief who'd seen the error of his ways and handed the stuff back; Ben the shocked and disappointed friend. And when Ben finally gave his word that the secret was safe with him, Jacob looked as though he might sink to the floor in a faint. He didn't though, he said 'Thank you' over and over, dried his eyes then left the changing rooms.

Ben allowed himself a satisfied smile the moment the door swung shut on its pneumatic hinge. The plan had worked perfectly. Everybody would get their stuff back, and he now had something he could hold over Jacob.

The sudden sense of power caught him by surprise; he hadn't expected it to feel quite so good. Deep down, he knew why it did. Their relationship had shifted in the past year, not so much at school, but at home, where Jacob had begun to assert himself in ways he never had before. He had even taken to playing Ben's parents off against him in order to show himself in a good light or to get his own way. Ben had almost become a figure of fun in his own home. There were definitely more jokes at his expense. Even Emily felt entitled to mock him whenever she wanted to, and he couldn't help thinking that in some way Jacob was to blame for this too.

Well, maybe that would all change now, maybe he could make it change. He had given his word and he knew he wouldn't break it, but Jacob wasn't to know that. If Ben's father ever found out that the boy he'd welcomed under his roof had stolen from him, well, even Jacob wouldn't be able to wriggle out of that one. It would all be over. He'd be gone.

Ben didn't feel too bad thinking these things, not after the hurtful words he'd read in Jacob's diary. He had found the exercise book tucked away with everything else under the floorboards upstairs.

Scrawled across the cover in felt-tip pen was: *JACOBS DIARY . . . READ AT YOUR PERILL!!!* (spelling had never been Jacob's thing). Ben knew immediately that he would have to get rid of it; it would identify Jacob as the thief if he included it with the other stuff. He was desperate to read it, but he thought of his mother and what she would do. She was a good woman, big on morals and principles, which is why he managed to hold out right up until the very last moment, just as he was about to drop the diary into one of the big stinking bins out the back of the kitchen.

The opening paragraph read:

Its the first day of term and Ben has got the best bed in the dorm OBVIUSLY!!! Its the one by the window and we all had to arm wressle for it and he won OBVIUSLY!!! God he can be so cocky. He has to win everything.

It wasn't anything he hadn't already heard from Jacob at one time or another, face to face, during one of their spats, but there was something about seeing it written down that really hurt. He didn't read on because he knew their friendship would be destroyed if he did.

He dropped the exercise book on to the heaped slops of that day's dinner at the bottom of the bin.

The identity of the thief was the talk of the school. Ben was puzzled at first to see Jacob put himself right at the centre of the debate, keeping it alive, stirring up rumours, but he soon came to understand. How could Jacob possibly be the thief when he was the one leading the hunt?

Jacob didn't seem to care that Ben knew he was lying through his teeth, and he didn't let up. Again, it took Ben a while to catch up with Jacob's thinking. Jacob was furious, desperate to find the real thief, the boy who had stolen his stash and turned it over to Burroughs.

If Jacob suspected it was him, he never let on, and Ben was pretty sure he'd played his role convincingly. He hoped he had, because Jacob's obsession only seemed to grow with time. People even began to talk about it.

Ben waited until an exeat weekend, until they were back at home, to warn him. It wasn't an easy subject to bring up. Almost two weeks had passed since Jacob had begged in tears for his forgiveness and silence, and in all that time there had been no more talk of it between them.

'You're safe now. I think you should let it go.'

'Let what go?' asked Jacob.

'You know.'

Their words were spoken across the darkness, each of them lying in their beds.

'Why do you say that?' demanded Jacob.

'It's a bit weird the way you keep going on about it. Other people think it's weird.'

'Who?'

'It doesn't matter who.'

'Yes, it does. Who thinks it's weird? Tell me.'

Ben could see that for Jacob the answer might offer some clue as to who had handed his stash in to Burroughs.

'No,' he said.

'Why not?'

'Because it's not important. You gave the stuff back. It's over now.'

There was a short silence before Jacob replied. 'Maybe I didn't.'

'Didn't what?'

'Give the stuff back. Maybe someone else found it. Maybe someone else dumped it with Burroughs.'

Ben hadn't expected that. He needed to be alert. 'If you lied to me I'm allowed to break my promise to you.' He was pleased with his reply. It had just the right mix of indignation and menace.

Jacob gave a forced whinny of a laugh. 'Don't worry, I was joking.'

And that was that, or so Ben thought. A couple of minutes later Jacob's voice cut through the darkness.

'You never asked why I put your things in the bin bag for Burroughs. I mean, if I hadn't you'd never know it was me.'

Ben felt a twinge of alarm. 'Why didn't you?'

'The point is, you didn't ask before.'

Attack suddenly seemed like the best form of defence.

'Yeah, and I didn't ask you why you stole off me in the first place . . . me and my family,' he added, with a twist of the knife.

He might have silenced the mouth, but he could hear the cogs turning in Jacob's head, grinding away.

ten days to go . . .

MOST PEOPLE IN his position would have written off the Friday, tacking it on to the weekend, but Victor was long gone, whisked off to London by Lance before the rest of them had even stirred from their beds. He would be staying that night at the house in Mayfair; he had a theatre engagement with a client as well as a Saturday morning breakfast meeting.

Victor's work ethic was shaming, although Mo did a good job of running him a close second, skipping breakfast and turning down Ben's suggestion of a flying visit into Oxford. Mikey would be providing the shirt for the match on Sunday, but Ben had to buy himself some cricket trousers and boots.

'I'd love to,' said Mo. 'Just not today.'

He opted for the Honda over the BMW, almost out of sympathy for his old motorcycle. It looked so tatty and forlorn standing there, like a beggar at the steps of a palace, dwarfed by the gleaming new German monster.

Elmer Cotton Sports was on Turl Street, near the junction with Broad Street. Memories of past purchases assaulted Ben as he made a tour of the cluttered shop. There had been a squash racquet (when most were still made of wood and had towelling grips), an Adidas tracksuit (a birthday gift from his parents), football boots, a hockey stick, and any number of tennis balls. When he thought about how much sport he'd played, it was amazing there'd been any time left over for studying.

The entrance to Trinity College was just across the way. He found a different porter on duty in the Lodge, an older man than the one who'd treated him with such casual disdain on his last aborted visit.

'Before my time, sir,' he said, when Ben offered up his credentials. 'Welcome back.'

It was out of term and he expected the place to be deserted, but there were students milling around the college, many of them Asian. He made a brief tour, poking his head into the library, the chapel and the dining hall, before heading for the gardens.

He was breathing in the airy elegance of Garden Quadrangle when he saw someone he recognised hurrying towards him. It was the walk that did it, the urgent, pigeon-toed shuffle. Professor Swift had lost almost all his hair in the intervening years, and what little remained of it was optimistically styled to conceal this fact. His eyes were turned towards the ground, and for a moment Ben considered letting him pass by.

'Professor Swift . . .'

The professor looked up suddenly, searching Ben's face with rheumy eyes.

'Ben Makepeace.'

'Ah, Makepeace, yes . . .'

Mark Mills

It wasn't convincing, and Ben was about to help him out when the professor raised his hand. 'No, don't. I have it. The early nineties. Makepeace. Although I'm not sure I'd remember if your name had been Jones, say.'

'I wasn't a stand-out student, sir.'

'Loved your Milton. Tell me I'm wrong.'

Ben was pleasantly surprised by that. 'Yes, I did. I still do. I have you to thank for that.'

'Most unlikely. Wait. Early nineties? Possibly. I've gone off him since then. Humourless old fart.'

Ben laughed, which seemed to warm Professor Swift towards him.

'Yes, Makepeace. Enjoyed yourself far too much, as I recall, always playing sport. What brings you back to the old place?'

Ben opened up his shopping bag.

'Cricket boots?' chuckled Professor Swift.

He was heading for the Bodleian Library but asked if Ben would like to join him for a coffee at Blackwell's. 'Coffee houses in bookshops. I never saw that one coming. Don't get me wrong, I'm all for it.'

The professor was known at the Caffè Nero franchise in Blackwell's.

'Good morning, Svetlana.'

'Professor Svift.'

'This is Ben, an old student of mine.'

Ben and Svetlana smiled politely at each other. She was attractive in an undernourished sort of way, the tips of her ears poking through her long, lank hair.

'Svetlana is Macedonian, although she also has Greek

blood. Her great-grandfather was a Macedonian communist who fought in the Greek civil war alongside her great-grandmother, who was a Greek communist. How romantic is that? Love born of beliefs and warfare.'

'Skinny latte and cvoissant, Professor Swift?'

They found a table by the windows overlooking Broad Street.

'I thought you'd be in Italy,' said Ben. The professor had always been very vocal about his love of the country.

'Times have changed, Makepeace, times have changed. Gone are the days of drinking the college dry of claret while patronising a few undergraduates.' He said this with an amused and self-deprecating twinkle. 'No, the buggers have got us working for our keep.'

He planned to make a trip to Bologna in September, but until then he would be teaching a summer intake of Korean students. 'Fiercely intelligent people, take my word for it. Terrifyingly bright.' He was also putting the finishing touches to a book. 'Publish or perish, that's the word from the new Master. It doesn't matter if no one reads the bloody thing – thank God, because I'm not sure that four hundred pages on the lesser-known poems of John Dryden is destined for the bestseller lists.'

'You may be wrong.'

'Yes. No, I'm not. It doesn't matter. The point is, I'm "on message".' He uttered the words as though they were a curse that would send his dearest love to their grave. 'I'm "engaging" the students in a "dialogue", "facilitating" them on their "journey".'

Ben laughed. 'They'll have you Tweeting next.'

'You joke, but some of the younger dons are already at it. By God, there's so much useless chatter in the world. Everything we need to know has already been said.'

'"The superior man acquaints himself with the many sayings of antiquity . . ."'

'Ah, Milton,' observed the professor. 'I never said he didn't know a thing or two.' He broke off a piece of croissant and dunked it in his latte. 'I seem to remember that most of your lot went into finance. What allows you to swan around Oxford on a Friday morning buying cricket boots?'

Ben delivered a potted history of his chequered career as a screenwriter. Professor Swift had never been a good dissimulator. 'Well, if it pays the bills and doesn't add to the surplus of human misery . . .'

Ben didn't say that a couple of critics had accused his first film of doing just that. 'Actually, I'm in a position to do quite the opposite.'

'The opposite?'

'To reduce the surplus of human misery.'

He spelled out the circumstances and details of Victor's offer. Professor Swift looked genuinely startled.

'Forty million pounds a year for ten years?'

'That's right.'

'And he's willing to pay you to scatter this fairy dust around?'

'Way more than I've ever earned before.'

'Well, you have to do it, of course,' came back the immediate reply.

'You really think so?'

Professor Swift laid a liver-spotted hand on Ben's forearm and said with a strange intensity, 'My dear fellow, the wonders you could perform, the miracles . . .'

They parted company with a handshake on the steps by the Sheldonian Theatre. 'Thank you, Professor. You were always a great inspiration to me.'

'Oh, I doubt that's true.' He released Ben's hand. 'Just one note of warning. It's about the only thing I've learned during my seventy-odd years on this spinning ball: if something seems too good to be true, it usually is.'

Mo and he had discussed it and decided there was no harm in Victor knowing about them. Unfortunately, the opportunity to tell him hadn't come up before he'd disappeared off to London. This left them stranded in a frustrating limbo, still playing charades with Annabelle. He could handle it. Mo was so absorbed in her work that another twenty-four hours here or there wasn't going to make a blind bit of difference. She barely showed herself at dinner, not even bothering to change out of her overalls when she dropped by the back terrace briefly for a glass of wine and a bowl of Gregoire's homemade tortelloni.

The leering devil on Ben's shoulder whispered in his ear that the work was just an excuse, that Mo was having doubts, that she'd changed her mind, that Connor had got through to her with his tearful pleas. However, when he returned to the library after dinner and opened up his laptop he found a note resting on the keyboard. She must have secreted it there on her way back to the studio. It read:

I'll make it up to you in ways you can't imagine (although I'm also open to suggestions) XX

P. S. If this message doesn't self-destruct in five seconds, eat it.

It made him smile. It made his heart soar. It made him text her: **Message received. I hope you choke on the dust xx**

He knew why he was so eager to get the matter settled. On Monday he would be scooping Toby up from London and bringing him out to Stoneham Park for the week. He didn't want to have to fudge things with his son; he wanted to be clear and honest. It had occurred to him that this might be the last thing Toby needed right now, coming hot on the heels of Madeleine and Lionel's engagement, but he also suspected that buried beneath the tangled mesh of Toby's upset lay a touching concern for how he had taken the news.

He wanted Toby to know that he was just fine, that life was moving in the right direction for him too.

nine days to go ...

I⊤ CAME TO HIM while he was asleep, or rather, floating in that liminal state where it's sometimes possible to intercede in your dreams. This wasn't a dream, though; it was a stark epiphany, and it jolted him awake.

His subconscious brain must have been grappling with the issue ever since his lunch with Victor. He also wondered if Professor Swift's parting words had somehow played a part. 'Just one note of warning,' the professor had said, but that single note had been ringing in his head ever since.

He knew he wasn't mistaken. He could picture Dominic leaning forward on the bench at the playing field and saying it in that superior, slightly mocking way of his: 'I believe the young lady picked up the tab at the restaurant.'

There were a number of possible explanations, but only one question: how the hell did Victor's head of security know about Chiara?

He waited until after his morning run before phoning the Villa d'Este, and he made a point of calling from his own phone.

He explained to the receptionist that he'd recently stayed at the hotel, and that his phone had been stolen since then, which meant he'd lost the contact details of a fellow guest.

As he'd anticipated, the best they could do for him was pass on a message to Signora Bonetti.

He had toyed with the idea of shock tactics before settling on something more composed, more intriguing, but hopefully just as alarming. He was playing on the fact that the fourth and final time they had made love it had been unprotected sex.

'Please call me. There's something important you should know.'

He left his email address along with his mobile number, and the moment he hung up he went online.

He had searched the Web before, but it had been a cursory hunt for a picture of her. This time he was considerably more thorough. There were any number of Chiara Bonettis out there, but none of them appeared to be her. Was it really possible that someone who held an important position at the heart of the Italian silk industry could stay below the radar: no conferences attended, no interviews with journalists? It seemed unlikely.

What seemed increasingly likely was that Chiara Bonetti, buyer of Chinese silk threads, was a fabrication, a creation. And if Victor's head of security knew of her existence then she had to have been a plant. Dear Dominic, so full of himself, had screwed up royally.

God only knew what it all meant, and where exactly Victor

fitted into the scheme of things, but Ben had to tip his hat to Professor Swift, stooped and wizened sage.

Too good to be true.

By lunchtime, having tinkered distractedly with the script, he had decided that the best course of action was to hold off until he'd heard back from Chiara (or whatever name she really went by). It might never happen, but he would give her a few days' grace before making his move. A couple of weeks ago he might have gone in all guns blazing, letting the bodies lie where they fell, but there was far more at stake now, not least of all eight million pounds. Only an idiot of the first order would jeopardise that on an unsubstantiated hunch.

Mo was still in lockdown and didn't show for lunch, which pissed him off. He was beginning to doubt her words about making it up to him. How could she share herself with him then disappear so suddenly, so completely, from his life? In a pique of paranoia, rapidly quashed, he even started drawing parallels with Chiara's vanishing act.

Anxious as he was about seeing Victor again, it was almost a relief when Lance delivered him back from London soon after lunch. An hour later, the two of them were trading shots on the grass tennis court. It was to be their first match in almost thirty years, and Ben knew even as they were warming up that he would lose it.

Victor's groundstrokes had been coached to near-metronomic perfection: knees bent, eyes on the ball, which he hit hard and with a lot of top spin. No wonder he hugged the baseline. Why approach the net when you could destroy your opponent from a distance?

Back in their youth, Ben had always taken the edge off his game to allow Jacob a fighting chance. The reincarnated Jacob was a much more formidable beast: determined, mobile, and clearly set on annihilating him. There was nothing to be gained from hitting the ball hard; Victor simply stole the energy and fired the thing back with interest. Ben tried sucking him in short with sliced shots, obliging him to play the ball on the move, but Victor proved more than up to the task, putting away the winners from mid-court, swatting flies.

Ben lost the first set 6–3. A single break of serve had separated them, and he quickly figured he needed to mix up his service game, concentrating on Victor's backhand, which came back flat and floated and could be volleyed away easily enough if he committed to following his serve in. The second set went to a tiebreak, which Ben shaved 9–7. No honourable draw for Victor, who wanted a decider. This was fine by Ben; he was on a roll, in the ascendancy.

The third set showed just how wrong he was. He was 3–1 down before he realised that Victor had been doing to him exactly what he'd done to Jacob all those years ago: allowing his opponent a tantalising taste of victory. Ben couldn't say how it happened – no counter-strategy came to mind – but Victor simply shifted up a gear, breaking him again then serving out to take the match.

Aside from the odd clenched fist, there had been no crass displays of competitiveness from Victor during the match, but as soon as he had fired off the winning ball he emitted a triumphant, 'Yes!' and bounded to the net. 'Every dog has its day,' he grinned.

Ben shook his hand. 'Well done.'

'You really wanted that, didn't you?'

'I was taught never to beat a man on his home turf.' Victor's childishly delighted expression clouded over before he realised Ben was joking. 'You want revenge?'

'Who doesn't?'

'Bring it on, buddy.'

'Just say when, pal.'

'Tomorrow afternoon.'

'Can't. I'm playing cricket for Stoneham.'

'You're kidding!'

'Didn't I say? Mo landed me in it.'

Victor gave an amused snort. 'Now *that* I've got to see.'

They showered then swam, and afterwards Victor mixed them a couple of strong mojitos at the poolhouse bar, using a fistful of mint torn from a bushy clump of the stuff out front. They lay back on loungers in the hazy evening sunshine.

'I love this place,' reflected Victor. 'It already feels like home.'

'Where was home before?'

'The house in Mayfair, I guess, although in my mind it's always been the villa on Cap Ferrat.'

'Mo says it's an amazing place,'

'Yeah, she really took to it.' Victor savoured a sip of his drink. 'Tell me, how are you two getting along?'

'Well.' Ben paused before taking the plunge. 'Actually, a bit more than well.'

Victor shifted on his lounger, intrigued. 'Is that the sound of two people going at it I hear?'

'It might be.'

Victor offered his glass for Ben to clink. 'Congratulations.'

'You don't mind?'

'Two of my favourite people? Why would I mind, for Chrissakes? And it was kind of predictable.'

'You think?'

'No, totally predictable. Annabelle thought so too. Don't look so surprised, she's a wise old bird.'

'No, it's just that we've been playing it down with her. Mo thought she wouldn't approve.'

Victor laughed. 'Listen, Annabelle's like me, she thinks Mo's wasted enough of her life already on Connor. He came to stay once. The guy's a jerk.'

Ben doubted it. Somehow he couldn't see Mo spending eight years with a jerk.

'I'm happy for you, happy for her. You don't need Annabelle's approval, and you don't need mine. Just enjoy yourselves.'

A burden lifted – they were free to be. He was surprised he didn't feel more elated. Maybe he would once the Chiara issue had been settled.

*

It was confirmed over dinner that Victor's son, Marcio, would be arriving from Paris on Tuesday, his visit timed to overlap with Toby's stay at Stoneham Park.

'They'll have a ball together, I know they will,' said Victor.

Annabelle, Ben noted, didn't look quite so convinced, although she did chip in, 'There's loads of stuff for them to do here. It's boy paradise.'

'I'm sure they'll get by,' said Ben. 'We did, and with a lot less.'

'We sure did.'

'Oh God,' groaned Mo. 'Please no more stories about marbles and paedophiles.'

'I second that,' said Annabelle.

Mo turned to her. 'What, you too?'

'What was his name again? Ronson? Johnson?' Annabelle was addressing Victor, who shrugged uncertainly.

'Could have been pretty much any one of them.'

Annabelle had been throwing back the wine and was too merry to be deterred. 'You know, the hairy one . . .'

'Jobson.' The word was out of Ben's mouth before he knew it.

'Yes, Jobson, that's him,' chimed Annabelle.

Ben looked at Victor. 'You think Mr Jobson . . .?'

'You don't?'

'God knows. Maybe. I wouldn't put money on it. Mr Delafont, on the other hand . . .'

'Oh, shit, they're off,' sighed Mo, holding up her hand across the table for Annabelle to high-five. 'Sisters in suffering.'

It was more of a tap than a slap from Annabelle. 'Ooh, I don't think I've ever done that before.'

'Well, you're a natural.'

'No, she isn't,' said Ben. 'She looked like she was testing the heat of an iron.'

eight days to go . . .

B EN'S EYES WERE closed, his head back, so the first he knew of it was the tap-tap on the shower door.

'Room service.'

Mo slipped inside the steamy cubicle and pressed herself against him.

'I tried not to wake you,' he said.

'I wasn't asleep. I was thinking.' She squeezed some shower gel into her hand and smeared it across his chest, working it into a lather. 'What are you going to tell Toby?'

The question caught him off guard. 'Not what you asked me to do to you about two hours ago.'

She slapped his chest in rebuke. 'Well, you didn't have to do it.'

'It would have been impolite to refuse.'

Her hands worked their way downwards until they were cupping him, cleaning him. 'I'm scared.'

'Of what?'

'Toby.'

'You won't be when you meet him.'

'I'm sure he's a really sweet boy, but you know how it is with kids – all they really want is for their mum and dad to be together.'

'He knows that's not going to happen.'

'It doesn't matter. Deep down it's still what he wants.'

They had ended up spending their first full night together in Ben's room less by design than by default. After Victor and Annabelle had turned in, they had sat on the back terrace and chatted deep into the night about Mo's family, her over-weight mother and her three brothers and her grandfather, Grampy Shorrock, who had worked down the coal mines. He had been her chief supporter over the years, possibly because he'd also earned a living hacking into rock. She had grown quite impassioned at one point, when describing the eloquence of different stones and how she felt her work connected her to a deep, deep history. One of the first things Homo sapiens had done as a fledgling species was work stone. There was a hand axe in the British Museum that had been crafted from a block of volcanic rock more than a million years ago.

When the last of the candles had guttered, sputtered and died, the prospect of making their way back to Mo's apart-ment in the stable block had seemed like a step too far, so they had headed upstairs to Ben's room. It had started with a massage – Mo's shoulder muscles were taut as twisted rope after her recent exertions in the studio – and it had gone on from there: not sex, not sleep, but a loose fusion of the two, which had carried them right through to the dawn chorus and beyond.

Now it was ten thirty, and Mikey wanted Ben at the cricket ground by eleven to help roll the wicket before the match.

'Then you'd better hurry,' teased Mo, still soaping him.

'That's not fair. You can't leave me like this.'

'This'll help.'

Mo twisted the shower lever and darted from the cubicle before the blast of icy water hit him.

'Jesus!'

Mikey was unloading a bunch of cricketing gear from the back of his tatty hatchback when Ben pulled up in the car park on the BMW. He kicked down the side stand and tugged off his helmet.

'Flash bastard,' said Mikey.

'Fat bastard,' said Ben.

The opposition was a local village side, Steeple Aston. Like Stoneham's team, they covered everything from rangy teenagers with skin conditions through to balding elder statesmen with paunches and knee supports. There was history between the two sides, something to do with the Steeple Aston captain not giving out his star batsman leg-before-wicket while umpiring last year. The fellow had gone on to score a century and effectively take the match.

Mikey won the toss, electing to bat first. Ben was relieved to find himself put down as number six; it meant there would be time for some much-needed batting practice in the net. Ominously, they lost their first wicket in the second over – clean-bowled, centre stump – and Mikey waddled out to take his place at the crease. To a resounding cheer from the pavilion, he smashed the first delivery through the covers for four runs. It wasn't a fluke. He had a good eye, great timing and a strong arm. Anything loose was picked off and punished. The runs were beginning to clock up when they suddenly lost two cheap wickets and Ben was hurrying to get kitted up and into the net.

It was years since he'd strapped on some pads, but it came back surprisingly quickly, probably because he'd always been a dull batsman, determined to protect his stumps at all costs: watch the ball out of the bowler's hand, pick the line early and get the front foot forward. It worked well enough in the net; out there it would be different. He didn't have to wait too long before finding out.

Another wicket fell – not Mikey's, thankfully – and Ben found himself heading straight out to the wicket from the net. Mikey came to meet him.

'Fucking muppets . . . fifty-eight for four . . . we're in all kinds of shit now. You and me need to dig in, mate. Think the Alamo, think Custer's last stand.'

'Everyone died at both of those.'

'Yeah? Well, we won't.' Annoyingly, Steeple Aston had just brought their lanky young pace-bowler back on. 'But you're a leftie,' said Mikey. 'He won't like that.'

Ben couldn't resist it; Mikey obviously hadn't seen him practising in the net. 'I thought I'd bat right-handed, give the poor bastards a chance.'

'Very funny.'

'Seriously, Mikey.'

'And I'll seriously kick your arse if you do.'

Mikey's face was a puce picture of murderous intent as Ben called for a right-handed guard.

He safely defended the first two balls, before turning the third away for two runs backward of square on the leg side. It was a huge relief. He'd avoided all three of the dreaded ducks and could begin to relax. Mikey looked stunned and gave him a thumbs-up.

By lunch they had put on a solid partnership of thirty or so runs. More importantly, they had stopped the rot. Mikey slung an arm around Ben's shoulders as they made their way back to the pavilion for the break. 'You fucking beauty.'

Their teammates and a smattering of supporters clapped all the players in. Ben hadn't seen Mo and Victor arrive, but there they were, hovering at the back of the throng. The Colonel was also present, and he stepped forward to shake Ben's hand.

'Excellent work, young man.'

'Damn right,' said Mikey. 'And batting off his wrong hand! You ever see anything like it?'

Ben caught Mo's eye. 'Do you want to tell him or shall I?'

'He's a mix,' said Mo. 'Left-handed for most things, right for others.'

This earned Ben a bone-numbing thump to the shoulder from Mikey.

Victor was casually dressed in T-shirt, shorts and sneakers. For a man who was known to all but who rarely, if ever, showed his face in Stoneham, he entered into the relaxed spirit of the occasion like an old hand, chatting freely as he sat crossed-legged on the grass with a bottle of beer and a paper plate piled high with chicken thighs, salad and new potatoes.

You could sense people's bewilderment. Was the bloke mucking in and making them laugh really the remote and mysterious figure they'd been bad-mouthing all this time? When it emerged that Victor had played cricket as a young boy they even tried to sign him up.

'I never really had it, not like Ben.'

'Strongest arm in the school, though. He smashed the record in the cricket ball competition.'

'Oh, yeah?' said Mikey. 'Let's see.' He tossed Victor a cricket ball.

'It was only thirty years ago.'

'No excuses. A tenner says you can't hit the stumps from the boundary here.'

Victor eased himself to his feet, his eyes narrowing as they turned themselves on Mikey. 'If I dislocate my shoulder, it's your fault, big man.'

'I'll drive you to A&E in Banbury myself,' grinned Mikey.

It was some forty or fifty yards from the boundary to the wicket – well beyond Ben's range, and Victor's too, he guessed. Unlike his tennis strokes, which had been completely remodelled by some pro, Victor's throwing technique hadn't changed at all. It was a glimpse of the old days: the way he windmilled his arm to loosen his shoulder before setting off on his short run-up, hingeing so far back at the waist that the ball was down near his right knee before he finally let fly.

'Holy shit . . .' muttered someone as the ball arced high across the blue backdrop of the sky.

It didn't hit the stumps; it overshot the wicket and skittered off towards the far boundary.

'Whoa . . . respect!'

'Get your wallet out, Mikey.'

'I said *hit* the stumps. He missed.'

'He did,' said Victor, graciously. 'And I did.' He winced as he shook out his arm. 'Oof, I'm going to feel that tomorrow.'

Wandering back out to the wicket after lunch, Mikey turned to Ben. 'Your mate . . . he's not as much of a cunt as I thought.'

'Don't go soft on me now, Mikey, we've got a job to do.'

They added another forty runs to their partnership before Mikey was caught in the slips. And when Ben was run out a few overs later – quite unnecessarily, after a stupid call from one of the youngsters – there were 162 runs on the board, 38 of which had been knocked up by Ben.

He was surprised to find Victor still hanging around.

'Nothing better to do. And it's shaping up to be a real classic,' he added with an ironic twinkle.

They were all out in the forty-ninth over for a respectable total of 178, their best score of the season. Sniffing victory, Mikey set a cautious field for Steeple Aston's opening batsmen.

The wind had died, and it was blisteringly hot in the

outfield. The youngster who had run Ben out more than redeemed himself with the ball, bowling fast, varying his line and length to unsettle the batsmen. Ben, on the other hand, when eventually called on to try his arm, bowled somewhere between slow and medium, usually short, and mostly down the leg side. You could almost hear the batsmen licking their lips each time he ran up to the crease. They were a costly couple of overs, but just before tea he took a good catch at midwicket, which went some way towards appeasing Mikey for his shoddy performance with the ball.

A couple of wickets tumbled quickly after tea, but the match then swung back in the opposition's favour when a young fellow with the broken face of a bare-knuckle fighter took to the crease. He was a slogger, and his eye (lost in the shadow of his Neanderthal brow) was in. The runs came freely. He was dropped twice. Mikey grew dangerously sullen. The match was slipping away from them. Then slogger was dispatched, his off-stump uprooted. The lower order collapsed and Stoneham took the day by eight runs.

Victor had been joking, but it had indeed turned out to be something of a classic, victory and defeat hanging in the balance until the very last moments. Mikey was like a man possessed, hugging his troops, even promising to stand a round at the pub.

'He must have sunstroke,' called some wag.

Victor spread his congratulations around, along with his farewells; he was going to give the pub a miss. Ben accompanied him to the car park, suggesting that they make a quick detour en route.

'Intriguing . . .' said Victor, as they took the path through the trees that cut the corner to the village green. It brought them out by the lychgate of the church, and the big board indicating the progress of the church appeal.

Victor understood immediately.

'I'm an atheist.'

'So's the treasurer of the appeal. You met him – Colonel Armitage. I saw you two talking while we were fielding.'

'He didn't say anything.'

'He's too classy to go for the hard sell. I'm not.'

He explained that the roof lead needed replacing, and the longer it took, the more the costs kept climbing because of the water damage inside. Victor listened attentively before asking, 'Why's he doing it if he's an atheist?'

'I don't know. For tradition's sake. Something to fill his days. He's alone now. His wife's buried just over there.' Ben nodded towards the overflow cemetery. 'They've saved him a plot next to her because he's treasurer of the appeal.'

Victor glanced up at the board. 'Fifty thousand to see the Colonel buried next to his wife?'

'There are worse reasons. He's a good man.'

Victor weighed his words. 'Is this your way of saying yes to my offer?'

'It might be.'

A slow smile spread across Victor's face. 'That's great news. It's also the best reason yet. OK, I'll give you a cheque for sixty.'

'Fifty will do it.'

'These things always run over. And if it doesn't they can keep the rest back for a rainy day. How's that?'

'Just dandy,' said Ben.

Victor laid an affectionate hand on his shoulder. 'Welcome aboard.'

one week to go . . .

'Y<small>OU'RE LATE</small>,' <small>SAID</small> Madeleine, even as she pulled open the front door.

'By five minutes.'

'Seven. And what on earth is that?' She peered past him at the driveway.

'A Maserati. A VW Polo just wasn't me.'

'Very funny.' She stepped aside to let him enter. 'I'm going to be late for work now.'

'It's good to see you too.'

Closing the door, she sighed then kissed him perfunctorily on both cheeks. 'Sorry, I'm just a bit strung out. Toby had a friend staying last night – Alice, the little French thing I told you about – and I've got to drop her home on my way in.'

'I'll do it.'

'Really? Would you? It'll save me fifteen minutes.'

'Which leaves you eight minutes for a quick coffee with your ex-husband.'

Toby and Alice were finishing off their breakfast.

'Dad!' called Toby, hurrying over from the table and hugging him. Alice was even prettier in the flesh – a perfect little sprite demurely perched on the edge of her chair.

'*Enchanté, mademoiselle. Je suis le père de cet imbécile.*'

Alice giggled, Toby rolled his eyes, and Madeleine called from across the kitchen, 'What colour Nespresso capsule do you want?'

They took their coffees outside to the table on the back terrace.

'You look well. No, more than well.'

'The country life,' replied Ben. 'And I've started running again.'

'Come on, what's her name?' She was joking.

'Mo. It's short for Molly.'

Madeleine straightened in her chair. 'And where did you meet her?'

'She's a sculptor, a stone carver. She's working on a big piece out at the estate.'

'A sculptor, I should have guessed.'

'What's that supposed to mean?'

'What's she like? Is she pretty? How old is she?'

'She's thirty-three.'

'Cradle-snatcher.'

'Hardly.'

'Is she pretty? I bet she is. She sounds pretty . . . Mo the sculptor. No, she sounds more than pretty, she sounds beautiful.'

'Mads—'

'I'm fine with it, OK?'

'Good, because you've no right not to be.'

Madeleine made a show of replacing her cup on its saucer. 'Actually, Ben, I think I have every right to know that my son is going to be spending a week with your new squeeze. I'm just surprised you didn't warn me before.'

'There was nothing to warn you about two days ago.'

'What, you've only just fucked her?'

Ben held up his hands. 'This conversation's over.'

'Do you plan on fucking her while Toby's there?'

'God knows what you and Lionel get up to at night, but I don't suppose it's Scrabble.'

'Actually, Lionel doesn't like to fuck very much, especially when things are going badly at work, which they are right now.'

'Mads, I don't need to know. I don't *want* to know. It's your life.'

She scrutinised him with granite eyes. 'You've changed. You're different. You're harder.'

'Or maybe I'm just happier.'

'That's cruel.'

'It's not a dig at you.'

'For once.'

'Oh God . . .' he groaned. Madeleine had never had a problem with contradicting herself in arguments if it scored a hit.

'What?' she demanded.

He foolishly opted for logic. 'So you agree with me, it wasn't a dig at you, I wasn't being cruel. I was talking about me – my happiness.'

Madeleine adopted an expression of puzzled concern. 'Why are you so keen to rub my face in it?'

Ben pointed at his watch. 'Damn, look at that, our eight minutes are already up.'

They left the house at the same time, Toby and Alice piling excitedly into the back of the Maserati. Madeleine stuck her head through the window. 'Alice, call your mother and tell her you're going to be a bit late.' Standing, she turned to Ben and said for his ears only, 'I'm sorry.'

'Forget it.'

'I think I must have been a witch in a former life.' She kissed him on the cheek. 'I'm happy for you, and for Milly Molly Mandy. Shit, there I go again.'

Ben reversed the Maserati into the street but didn't drive off immediately. He wasn't going to pass up the chance of spending a bit of time with Toby and Alice together. 'Alice, what are you up to this morning?'

'Nothing.'

'Who wants to see the Gates of Paradise?'

'Er, no one, Dad.'

'I do,' said Alice, with an apologetic glance at Toby.

'Yeah, sounds cool,' shrugged Toby.

The Victoria and Albert Museum could hardly be described as cool, but Toby and Alice both fell silent when they entered the first of the two enormous Cast Courts.

'The Victorians were pretty good at stealing other people's stuff, and if they couldn't nick it they took plaster casts instead. That's Trajan's Column, from Rome.'

The gallery's glazed barrel roof was high overhead but not a full thirty metres up, and the copy of the column, intricately carved with battle scenes, stood in two towering sections which dwarfed the casts of burial tombs and statues scattered around them. Against the end wall stood a huge medieval church portal, its four recessed doors trimmed with figures of the Apostles and the Prophets and crowned by a tympanum showing Christ in Majesty.

'Are those the Gates of Paradise?' Toby asked.

'No, the Gates of Glory, from the cathedral at Santiago de Compostella in Spain. This way for paradise . . .'

'Santiago de Compostella is where the pilgrims go,' said Alice as they strolled on.

'Bravo,' said Ben. 'Have you been there?'

'No, I read it in a book.'

'She's very clever,' grumbled Toby, bringing a blush to Alice's cheeks. 'It's really annoying.'

The East Court was devoted to Italian works of art. Toby and Alice glanced around them – wide-eyed Lilliputians – as Ben picked a path through the statues and portrait busts, pulpits and other monuments, pointing out the better known masterpieces. It struck him suddenly that Mo should be there with them, acting as tour guide. After all, the place was one giant tribute to her craft.

'That's Michelangelo's statue of David. And somewhere there's a plaster fig leaf they used for covering up his privates when royal ladies visited.'

It was Michelangelo who had dubbed Lorenzo Ghiberti's doors for the Baptistery in Florence 'The Gates of Paradise', but Toby and Alice looked underwhelmed by the early Renaissance relief panels with their tales from the Old Testament. Even when Ben pointed out how Ghiberti had cleverly combined several moments from the same story in some of the panels, Toby said, 'I still prefer the Gates of Glory.'

'Fair enough, but these are plaster replicas. See how you feel when we're in Florence, standing in front of the real thing. We'll do it one day, and soon.'

'Can I come too?' asked Alice brightly.

'What do you reckon, Tobes?'

'I don't know. It's a tough one.' Alice's affronted look turned to one of outrage when Toby added, 'She snores.'

'I do *not* snore!'

Toby pulled out his phone. 'Proof. I recorded you.'

It wasn't loud, but it certainly qualified as snoring.

'*Oh, non,*' gasped Alice, her hand going to her mouth. '*Quel horreur!*'

Their laughter echoed round the gallery, earning them a sharp look from the uniformed attendant on duty.

Alice turned out to be a miniature version of her mother. Sabine was dressed in tight black running gear when she greeted them at the door of the mews house tucked away off Eaton Square. Ben turned down her offer of a coffee.

'Thanks, but we should hit the road, we're expected for lunch.'

They had barely pulled out of the mews when a text landed in Toby's phone with a frog-like croak.

'Alice says thank you.'

Ben knew better than to probe too much. 'She's very special, Tobes.'

Another croak – another text. Toby read it. 'She thinks you're OK too.'

It wasn't the last time the phone croaked before they reached Stoneham Park.

'Oh my God, Dad . . .' gasped Toby as the main house and the stable block hove into view at the end of the driveway.

'I told you it was big.'

'Not *this* big! It's like that hotel we stayed at with Mum once.'

'You remember that?'

'That was the best weekend of my life.'

Not for Ben. Far from it. That was the weekend Madeleine had come clean with him about her infidelity: a one-night stand with a stranger, a Frenchman staying at the same hotel near Amiens where her legal conference had taken place.

Ben had phoned ahead and told them not to wait, but that's exactly what Mo and Annabelle were doing, chatting at the table on the back terrace.

'You should have started.'

'Toby's first meal?' replied Annabelle. 'Whatever would he think of us?'

If Mo was nervous, she didn't show it, and Toby rose to the occasion, not just fielding the many questions the two women fired at him, but taking the initiative too.

'Dad says you're a sculptor.'

'That's right.'

'You don't look like a sculptor.'

'No? What do I look like? Actually, don't answer that, I'm not sure I want to know.'

'He says you're very good.'

'She is,' chipped in Annabelle.

'I'll show you what I'm working on afterwards, if you want, then you can make up your own mind. There's just one thing you have to remember.'

'What's that?' asked Toby.

'If you don't like it, lie.'

Judging from the look in Mo's eye, Ben wasn't the only one who sensed some greater significance in the sound of Toby's laughter.

A connection of the very best kind had just been made.

'He's gorgeous,' said Annabelle. 'I want him.'

'Sorry, he's already taken.'

They were heading downstairs after showing Toby to his room, the one he would be sharing with Marcio, and where he was now unpacking his things.

'Have you told him about Mo yet?'

'No.'

'Why not?'

'I want him to form his own opinion of her first.'

'I think he already has.'

'Maybe I'm just worried about how he's going to take it.'

Annabelle laid a hand on Ben's arm, holding him back on the landing. 'I know there's not much an old spinster like me can teach you, but from what I saw at lunch I'd say if you're happy, he's happy.' She paused. 'Don't leave it too long or he'll wonder why you did.'

'Sounds advice . . . for an old spinster.'

Annabelle smiled. 'We have our uses.'

Mo's studio was the first stop on the tour, and they were greeted by the deafening sound of the pneumatic chisel.

She had spent the past few days lending shape to the back of the sculpture, blunting the angularity of the raw block, removing a large amount of material in the process.

'It's amazing,' said Toby, staring at the face.

'Liar,' quipped Mo.

'Really.' Toby told her about their visit to the Cast Courts at the V&A. 'It's much better than anything we saw there, isn't it, Dad?'

'It sure is.'

'Thank you, Toby, you can come again. Hey, you want to have a go?'

Kitted up with a mask and goggles, and with Mo guiding the pneumatic chisel in his hand, Toby stripped some stone from the back of the block.

His 'Wow!' was muffled by the mask. So was his, 'Can I try it by myself?'

'Sure, go for it.' Mo pointed. 'That lump that's sticking out there.'

Toby dealt with it.

'Yep, he's history,' said Mo.

From the stable block they cut through the farm buildings,

Ben pointing out the modern, low-rise structure discreetly tucked away in the trees at the back of the complex. 'That's where Victor keeps his vintage cars. The temperature and the humidity are controlled by a computer.'

'Sweet,' said Toby. 'What's he got?'

'No idea.'

'Dad . . .' came Toby's pained reply. Like a lot of boys his age, he knew way more about cars than was healthy.

'Honestly, I haven't seen inside. But he did mention an old Ferrari.'

'Which one?' asked Toby excitedly.

'I can't remember, maybe a two-seven-something . . .' teased Ben.

'A 275 GTB!'

'Yeah, that could have been it.'

'You're winding me up.'

'No, definitely rings a bell.'

'I'll kill you if you're lying.'

'Perspective, Tobes – it's just a car.'

'Just the best car *ever*.'

They took the track past the run of cottages and set off through the fields, skirting the woods at the centre of the estate. They stopped for a while to watch a combine harvester, shrouded in a pall of dust, stripping a field of wheat back to stubble. They looped back on themselves towards the lake. Toby's eyes lit up when he saw the inside of the boathouse, especially the jet ski tied with a blue ribbon.

'You mustn't say anything – it's Victor's birthday present to Marcio.'

'What's he like?'

'Marcio? A bit older than you, and very sporty, Victor says. I guess we'll find out tomorrow. It's got to be better than having no one to play with.'

'Not if he's a dork.'

Ben had purposely held the swimming pool and the two tennis courts back till last, figuring that it was where Toby would be spending most of his time with Marcio. 'Not bad, huh? There's even a small football pitch on the other side of that hedge.'

'I want to live here.'

'You can buy your own when you're older. All you need is twenty-five million quid.'

'Twenty-five million!'

'Something like that, according to Annabelle, but keep it under your hat.'

Work would have to wait until tomorrow; it was his last chance to spend any real time alone with Toby before Marcio showed up. After two hours of tennis, some keepy-uppy and some lazing by the pool Ben still hadn't rustled up the courage to break the news about Mo. Later, he told himself. Besides, there was only just enough time to shower and change before their six o'clock croquet appointment with her on the back lawn.

She was already there, practising on her own, when they came downstairs. 'You guys are in serious trouble,' she said. 'I'm on fire.'

Ten minutes later, and with Ben leading by a hoop and a half, she had changed her tune.

'OK, Toby, here it is. The only way we're going to wipe that smug grin off your dad's face is if we work together. A word of warning, though – watch your back, 'cos as soon as we've caught him up I'll turn on you in a flash.'

It was where the real joy of croquet lay, in the delicious contrast between the surface gentility of the game and the ruthless betrayals required for victory.

'Not if I turn on you first,' said Toby.

Mo squared off. 'Big words for a small man, buster.'

They were close to catching Ben up when his phone buzzed in his pocket. Unknown number.

'Hello.'

'It's me,' came a woman's voice. 'Chiara.'

'Chiara . . .' The word slipped from his lips. 'Hold on a moment.' He raised a couple of fingers to Mo and mouthed, 'Two minutes,' before strolling off, out of earshot. 'Thanks for calling,' he said. 'How are you?'

'OK,' Chiara replied, guardedly.

'How was China?'

'China was—'

'Don't bother,' Ben broke in. 'I know.'

There was a brief silence. 'Ah . . .'

'I hope you were well paid.'

'And I hope you enjoyed it.'

'I did. A lot.'

'*Anch'io*,' she said softly in Italian: me too. 'I'm sorry he told you.'

'He didn't. I figured it out for myself.'

'Is that what you wanted me to know?'

'No,' he replied, fearing she'd hang up if he didn't keep her guessing.

At that moment Victor, fresh back from London, appeared at the top of the rear staircase. He gave a wave, which Ben returned with mechanical brightness.

'Ben?'

He was strangely touched that she'd used his name. 'What did you mean by *chi va piano*?' This was the cryptic message she'd left for him at the hotel.

'*Chi va piano va sano e va lontano.*'

'I know what it means, I looked it up.' *He who goes slowly goes safely and far.* 'It sounds like some kind of warning.'

'It's like when you say "Take care" in English.'

'No, it isn't, that's *Stammi bene*. There's something you're not telling me.'

He thought for a moment that she'd hung up on him.

'How well do you really know Victor? That's all I'm going to say.'

'Chiara, please—'

'That's not my name. And this conversation never happened. I mean it. We never spoke.'

Victor had descended the steps and was now making his way across the lawn towards them.

'At least tell me your real name.'

'Raffaella.'

'It suits you.'

'Goodbye, Ben.'

She was gone, and Victor was offering his hand to Toby. 'You must be Toby. I'm Victor.'

Toby shook Victor's hand. 'Pleased to meet you. Is it true you have a Ferrari 275 GTB?'

Victor laughed. 'Yes, yes I do.'

'Which one?'

'You know about cars?'

'Not much.'

'Well, it's a GTB/4 N.A.R.T. Spyder.'

'No way! They only made ten of them.'

Victor tilted his head at Toby. 'Not much . . .?'

'Well, a bit,' came Toby's bashful reply.

'What do you say we take it for a spin when Marcio's here? He hasn't seen it yet.'

'I'd love to join you,' said Mo, 'but I'm flossing my teeth then.'

'Cars don't do it for Mo,' explained Victor.

'What can I say? I'm a freak, me and six billion other people on the planet.'

Victor turned down their offer of making up a foursome; he had an urgent call to make to the States. Ben only just managed to hold on to his lead to take the first game, but the phone call had shaken him badly and he wasn't even in the running for the next one. It didn't help his concentration when Mo asked, 'So, who's Chiara?'

She had just ruthlessly dispatched Toby's ball to the far end of the lawn, quite possibly with a view to a bit of privacy.

'An Italian friend.'

'From Como?'

'No, not from Como.' He hoped the note of genial

tolerance was convincing. 'From London. She's been having problems. I had to take the call.'

'Man trouble?'

'Work. She missed out on a promotion and now she thinks she's going to be fired.'

Too much information, he told himself. Less is more.

'I look forward to meeting her.'

'And you will.'

He knew he had just dug a big hole for himself. Far worse than that, though, he had just told his first lie to Mo.

Toby loved to be read to in bed. It was an indulgence inherited from Madeleine, who had demanded the same service from Ben. God only knew how many hours he had spent propped up on pillows, reading to one or other of them.

He didn't mind. He enjoyed speaking other people's words, breathing his own life into them. It played to his private passion. His father had always done his best to kill off his interest in acting. 'All actors are narcissists,' he had declared on hearing that Ben had been cast as Iago in the Fifth Form production of *Othello* at Dean House. Ben had looked the word up later, struggling to square the dictionary definition of 'narcissist' with the pleasure he got from performing. Acting, it seemed to him, had nothing to do with an excessive interest in oneself. Quite the opposite, in fact. It was about emptying yourself and allowing someone else to inhabit you. It was a game of make-believe in which you hardly figured at all, even when you took a bow at the end.

His father needn't have worried. In his second year at

Charterhouse stage fright had put paid to Ben's secret ambition. Looking back, it was probably no more than paralysing adolescent self-consciousness, and it had taken him twenty years to understand that writing words for actors was the consolation prize, the next best thing to the career which had slipped through his fingers.

'Just a few pages, Dad. I know the others are waiting.'

Ben could tell that Toby wasn't really listening, which only made sense when he asked suddenly, 'Is Mo your girlfriend?'

'Why?'

'Mum asked me about her when we spoke earlier.'

'What did she say?'

'Nothing. But she asked.'

'And what did you say?'

'That she's OK.'

'OK?'

'I didn't want to say I really liked her. I mean, really, REALLY like her.'

'You're such a sweet boy, Tobes. I don't know what we did to deserve you.'

Toby laid his head against Ben's chest, draping an arm across his midriff. 'She's just the best thing, Dad.'

'Yeah, she's all right, isn't she?'

It had chilled off outside, and when Ben made his way downstairs he found that the others had decamped from the terrace to the table in the kitchen.

'What a great kid,' said Victor. 'And so grown-up for thirteen.'

'He hasn't had much choice in it.'

'Same goes for Marcio, but there's no way he could talk to adults like that.'

'You don't know that,' said Annabelle. 'They change so quickly at this age, and it's been a while since you last saw him.'

'Not for lack of trying,' replied Victor defensively.

'I know. I didn't mean it like that.'

Victor turned to Ben. 'His mother doesn't make it easy.'

'Understatement of the year,' said Mo.

'Mo and Luciana didn't exactly hit it off.'

'It was all going so well until she called me a *puta de merda*.'

'That's practically a term of endearment for Luciana,' chuckled Victor. 'You should have heard what she called me on the phone the other day because I wouldn't send the jet to Paris to pick up Marcio.'

The moment the whisky bottle hit the table, Annabelle bade them goodnight. Mo wasn't far behind, which left Ben torn. He wanted to fall asleep and wake up beside her as he had last night, and yet he also needed to have it out with Victor. A lot of good things had come his way recently, and he'd held himself in check because of it. Raffaella was in a whole different league, though. He couldn't just let that go.

Victor suggested they move through to his study.

'Sure' said Ben. 'I've just got to shake hands with an old friend.' It was the euphemism they'd used as kids.

He arrived in the study to find Victor seated at his desk, bathed in an eerie glow from the bank of monitors. Music was playing, something classical.

'Here.'

Victor tore off the cheque he'd been writing and handed it to him. It was made out for sixty thousand pounds, the payee left blank.

'It's the Stoneham Village Church Appeal.'

Victor took the cheque back and filled it out. 'Don't want to put temptation in the Colonel's path.'

Ben glanced at the screens. There were multi-coloured graphs and columns of flickering, ever-changing numbers.

'Make any sense?' Victor asked.

'About as much as sheet music.'

'That's a good analogy. It's like music, a giant symphony that never stops.'

'How's it sounding right now?'

'Disturbed. Like the third movement of Mahler's Seventh.'

'I wish I could give a knowing laugh, but I have no idea what you're talking about.'

'That's easily fixed.' Victor reached for an iPad on the desk.

They settled into the leather sofas that split the room in two and listened in silence to the third movement of Mahler's Seventh Symphony. Even to Ben's untrained ear there was something unhinged about its efforts to sound stirring, as if order and anarchy were locked in battle, a dirty struggle for the upper hand that neither of them could ever win.

Five minutes in, Victor produced a box of cigars, and they were puffing away merrily when the movement ended.

'That's what it sounds like.'

'I'd get out now, if I were you,' suggested Ben.

Victor laughed. 'Challenging, isn't it? Like all the best things.' He turned down the volume for the next movement, which was quite different, almost romantic in its mood. 'It was the Seventh Symphony that convinced Schoenberg Mahler was a genius.'

'When did you learn so much about music?'

'It's been more than twenty-five years.'

'True.'

Victor drew on his cigar, tilting his head back and emitting a long plume of smoke which faded into nothingness beyond the tight pool of light thrown by the two standard lamps. 'I've worked hard at it. I've had to. My parents never once took me to a concert. They thought it would be wasted on me.'

'I'm sure that's not true.'

'I didn't say it for the sake of it,' replied Victor darkly. 'They were never happy with what the stork brought them – two academics lumbered with a dunce of a son.'

It was all beginning to sound rather self-pitying, although there was no catch in Victor's voice.

'Remember "Thicko Hogg"? Of course you do. I struggled. I've always struggled. I was never like you. Things didn't come easy to me.' He paused to take a sip of whisky. 'I was born with a mix of visual and auditory processing issues. I know that now, and I've learned ways to get around them. I've had help, a lot of help, but never one thing from my parents, just a sort of . . .' he searched for the right words, – 'embarrassed silence.'

'Are you talking about a sort of dyslexia?'

'A stupid catch-all term, like "autism". But yes, something like that.'

'It was a different time. There was so little talk of it back then.'

'There was enough. They chose to ignore it.' Victor paused thoughtfully. 'I once overheard them talking to some friends of theirs. It was before I moved back to the States, while I was still at Dean House. I can still hear my father saying it: "Jacob's the flower of the class," and my mother saying, 'The bloomin' idiot."'

'Jesus, it's not even funny.'

'What really got me was the double act, like it was some kind of comedy routine they'd worked before and would work again.'

'Are they still together?'

'Last I heard. That was twelve years ago, so who knows?'

He had severed all ties with his parents, but not before sitting down and calculating just how much he had cost them over the years. 'I even accounted for lost interest and added five per cent to cover any oversights. Then I sent them a cheque for the full amount, with a thank you card. It had a drawing of three pears on the front – two big, one small. Inside it said, "You're The Best Pearents In The World". You have no idea how good it felt.'

'No regrets?'

'None. It freed me to get on with my life. I haven't looked back since.'

Maybe it was true, but it seemed to Ben that looking back was something Victor did a fair bit of. Their conversations had always been informed by a keen sense of memory on Victor's part, right down to the exact scorelines in tennis matches Ben had played at Dean House.

'Do you ever wonder if my father was screwing your mother?' Victor asked unexpectedly.

'No! Why?'

'I don't know, there was something there. The times he flew in to take me back for the holidays he always stayed at your place, often when your dad was away on business.'

'My mother's not like that.'

'What if I said I knew for a fact they'd had an affair?' Victor's face was still as stone.

'I'd say Mo was right – your nostrils flare slightly when you're lying.'

Victor laughed. 'Damn, I've got work on that that "tell".' He pinched his nose. 'You know, I used to wish there was something going on between them, that it would turn into something bigger. We would have been brothers, then.'

'Stepbrothers.'

'Don't take it the wrong way, we both know I was a fucked-up kid.'

'Not that fucked-up.'

'Kleptomania doesn't exactly scream stable and happy child.'

That caught Ben by surprise. It was an uncomfortable subject, the root cause of all the bad things that had happened between them back then. 'No, I guess not,' he replied warily.

'You don't want to talk about it?'

'You do?'

'No point in pretending it didn't happen,' shrugged Victor. 'And I'm sorry. I never really apologised to you, not properly.'

'No, fuck you, you stole my catapult. Apology rejected.'

Victor threw his head back and laughed. 'God, what was I thinking?'

'It doesn't matter now.'

Victor leaned forward and tapped the ash from the end of his cigar. 'Hey, I've got to ask. It *was* you, wasn't it, who found the stuff in the attic and handed it in to Burroughs?'

'What? No.'

'Come on,' Victor drawled. 'Like you say, it doesn't matter now.'

But there was a flicker of something in his eyes that didn't square with the matey tone.

'It wasn't me. And we should probably leave it at that. Remember what happened last time we had this talk.'

'Yeah, you kicked my ass.'

'Not exactly.'

'Close enough. You know, I was sure I had you. I was bigger than you then, just for that one year. You hadn't started to grow yet. But you were quicker. You were always quicker.'

'I had to be. You were pretty worked up.'

'You remember it?'

Ben leaned forward, reaching for his glass. 'Who knows what any of us really remembers. I read this piece recently on the fallibility of memory. It was in *Nature*, I think, or maybe it was the *New Scientist*—'

'Point proved.'

Ben smiled. 'They reckon there's no such thing as an unchanging memory, not like we think of a file on computer, say – something that can be pulled up over and over in exactly the same form. Apparently our memories are assembled from different parts of the brain, bolted together from thousands of different places in a moment. One of those places is our sense of our self in the past, which is changing all the time.'

'You're saying we didn't have a fight in the woods?'

'No, but the fight I had isn't the one you had. And in a year's time it'll be different again for both of us.'

He was pleased with himself. He'd successfully killed off the discussion, drowning it in layman's science he'd lifted from a magazine. He also saw an opportunity.

'I have a memory, a recent one. It's of my meeting with your head of security.'

'Dominic.'

'Yes, Dominic, when he was posing as some bigwig at the Serious Fraud Office.'

'You're not still pissed about that, are you?'

'No. Yes. A little.

'Think about the eight million pounds,' Victor replied, his voice cool and removed. 'That should help.'

It was a warning shot across Ben's bows, but he stuck to his course. 'That's not why I brought it up.'

Victor spread his hands. 'Fire away.'

He had to play it carefully, if only for Raffaella's sake. There had been a note of fear in her voice when she'd told him Victor was never to know that they'd talked.

'He was laying it on thick at the time, how he knew about the trip to Como, how I hadn't booked the flight or paid for the hotel – stuff he'd got from you, I guess.' When Victor didn't react, he went on. 'He even knew that the woman I had dinner with on Saturday night had picked up the tab at the restaurant.'

'What woman?'

It wasn't convincing.

'I think we both know what woman.'

Victor sank back slowly into the sofa. 'Oh, Dom, Dom, Dom . . .'

'He fucked up.'

'He sure did.'

'You hired me a hooker?'

Victor winced. 'Ooooh, she wouldn't like that. And hooker hardly does justice to her special talents, wouldn't you say?'

Special talents which, by implication, Victor had also sampled.

'I wouldn't know, never having slept with one before.'

Victor snorted derisively. 'Come on, Ben, don't be so fucking self-righteous.'

'I'm not. People can do what the hell they like in my book. It's their choice. All I'm saying is it wasn't mine. You made it for me.'

'Tell me it wasn't amazing. She says it was.'

He resisted the flattery. 'What, you have a post-mortem every time you farm her out to one of your friends?'

'If you really want to know, that's the first time I've ever asked Raffaella to do me a favour.'

'Raffaella?' he replied in the nick of time, wondering if he'd just slipped a trap.

'Or whatever she called herself.'

'Chiara.'

Victor's tone softened to one of apology. 'Look, it was a misjudgement, OK? But she was meant as a gift. You'd been banging on to me at the Wolseley about your crappy love life.'

'Hardly banging on.'

Victor seemed both amused and exasperated. 'Ben, listen. Everyone had fun, no one died. Let's face it, worse things have happened to better men.'

Mo had fallen asleep with the light on while reading Ben's book in bed. He woke her with a kiss.

'*Mmmm*, whisky and cigars,' she said groggily.

'I'm sorry.'

The bedside light was off by the time he returned from the bathroom.

'Just hold me,' she said, nestling against him. He slid his hand beneath her T-shirt and stroked her back with his fingertips.

'I told Toby about us.'

'What did he say?'

'What do you think? He's totally sold on you.'

'That's because I let him loose on dangerous machinery.'

He smiled. 'Yeah, that must be it.' He hesitated before adding, 'I also told Madeleine.' He felt her stiffen slightly.

'How did she take it?'

'Nowhere near as well as Toby, but she knew she was being an arse.'

'Do you still love her? I'd understand if you did.'

'You really think I'm going to fall for that?'

He couldn't see her smile in the darkness, but he could hear it.

She fell asleep almost immediately. Listening to the gentle ebb and flow of her breathing, he found himself reflecting on the conversation with Victor. It had marked a shift away from the good-natured exchanges of the past weeks. In fact, there had been a distinct taste of the old days about it, a sort of smouldering antagonism.

thirty years before . . .

J ACOB WAS ALMOST unrecognisable when he stepped through the arrivals gate at Gatwick airport. His hair had grown over the summer holidays, and so had he, by a good three or four inches.

'Excuse me, sir,' joked Ben's father. 'We're waiting for a young boy called Jacob Hogg. You haven't seen him, by any chance, have you?'

'Leonard . . . Ben.' Jacob's voice had broken too, plunging a couple of registers, and there was bum fluff on his top lip.

These physical changes earned Jacob membership of a select club of three during the autumn term of their last year at Dean House. There had been little to connect the three boys before then, but they now seemed to gravitate towards each other, an alien triumvirate outnumbered by hordes of shrill and hairless midgets. They soon came to understand that their extra size and strength counted for something, although these advantages were offset by a gawkiness which did them few favours on the football pitch. Jacob was angrier than ever that he didn't make the First XI, demanding that Ben do something to rectify this injustice, whereas in the past he had pleaded.

Ben might have been more irritated by such antics if he'd had time to dwell on them, but his position as head boy filled his days and evenings with duties, everything from assigning tasks to his troop of prefects and monitors to doling out punishments for minor offences. He was also studying for the scholarship exam to Charterhouse, which he and Henry Clayton were due to sit at the end of term. Even if they weren't successful they would probably be offered places, sparing them the standard entrance exam in the summer, and the thought of two idle terms after Christmas was enough to make him study like a medieval monk now.

It paid off, the letter arriving at home a week after they'd broken up for the holidays. His father failed to mask his disappointment that Ben had only been awarded a Junior Scholarship (whereas he, of course, had been a Senior Scholar at Charterhouse). This stung. His father seemed to take all his achievements as given, and therefore not worthy of comment, let alone praise. He hadn't come to one football match during the term, choosing to shoot pheasants on Saturday afternoons rather than watch his son captain the 1st XI to their first unbeaten season in more than ten years. Hardly one mention of that success, but the moment he felt Ben had failed in some way he was all over it.

Ben wasn't conscious of it, but the resentment must have sat there and simmered away. He was as surprised as anyone by his sudden outburst during lunch on Christmas Day.

Grandmother was staying with them, as she always did. It was her second Christmas as a widow, and this year she felt up to going to church, which was always followed by drinks at the Flanagans', in their big house beside the village pond.

Back at home, the phone rang as the turkey was about to hit the table. It was the Hoggs, calling from America. Ben hovered in the hallway, trying to make sense of the conversation between the two fathers once the standard festive greetings had been exchanged: 'That's wonderful news! . . . No, no, it'll be a pleasure . . . (a little chuckle) . . . We love having him here . . . Anything we can do to help. It goes without saying . . . Of course, of course, I'll go and get her. Ben's here, I'll put him on.'

Ben's brief conversation with Jacob didn't do much to clarify things.

'Happy Christmas.'

'You too,' said Ben.

'What did you get?'

'Don't know. We haven't done presents yet.'

'I got a Sony Walkman. It's the WM-F2, the one with the radio.'

'Cool,' said Ben.

'And you can record on it as well.'

His mother appeared in the hallway, drying her hands on her apron. 'I think my mum wants to speak to your dad.'

'OK. Have a good one.'

'You too.'

Ben soon discovered that Jacob's parents' plans had changed.

They would now be returning to England in a year or two's time, and rather than yanking Jacob back there after Dean House, it made sense for them to leave him in the English schooling system.

This was the cause of much celebration over lunch, and a fair bit of speculation. Which school should Jacob go to after Dean House? And could he achieve the sixty per cent average required by Charterhouse? Ben suspected not, but he didn't say anything.

Mention of Charterhouse set Grandmother off. 'It's most unfortunate you weren't awarded a Senior Scholarship.'

'I'm sure it was a close-run thing,' his father replied. 'In fact, I know it was.'

'How?' asked Ben.

'I spoke to them. Your Latin was a bit below par.'

'My Latin?'

'That's what they said. And they set great store by Latin.'

'They always have,' said Grandmother. 'I'm just sorry you didn't know that.'

His father seemed to take this as a criticism. 'I can assure you he did.'

'That's not true. You never said anything.'

'Ben.' There was a snap in his father's voice.

'I tried my best.'

His mother came to his defence. 'Exactly, he tried his best.'

'And on the day he fell short,' retorted Grandmother. She turned her gaze back to Ben. 'Well, you know how to make up for it, don't you?'

'No, Grandmother, I don't.'

'Then let me tell you,' she replied tightly. 'When it comes to your O levels you beat them all hands down. All of them.'

She was talking about a set of exams more than three years away, and he felt breathless, squeezed in the grip of her expectation.

'What if I can't?'

'Can't isn't a word in this family's vocabulary.'

'And what about "Well done, Ben"?'

'That's three words.'

Ben counted them out on his fingers. 'Well . . . done . . . Ben. Sorry, you're right.'

'Ben . . .'

His mother's gentle plea was drowned out by his father. 'Don't be sarcastic with your grandmother!'

He knew the signs. His father had drunk enough to start raising his voice. He knew he should tread carefully. But something drove him on.

'Will Jacob get in? Won't Jacob get in? Well, I've already got in, and with a scholarship.'

'Jacob doesn't have your gifts,' countered his father.

'Jacob's got loads of gifts, you just don't know what they are.'

'And what's that supposed to mean?'

Ben caught his mother's warning look out of the corner of his eye and he back-pedalled. 'It means why don't you ever come to watch me play football?'

It was Grandmother who replied. 'Do you think those poor boys who fought for King and Country in the First

War needed their fathers beside them in the trenches? No, they didn't. They got on with it.'

'But I bet their fathers weren't at home drinking too much and killing innocent birds.'

The words were stolen from his mother's mouth, and he'd heard her say them enough times to know what his father's reaction would be.

'Go to your room!'

He didn't protest. He placed his napkin beside his plate, glanced at Emily (who had had been silent throughout and whose jaw was now practically on the table) then left the dining room.

'Hormones,' he heard his grandmother say as he stumped upstairs. 'It has to be. He's at that age.'

Maybe she was right. He had never pushed things so far before, and he hadn't intended to. It had just happened, the words rising up from somewhere deep inside him. He felt strangely calm. He could have destroyed all their illusions about Jacob in a moment. He could have destroyed Jacob. He hadn't, though. He had wandered to the edge of the cliff, peered over the drop and then walked away.

He tried to lose himself in his book. He was reading *Of Mice and Men* by John Steinbeck. If nothing else, the Great Depression helped put his own hunger in perspective.

An hour or so later his mother appeared in his room. 'Dad says you can come down now. *Chitty Chitty Bang Bang* is about to start.'

It was tempting, but George had just gone into town with the other ranch hands and Lennie was talking to

Crooks in the stables. He could tell things were about to turn nasty.

'I'm OK,' he said, holding up the book.

His mother came and perched beside him on his bed. She stroked his hair. 'Are you, *piccinino*? Are you really?'

He loved it when the Italian words of her youth popped out. He loved it when she stroked his hair.

'I'll never be like that with my son,' he said, tears threatening to spill from his eyes.

'It's not his fault, it's her fault. And it's probably not her fault, it's someone else's. *Così va il mondo*.' She lay down beside him and kissed him on the cheek. 'Read to me.'

Jacob had grown another inch over the Christmas holidays and he seemed to have changed shape around the neck and the shoulders. He easily won himself a place in the 1st XV rugby team, playing number 8, which meant working closely with Ben at scrum half. Jacob loved to pick up and go from the back of the scrum, and Ben was always at his heels, ready to recycle the ball. A sort of sixth sense quickly sprang up between them. They just seemed to know where the other one was, to the point that blind passes and offloads became a feature of their game. Together, they wreaked havoc on the opposition.

It was a special time, not just for the team but for their friendship. The rugby bound them together in a way that nothing else had before now. During exeat weekends at home they worked on special routines in the garden, inventing their own coded calls for dummy, reverse and pop passes. Their only defeat came just after half-term, but that was down to a biased referee who blew up for every infringement Dean House committed (and many they didn't) while allowing his own team to knock-on and stray offside. At the final whistle Ben had to restrain Jacob, who looked as if he might take a swing at the bow-legged little Scotsman who had robbed them of victory.

Ben's parents came to watch the last match of the term – the local derby against their arch rivals, Barton Court. Jacob played out of his skin, marauding like a man possessed, making barnstorming runs. Last year they had been thrashed, but with a couple of minutes left to play they were trailing by just three points and their pack was driving for Barton Court's line. They won themselves a penalty which Gideon Shorrock could easily have converted for an honourable draw. As captain, it was Ben's call. His forwards were braying for a scrum and a shot at a winning try, which was just fine by him. Victory or bust.

Their pack soaked up the determined push from Barton Court and even gained a few more yards of territory. The ball was at Jacob's feet and Ben was judging his options. He drifted off the back of the scrum, sending a message to the opposition that Jacob was about to pick up and go. Their scrum half yelled for more support on the blind side. That's when Ben saw the opening in the defensive line.

'Atticus!' he called.

Atticus was their secret weapon, never before deployed: a feint from Jacob followed by a blind handoff pass to Ben on the open side. They had worked the move over and over in the garden, refining it, but as Ben burst forward the ball never came. He was past the scrum before he knew it, ghosting through the gap and shrugging off a desperate lunge from Dean Court's fly half. If he'd had the ball in his hand he would have scored the winning points. As it was, Jacob came hurtling past him and dived over the line for the try. The referee blew the whistle and Jacob was smothered by his fellow forwards.

The referee had to blow his whistle many more times before he had everyone's attention. He pointed at Ben. 'Obstruction on Dean Court's fly half. Try disallowed.'

Ben couldn't argue with the call, that's how it must have looked, as if he'd bulldozed a path for his big number 8. At best, Jacob had gone for glory; at worst, he'd sacrificed victory to make Ben look foolish in front of his teammates and the supporters.

'Did we lose because of Ben?' he heard Emily ask his father as they all trooped off the pitch.

It was his mother who replied. 'No, darling, they were just unlucky.'

Jacob was rightly awarded man of the match, and Ben did nothing to sour his moment or feed the general disappointment. He bided his time, waiting till after supper, falling into step beside Jacob as he made his way towards the table-tennis room.

'Atticus.'

'What about it?'

'We would have won.'

Jacob stopped and turned. His left eye was swollen from battle, giving his face a lopsided look.

'It's just a game of rugby,' he said. 'Get over it.'

Ben found himself alone in the corridor.

Maybe Jacob was right. Maybe he was overreacting. But even if he was, why had Jacob soaked up every single word of consolation for his disallowed try? Why hadn't he deflected at least some of the blame away from Ben?

six days to go . . .

B EN KNEW WHERE the Colonel lived, because he and Mo
had seen the old fellow safely home on Sunday night after
the victory celebration in the pub. Someone had needed to.

He rang the front-door bell of the old stone cottage and
pinched the sweat from his eyes. He had pushed it hard from
Stoneham Park. The Colonel answered the door in khaki
trousers, penny loafers and a pale green button-down shirt
– dapper as ever, even at this early hour. He peered over the
tortoiseshell spectacles perched on the end of his nose.

'My dear boy, what can I get you? A glass of water? A
doctor?'

The Colonel was having his breakfast at a cast-iron table
in the back garden: toast, orange juice, a pot of coffee and a
boiled egg (trepanned but not yet eaten).

'I'm sorry to interrupt you.'

'Don't be silly, it's a pleasure to have some company.'

The Colonel poured him a cup of coffee. A copy of *The
Times* was open at the obituary notices.

'It's the first thing I do every day – check to see who's died.

No one today. Lost an old friend last week, though. Roddy Inglewood. Such an amusing chap when we were younger, but he never managed to reconcile himself to the advancing years. Became a caustic old bugger towards the end.'

The Colonel took a mouthful of egg then dabbed at his mouth with a napkin. 'Plato was right when he said an old man may become twice a child, but I don't see there's any earthly reason why he shouldn't be a good child – polite, intelligent, considerate. It's one of the many things Felicity taught me.'

They chatted away, chiefly about the Colonel's garden, with its bowling-green lawn and its immaculate flower beds festooned with roses. It was a while before the Colonel finally asked what had brought Ben there.

Ben reached into the pocket of his running shorts and handed over the cheque.

The Colonel appeared genuinely shaken. 'Oh, my goodness. Oh, my goodness . . .'

'He added a bit extra for overages.'

'You know what this means, don't you?'

'That you can start work immediately.'

'No, it means I can *stop* work immediately. No more endless committee meetings and quiz nights and raffles and bobbing for bloody apples in the village hall.' For all the Colonel's efforts to make light of it, he looked moved almost to tears by the gesture. 'I'll write Mr Sheldon a letter he won't ever forget, but thank *you*, Ben.' He reached across the table and gripped Ben's forearm to reinforce the message. 'You've made an old man very happy.'

If this was a foretaste of what he could expect in his new role as Victor's head of philanthropy then the future promised to be very rewarding. Sixty thousands pounds was a mere fraction of the sums Victor was proposing to give away.

'There's one condition,' Ben explained. 'It has to be an anonymous donation. He doesn't want people thinking he's trying to win favour in the village.'

'I'm not sure I can guarantee that. There are some accomplished gossips on the committee.'

'I don't suppose he'll mind too much if there are rumours.'

'Ah, generosity coupled with humility,' said the Colonel knowingly.

'It's just a guess, so try and keep it under wraps.'

Ben had walked home on Sunday night with Mo, leaving the BMW parked at the sports ground. He had the motorcycle keys with him, and the Colonel accompanied him most of the way, bearing a freshly cut rose for his wife's grave. They parted company at the wooden gates to the overflow cemetery.

'I've already told her what a fine young man you are. She'll have to believe me now.'

'Don't sit on the cheque,' Ben found himself saying. 'Bank it quickly.'

'Why do you say that?'

'No reason.'

Marcio was on an early morning flight from Paris Charles de Gaulle, and Victor made a point of picking him up in person from Heathrow. Father and son were back at Stoneham Park by late morning.

Marcio was a handsome boy, tall and honey-skinned, with large dark eyes which seemed incapable of settling on anything for more than a moment or two – not so much shy as mistrustful.

The two boys greeted each other in the way that boys of that age did: with a nod and a grunt and an appraising glance at each other's shoes. Both were wearing DC skate shoes, which boded well, and when Marcio produced a skateboard from his big black travel bag, they slouched off upstairs to their room, speaking a foreign language of decks, trucks, ollies, kickflips and frontside fakies.

'Well, that's them sorted,' observed Annabelle drily.

Lunch was homemade burgers down by the pool. The smooth travertine pool surround was ideal for skateboarding, and the boys laid on a display while Gregoire toiled away at the barbecue, grilling peppers and courgettes before moving on to the meat.

Marcio was a proficient skateboarder with a limited bag of tricks which he insisted on performing over and over until Victor finally called, 'Let Toby have a go.' Ben had sat and watched Toby do his thing at the Stockwell skatepark enough times to know exactly what he was capable of, and he looked on with pride as Toby toned down his act, sticking to basic tricks, even fumbling landings he would normally have nailed so as not to outshine Marcio.

Mo didn't hang around for the unveiling of Marcio's birthday present after lunch. It was hard to say whether Marcio was disappointed or just puzzled by the jet ski. He'd never heard of the make before.

'That's because it's electric,' Victor explained. 'One of the first of its kind.'

As a rule, Ben detested jet skis, but this machine was a revelation: speedy as hell and yet almost entirely silent. Marcio was beaming by the time he and Victor returned from a training spin around the lake. The batteries were good for a couple of hours of fun, and after dishing out the usual stuff about not showing off and always wearing life vests, they left the boys to it and strolled back to the house.

Victor knew that Ben liked to get to the end of a script before showing it to anyone, but he was desperate to read the changes so far. 'It's eating me up.'

Ben was happy to make an exception. For once, he was actually quite proud of the work he'd done. He read through the revisions, made a couple of minor adjustments then printed out the first forty pages in Annabelle's office. He dropped them off with Victor, who was on a conference call in his study, padding around the room in his bare feet.

An hour later, Victor appeared in the library. He didn't say anything. He wandered over, dropped the pages on the table and planted himself in a chair.

'Fucking amazing.'

'You think so?' asked Ben, feeling the warm glow spread through him.

'Way better than I ever dreamed. It's crisper, funnier, more menacing, and as for the relationship between Malik and Amy . . .'

'Yeah, that's coming along, isn't it?'

'Coming along? It's Romeo and Juliet. They've got to die, of course. Just kidding.'

'Phew.'

Victor leaned forward and drummed his fingertips lightly on the table. 'I've been thinking about what you said and I've got a proposal to make. You're worried about your writing taking a back seat, so what about this . . .?'

'This' turned out to be an offer from Tortoise Pictures to buy up Ben's other spec script along with the three feature film ideas Stella had sent them.

'That's everything I have.'

'They're all strong, commercial ideas, and this way you know they'll have a life, you'll know I'm serious about making the writing fit in with the other stuff.'

Ben didn't want to sound ungrateful, but he had been talking about a different kind of writing. He had imagined himself in his book-lined study in his smart new flat in South Kensington penning plays, or possibly a novel, when not distributing Victor's fortune to worthy causes.

'You don't look convinced,' said Victor. 'But you'll make it work. We'll make it work.'

Ben found Mo slumped in a chair staring at her sculpture.

'What's up?'

She turned, dead-eyed. 'I think it's finished.'

He wandered up behind her and rested his hands on her shoulders.

'What do you reckon?'

'It looked finished to me two days ago.'

'Well, it wasn't. It still isn't.' She gathered up a mallet and chisel, advanced on the sculpture and removed the barest chip of stone.

'Yep, that's much better,' said Ben.

He followed her as she made a tour, stopping to tap away every so often. He could sympathise. The minute refinements were the sculptor's equivalent of him neurotically changing commas for semi-colons, semi-colons for colons, colons for dashes, before firing off a script.

She must have sensed something in him because she turned and asked, 'Are you OK?'

'Victor keeps offering me things, my son is rocketing around a lake on a battery-powered jet ski and my girlfriend has just finished her sculpture. The world's turned very weird very quickly.'

'Your girlfriend?' she asked teasingly. 'Come on, I've got a bottle of champagne in the fridge to celebrate. I figure you deserve a glass for saving me God knows how many months of carving hair.'

'I hope your client doesn't feel cheated.'

'He saw it yesterday and he's very happy with my new direction. It *is* mine, by the way. I'll swear you had no hand in it.'

They lay low in the water, facing each other from opposite ends of her big bathtub, legs intertwined. Ben savoured a sip of champagne. 'What will you do now?'

'There's talk of another commission for Victor. And the gallery's leaning on me for a show next year.'

'Could you even live in London?'

'I couldn't afford the rent. Rents. There's the studio to think of too.'

'Come and live with me . . . us . . . me and Toby.'

There. He'd been thinking it, and now he'd said it.

Mo didn't reply immediately. 'That's . . . kind of sudden, isn't it?'

'You don't think it would work?'

'I didn't say that.'

'I'm not asking you to marry me.'

'Two proposals from two different men in one week – that would have been something.' She reached out and rubbed his knee. 'I'm sorry, I didn't mean to bring him up.'

'Connor proposed? You could have said.'

'I just did.'

'What did you tell him?'

'Yes. And that the best way to break it to you was naked in the bath . . . idiot.'

There was nothing in Mo's behaviour that evening to suggest he had freaked her out too badly. During dinner at the kitchen table she touched him several times, the tender, unthinking gestures of a couple.

Dinner was fun, with a lot of laughs and some spot-on impersonations of well-known actors from Marcio, who turned out to be a gifted mimic. He soon blotted his copybook, though, kicking up an embarrassing fuss when they all traipsed through to the saloon to watch a film and the sci-fi thriller he was desperate to see didn't win the vote.

Annabelle's reasoned approach failed, and in the end only a sharp rebuke from Victor silenced him.

While Marcio sulked, Ben found his thoughts straying from the screwball comedy on the giant flat-screen TV. What had driven him to make such an impulsive offer to Mo earlier? She was barely out of a serious relationship. They hardly knew each other. Move in with him? Was he mad?

He wondered if his rash behaviour owed something to his conversation with Raffaella, and the sense of misgiving he hadn't been able to shrug off since: 'How well do you really know Victor?'

Almost everything good and new in his life he held by the grace of Victor. The benefits had been freely given, but they could just as easily be withdrawn. Mo was the one exception. She wasn't Victor's to give or take away. Maybe that's why he had lunged at her. He had needed to know that if all else vanished, she would still be there.

five days to go . . .

THE DAY STARTED badly with a distressed call from Madeleine.

'Basil's dead.'

'Basil? How?'

'I don't know. She's gone.'

'What, escaped? Maybe she'll show up.'

'There's blood, Ben, and bits of fur. Oh God, I really fucked up. Toby was right.' She was close to tears.

They had always teased Toby about his fear of urban foxes, but a mistake had been made – Madeleine had forgotten to shut Basil up in her hutch at night and somehow the rabbit had been snatched from its run. 'What are we going to tell him?'

'Nothing for now.'

'We can't lie to him,' protested Madeleine.

'Mads, we're not lying to him, we're delaying the release of painful information. It'll ruin his time up here.'

'Well, I'm sorry if it can't be the happy little gathering you hoped for.'

Ben refused to be drawn. 'OK, you tell him. It should come from you. I'll just go get him.'

His no-nonsense approach had the desired effect.

'Wait,' said Madeleine. 'Don't.'

They agreed they would shield Toby from the news until Ben drove him back to London on Friday. That wasn't the end of it, though. Madeleine felt the need to explain why she'd failed in her duties.

'It's a bad time. There's a lot going on here, stuff with Lionel's work I can't tell you about. Yes, I screwed up, but if you knew, you'd understand.'

'I do. It's an easy mistake to make.'

There was a brief silence. 'Aren't you even going to ask?'

'About the stuff you can't tell me about?'

'Oh, for God's sake, Ben, you know me far too well to take that literally.'

'Look, I'm sorry if Lionel can't pay himself a two million pound bonus this year.'

'A bonus? We'll be lucky if we get to keep the house.'

She had always had a tendency toward melodrama and exaggeration.

'What do they say? If you dance with the Devil . . .'

'Meaning?'

'Meaning Lionel got his fingers burnt. I'm sure they'll heal.'

'Don't bank on it.'

He wanted to say that 'Multi-millionaire Financier Loses Money' wasn't going to have anyone weeping in the aisles. 'It'll be OK. Remember what we used to say? It's only life.'

'Chaff in the wind.'

'Chaff in the wind,' he repeated.

'Gone in a puff.'

'Exactly.'

'God, I miss you,' she said unexpectedly. 'Tell me you think about me sometimes.'

'Once a month, when the money leaves my account.'

She laughed. 'It all goes to Toby. And you didn't do too badly. I could have asked for more. I might have to now.'

'Don't worry, I can take up the slack.'

He told her about the charitable foundation Victor was setting up and which he would be overseeing in parallel with the writing.

'Sounds like a lot of work.'

'I feel ready for it.'

'Are you on drugs?' she asked.

'Oh God, do you think I'm finally growing up?'

'I hope not, Mouse. I like you just the way you are.'

Ben was on his own with Annabelle and the boys for the day. Mo had hitched a ride into London with Victor to have lunch with a friend and catch a couple of exhibitions.

The boys spent the morning helping with the harvest, returning at lunchtime with tales of driving the combine harvester and riding around in trailers filled with corn. It was good to see them getting on well. Toby was a gentle boy by nature, unthreatening to other kids, and possibly because of this, Marcio seemed to have dropped his guard a touch.

The afternoon passed funereally, time slowing to a trickle

in the library as his thoughts kept drifting towards the phone call with Madeleine. It was years since she'd last called him 'Mouse', the pet nickname she'd coined for him in Sicily during the early days of their relationship. He saw the pensione in Noto, and he saw himself on his hands and knees in their poky bedroom, searching for her contact lens. Disposables were a thing of the future, and if he didn't find it soon it would be dried out and done for. That's why the bedside lights were on the floor and his nose was pressed close to the terrazzo tiles.

'You look like a mouse.'

It had stuck. She had made it stick. One of the readings at their wedding had been 'Mice' by Rose Fyleman, which Edwin had played for laughs, especially the line about mice nibbling things they shouldn't.

Good memories summoned up by a single word, just as Madeleine had intended, he suspected.

Annabelle joined him when he went looking for the boys. They found them down at the lake, back on the jet ski, or rather, Marcio was on the jet ski and Toby was in the water, bobbing about in his life vest.

He must have just fallen off because Marcio was making a long looping turn to pick him up. Pulling alongside, he offered Toby a hand, only to snatch it away and take off again. Funny, but not that funny, thought Ben, picking up his pace. When Marcio made a beeline for Toby, swerving away at the last second, he started to run.

'Marcio!' called Annabelle from behind him.

'Hey!' shouted Ben.

Marcio didn't hear their cries, too absorbed in his game of terrifying Toby, making close pass after close pass. When he finally spotted them, he stopped and hauled Toby from the water. He was laughing, making light of it. Toby wasn't. Ben signalled for them to come in.

He was ready to let rip as the jet ski nudged against the jetty, but Annabelle beat him to it. 'What on earth are you playing at? You could have hit him!'

'It was a joke. And I didn't hit him.'

'It's OK,' said Toby, a slight catch in his voice.

'Yeah, chill,' said Marcio.

'You chill!' snapped Annabelle, which sounded ridiculous. 'And give me that key.'

'It's my jet ski.'

'You don't deserve it. I knew it was a terrible idea.'

Ben helped them both on to the jetty and set about tying up the machine. He saw Annabelle hold out her hand for the key and he saw Marcio dangle it from its cork keyring before letting it fall to the boards just shy of her hand.

'Pick it up,' demanded Annabelle.

'You can't tell me what to do.'

'Oh yes I can, young man – I just have.'

'I've got it,' said Toby, scooping up the key.

'*Baitola*,' Marcio muttered, stalking off.

Annabelle's fury had dropped a notch or two by the time Victor and Mo returned from London. They came bustling into the kitchen with two boxes.

'Quadrocopters for the boys. Where are they?'

'In their room,' said Annabelle. 'Marcio's refusing to come down.'

Victor listened impassively to her account of the incident. 'Sounds like he was just fooling around.'

'Maybe, but it was very dangerous. One small misjudgement . . .'

Victor glanced at Ben who nodded grimly in confirmation. 'I'll go and have a word with him.'

Annabelle followed him from the room.

'Sounds like I chose the right day to be away,' said Mo, approaching. She pecked him on the lips. 'Miss me?'

'Eight or nine on a scale of ten.'

'Then you can have the present I bought you.'

'Enjoy the exhibitions?' he quipped when he saw the shopping bags lined up in the entrance hall.

'It's Charlotte's fault. She led me astray.' She produced a tan leather belt from one of the bags. 'I know it's a bit boring . . .'

'No, it's beautiful. Thank you.'

His offer to help with her shopping bags was really an excuse to get her on her own. When it was rejected, he wandered through to the library and went online, searching for '*Baitola*'.

Marcio's parting insult to Annabelle down at the jetty turned out to be Brazilian slang for 'sissy' or 'faggot', which meant it hadn't been directed at Annabelle but at Toby, presumably for picking up the key.

'Little fucker,' Ben muttered.

He stared blankly at the screen.

He hadn't said anything before, but he could have sworn Mo had told him that the friend she was meeting for lunch in London was called Maggy, not Charlotte.

Peace was quickly restored by Victor. Apologies were made and accepted on all sides, and any lingering stink soon faded as the boys threw themselves into the task of getting the quadrocopters airborne. Annabelle helped, loading up the necessary software on to a couple of iPads. Ben had never even heard of a quadrocopter, but apparently the gadgets could be operated simply by tilting the iPads in the direction you wished them to fly. They were also equipped with cameras which beamed high-definition footage straight to the iPad screens. It was hard to believe, until the two machines rose gracefully from the turf on the back lawn.

'Look, Dad!' exclaimed Toby.

On his screen was a bird's-eye view of the two of them. Ben approached the hovering quadrocopter. He was almost nose to nose with it when it turned and set off down the lawn, pursued by Toby.

Ben and Victor stood watching as the boys got to grips with their new toys. 'What we wouldn't have given for a couple of those,' said Victor.

'Nothing beats dropping an Action Man out of a tree on a parachute made from a handkerchief.'

'Ah, the big cedar tree by your folks' tennis court.'

'You almost killed yourself falling out of that tree.'

'You're right,' said Victor, 'I did.'

'You almost killed yourself on a sledge too.'

'You remember that?'

'I'll never forget it. Scared the living shit out of me.'

Victor glanced off down the lawn. 'I never told you . . . I did it on purpose.'

'What?'

'Steered the sledge off the path.'

'No, you didn't,' scoffed Ben.

Victor shrugged as if to say he didn't care whether Ben believed him or not.

'Why?'

Victor hesitated. 'It was a kind of test. I'll tell you some day.'

'What's wrong with now?'

'When the time's right.' He nodded towards the house. 'Let's go get a drink.'

Mo joined them for dinner but excused herself early, almost as soon as the boys had headed off to watch a film. She wasn't feeling well and wondered if it was the oysters she'd had at lunch.

'Can't be,' ventured Victor. 'The second a bad oyster hits your stomach you know it.'

Either way, Mo was gone for good with a, 'Sorry, I'll see you in the morning,' to Ben.

He knew he wasn't imagining it; there had been something remote about her since her return from London. Oysters? Possibly. He poured himself another glass of wine and forced himself back to the conversation. Annabelle and Victor were discussing which bedrooms to assign to which guests at the weekend.

four days to go . . .

IT WAS PROBABLY the lack of any meaningful sleep, but Ben woke with the feeling that Stoneham Park was fast losing its appeal. For all its obvious beauty, for all the silence, where was the peace? Wasn't that the point of living in a place like this? Why cut yourself off from the frenetic churn of city life only to find yourself tossed on a choppy sea of maudlin introspection.

He lay there and let the black thoughts flap in to roost.

Victor who wasn't even called Victor with his high-class whores and his money and his stories of giving it away (when he wasn't buying vintage speedboats) and of steering sledges off pathways and his weird son who had called Toby a faggot in the tongue of his mother who was a crazy Brazilian cow by all accounts – well, Mo's account anyway – which he probably shouldn't trust because for all her earth-mother posturing she wasn't exactly rock-solid reliable and thanks for the belt by the way but a real kiss would have been nice rather than the firm-lipped pucker you plant on the forehead of an elderly relative about to turn up their toes in some hospital ward.

That'll do for now, he thought, swinging his legs out of bed and making for the bathroom.

The boys spent most of the morning playing tennis and football, which was irritating because Ben was keen to get Toby on his own and talk about yesterday. Toby had handled himself impeccably, heading upstairs in the immediate aftermath of the spat to appease Marcio. This had been fine by Ben at the time, but the thought of his son pandering to that charmless and obstreperous little shit now nettled him. Stand up for yourself, he wanted to tell Toby, don't be a pushover.

He knew he should probably let it lie. Why stir up trouble with only twenty-four hours to go? Tomorrow afternoon he would be driving Toby back to London. He had planned to turn right round and crawl back to Oxfordshire in the Friday rush-hour traffic, but the prospect of staying over suddenly seemed very appealing. He called Edwin.

'What now?' replied an irritated voice.

'Edwin, it's me – Ben.'

'I know, you prick, you're in my phone.'

Edwin was free and up for a night on the tiles. Cassandra and he were no longer an item.

'What happened?'

'I'll bore you with it tomorrow. Bring a hankie.'

Mo didn't appear in person, as she usually did, choosing instead to text him just before lunch with a bland and non-committal: **Hi**

Hi
What's up?
Same old, same old
I'm feeling better
Glad to hear it
Want to pop round and take my temperature?
Can't. Running boys into Oxford
You OK?
Tickety-boo
Rhymes with fuck you
Also rhymes with fuck you too

He guessed she'd be round at any moment, and he was right. Her reply arrived as he was leaving the library: **Don't move**

He was on his fourth length by the time she found him down at the pool. She stood waiting for him at the shallow end, dressed in her overalls, feet stubbornly planted.

'What's going on?' she demanded.

He peered up at her through his swimming goggles. 'You first.' When she didn't respond he turned and pushed off. He was on the return length when the clear water ahead of him was shattered by an explosion of bubbles and limbs. It was Mo, and she was naked.

'What's the matter?' she demanded, pushing her hair out of her eyes.

'Take a wild guess.'

'You lied, you hate the belt.'

He tried not to smile. 'No, just everything else about you last night.'

'I can't keep this up.' She meant the talking while treading water, so they both kicked for the shallows.

He tugged off his goggles. 'You know what I mean.'

'OK,' she conceded. 'I was a bit freaked out by what you said . . . about moving in with you.'

'I'd already figured that.'

'So?'

'So, don't freeze me out. We're too old for that shit. Well, I am.'

She held his look. 'You're right. It was pathetic. I'm sorry.'

'If you've got something to say, just say it. I can take it.'

'OK, but don't hate me for it.'

'Hey, I never said I wouldn't hate you for it.' A little jest squeezed out in spite of the sudden chill in his chest.

'My girlfriends think I'm mad, the ones I've spoken to, which is three. They think I should live a little before rushing into something new. But I woke up this morning and I knew I didn't want to lose you. Yes, I'll move in with you. I want to live with you. I want to give it a go and see what happens.' She broke off briefly. 'There, who's freaked out now?'

Ben sunk low in the water until their heads were level. 'Not me.'

They kissed, his hands straying to her hips, her thighs.

He was aware of a noise, both alien and familiar, but he shut it out. Only when he heard Toby's distant cry – 'Oh gross!' – did he turn and see the quadrocopter hovering nearby, spying on them.

★

Mo fell in with their plans. The boys had searched out a skatepark in Oxford on the internet and she came along for the ride. The 'skatepark' turned out to be one large wooden ramp covered in graffiti in a field near the Iffley road. It was mobbed with older boys, some shirtless and tattooed, leaping about on BMXs, staking their claim. The skateboarders were having to pick their moments carefully. It didn't take much to realise that two thirteen-year-old outsiders with one skateboard between them weren't going to be a welcome addition to the mayhem. If there was any doubt, the hostile glances from a huddle of kids seated in the shade near the trees, smoking and handing round a two-litre bottle of cider, settled the matter for Ben.

'It's too crowded. I think we should go.'

'Dad!' pleaded Toby. 'We've come all this way.'

It was about the first time Ben had seen Marcio looking uncomfortable and he exploited it. 'Marcio?'

Marcio shrugged: couldn't care less either way. He wasn't going to lose face in front of Toby.

'OK, go for it. I hear the food at the JR's pretty good.'

'What's the JR?' asked Marcio.

'The John Radcliffe. It's a hospital, not too far. I can probably get you there in about ten minutes at this time of day.'

'Dad, we'll be OK.'

'Remember, you don't have helmets.'

'Just . . . don't get too close.'

It was Toby's diplomatic way of saying: *Go away, you're destroying our street cred*. He even nodded towards the trees.

'Why are you smiling?' Ben asked as he and Mo were removing themselves to an acceptable distance.

'He's embarrassed by you.'

'No, he's not.'

'Yes, he is.'

'Shit, it's finally started. When does it stop?'

'Twenty-five. Thirty. Never.'

It was the first time Marcio had ever let Toby go first on his skateboard, and for ten minutes nothing happened. Ben knew what Toby was like, though. Marcio or no Marcio, he was going to put down a marker with his first run, he wasn't going to hold back.

'Oh God, here he goes . . .'

Mo was rolling a cigarette. She looked up as Toby dropped in hard, catching a lot of air off the central spine, landing the jump perfectly before sailing up and out of the ramp on the other side, grabbing the board as he cleared the coping. This earned him a couple of nods from some other skaters waiting their turn.

'Way to go, Tobykins!' screamed Mo in a stage whisper. 'He's good.'

His return run was even better. He flipped the board beneath his feet as he shot over the spine. Even Marcio looked impressed, before he remembered himself. Just like his father used to be, it struck Ben. Jacob had always struggled to enjoy other people's prowess and success.

Marcio wasn't going to risk making a fool of himself. He rejected the board every time Toby offered it to him, and when Toby tried to show him how to drop in he wouldn't even step up to the coping. It didn't matter; they had hooked up with a couple of the younger skaters by now and Marcio seemed happy enough to chat and, from the way he kept pointing at his foot, make his excuses. Toby, meanwhile, was trading tricks with the better of their two new friends, trying out some new things. When he fell, which was often, he picked himself up, dusted himself down and tried again until he'd mastered it.

'He's fearless,' observed Mo.

'God knows where he gets it from. Not from me. He popped out like that. Having kids rather blows the whole nature/nurture debate out of the water.' He suddenly realised what he'd said. 'I'm sorry.'

Mo reached for his hand. 'I'm OK with it. Anyway, if what you say is true I'd probably have ended up with one like Marcio.'

Thursday was Gregoire's night off and Ben had offered to cook. This meant picking up a couple of ducks from the butcher in the covered market as they made their way back through the centre of Oxford.

Victor was already back by the time they got home, and the Ferrari was primed and ready to go out front. Toby made a reverential tour of the vehicle, keeping his distance, as though it were a sacred object.

'You're allowed to touch it,' joked Victor. 'I might even let you drive it.'

'No way.'

'If it's OK with your dad.'

'I'm sorry, I can't allow that.'

'Dad!'

Ben heaved a sigh. 'Oh, OK.'

Thursday was also Annabelle's night off but she had decided to forgo it in favour of Toby's last dinner. She joined Mo and Ben on their raid of the vegetable garden and even insisted on playing sous-chef. The jollity in the kitchen, fuelled by a bottle of vintage Bollinger, took a knock when Victor stalked in with a face like thunder.

'Everything OK?' asked Mo.

'No, everything is not OK. Marcio made a scene.' Victor poured himself a glass of champagne and raised it. 'To his imminent departure.'

'To Toby,' seconded Annabelle.

'I meant Marcio.' Victor sunk half the glass with two gulps.

Ben caught a startled glance from Mo. 'What happened?' she asked.

'He flipped out because I let Toby drive the Ferrari before him. He wanted to go first. Pathetic.'

'It's a difficult age,' soothed Annabelle.

'Is it? Let's ask Ben, shall we? Do you find it a difficult age, Ben? No, you don't, because you have a son with manners, a son who hasn't been spoiled rotten by his fucking mother.' He drained the rest of the champagne. 'Were you like that? Was I like that? I've got to get him away from that bitch.'

It couldn't have been worse timing, Marcio materialising in the doorway at that same moment, his hands jammed into his pockets. Ben was the only one positioned to see him standing there, and he gave Victor a warning tilt of the head.

Victor turned in time to glimpse Marcio hurrying away. 'Oh, shit . . .' He placed his glass on the counter and disappeared. The atmosphere didn't. It lingered like a noxious smog, stifling them.

Mo was the first to find her voice. 'Was he like that?'

She might have asked the question, but Ben could tell that Annabelle was waiting just as eagerly on his answer.

'No,' he finally replied.

thirty years before . . .

T HE Q DAY vote took place in the dining hall on the first Wednesday of the summer term, the eight tribe leaders being elected by a system of one man, one vote. The silent ritual was presided over by Headmaster Burroughs, the boys filing up to High Table and dropping their folded pieces of paper into a pith helmet which had once belonged to the founder of the school, a man who had served as an administrator in India.

This year there were eight clear winners and no need for a second vote. Jacob had been campaigning hard for the past couple of days and looked shocked when he didn't make the cut. Ben did, topping the list, which gave him the right to pick first. It was an awkward moment, standing there scanning the faces, knowing he was about to offend a number of people, not least of all Jacob.

Memories of the rugby match at the end of last term still rankled, possibly because his father had brought it up a couple of times over the Easter holidays. No, he wanted team players not glory hounds, and anyway, little Felix Malthouse was the best cross-country runner in the school by a mile, which was going to count for a lot on Sunday.

Jacob was picked by Clive Bishop in the first round, which wasn't surprising. Playing first lieutenant to a good friend should have been enough for him, but when it was all over and they were getting ready for cricket practice he collared Ben in the boot room.

'Malthouse? Before me?'

'It's just Q Day,' said Ben. 'Get over it.'

There were eight camps scattered through the woods, not that much remained of any of them after two terms of bad weather and boys cannibalising them for rafts and firewood at weekends. All you really got was the right to build again on the same spot. Some of the sites were more prized than others, and Ben guessed he wasn't the only tribe leader who wanted the one just above Top Lake. Set on rising ground and with water on one side, it was about the easiest to defend. The race on Sunday would settle it; until then it was a game of lies and spies and spreading false rumours – anything to keep your own plans private.

The big day finally arrived. At three o'clock the Fifth Form gathered in their sports gear at the top of the steep pasture behind the chapel. Burroughs reminded them of the rules. There was to be no interference until they had crossed the bridge at the bottom of the pasture and were into the woods. After that it was a free-for-all; they could trip, tackle and wrestle at will. No punching, though. A master was waiting at each of the eight camp sites, and the first boy to shake his hand got the camp. It was that simple.

Malthouse was quick, but a downhill sprint was a great leveller. It was going to be about protecting him, seeing him safely through the big skirmish which always erupted on the other side of the bridge. If they could just do that, Malthouse would be home free. No one could match him over distance.

'Hey, Ben!' called Clive Bishop from down the line. 'I hope you've got a Plan B 'cos we all know what Plan A is!'

'It's Plan C you should worry about,' Ben shouted back, to another burst of laughter.

Burroughs raised the starting pistol and they were off, a stampede of boys, some stumbling and falling as they swept over the rise by the big oak tree. Nearing the bottom of the field they began to hear the cheers of the lower years, who were in the woods waiting for the spectacle to begin.

Ben and Malthouse were in the leading pack over the bridge. Two of the boys just ahead of them – Andrews and Hinksey – turned suddenly, lunging at Malthouse, a co-ordinated move planned in advance, an allegiance between two tribes. Malthouse feinted past Hinksey and Ben dropped his shoulder, sending Andrews flying, although he stumbled, losing precious momentum in the process. Malthouse was tearing off up the track, coming into his own, but there were others hot on his heels. There was also someone in a blue plaid shirt bounding off through the trees at an angle. Ben had just registered the shirt as Jacob's when he heard a voice behind him, 'Tap tackle . . .'

A second later he was sprawling forward, clawing at air.

He hit the ground hard and turned to see Clive Bishop already scrabbling to his feet, grinning triumphantly. 'Gotcha.'

Ben liked Bishop but he had no qualms about sticking out a leg and tripping him up as he shot past.

There was chaos all around, boys were wrestling each other to the ground and the spectators were going wild, but Ben's mind was elsewhere, making rapid calculations. He had lost vital seconds . . . Malthouse was out of sight, out of range . . . there was nothing more he could do for him, he'd never catch him now.

Instinct told him to set off after Jacob. Even at a distance, Ben could see him weaving through the trees with purpose. Something was up. But what? It didn't make any sense. Ben knew the woods intimately, they all did, and there was no hope of cutting Malthouse off. Yes, he had to loop round the back of the big bracken heath on his way to Top Lake, but the only way to intercept him meant cutting through the bracken, which was out of the question. It was impassable, a chest-high jungle of dead growth laid down year after year. Everyone knew there was no path through it—

Not unless someone had made one. Someone or several people. Possibly yesterday afternoon. Not Jacob, because he had been knocking up twenty-four runs for the 2nd XI against Grange Manor.

Ben had lost sight of Jacob, but he was dimly aware of a strip of red cloth dangling from a tree branch. Only when he saw another flash of red off to his right did he change direction. They must have laid a trail for Jacob, marking the way for him. Was it too much to hope for? No. Another strip of red cloth, and another, then the trees gave way to the heath and there it was: the fresh path, a narrow slice through the bracken.

It was an ingenious idea. You had to admire them, not just for thinking it up and pulling it off, but for managing to keep it secret. Ben stayed low, running in a crouch, shoulders forward, moving as silently as he could. He was halfway across the heath when he first stood up, catching a glimpse of Jacob's blue shirt bobbing through the bracken up ahead. The second time, he took a longer look. There was no sign of Jacob, but he did see Malthouse racing along the track that bordered the heath on the south side. Malthouse glanced over his shoulder, unaware that the real danger lay just in front of him, that he was about to be ambushed.

The warning cry died in Ben's throat. No. Let it happen. Ducking back down, he set off as fast as he could.

He didn't see Jacob make his move but he heard it. There was a wild roar then a startled cry from Malthouse followed by the sounds of a scuffle. Ben burst from the bracken to see Malthouse face down in the dirt, pinned to the ground beneath Jacob, who had him in a half-nelson. 'Move it!' yelled Jacob, gesticulating to someone back down the track.

Rory Cutler, his fellow tribe member, was some thirty or forty yards off but approaching fast. Cutler pointed and yelled, 'Makepeace!'

Jacob's head snapped round. Ben just had time to register his look of utter confusion before breaking into a sprint, giving it everything he had.

The master waiting at the camp above Top Lake turned

out to be Mr Jobson. He was wearing baggy khaki shorts and was smoking a cigarette.

'Good afternoon, sir,' gasped Ben, offering his hand.

Mr Jobson took it in his hairy paw. 'Well done, Makepeace. Do you have a name yet?'

'The Mau Maus, sir.'

'Not funny, Makepeace.'

'The Hyksos.'

'The Hyksos?'

'They were a warrior tribe who conquered ancient Egypt.'

Mr Jobson nodded. 'Well, congratulations.'

They were alone and Ben took the opportunity. 'I have to ask, sir. Did you kill any Mau Maus in Africa?'

Mr Jobson tapped the ash from his cigarette. 'That's for me to know and you to wonder.'

'Please, sir, it's my last term.'

'And our loss is Charterhouse's gain.'

'Please, sir.'

'Sometimes it's best not to know. The truth can be very disappointing. Here, have a sip.'

He handed Ben his old army canteen. The water was slightly salty but refreshing. Mr Jobson took a long gulp of it himself before screwing the lid back on.

'It's like a card trick.'

'Sir?'

'A card trick you've been puzzling over for years then someone shows you how it's done. The mystery's gone.'

Cutler must have been dispatched to claim another camp because it was Jacob who came running up at that moment.

He slowed to a halt, glaring at Ben. 'Who told you?'

'No one.'

'Someone sneaked. Who the hell sneaked?'

'Jacob . . .' said Mr Jobson, a warning note in his voice.

'What?'

No one said 'What?' to a master, not even one who'd called you by your Christian name, which hardly ever happened.

'Control yourself, Hogg, or there'll be consequences.'

Jacob dropped his gaze. 'Sorry, sir.'

Jacob was able to laugh about it later, after he'd heard that Cutler had claimed the camp near the quarry, which was almost as good. And as they traipsed back to school they joked that the scary look in Mr Jobson's eyes proved beyond doubt that he had indeed killed Mau Maus in Africa.

three days to go . . .

M O DIDN'T JUST work all morning, she demanded privacy. This only made sense when she showed up at lunch bearing a farewell gift for Toby. It was a small abstract figure, some ten inches tall, carved from white marble. She stood it on the table. 'What do you think it is?'

'Someone falling?' offered Toby.

Ben had read it the other way, as someone stretching, arching their back, but he saw now that the weight, the torso, was at the bottom (not that there was anything as obvious as a head or an arm to help you out).

Toby looked up at Mo and smiled. 'It's me falling off the skateboard.'

'It's called "Face Plant".'

When it came time to leave, Toby received hugs and kisses from the women and a hip-hop handshake from Marcio which was way too elaborate for them not to have worked it out together beforehand.

Ben got a kiss too, from Mo. 'See you tomorrow. Enjoy your night on the town.'

Victor had driven himself into London that morning in the Maserati so they took the Mercedes. The car's nonchalant purr seemed to reinforce the silence that sat between them as they made off down the driveway.

'Thanks, Dad, I had a really great time.'

'Yeah? I wasn't sure. Marcio's not the easiest of people.'

'He's cool, just a bit weird. But his life's a bit weird. His mum's never around. There's an old woman who looks after him. He doesn't like her.' He paused. 'I feel sorry for him.'

Ben stopped at the end of the driveway and checked the road both ways. 'You're a better man than I am, Gunga Din.'

'Who's Gunga Din?'

'It's a poem. I'll read it to you some time.'

He tapped the throttle and the Mercedes stuck them to their seats.

'You know, Tobes, there are people in this world who feed off other people's goodness. It's OK to stand up to them.'

'I know.'

'I don't mean slap them down, but they need to know there are limits to what they can get away with. It's why Victor gave Marcio that talking-to about the jet ski thing.'

This was the stuff he had always struggled with, the 'mark my words, son' proselytising which he'd been brought up on. It made him feel like a fraud.

'Marcio said his dad didn't tell him off.'

'Really?'

'Yeah, he told him not to worry about it, that he was a Sheldon and that made him special.'

'That's what Marcio said?'

'He said more than that.'

'I don't need to hear it because it's rubbish. He was just playing the big man with you.'

'If you say so, Dad.'

Was that the makings of an ironic smile playing at the corners of Toby's mouth? Toby was no fool. If Marcio had convinced him of it, then maybe it was true. It wasn't impossible. He could see it.

It felt good to have Toby to himself again, but he'd also been dreading the journey back into London, knowing what was waiting for them at the other end. They were halfway there when he finally mustered the courage to say it.

'Tobes, I've got some bad news, I'm afraid. It's about Basil.'

He had spoken to Madeleine earlier and warned her he might say something. She hadn't been against the idea, but she *had* insisted that he tell it as it had been. So he did.

'Mum's sick with guilt. You mustn't hold it against her.'

'Why not?'

'Because one day you'll make the same sort of mistake.'

'No, I won't.'

Toby was holding himself as still as he could to keep from crying. Ben reached for his hand. 'I hope you're right, because it's a horrible feeling.'

The tears didn't last too long, a few minutes at the most.

'Poor Basil,' Toby finally managed to say. 'Is that where she bit you?' He traced the scar on the back of Ben's hand with his fingertip.

'Sure is.'

'Something to remember her by.'

Toby buried himself in Madeleine the moment she opened the front door of the house to them. Ben gave a nod to her inquiring look.

'I'm so sorry, little big man.' The words caught in her throat.

They made a tour of the garden. Unsurprisingly, there were no signs of the fur Madeleine had mentioned to Ben. The hutch and the run now stood beside the garden shed.

'I know there'll only be one Basil, but if you want another rabbit . . .'

Toby turned to her expectantly. 'What about a dog?'

A suggestion Madeleine had shot down many times before, Ben knew. She was going to find it harder to do so now.

'A dog?'

'Only joking, Mum.'

'You beast!'

Ben was in no hurry. He wasn't meeting up with Edwin until eight thirty.

'How is the old bastard?' Madeleine handed him the wine and the bottle-opener. They were alone in the kitchen, Toby having drifted off upstairs. It was something he had always done instinctively since the separation: allow them time to themselves.

'I don't know, I haven't seen him for a bit.'

'Who *have* you seen of the old gang?'

He shrugged. 'I don't go out much.'

'I know. People are worried.'

'How do you work this thing?' It was some state-of-the-art bottle-opener with levers all over the place. Madeleine took it from him and popped the cork in a flash.

'Georgia says you always make some excuse when she invites you to dinner. She thinks you're depressed.'

'I would be if I went round there. Matthew's insufferable since he sold his company.'

'He's not so bad.'

'Mads . . .' He trailed off. No point in going there.

'What?' she demanded. 'What?'

'You used to think he was an arsehole. He's now even more of an arsehole. Why are you defending him?'

'Why are you so down on him? Why can't you just be happy for him?'

'The guy made a small fortune selling party-poppers online.'

'Not just party-poppers.'

'I know, hats and bunting and other stuff too. That doesn't give him the right to start mouthing off about the "makers" and the "takers" in society. Why would I want to listen to that crap? Why would anyone?'

Madeleine was stripping the skin from a small salami. It was an ugly, misshapen thing, like the desiccated penis of some animal or other. No doubt it had cost a small fortune from a fancy Chelsea delicatessen.

'You're right. He's a fucking arsehole. He always was.'

'Thank you,' he said.

'For what?'

'For agreeing with me for the first time in two years.'

His words seemed to suck the life out of her. Her shoulders slumped and she stared blankly at the chopping board. 'What happened to us? What happened to me?' She held up the knife. 'You know how much this knife cost?'

'I don't care.'

'Good for you,' she said. 'Me neither. You know, I'm not even allowed to put a coffee cup down on the surface in case it stains. It stains easily, travertine, sucks up the marks like a sponge. Luckily there's a special bleach under the sink for emergencies, just in case. It's all perfectly planned, just as it should be.' She turned and surveyed the kitchen. 'Everything just as it fucking should be.'

They weren't unwelcome words, but it pained him to see her unhappy. 'Mads, come here . . .' It was a gamble; they hadn't hugged or held each other in two years. She didn't resist when he took her gently in his arms. 'It's normal to have doubts.'

'Not like this.'

'You mean, not like wanting to call off our wedding with three days to go?'

'Oh God, I'd forgotten that.'

'It'll be OK.'

She looked up at him. 'What if I don't want it to be OK?'

'I can't help you with that.'

'Yes, you can,' she said.

He knew she didn't mean it. She just wanted to gauge the power she still held over him. She wanted to know she could have him too.

'Mads . . .'

She pulled away from him, recovering some of her dignity with a dose of humour. 'Shit, I think I just made a pass at my ex-husband.'

'Don't worry, hardly anyone will ever know.'

'If you breathe one word of it you're a dead man.' She brandished the knife at him. He placed his finger against the tip of the blade and examined it.

'Fifty pounds. Sixty tops.'

'One hundred and ninety.'

'For a knife?'

'It was Lionel's Christmas present to me.'

'Sexy.'

'Almost as sexy as the suitcase you bought me for my birthday.'

Ben laughed. 'OK, I screwed up on that one.'

They carried the white wine and the ugly little salami outside to the table on the terrace.

'Thanks for breaking the news to Toby.'

'He took it better than I thought he would.'

'Our brave little big man.' She poured them both a glass of wine. 'You know, I was thinking the other day about that card he wrote you . . . the birthday card: *Dear D-d-d-d-dad*.'

Toby had developed a stammer when he was seven. It had lasted about a year before vanishing as suddenly as it had appeared. It was remarkable that he'd been able to joke about something that had caused him so much distress, and so soon after the demon had left him.

'I still have it somewhere.'

'Filed away?' she teased.

'You know me.'

'That's one thing I don't miss about you – shopping bags full of your crap all over the house.'

'What are the other things?'

'God, where to begin? That you never changed the loo roll when it was finished . . . and always left the hot tap running when you shaved . . . and never noticed when I'd had my hair done.'

'The big stuff, huh?'

'You want big? OK. You could never admit my Bart Simpson voice was better than yours.'

'Mom, can we go Catholic so we can get communion wafers and booze?'

'Worse than ever,' scoffed Madeleine. *'I didn't do it. Nobody saw me do it. You can't prove anything!'*

To which Ben replied in his best Bart: *'I didn't think it was physically possible, but that both sucks and blows.'*

Madeleine laughed. 'Not bad, but I'm still better.' She took a sip of wine and eyed him fondly. 'It's good to laugh. There hasn't been a whole lot of that sort of thing around here recently.'

'So what's up with Lionel? What's he gone and done?'

'Oh, only gambled away the family silver on some dodgy deal. It's bad. I've never seen him like this. They've been in crisis talks all week. It was a good time for Toby to be away.'

'How bad really?'

'Like "goodbye to all this" bad.' Her eyes flicked up at the house looming over them. 'He's not saying much but he moved out some of the artwork the other day, the more valuable sculptures and paintings.'

'Jesus, Mads . . .'

'I've already put a call in to him but I'm not holding out much hope.'

'Yeah, the atheism thing might be a deal-breaker.'

She laughed a little too loudly. He couldn't help wondering, probably unfairly, if the recent shift in her attitude to him was connected. She was one of the world's survivors, not the type to go down with a sinking ship.

'Toby will be OK, won't he?'

'Toby will be just fine,' he replied.

'School fees?'

'Not a problem.'

'That's good to know. And if the shit really hits the fan he can always move in with you in your new place.' She hesitated. 'Toby mentioned it when I spoke to him a couple of days ago. Comes with the new job, apparently. Very nice.'

'I haven't seen it yet, only the photos.'

'Where in South Ken?' she asked casually.

'Onslow Square.'

She looked impressed. 'Beats Clapham Junction.'

'Excuse me – Battersea.'

She topped up their glasses. 'Lionel's a bloody fool. Only invest in what you know. That's what he always said. What the hell does he know about Brazil?'

Ben felt a chill run through him. 'Brazil?'

'I mean, he hasn't even been there.'

'What did he get involved in?'

'I don't know. Something he shouldn't have. Like I say, he can hardly talk it about it he's so traumatised.'

When the subject turned to Toby's stay in Oxfordshire, Ben tried to remain focused, but he felt like a stranger eavesdropping on their conversation. And when Madeleine called upstairs to tell Toby his father was leaving, he asked, 'What's the name of Lionel's outfit?'

'Why, thinking about putting some money with them? Don't is my advice.'

He didn't push it. He didn't need to. Edwin would know.

The first thing he did was order a car from his local minicab company. He then opened some windows. It wouldn't make any difference. From the rotten sills he'd just revealed to the peeling cork tiles on the kitchen floor and the moth-eaten kilim in the living room, there was a forlorn mustiness to the place that was never going to be dispelled by a gulp of fresh air.

He had blitzed the flat before leaving, cleaning it down to its bones. It was looking its best, probably the best it had ever looked, but after only five minutes he already felt soiled. He flicked on the immersion in the airing cupboard. He knew the water took half an hour to heat up from a standing start, which would mean calling the cab company and Edwin and putting both of them back by twenty minutes.

He installed himself at the kitchen table with a bottle of warm beer from the cupboard and his mail, which Trisha had sweetly kicked into a corner in the entrance hall downstairs. There was nothing of any real note, but it struck him that for the first time ever he opened a credit card bill without trepidation. Whatever it contained, he was good for it, more than good for it.

He cast an unforgiving eye around the kitchen, glad that he'd decided to stay over in town. Being here shed a whole new light on his situation. He was never going back to this. How could he now?

The minicab had been waiting outside for five minutes when he hurried downstairs. He was double-locking his front door when Trisha appeared from her flat in black leggings and a T-shirt big enough to double as a kids' wigwam.

'Oh, it's you.'

'Hello, Trish.' He knew she hated being called Trish.

'Your gutter's leaking.'

'*My* gutter? Aren't *you* the freeholder?'

'It's leaking on to my patio.'

'Listen, Trish, God knows what you do with the service charge I pay you every year.' He spread his hands, taking in the worn carpet and stained walls. 'Are you seriously telling me there's nothing left in the pot?'

'How dare you?'

'You really don't want me to answer that. Get a man in, sort it out. Who knows, you might even get lucky. Have a good evening, Trish.'

'It's Trisha,' came her cry, more anguished than outraged, as he pulled the front door shut behind him.

It was an overcast but warm evening, and the streets of Soho were jammed with people spilling off the pavements, slowing the traffic to a crawl. Edwin had suggested they meet at a new hotel near Golden Square, and Ben found him perched on a footstool at the crowded bar, sipping a dry martini.

'Shaken not stirred, I hope,' he said in his best Sean Connery voice.

Edwin turned. 'Ben! Mate. God, you look good. Bastard. Are you on something? Don't tell me – nightingale shit facepacks, all the rage in Hollywood.'

'Water. It's all I drink now.'

Edwin deflated. 'Then you can fuck right off.'

Ben smiled.

'Arse,' said Edwin.

'I think I'll kick off with one of those.'

Edwin caught the barman's eye and indicated two more of the same. They weren't the oldest people in the place but it was a close-run thing. This didn't seem to bother Edwin.

'Top totty at three o'clock. Red skirt. Looks Italian to me.'

'She also looks about twelve years old.'

'Nah, twenty-one, twenty-two.'

'Are we really going to spend the evening leering at girls half our age?'

'Of course not. We're going to talk to them too. It'll be just like the old days.'

'Remind me.'

'We suck 'em in with your looks and then . . .' Edwin drove his fist into his palm.

'We punch them in the face?'

'I close the deal with my top banter.'

Ben had to laugh. 'Come on, when did we ever close a deal? We always went home alone.'

'Not tonight, mate, not tonight.'

Edwin got a chance to try out his top banter twenty minutes later. He had slipped the maître d' twenty quid and when the next table came free, it was theirs. A couple of girls soon pounced on their spare chairs.

'Can we?' one of them chirped.

'Sure, go ahead,' said Edwin. 'As long as we can have them back when Brad and Angelina show up.' The girls giggled politely and disappeared with the chairs.

'That went well.'

'Hey, I'm working on the hoof here. What would *you* have said, Casanova?'

'I'd have said "No", because now no one can sit with us.'

'Shit,' spat Edwin. 'Shit.'

Edwin only began to relax once they'd moved on and were no longer hemmed in on all sides by young flesh. Wisely, he'd made a reservation at a restaurant on Lexington Street, because queues were already beginning to build outside every eatery. Up until now Edwin had resolutely refused to speak about anything other than the present and the future. This was on the advice of the 'life coach' he'd been seeing, a woman called Beverly who lived in Elephant and Castle.

'You can't move forwards if you're looking backwards.'

To which Ben had replied, 'Unless you're a rower.'

'Yeah, yeah, smart arse. I'm telling you, she has more wisdom in her big toe than the two of us put together.'

'So what's she doing in Elephant and Castle?'

'She warned me about people like you. You're "emotional vampires".'

It would pass, like tae-bo and self-hypnosis and all the other fads Edwin had thrown himself into since his divorce. In fact, by the time their first courses arrived he was already droning on about Cassandra and what had gone wrong with the relationship.

'She was bat-shit crazy, in the nicest possible way, mind. It wasn't that. No, one night she mentioned the B-word.'

'The B-word?'

Edwin lowered his voice to a conspiratorial whisper. 'Babies . . . how much she loves them, loves their podgy little hands and their funny little noses.'

'Ahhhh.'

'Mayday, mayday. Actually, you would have been proud of me. I was very grown-up. I didn't say no. But I couldn't promise her yes either. And that was that – adios, Edwin.'

There were no hard feelings, apparently. Edwin still bought his lunch at the sandwich bar where Cassandra worked.

'It's weird, it always gets me with the exes how you go, you know, from the most incredible intimacy to, well, nothing. Polite formality at best. I mean, I was in there yesterday, and she's making me my mozzarella and Parma ham ciabatta, and she's putting it in the grill thing and giving it all this "*Dos minutos*, Edwin" stuff, kind of friendly and knowing at the same time, and all I'm thinking, I mean, *all* I'm thinking is that a week ago, not even, the tip of my tongue was in her tight little anus.'

'Jesus, Edwin!'

'I'm making a serious point here.'

'Yeah, just not when I'm eating squid rings.'

Edwin glanced down at Ben's plate, slapped the table and erupted in laughter.

'It's always the way. Just when I'm beginning to think you're a bit of a cunt you come out with something like that.'

It was all about timing. He had to strike when Edwin was too drunk to question what was being asked of him but not so drunk that he'd forget it by the morning. He judged the arrival of the coffees to be that moment – incorrectly, as it turned out.

Edwin had already heard through the grapevine about Madeleine's engagement to Lionel but he hadn't yet got wind of Lionel's business predicament.

'That surprises me,' he said. 'Quercus is thought of as a safe pair of hands, low-risk low-return, kind of boring.'

'Well, something happened to suck them into this Brazilian thing.'

'What exactly?'

'I don't know. Lionel's not saying much and Mads is tearing her hair out.'

'I'll ask around, check it out.'

'Thanks.'

'No problem.'

That was the easy bit. There was more he needed from Edwin, though, and he cursed himself for not sitting down beforehand and working out a more subtle way of broaching the subject.

'Another thing . . . she thinks some guy called Victor Sheldon might be involved.'

Edwin leaned forward in his chair. 'Victor Sheldon? I doubt it, not if the deal's gone tits up. The guy's a genius, a legend.'

'It's just a name she threw at me. And even geniuses screw up.'

That's when the suspicion bit, Edwin's eyes narrowing as he said, 'I'm pissed, but I'm not that pissed. What's going on?'

Ben could have lied, fudged the facts – it's what he had pictured himself doing – but as he looked into his friend's face he felt a sudden urge to come clean.

'I know Victor Sheldon. I was at prep school with him. He was called Jacob back then.'

'Jacob? Not the guy who lived with you?'

'I told you about him?'

'Sure, he was like a brother to you. That's Victor Sheldon?'

'It is now.'

He filled Edwin in on the events of the past few weeks: the reunion with Victor, the film script, his time at Stoneham Park, the offer to head up the charitable foundation.

'He's turned my life around.'

'I'll say!'

'I think I'm going to say no to the job.'

'Do it. Give him my number.'

'I mean it. There's something not right about it.'

Edwin leaned forward on his elbows. 'Listen, for eight million over ten years you find a way to make it feel right.'

'It's not just that, it's everything.' Ben emptied the rest of the red wine into their glasses. 'Remember when I called you about the script I was working on? I lied. That was my postcode in his satnav. It was entered months ago, way before any of this.'

'So?'

'I remember what you said: *plain fucking creepy whichever way you slice it.*'

'I was being polite, encouraging about the idea.'

'You don't find it weird?'

'A bit,' conceded Edwin.

'It's been deleted since – the postcode. There's other stuff, too.' He told Edwin about the Serious Fraud Office ruse to test his loyalty.

'So, he's a private guy, a bit paranoid. I've heard that about him. Some of it's obviously rubbed off on you.'

'What else have you heard about him?'

'Bits and pieces, not all of it good. But you don't get to where he's got without playing rough and loose, pissing some people off. It's just rumours. Not even. Sour grapes and Chinese whispers, more like. There are people out there right now saying the same sort of things about me.' Edwin's eyes narrowed menacingly. 'But I know who they are.'

Ben laughed, going with it. He knew what Edwin was like. He'd taken his stance and was warming to his theme. There was no point in resisting him.

'Listen,' said Edwin. 'Don't turn your back on Lady Luck or she won't come calling again. Bank your fucking chips and walk away a winner.'

Ben nodded. 'OK. But you'll check it out, this thing with Quercus?'

'Mother of shit! Yes. If it'll shut you up.'

They ended the night on the roof deck at Soho House, where Edwin's banter went down considerably better with an older crowd.

When an attractive woman with close-cropped hair approached them and asked if they had a light, Edwin said, 'Sadly not, but if you don't mind keeping an eye on my severely autistic brother I'll go and find you one.'

Her name was Finola and she didn't really want the cigarette; it was an excuse to flee a big dinner downstairs. She was a planner in an advertising agency and a client had been hitting on her.

'You don't have to worry about us,' said Edwin. 'We're gay.'

'My first thought when I saw you both.'

'And your second?'

'Or maybe they're just repressed heterosexuals.'

It was quick and it was right up Edwin's street. His laugh was loud enough to turn heads.

Finola popped downstairs, supposedly to make her excuses. When she didn't return, Edwin grew sullen and morose. 'I can't believe she lied to us.'

'Remember Beverly. It's in the past. Eyes front.'

'Fucking Beverly. A hundred and fifty quid an hour.'

'A hundred and fifty quid an hour!'

'For what?' asked Finola. She had crept up on them through the shadows.

'Ben's life coach.' Edwin rolled his eyes.

Ben was happy to take the fall for his friend; Finola didn't seem like the sort of person who looked kindly on life coaches or, for that matter, the people who employed their services.

'Yes, it's a lot, but she's worth every penny. There's more wisdom in her big toe than the three of us put together.'

'Oh? Want to share some of it?'

'Sure. You have to look backwards in order to move forwards – like a rower.'

Finola was intrigued. 'That's . . . crap, obviously. But kind of interesting.'

'That's what I was telling him.' Edwin gripped Ben's arm. 'Stick with it, mate. She's got to be better than that anger management bloke you were seeing.' Ben fired him a look: don't push it, pal. 'That was a joke – the anger management thing.'

'I thought it might be,' said Finola.

'I thought you thought it might be, but just in case.'

'Well, thank you for your . . . condescension.'

'No problem,' replied Edwin. 'I also do a fine line in pretension and hypocrisy.'

'Oh my God, you have so got to meet my husband.' Edwin wilted, but only momentarily. 'That was a joke,' Finola added.

'I thought it might be.'

Finola's lips curled into the slightest of smiles. 'No, you didn't.'

Ben couldn't have kept up with them even if he had wanted to, even if they had wanted him to, which they clearly didn't.

They were up and away, soaring together, riding their own thermal. He said his farewells and stood swaying on Shaftesbury Avenue for fifteen minutes before an empty cab picked him up.

Draped across the back seat, staring at the world flashing by outside, he found himself smiling. He'd had a great evening, a fun evening, and he'd just witnessed his old friend lose his heart to yet another woman. Finola was special, though, smart and very amusing and more than a match for Edwin. Yes, he could see it going the distance. He toyed with the opening of his speech: 'The last time Edwin asked me to be his best man . . .'

Edwin, who knew him better than anyone else did, maybe better even than Madeleine. Edwin, who had never been afraid to knock hard sense into him, who had fought tooth and nail to save his marriage, even as his own was disintegrating. Bad memories, which now crashed over him in waves.

They were stilled by a single thought so dreadful, so unimaginable . . .

He was vaguely aware of Buckingham Palace blurring by on his right as he fumbled his BlackBerry from his pocket.

I have to see you. Can you slip away in the morning?

He didn't expect her to be awake, but Madeleine's reply came back almost immediately.

Where and when?

two days to go . . .

A s luck would have it, Ben was unloading the shopping from the Mercedes just when Trisha appeared from the house.

'Good morning, Trisha.'

There was a charged moment of silence as she eyed the Mercedes, looked at Ben and nodded. 'Ben.' She had never used his name before. 'New car?'

'Not mine.'

'No point in me keying it then.'

There was a definite twinkle in her eye.

'Friends again?' he asked.

Trisha strolled off. 'Don't push your luck, pal.'

Weird. He obviously should have stood up to her before.

His BlackBerry PING-ed as he was loading the coffee machine in readiness. He guessed it was a text from Madeleine to say she was running a bit late. It was Edwin.

Your friend has the most enormous cock. Finola X
My friend IS the most enormous cock.

The doorbell rang.

Madeleine was looking waifish in the short gauzy cotton dress he had bought her in Perugia. 'Hi.' She glided over the threshold, landing a kiss on his cheek.

'I've never seen it so tidy.' She was poking around in the living room and he was in the kitchen, making the coffee.

'Yeah, I don't know what came over me,' he called back.

His mobile rang: Edwin again.

'Take it, I don't mind.' She stood in the doorway, holding a book.

'It's just Edwin calling for a post-mortem.' He let it go to message.

'Remember this?' She held up the book: *Invisible Cities* by Italo Calvino. 'What's it doing on your bookshelf? It's mine, you gave it to me.'

He shrugged. 'You never read it, so I figured . . .'

She opened the book. '"My dear, darling Mads. Not one of these magical cities comes close to the place we've built together. Forever. Mouse."' She closed the book and looked up. 'Nine kisses.' Their private code. 'Forehead . . . eyes . . . lips . . . throat . . . breasts . . . belly button . . .' She didn't finish.

He wished she had never started, because he knew what was coming and she wasn't going to like it. He was saved by the milk rising suddenly to the boil in the saucepan.

'Shit.'

The cloth hissed on the hob as he wiped away the spillage. Burnt milk. The odour of childhood.

'So, how was your boys' night out?' she asked.

'Great. I think Edwin might have found the woman of his dreams.'

'Again?'

'This one's special. Finola. She's the real deal.'

He was adding the milk to the dark pools of espresso in the bottom of the cups when she gently pressed herself against him from behind, resting her head against his shoulder.

'Tell me about her. What does she look like?'

God, it felt good. It felt far too good.

'Well, she's kind of tall. Your height. And she has short hair. And a long nose.'

'I know you like a long nose on a woman. No ski jumps for Ben Makepeace.'

She ran a hand under his T-shirt and across his stomach.

'She's a planner at an ad agency.'

'A planner? What does a planner do?'

'Well, as far as I could tell they . . .' He trailed off as her hand dropped to his crotch, grazing lightly over the denim.

'Plan things?' she suggested.

He was getting hard and it had to stop. He swivelled to face her.

'I'm sorry, Mads, it's not why I asked you here. I should have said.'

Her embarrassment morphed swiftly into anger. 'Yes, you should have.'

'There's something we need to talk about.'

They carried their cups through to the living room in

frosty silence. She sat on the sofa; he dropped into the leather
club chair, regretting it immediately. It was one of the few
items they'd fought over.

'I'm all ears,' she said crisply.

'It's about the Frenchman.'

She gave a short, bitter laugh. 'Oh, God, not this again.
Please tell me you're joking.'

'It's important.'

'Like last time? And the time before that? And the time
before that?'

'No. Different.'

'It was a one-night stand, and the biggest mistake of my
life. What more do you want to know? Why I did it? I can't
tell you. I didn't want to, but I did it anyway. My therapist
thinks my father's death is to blame, but what does she know?
What do I know? We've been over this a thousand times.'
She broke off, but only to regather her forces. 'I've paid the
fucking price, Ben. I've done my time. How dare you keep
coming at me like this? I'm sorry, OK? It cuts a hole in my
heart every time I look at Toby, every time I see you, and
there's nothing I can do about it. It's there. It's always going
to be there. I don't need you to remind me it's a life sentence,
I really fucking don't.'

Her eyes shone with tears and his instinct was to get up
and go and hold her. Maybe he would, but not yet.

'Mads, I don't blame you.'

'Yes, you do.'

'A bit, not really. And I'm not trying to punish you. There
are just a couple of things I need to know.'

She delved into her bag and pulled out a packet of ten cigarettes. His fingers itched for one, and he helped himself once she'd lit hers, offering up his saucer as an ashtray for them both.

'You said it was just the one time, at the hotel.'

'Yes,' she replied robotically.

'You never saw him again.'

'No.'

'Did you try to?'

'No.'

'And you didn't speak to him again?'

'No.'

He sat back in his chair. 'I find that hard to believe, knowing you — a night of passion then *au revoir*.'

'It wasn't *au revoir*, it was *adieu*. And it wasn't passion, it was just sex — OK sex, nothing special.'

'Last question. Please be honest. Did you try and speak to him again?'

'No.'

But there had been a momentary hesitation; they were both aware of it.

She drew on her cigarette, exhaling hard before admitting, 'He gave me his number. I didn't want to see him again, I just wanted to . . . I don't know, acknowledge it or something, draw a line under it. It didn't make any difference because the number didn't work.'

'Did you try and get a message to him via the hotel?'

'I thought he might have written the number down wrong.'

'So, you did?'

'Yes.'

'But you never heard back from him.'

She crushed out her cigarette. 'No, Ben, I never heard back from him.' He saw the anger rising once more in her face. 'Quid pro quo. What's this about?'

'What if I told you he was paid to sleep with you?'

When she finally replied she was already on her feet and reaching for her bag. Her voice was cold, unearthly.

'You need help. I mean it, Ben, you need some serious fucking help to sort your head out. You've been weird and withdrawn since the beginning of the year. I'm not the only one who thinks it, everyone does, even Edwin. He's phoned me a couple of times to talk about it. No, don't look at me like that. It's true. People are worried about you, and they're right to be. I thought you'd turned a corner in the past few weeks – the script work, the money, the new job – but all it's done is push you over the edge.'

He took it in silence, without a fight, because he should never have said it in the first place. It was a mistake.

Long after he'd heard the front door slam shut downstairs, he was still sitting in the chair, pinned there by creeping doubts. Maybe she was right. Maybe his brain had buckled. Maybe he'd been possessed by the malevolent spirit of DC Leon Grosse. All he had to go on were a couple of cryptic comments from Raffaella which he'd chosen to read as warnings, and a memory which might or might not have been reliable: a brief snatch of their conversation over dinner at Harry's Bar in Cernobbio.

'When was this?' Raffaella had asked when he'd told her about Madeleine's infidelity at the conference in France. She hadn't said, 'That's terrible,' or, 'Have you never been tempted yourself?' or a bunch of other things which would have made more sense under the circumstances. No. 'When was this?' And when he told her she had given a thoughtful grunt before moving the conversation on. It had struck him as mildly curious at the time. In light of everything that had happened since, it now seemed deeply odd.

In her haste to leave, Madeleine had left her cigarettes and lighter. What the hell? Just one more.

He had to pick the words carefully if he stood any chance of a response. Raffaella might have called him back before, but there had been a clear note of finality in her parting words that time. He tamped out the cigarette, searched for the Villa d'Este's number on his phone and called it.

He used the same excuse – that his phone had been stolen, and, like the last time, they were quite happy to forward a message to Signora Bonetti. The accommodating tone of receptionist's voice wavered slightly when she checked if she had heard him right: *Do you know the Frenchman? This is my life we're talking about.*

Annabelle had told him that most of the weekend guests would be arriving at Stoneham Park in time for Saturday lunch. He delayed his return accordingly. He didn't want to face them all at once, ranged around a table. He didn't want to face them at all.

He was aware that a switch had been flicked in him, but

he was still surprised when the house swung into view at the end of the driveway. It seemed to have changed during his brief absence, as if a shadow had fallen on the place with no promise that it would ever lift. The house itself now looked squat, bloated, pretentious – quite possibly not unlike the man who had first built it, he reflected.

Mo wasn't in her studio but she had evidently been hard at work there over the past twenty-four hours. The place was spotless, stripped of its heaps of stone chippings and its ghosting of white dust. There were colours he'd never seen before: the red of the generator, the silver of the extraction pipes, the tawny hue of the wooden pallet on which her sculpture stood proud. It even seemed to him that someone had run a flannel over the face itself.

He tilted his head and stared. Maybe he had brought it with him, but there was a whisper of something behind the aloof dignity of those heavy-lidded almond eyes which he hadn't detected before: pity, coupled with understanding. No, it was more than simple understanding, it was fore-knowledge. *I'm sorry*, the fallen figure seemed to be saying to him. *I wanted to tell you before but I couldn't*.

The more he stared, the more he became convinced of it. Had Mo planted it there as a warning, the plastic counterpart to Raffaella's grunt? Were they both women who couldn't quite bear the burden of deceit?

No, that way lay madness. Mo wasn't involved. She couldn't be. He needed to stay level, focused. He also needed to take a leaf out of Victor's book, the page headed PATIENCE. He wouldn't be hearing from Edwin until

Monday at the earliest, and he suspected he wouldn't be hearing from Raffaella at all.

He found the others down at the pool and slipped into hail-fellow-well-met mode. Only one of their names stuck: Douglas, a big breezy man with a prodigious moustache. Victor and Mo were paired together, playing mixed doubles on the grass tennis court.

'Go get your gear on,' called Victor. Mo blew him a kiss then set herself to serve. It was deep and hard, and the bald man receiving fired it back with pace. Victor, poised at the net, lunged and volleyed the ball away. Mo squealed, scampered towards Victor and high-fived him.

No need to overdo it, thought Ben – the return would have been long by a good few feet.

The afternoon fractured into bouts of tennis doubles and swimming and roasting by the pool. Ben had a suspicion about how it would all come back together. Sure enough, Victor challenged him to a game of singles.

Their match drew a small crowd of spectators which included Mo. It played in Ben's favour that winning in front of his guests mattered so much to Victor. He was tight and urgent, his timing all out. He swung too early, driving the ball long, and when he tried to adjust, he forced his strokes, turning the ball into the net.

Ben showed no mercy, mixing up his shots so that Victor never got a chance to settle into any kind of rhythm from the baseline. He was rewarded with a 6–2 scoreline.

'Every dog has its day,' said Ben, approaching the net.

Victor ignored his hand. 'Want another?'

'Sure.'

Ben killed himself chasing down balls, fighting for every point, and although Victor started to come back into it in the last couple of games, even breaking Ben's serve, he still lost 6–4.

They were both drenched in sweat by now. Victor was riled, grudging in defeat, complaining that the pro at his club in London had strung his racquet too high.

'All four of them?' asked Ben, not so innocently.

'All square. One match apiece.'

'Or three sets to two, depending how you look at it.'

It was a return to the language of their youth, and they both knew it.

Mo must have sensed something.

'Are you OK?' she asked when she stopped by Ben's room later as he was getting dressed for dinner.

'Sure. Why?'

'Sure. Why?' she parroted. 'Because you looked like you wanted to kill him out there.'

'He plays a tough game. I didn't have much choice.'

'You could have let him win in front of his friends.'

'They're not his friends. You should have heard what he said about the last lot that was here.'

'OK, if Mr Grumpy doesn't want to play, I'm off.'

God, she looked more beautiful than ever, slightly flushed from an afternoon in the sun.

'Define play,' he said.

'Well, it would mean me having to do this.' She reached beneath the hem of her little black dress then raised her fingers to her lips in a gesture of demure surprise. 'Oh, I forgot, I'm not wearing any.'

'Come here.'

'No, come and get me.'

It was a short chase, all of two metres to the bed.

Ben did his bit at dinner, but no more. He was seated next to Douglas, he of the huge moustache, who turned out to be the boss of a biomedical research outfit near Cambridge which Victor had invested in. Their big thing was synthesising anti-cancer medicines from fungi, but he spoke with engaging enthusiasm about science in general.

At the very least, Douglas spared him having to talk to his other neighbour, a tiny, leathern woman with some offensive views on rape and immigration.

Night fell cool and scented, and Ben began to flag. He had fought for sleep the night before, his mind going in five different directions at once. He caught Mo's look as the coffee was being served. They were soon saying their goodnights.

'I thought you artist types had stamina,' said the bald man.

'I don't think their evening's over quite yet,' drawled leathern lady, to a gust of laughter. The most Victor could produce was a thin smile, Ben noted.

At Ben's request they made for Mo's apartment. He wanted to be far away from the house, from them all, alone with her. They smoked a joint while listening to Siouxsie and the Banshees and he let the pleasure of her company wash over him. She was slightly anxious about tomorrow. It was her big day. The lorry was arriving at eleven to transport her sculpture to its concrete perch in the copse by the lake. Sunday morning seemed an odd time for such an undertaking, but Victor was off again next week on his travels. This was news to Ben.

'When's he leaving?'

'Wednesday. And I guess he thinks it'll be fun for them to see.'

'Right, a bit of light entertainment before lunch.'

They were curled up together on the sofa, her head in his lap, his head filling with thoughts of Wednesday, and how soon that was, and how he hoped he had some answers by then, because he was going half-mad with the anticipation, the not-knowing.

'You must tell me if you've changed your mind,' said Mo.

'Changed my mind?'

'About us. About me moving in with you.'

'Of course I haven't.'

But the offer had been born out of a now fading vision of life in a large apartment in South Kensington and enough money to secure Mo the workspace of her dreams. A penniless existence in a shoebox in Battersea might not be quite such an appealing prospect for her.

Mo twisted herself into a sitting position. 'You don't seem yourself.'

'I had a heavy night with Edwin, that's all.'

She cradled his face in her hands and kissed him. 'Come to bed.'

They made love tenderly, silently. And afterwards he

turned his mind again to the big question, the one that had kept him awake for much of last night and tormented him for most of the day: why?

Lying on his back, Mo's arm draped across his chest, he let the memories unfurl.

thirty years before . . .

THE LIGHTS HAD been out for twenty minutes and sleep was billowing over them all when Ben heard the cry outside in the corridor: 'Herodotus! Herodotus!'

The Q Day code word, known only to the eight tribe leaders. They knew it was coming, just not when, or to which of them Burroughs would say it.

Clive Bishop burst into the dormitory and flicked on the lights. 'Herodotus! It's Q Day!'

The madness spread like wildfire through the senior dorms. They'd had their clothes ready for days, their sleeping bags rolled beneath their beds, their torches tucked away in their washbags just in case tonight was the night. Exams were over; the results were in; most had made the grade for the schools of their choice (Jacob had been accepted by Ardingly, where many of his friends were going). It was time to play, to run riot.

It was a cloudless night, the moon almost full, and there was no need for torches as they gathered on the tennis court. They formed themselves into eight orderly lines behind the heaped boxes of provisions and cooking utensils. Headmaster Burroughs called them to silence with a blast on his whistle. He reminded them all of the rules of night warfare. You could sense the buzz of excitement building as Mr Jobson then distributed the bangers and the boxes of matches to the tribe leaders. This was the only bit of Q Day anyone really cared about. Tomorrow's orienteering, cycling and canoeing competitions were the price they paid for the right to go rampaging through the woods with explosives in their pockets.

They travelled in one giant pack which began to break up once they were in the woods, the tribes peeling away into the night, filing off to their respective camps. They had an hour to prepare before the flares went up and they had to move quickly. It was just enough time to light the fire, check the traps, rig the tripwires and go over their battle plan.

The rules of the game were simple, the scoring system almost incomprehensible. There were points for dropping bangers into other tribes' fires, and slightly fewer points for taking prisoners during an assault, and even fewer for taking prisoners beyond the camp perimeter. There were more points to be added when it was all over: for the tribe who'd had the fewest bangers dropped in their fire; the tribe who'd taken the most prisoners etcetera etcetera. There were no points for hurling lit bangers to flush out, disorientate and generally terrify the enemy (which was the best bit, of course).

Prisoners could be taken anywhere and at any time. All you had to do was raise the boy off the ground and speak the opening lines of the hymn 'Jerusalem': *And did those feet in ancient time walk upon England's mountains green*. This took a while, which was the point. One on one, it was almost impossible to pull off against a struggling opponent. It usually required two of you to take someone out of the game.

Ben had sat down in secret with Malthouse and worked out that defence was the key to winning. Most tribes put far too many people in the field, which left them vulnerable to attack and filled the woods with raiders. There were groans when Ben announced that they were going for an almost even split of five defenders and two raiding parties of two.

'I know it's a lot of defenders, but it's the right thing to do, and we'll switch places every half an hour.'

This was only possible because Fawcett was scared of the dark and happy to defend the fire all night.

It was blazing furiously now, sending sparks shooting up into the trees and flooding their faces with orange light. Ben handed out fistfuls of bangers. They then formed a hill of hands at the centre of the circle.

'We're the Hyksos,' said Ben. 'We took out the ancient Egyptians, we can take this lot out.'

'Yeah!' came back the chorus.

'Do you want to know what the Hyksos used to shout before they went into battle?'

'Yeah!'

'I don't hear you.'

'YEAH!'

'Tell them, Freddie.' Ben glanced at Malthouse.

'I don't know.'

'Yes, you do, Freddie.'

Titters of laughter rippled around the circle.

'Oh, OK. How about this?' Freddie thought on it for a second or two. 'Aba goo bam aba foo da.'

It was perfect. It sounded even better when chanted over and over, louder and louder, by nine boys.

'What does it mean?' It was the sort of question only Fawcett would think to ask.

'Freddie? Anyone?'

Bardwell nailed it first time. 'Your blood shall forever feed our crops.'

They were still laughing when the flares went up.

Ben had assigned himself to defend for the first phase, and with Fawcett on fire duty the rest of them each took a quadrant, slipping into the trees beyond the perimeter. They lost themselves in the shadows, their eyes slowly adjusting to the darkness of the moonlight-dappled woods.

This was their territory, they knew it better than anyone: the fallen trees, the ditches, the clumps of thick underbrush which the enemy would probably make for in search of cover. The anticipation was unbearable – Ben could feel his heart pulsing in his throat – and it was almost a relief when the first attackers came slinking through the trees.

It had been Campbell's idea to scatter dried twigs in a ring far out beyond the perimeter. Clever boy, thought Ben, as a brittle SNAP alerted him to someone approaching over his right shoulder. There were two of them and he forced himself deeper into the hollow of the tree, letting them pass. They crouched behind a bush, eyes on the camp, on Fawcett patrolling the fire. He heard the nerves in their whispers. Everyone was scared; no one wanted to be taken out of the game at such an early stage.

He had felt a bit bad about stealing one of his mother's disposable lighters, but he didn't now. The rasp then sudden flare of a lit match would have ruined the surprise. As it was, they first they knew of him was when two fizzing bangers landed right between them.

BOOM! BOOM!

They panicked, breaking cover, one of them fleeing, the other one, braver, making a beeline for the camp.

'Aba goo bam aba foo da!' Ben bellowed, hot in pursuit.

The attacker shot a look over his shoulder at exactly the same moment he hit the tripwire.

Ben was on him immediately.

'Don't. Don't. I think I've broken something.' Ben released him. It was Riley. 'My hand,' he groaned. He knelt hunched in a ball, holding his wrist. Campbell came running over from his quadrant to help out.

'It's Riley. He's hurt.'

Riley took off so quickly that Ben only just managed to trip him up.

'You faker!' yelled Campbell.

Riley struggled, but together they lifted him off the ground: '*And did those feet in ancient time walk upon England's mountains green.*'

They made a point of dropping him when they were done.

This early success convinced Ben that defending was

actually more fun than attacking. He still went out when it was his turn, though, he and Campbell together, making straight for the big prize and picking up a smaller one en route in the form of Cullen, who was foolishly out on his own. They took him prisoner then left him to traipse back to the camp and hand himself in.

Clive Bishop had decided to call his tribe the Haestingas, because he lived near Hastings and that was the name of the Saxon tribe that had once ruled the area. Ben and his lot openly referred to them as the 'hasting-arses', or more simply the 'Arses' – all part of the friendly rivalry that had sprung up between the two tribes following their battle for the Top Lake camp at the beginning of term.

They came at the camp through the quarry because no one would be stupid enough to mount an assault from that direction. It was a steep and treacherous climb to the lip, but they'd scouted it in secret and knew the best, the only, route up. Sure enough, they slipped in unchallenged, and dropped their bangers in the fire. The explosions and the cheers from the prisoners huddled inside the camp itself brought Jacob running out of the darkness.

'No one on fire duty?' said Campbell. 'Tut-tut.'

'How did you . . .?' Jacob saw the dirt caking the front of their clothes. 'The quarry.'

'Like it, Campbell, like it,' shouted one of the prisoners.

Campbell took a bow; he had always been a showman. 'Thank you, folks. Some are born great, some achieve greatness, and some have greatness thrust upon them. I was born great.'

'You've got one minute,' said Jacob over the laughter.

That was the rule: a sixty-second head start after a successful assault, then they could come after you.

It was enough for Ben: a double hit on the 'Arses' followed by another double hit on the 'Navajo' while heading home. He was happy to defend for the last hour.

They'd lost a couple of men by now, including Freddie, but they'd protected their patch, taking seven prisoners, eight including Cullen, which couldn't be bad. That was almost a whole tribe of prisoners.

With only ten minutes to go, Ben began to grow nervous. The 'Arses' had made one unsuccessful attack, almost losing a man. He knew Clive Bishop wouldn't leave it at that. They were coming, no doubt about it. They were probably closing in right now.

'Fawcett, I need you.'

'What about the fire?'

'I need you over here. Now.'

Fawcett reluctantly joined Ben at the perimeter.

'Don't worry, all you have to do is stand here and keep throwing bangers down there.'

Way below them, down the slope, moonlight silvered the surface of Top Lake.

'They won't come from there,' said Fawcett.

'They won't if you keep throwing bangers.'

He figured that's exactly where they would come from, although they would now be forced to work their way round to the left. They couldn't go right because of the brambles.

He slipped over the perimeter and into the trees. Better to flush them out than wait for the inevitable.

He was beginning to think he was mistaken, that any moment now he would hear a warning cry from Campbell on the other side of the camp, but then a shadow moved. His eyes locked on to the spot. Yes. There it was again, the merest shimmer. Someone was crawling across the slope on their belly.

He had the advantage of the high ground, so he lit six bangers at once and released them into the night, darting behind a tree as they went off like a giant Chinese firecracker. The attacker came charging up the slope. Ben ghosted in behind him, tripped him, then seized his ankles and began dragging him on his belly back down towards the lake. It was almost comical.

'Come on, doggy, let's go walkies.'

The boy clawed at the ground and lunged at the passing trees but there was nothing he could do to slow his descent. He was only saved by a root which caught Ben's heel and sent him tumbling backwards.

He cracked the back of his head hard on the ground and the world slowed for a moment. He knew he had to get up quickly but his limbs had turned to rubber.

'Come on, doggy, let's go walkies.'

His dazed brain recognised the voice, and a second later Jacob was groping for his ankles. Ben kicked out, twisting away, but Jacob was all over him, smothering him like a blanket – just like in judo lessons, except he wasn't trying to pin Ben's shoulders to the floor, he was trying to lift him off the ground.

'And did those feet in ancient time—'

Ben squirmed free, darting off down the slope, Jacob crashing after him. There was a strip of flat open ground between the trees and the lake, boggy as anything in winter, but hard and rutted at this time of year. The second they hit it, Ben turned suddenly, staying low as he drove at Jacob, leading with the shoulder. Winded, Jacob still managed to get hold of his shirt and drag him to the ground. They had wrestled before – there had been any number of play-fights over the years – but they had never used their fists.

'No hitting!' cried Ben indignantly. 'You know the rules!'

Jacob was astride him, but he only stopped his pummelling so that he could seize Ben by the throat.

'I know it was you,' he spat. 'You gave my stuff to Burroughs.'

Burroughs? What did Burroughs have to do with anything? Ben felt Jacob's nails score his windpipe as he yanked the hand away. 'Get off me!'

'Not till you admit it.' Jacob clamped both hands around his throat this time. 'I know it was you.'

This wasn't about Q Day and tribal rivalry, it was personal, and it was getting out of hand. Ben bucked and twisted with an animal frenzy, unsaddling Jacob and scrabbling to his feet.

'It wasn't me, OK? And it wasn't your stuff, you stole it!'

Jacob snatched up a broken branch and advanced on Ben, wielding it like a club. 'Admit it.' He swung the branch, forcing Ben back towards the water's edge.

'No.'

'Admit it.' Another swing of the branch. 'It was you.'

Ben might have admitted it if the next time Jacob swung the branch it hadn't missed his face by only a few inches. He pounced, driven by a sudden rage, catching Jacob off guard, off balance, seizing his wrist and spinning him round so that he went stumbling back towards the lake. His heels caught in the mud and he toppled into the water.

Time to go. But as he turned to flee he saw Clive Bishop step from the trees. Campbell was with him.

'Guys, guys,' said Bishop. 'The flares went up. Didn't you see them?'

Their arrival broke the spell. There was surrender in the slope of Jacob's shoulders as he stumbled dripping from the lake, the branch still in his hand. Campbell snatched it from him and hurled it far into the lake. 'No weapons, cheat.'

'Don't call me a cheat.'

'Why not, cheat?

Jacob shoved him away. 'It was just a bit of fun.'

'Liar,' said Ben. 'Liar. Cheat. Thief.' He levelled an accusing finger at Jacob. 'He's the one. He's the thief.'

one day to go . . .

A BIG CHEER went up as the sculpture touched down on the concrete. It wouldn't be possible to make adjustments once the lorry and its hydraulic crane were gone, so Victor and Mo examined it from a number of different angles to check the alignment. They even wandered off down to the water's edge to view it from there. Ben didn't get involved. It was their moment, patron and artist together.

The straps were finally removed and two bottles of vintage champagne were cracked open. The workmen were treated to a glass each. Even Marcio was offered a splash. He had kept himself scarce since Ben's return from London, but he now wandered up and asked after Toby. The boys had already been in touch on Facebook and Toby had told him about the death of Basil. It was a sweet gesture on Marcio's part, out of character, and Ben found himself feeling something of the same compassion for him that Toby had mentioned.

Victor tapped his glass against the sculpture then said a few words about Mo. He talked about the first time he'd seen her work, how of one of her heads had stopped him in his tracks, transfixing him with its stare. He couldn't say why exactly, and he hoped he would never be able to. The tribute was so flattering that someone asked if he was on commission.

'Only twenty per cent.'

'That's almost as much as you take off me every year,' exclaimed the bald man, who clearly wished to be identified as a high net worth individual.

Ben didn't laugh along with everyone else. He was looking at Victor and searching for signs of Jacob.

His instinct was to tell Mo everything, but it was only when he got her on her own after lunch that he realised why he couldn't.

What if he was wrong? He'd lose her forever. Paranoid and delusional weren't two qualities women generally searched for in men, except as character traits to be avoided at all costs. He remembered the look of abject pity in Madeleine's eyes just before she fled his flat.

Even if he was right, what good would a warning be to Mo?

Victor is out to destroy me. It's a course he's been set on for a while now, and you're a part of his plan whether you like it or not.

Why does Victor want to destroy you?

It's hard to explain, but I have a hunch.

Where's your evidence?

I don't have any, not yet, but it could be coming anytime soon.

No, whichever way the bones fell, this wasn't going to end well for him and Mo. Best to sit on his suspicions and enjoy their last few moments of normality.

Victor and Marcio left with the first of the quests. Marcio was booked on an evening flight back to Paris, and Victor was carrying on into London after dropping him off at Heathrow. He wouldn't be back until the following evening.

It was a relief; Ben was struggling to maintain any kind of front with him. He knew Victor could sense something was up. He saw it in the quick glance Victor fired at him as the Maserati pulled away.

Mo had a little weep when they wandered round her deserted studio. They were the tears of an empty-nester, a parent who'd just lost a child to the big wide world. He was surprised that it hadn't occurred to him before: her sculptures were the children she could never have.

'Don't freak out . . . actually, freak out if you want to, but I'm going to say it anyway.'

They were lying on her bed, fully clothed, just holding each other.

'I know,' she said.

'Oh? What was I going to say?'

'You love me.'

'Wrong.'

'I don't blame you. It's understandable.'

'God, Little Miss Full of Herself.'

'Little Miss Mind Reader.'

'Actually, I was going to say if you haven't heard a grass-hopper warbler by the time you're fifty you never will. The frequency of their song is too high for older ears.'

She smiled, kissed his neck and whispered in his ear, 'I love you too.'

THE TEXT WAS waiting for him when he returned from his morning run. He stared at it for a long while, wondering how four simple letters could pack so much punch: **Yes. R**

Relief blunted his anger. He wasn't going mad. The voices of doubt and doom scuttling about his head like incubi were in fact his allies, not his enemy.

Raffaella knew the Frenchman. And if Raffaella knew the Frenchman then he was entitled to each and every one of his suspicions, because it meant Victor had been messing with his life for more than three years.

'*Grazie*,' he muttered.

He owed her everything. '*Chi va piano . . .*' It all sprang from those few veiled words of warning. Without them he would only have some vague misgivings, not enough to make a difference. No, she'd given him back his life.

He was entitled to some of the credit. Mistakes had been made and he'd picked up on them. He thought back to the discovery of his postcode in the Maserati's satnav. Knowing what he now did, he could draw out the thread, examine it in its entirety.

Victor had indeed come snooping in the Maserati months ago. He was abroad when he realised Ben might spot the postcode, so he got somebody – probably Lance – to delete the data. Why didn't he just leave it at that, though? Why did he go out of his way to draw attention to it when he was back, when they were driving into Oxford together? 'That's strange, someone's deleted the history.'

Why bother to mention it?

Because he knew, somehow, that Ben had seen the postcode before it was deleted, and he wanted to divert suspicion away from himself.

It was the only explanation that made any sense, and there was only one conclusion to be drawn from it: Ben's internet activity had been monitored. Victor must have returned from his travels to find that he'd been checking up on the other destinations stored in the satnav.

Ben had happily entered the network key for the house's wi-fi on his arrival, but the truth was he had no idea what system he'd been plugged into all this time. Victor could easily have rigged things to track people's browsing. And why stop with the internet? Stoneham Park had been gutted then put back together as an 'intelligent house', with sophisticated media systems in every room and sensors that tracked your movements. How hard would it have been to wire the place for sound too? There were clearly microphones in Victor's study because Ben had found him strolling around it on a conference call. Maybe that's why Victor hadn't used local labour for the renovation: he didn't want people knowing the full extent of the surveillance system he'd installed.

They were only details, fringe pieces of the puzzle, but the point was they fitted now. Everything fitted. He saw clearly what he'd been feeling dimly for the past two weeks.

He looked at the text again. It wasn't information he could use, not without betraying Raffaella's trust, which he would never do. It didn't matter. Knowing the truth was enough. He didn't need to present his evidence.

He got the Colonel's number from directory inquiries and called it. Victor's cheque for £60,000 had cleared on Friday.

'It even got a mention in church yesterday. I've kept shtum, but everybody has a hunch who it's from, I'm afraid.' The Colonel invited Ben and Mo for drinks at his house later. 'I make a mean Tom Collins.'

'I can believe it.' He politely declined the offer, though. Tonight was not going to be a night for cocktails, that much was certain.

Sixty thousand pounds wouldn't hurt Victor, but at least it was something. What else was there? Fourteen thousand pounds of fully-kitted BMW motorcycle, and the money he'd already received for the rewrite. That was about the sum total of Victor's downside. Or maybe not. Maybe Tortoise Pictures was a front, a device to lure him back into his life. That must have come with a hefty price tag – the fancy offices, the two salaries – but it was still peanuts for Victor in the grand scheme of things.

The script was dead and gone. It would never get made.

Then again, it was never going to get made from the moment Victor acquired the underlying rights. The offer to buy up his other ideas was probably part of the same plan – to strip him of all his assets. Thank God he hadn't signed the paperwork yet.

While showering, his anger built to a howling rage. It owed as much to frustration as anything. He was hamstrung. There could be no real retribution. A sociopath with deep pockets was a formidable enemy, almost invulnerable, and even if you walked away there was nothing to stop him coming after you again. Maybe the best revenge was to stay silent, play along, take Victor for as much as possible then get out before he could administer the coup de grâce. It had all been too carefully plotted for Victor not to have worked out some sick finale, some ultimate humiliation for him.

Well, at the very least, he could deny Victor that satisfaction. He was ahead of the game for once. He held the initiative. He could rewrite the ending.

Lying naked on the giant Jacobean bed, he began to see what he would do and how he would do it.

He reached for his phone and called the Colonel back.

Mo was in her kitchen, waiting for the kettle to come to the boil. She'd only just got up and she wasn't in the best of moods. He had kept her awake with his tossing and turning last night.

He kissed her and told her to go back to bed. He had to shoot off to London, anyway. The woman who lived below his flat had just called to say he had some kind of leak and it was soaking her ceiling with water.

'Do you want company?'

'Don't bother. If it's major, it'll just mean hanging around for a plumber to show up and rip me off.'

A little note of humour to add texture to the lie.

He took the Range Rover Evoque for a change; it was probably his last opportunity ever to drive one of the things. It didn't disappoint, whisking him effortlessly into town. An hour and a half later, while he was searching for a parking space in Knightsbridge, Edwin phoned. He was in raptures, having spent most of the weekend in bed with Finola.

'Has she mentioned babies yet?'

'Turns out she's already got one of the little buggers and doesn't want any more.'

'You know what? I can see it.'

'Yeah, me too. For real this time.'

He knew Edwin meant it because he offered no intimate sexual details whatsoever. Despite his euphoria, Edwin hadn't forgotten their conversation.

'Listen, I called a mate who knows what's what – *branché*, as my dull-as-fuck Swiss colleagues like to say. You were right about that Brazilian mining thing Quercus got skewered on. Sheldon was involved – well, sniffing around it at one time. Word got out, everyone piled in, but Sheldon had already struck camp.'

'How does word get out? I mean, could Sheldon have made sure Quercus got to hear?'

'Of course. Child. You think the City rumour mill runs itself?'

'Edwin, I don't know the first fucking thing about your world, OK? All I'm doing is asking.'

'Why?'

Ben hesitated. 'I can't tell you. Not yet. And I need your word you won't ever mention this to Mads. I mean, never.'

'Sure.'

'I need your word.'

'What is this, the nineteenth century? Pistols at dawn? What the fuck, Ben?'

'Your word.'

There was a brief silence. 'You have my word. OK, arsehole?'

'Thanks,' said Ben. 'For everything.'

It confirmed what he already suspected: that Victor, as in all things, had covered his tracks far too well for a case ever to be brought against him. It also confirmed that the course he was now set on was the only one open to him.

He had visited the shop only once before, when doing research for the script formerly known as *Gangs on an Island*. He still remembered the name of the scrawny young man who had patiently talked him through their many gadgets and gizmos. Roger had no recollection of him, but it made him no less obliging.

It was all arranged. Ben had billed it as a surprise to Mo and Annabelle. More importantly, the Colonel seemed to believe that he had hatched the idea himself: a discreet gathering of five people, drinks in his back garden by way of thanks for the man whose extraordinary generosity had topped off the church appeal. Even Lance was in on it. Annabelle had been in touch with him to establish exactly when Victor would be delivered back to Stoneham Park.

The plan, ostensibly, was that Ben would wait for Victor to return home then invent some excuse to drag him into Stoneham, to the Colonel's cottage, where Annabelle and Mo would be waiting with their host to greet him.

Annabelle hadn't been without her misgivings – 'Mr Sheldon's not the sort of man who does surprises' – but he had talked her round to 'the Colonel's idea'. There was no harm in indulging the old boy; Victor would understand.

He didn't dwell too much on what he was doing; he just hoped that the lies would make sense to them all later.

Lance called Annabelle from central London at around five o'clock. Their ETA was six forty-five, traffic permitting.

Annabelle and Mo left for the village just before six thirty.

'And you're sure you've got your phone with you?'

'Yes,' sighed Mo wearily, producing it from her pocket this time as proof.

'I'll text you when I'm leaving the house.'

'I know. And we'll all dance a jig when you show up with him.'

Her smile cut right through him, because he knew that after tonight she would never again be able to produce one quite like it for him.

Victor followed the same routine as he did every evening, dumping his attaché case in his study before wandering through to the kitchen for a glass of wine.

Ben was waiting for him. 'Good day at the office, darling?'

Victor smiled. 'Not bad. Where is everyone?'

'Mo and Annabelle are still in Oxford, and Gregoire's already made dinner.' He nodded to the big pot standing beside the stove. 'Thai curry. It just needs to be heated up.'

Victor suggested a visit to Mo's sculpture. 'I've been thinking about it all day.'

Ben was happy to go along with him. It made no difference where it happened.

They took their wine glasses with them, and they were making their way along the lake shore when Victor said, 'I've been meaning to ask, have you told your parents we're back in touch?'

'No.'

'Why not?'

'Honestly?'

'Or dishonestly if you prefer.'

'I don't know,' said Ben. 'You've gone to a lot of trouble to reinvent yourself, break with your past, changing your name and so on. I wasn't sure you'd want them to know.'

'And honestly?' asked Victor.

'I can't face my father bleating on about it, about you. You've achieved everything he wanted for me.'

'That's very honest of you.'

Ben shrugged. 'The truth is I'm not like the two of you. I don't have the ambition, the hunger.'

'You used to.'

'I guess.'

Ben glanced at his phone, as if checking it for messages.

What he really did was fire off the text he'd written to Mo earlier but not sent: **Dial the number below and just listen. X**

There, it was done. The endgame was afoot.

'I've been thinking about the job, the foundation.'

'You've had some ideas?' asked Victor.

'Just the one. I'm not going to do it.'

'You're not going to do it?'

'I've changed my mind.'

Victor almost laughed. 'You're saying no to eight million pounds?'

'Uh-huh.'

'You want more?'

'No. I'm just not cut out for juggling two things at once.'

They walked on a way in silence.

'I've got to say, I'm surprised. And disappointed.'

'You'll get over it,' said Ben.

He'd been thinking about it all day, but he hadn't imagined it might actually be enjoyable.

'I wouldn't be too sure about that,' replied Victor tightly.

'Oooh, that sounds ominous.' He gave Victor a matey slap on the back. 'Come on, cheer up, we'll still have the film work. We'll turn Tortoise into one of the hottest outfits in town. I know which of my ideas I'm going to write out next. Go on, have a guess.'

Victor shook his head. 'I'm sorry, I'm still reeling.'

'Hey, no reeling allowed. It's a beautiful evening, we've got wine, there's a warm wind, we're going to see Mo's sculpture. Look, there it is, through the trees there.'

Victor was almost trembling with the violent effort to control himself. 'No one walks away from eight million pounds.'

It was time to turn up the heat.

'They do if they know they were never going to see a penny of it anyway.'

'What?' snorted Victor.

'You heard.'

'You're losing me.'

'No, I'm not. You're wondering how I know, or whether I'm bluffing. What do you reckon? Am I bluffing?'

'This is a joke, right?'

'You can drop the act. I know it's bullshit, all of it – the films, the job, the friendship. You're screwing with my life, setting me up for a fall.'

'I'd stop now if I were you, before it's too late.'

'It's already too late. I just have one question: how fucked up does a person have to be to bear a grudge for thirty years, Jacob?'

The path through the trees gave way to the clearing. They instinctively drew apart, putting a bit of distance between themselves.

'It's over,' said Ben.

Victor was a cautious man. He approached Mo's sculpture and ran a hand over the stone, an excuse to check behind its massive bulk. He also glanced around him before speaking.

'It's not over till I say it's over.'

It was chilling to see the change in him. His whole body seemed to relax as the pretence of the past weeks left him. He even worked a kink out of his neck.

'I mean it. It's not over.'

'No, I don't suppose it is. Just leave Madeleine and Toby out of it.'

'It's a little late for that.'

'I know. You sucked Lionel into a deal that's bankrupted him.'

Victor tilted his head at him. 'I'm impressed. Have you figured out why?'

'Let me see . . . Could it possibly be because you're a sick fuck?'

'That doesn't do justice to the beauty of it. I wanted to see what Madeleine would do, what *you* would do when she came running back to you, which one of them you'd choose, her or Mo.' He paused before adding, 'Your ex-wife's a very predictable woman.'

'Meaning?'

'Meaning you're not as smart as you think you are.'

Thoughts of Raffaella flashed through his mind, but he was safe to say it without compromising her. 'The Frenchman in Amiens. Yes, I wondered about him.'

That surprised Victor. 'I've underestimated you.'

'Praise indeed from the grand puppeteer. Do you have any idea how pathetic you are? All this because of a schoolboy spat?'

'Spat!? You changed the direction of my life. I want you to know how it feels.'

He wasn't going to allow Victor even the smallest sliver of satisfaction. 'All I did was expose you for the thief you were.'

'After swearing you wouldn't!'

'You attacked me. My blood was up. And it's not like you were expelled. None of the teachers got to hear.'

'But the boys did. *Fingers* . . . even the juniors whispered it in the corridors when I walked past. You think I could stay in England after that? It would have followed me to the next school, to Ardingly. Fingers Hogg.'

This was a surprise to Ben. He'd always been led to believe that Jacob's parents had changed their minds and yanked him back to the States. 'That's why you went back?'

'To them. To hell. Thanks to you.'

'Here's a thought, take it or leave it. None of this would have happened if you hadn't stolen off other people in the first place.'

Victor came straight back at him. 'Here's another thought. We were friends. You should have been more compassionate, knowing what you did.'

'Knowing what I did?'

'My diary. The one you read.'

'I never read it.'

Ben realised too late it was the wrong thing to say. He should have said, what diary?

Victor gave a satisfied smile. 'Ah, the truth at last. It *was* you who handed the stuff in to Burroughs.'

'I never read the diary. I swear to God.'

'The same God you didn't believe in even back then? No, you knew about Mr Jobson.'

'Mr Jobson . . .?'

What did Mr Jobson have to do with anything? The balance

of power seemed suddenly to have swung in Victor's favour, and Ben's confusion wasn't helping matters.

'That's good,' said Victor. 'Almost convincing.'

'I never read the diary. I dumped it in one of the bins out the back of the kitchen.'

'Liar.'

They had been circling each other warily. Victor now turned and stalked off towards a bunch of tools propped against a tree. There were shovels, and picks, an axe and a crowbar, but it was the sledgehammer he selected.

Not much of a weapon, thought Ben – too heavy, too unwieldy, easy to dodge. It wasn't intended for him, though. Victor advanced on Mo's sculpture.

He was too slow to react, freezing in his tracks as Victor raised the sledgehammer above his shoulder.

'Don't you dare!' snapped Ben.

'The knight comes to the defence of his maiden. How touching. Do you want to know what your maiden was doing in London last week? Fucking Connor. That's right. They spent two hours in his hotel room. I couldn't help noticing she was a bit frosty with you that night . . . or maybe she was just sore.'

It made sense – Mo had messed up the names of the girl-friend she was supposedly having lunch with. It was a while before he found his voice. 'You bastard.'

'Hey, I just had her followed, I didn't make her do it. That was her choice.' Victor had rested the sledgehammer against his shoulder, but now raised it again as Ben advanced. 'One more step and I'll do it, you know I will.'

'What do you want from me?'

'The truth. I want to hear you admit it. You knew about Jobson and you still went and shopped me as a thief.'

'I'm sorry,' said Ben.

'I knew it,' spat Victor with disgust.

'No — sorry for you. I read the opening of the diary. I can't remember what you wrote, but it was about me, and it hurt, and it was enough. I never read the rest of it, but I can guess what it said now.'

Victor shook his head. 'No, you knew. You knew why I started stealing. You knew what it was really about. You knew what he was doing to me.'

Ben nodded at Mo's giant head. 'Go ahead, smash the sculpture. I hope it makes you feel better. I doubt it will. And there's nothing I can do to help, because you're wrong. I didn't know.'

And with that he turned on his heel and walked away. He heard the thud of the sledgehammer hitting the ground. He didn't hear the footfalls until it was too late.

Victor slammed into him from behind, sending him crashing forward on to his face. He felt something go in his wrist as he tried to break his fall, but any pain was quickly lost in the hail of kicks which Victor now began to administer to his stomach, his chest, his back, even his head.

Lying curled in a foetal ball, some atavistic impulse warned him that if he didn't do something, and quickly, he would die right there, stamped and kicked to death. He gave a wild cry and lashed out with all his limbs, rolling, rolling away now.

The kick was aimed at his head but he deflected it on to his shoulder and scrabbled to his feet. When Victor came at him again, he swung his fist. It made satisfying contact with Victor's jaw, jerking his head round and momentarily buckling his knees. Ben didn't wait. He went in with both fists, flailing wildly but focusing on the head. When he saw blood, he hesitated. It was a mistake. Victor charged him, bringing him down.

He felt fingers groping for his eyes — his eyes! — and he retaliated with his teeth, sinking them into Victor's wrist, tasting the salty tang of blood.

He wasn't sure if the cries were his or Victor's. He only realised they belonged to neither of them when Mo and Annabelle started beating them, pulling at them, trying to separate them.

'Stop it! Stop it!' yelled Annabelle. 'Stop it!'

They didn't, not immediately, not until each of them had landed one last blow they were happy with. Victor was first to his feet. His cheek was smeared with blood from a cut above his right eye.

'Stupid, stupid men!' snapped Annabelle.

'Go and get Lance,' Victor ordered in a tremulous voice. 'He accused me of a whole load of nonsense then attacked me.'

Annabelle didn't move.

'I said, go and get Lance.'

'I heard,' replied Annabelle. 'I heard everything.'

Made of black plastic, it was slightly larger than a box of matches. It had been in the breast pocket of Ben's shirt but was now lying on the ground nearby.

Ben picked it up. 'Know what this is? You should. It's in

the script. It's a GSM transmitter.' He could see the realisation dawning across Victor's face. 'That's right, they really exist, I didn't make it up. This one's top of the range: five hundred and sixty quid plus VAT. Oh, and a tenner for the SIM card.'

He didn't have to say any more. It was a key plot device he'd used near the end of the story. You simply dialled the number and listened in. The text he'd sent to Mo earlier had told her to do just that.

'Here, you can have it.' He tossed the transmitter to Victor. 'A case of art informing life.'

'Art?' scoffed Victor.

'I for irony. We both know the script's a piece of shit.'

It wasn't perfect, but it had worked. It was certainly the most he was ever going to get out of the situation. Victor had been too smart, too thorough, to leave any meaningful trail; Ben had just needed to find a way for those who mattered to hear it from the horse's mouth . . .

Mo was staring at Victor, her face twisted in contempt. She now walked over to her sculpture and examined it closely, running a hand over its features. She turned away, picked up the discarded sledgehammer and in the same movement spun back and landed a mighty blow.

The nose disintegrated.

Mo let the sledgehammer fall from her hands.

She didn't look at Victor as she passed him, but she did speak. 'I knew there was something.'

Ben glanced at Victor then followed Mo towards the house.

fifteen days later . . .

ANNABELLE HAD LEFT the choice of restaurant to Ben. He had picked an Italian place on Elizabeth Street, low-key and not too pricey. He made a point of getting there early, only to find Annabelle already seated at the table with a glass of wine.

She looked exhausted and he told her so.

'It hasn't been an easy couple of weeks.'

It was the only nod to what they'd both been through until they'd ordered.

She asked him if he'd heard from Mo.

'Not since she went back up north. You?'

Annabelle shook her head. 'They were together for a very long time. You mustn't hold it against her, Ben.'

'I don't. I told her that, but she still left.'

'Maybe she just needs some time to think.'

'Maybe.' He didn't admit that he'd given up on that thought, resigning himself to an agony of emptiness. 'Does Victor know you're here?'

'Yes.'

'Does he mind?'

'Probably. He didn't say anything. He's gone very silent in the last few days.'

'How can you . . .?' His words trailed off.

'Stand by him?' She glanced away briefly. 'I'm all he's got. And someone's got to keep the caravan rolling. Talking of which . . .'

She produced her notebook from her bag and opened it. There were a number of items written down.

Ben smiled. 'You and your lists.'

'Don't mock. I've had to work hard on this one.'

First up was the BMW motorcycle, which Annabelle had arranged to be delivered to Ben next week.

'You'll have to put it back,' he said. 'I'm on holiday with Toby next week.'

'Oh, where are you going?'

'Surf camp in Morocco.'

Next on the list was the delivery payment on the rewrite, which she had just sent through to the agency.

'But I'm never going to finish it. I'm not sure I could even look at it again.'

Annabelle put a tick next to it anyway. 'Just take what you can,' she said matter-of-factly. 'Number three: Colonel Armitage sends his best wishes. Despite you ruining his drinks party, he hopes to hear from you sometime soon.'

Ben could see that the remaining item consisted of one word: *Quercus*.

'It's not a done deal, not yet, but I think Lionel will get all his money back.'

Ben was stunned. 'How . . .?'

'Let's just say I know enough about Mr Sheldon to do him some harm. Lionel must never know. He doesn't need to. It's being arranged through Brazil. It'll look like a contractual error, a get-out-of-jail clause.'

Ben reached across the table and squeezed her hand. 'Thank you, Annabelle.'

She shrugged. 'Like I told you once, we old spinsters have our uses.'

He wondered if this was the real reason she'd stayed on, to make amends, to right the wrongs Victor had committed.

They talked about the many things that had happened, but the subject of Mr Jobson didn't come up until they were well into their main courses.

'I got him to talk about it, not in any great depth, admittedly.'

It still made for painful listening. Jacob had kept a secret hoard of his own things up in the attic since his arrival at Dean House. In his second year, he had been caught up there by Mr Jobson, who had threatened him with all kinds of horrors, including expulsion. It was a ploy to bend Jacob to his own sick ends, of course, and once it had started there was no stopping it.

'I suppose the stealing was some sort of cry for help.'

'Oh, God,' Ben muttered.

'What?'

He couldn't bring himself to say it, that his mother had methodically rifled through Jacob's suitcase at the end of every half-term and exeat, ignoring the signs he was flinging in her face, never once confronting him. Had she known, maybe guessed? It was too awful to think about, let alone voice.

'I could have done things differently. Maybe I should have. But I swear I never knew about Mr Jobson. I never read that diary.'

'I'm not sure you'll ever be able to persuade him of that.'

'It's the truth.'

'And I believe you, but you can't expect him to. Think what it would mean for him – that everything he's done to you was done in error, based on a misunderstanding.'

'Yeah, well, maybe he should have thought about that before doing it. Maybe he should have taken it out on Jobson instead. Maybe he did and we just don't know it.'

'I've looked into it. Mr Jobson died in Aldeburgh twenty-two years ago from natural causes.'

'Aldeburgh?'

'Yes, why?'

Ben shook his head as if to say, it's nothing.

He sat back in his chair and studied Annabelle. 'He destroyed my marriage and he came back to finish me off. God knows what he had in store for me, but it wouldn't have been pretty, you can be sure of that. Don't expect me to feel sympathy.'

'I don't.'

He had thought about it a lot recently, playing the scene over and over in his head, and despite the fierce hatred still burning him up it seemed only fair to let her know. He described in detail the sledging incident on the South Downs when they were younger, how Jacob had careered off the track but miraculously avoided being skewered by the sapling stumps.

'He knew they were there under the snow. I warned him.'

'What are you getting at?'

'He said something to me, when Toby and Marcio were staying. It didn't make sense at the time. He said he did it on purpose – steered the sledge off the track.'

Annabelle held his gaze. 'Don't worry, I'm keeping a very close eye on him. We all are.'

They parted company on the street out front. Ben hailed her a taxi, and as it was pulling in, Annabelle said, 'Send my love to Toby.'

'I will.'

'He's a very special boy. Look after him.' She stooped to talk to the cabbie. 'Marylebone Station, please.'

Ben opened the door for her. 'Goodbye, Annabelle.'

'Goodbye, Ben. I'll be in touch.' She pecked him on the cheek and dipped inside the taxi.

He stood and watched her disappear in the direction of Eaton Square, heading off to keep the caravan rolling. No, not a caravan, more like Mother Courage's wagon, trundling aimlessly along, drawing an ever-changing cast of grotesques. He had been a passenger for a while, long enough to lose sight of himself, but he had survived his stint aboard and was no worse off than before, just bruised and a bit wiser about the world. And maybe a bit more alive – yes, as if he'd been shaken awake.

He waited until the taxi was lost to view before turning and heading south on Elizabeth Street, already mapping out the route home in his mind. He would walk it, walk off his lunch.

His phone rang a few minutes later as he was cutting through Ebury Square. He answered without checking who it was.

'Hi, it's me.'

The sound of her voice stopped him dead in his tracks and sucked the air from his lungs. He only just managed to produce a response.

'Hi.'

'I thought I'd call.'

He smiled at the sublime pointlessness of the remark. 'Yeah, I'd figured that.'

'Is it a bad time?'

'No, no.'

'Where are you?' asked Mo.

'Out and about.'

'Where exactly?'

'Ebury Square.'

'That's weird.'

'Why? Where are you?'

'Ebury Square,' she replied.

He spun round. She was standing not even twenty feet away in jeans and a dark blue Lacoste polo shirt. Had she ever looked more beautiful?

'Stalker,' he said into his phone. 'I should put the cops on you . . . you *and* your accomplice.'

Mo dropped her phone into her shoulder bag and approached. 'It's not Annabelle's fault. I made her tell me.'

'Why?'

'I wanted to see you . . . look at you . . . from a distance. I hadn't worked it out after that, thought I'd go with my gut. How are you?'

'Oh, you know . . . tip-top.'

'You look thin.'

'You look fucking amazing. I like the hair.'

She ran her fingers through it. 'Not much of it left.'

'Symbolic chop?'

'Something like that.' She moved a little closer, close enough to touch. 'I got your text.'

'Oh.'

'I don't surf.'

'That's the point of surf camp.'

'Still, doesn't sound like my cup of tea.'

'That's because you don't know about the yoga and meditation classes.'

'Oh, God,' she groaned. 'Tell me you're joking.'

'There's also a day trip to Fez on offer.'

'Why the hell would I want to go to Fez?'

'To buy a hat, of course.'

She smiled. 'Of course. Silly me.'

notes on school days

THE PRESENT DAY narrative in *The Long Shadow* is broken up with chapters detailing Ben and Victor's childhood experiences at a boys' boarding prep school. Having been packed off to such a place at the age of eight, I drew to a large degree on my own memories when writing these passages. With hindsight, it's clear to me now that my own school was fairly liberal by the standards of the time (the 1970s); we were effectively allowed to run merry riot through the extensive grounds, which, like Dean House in the novel, incorporated a huge swathe of wild woodland, with lakes and quarries and a river running through it. For all the fun – and there was a fair amount of it – my ambivalence towards those years hasn't dimmed with time.

I never fully adjusted to being interned so far away from home at such a young age; I learned to cope with it; we all did, losing ourselves in a blitz of sports and clubs and gangs and sad little stabs at authority, which worked well enough most of the time. But forty years on, the wrench of returning to school after a weekend at home is a feeling I can still summon up all too easily from somewhere deep in my gut. In many ways, this notion sits at the heart of the novel, although Victor is haunted by memories far darker and more enduring than any I carry with me.

my top ten novels

1. *Lord of the Flies* – William Golding
Man's savagery to man played out with children.

2. *Stoner* – John Williams
A complex, moving and beautifully written portrait of one man's life.

3. *The Great Gatsby* – F. Scott Fitzgerald
Contains one of my favourite lines (and themes) in literature: *So we beat on, boats against the current, drawn back ceaselessly into the past.*

4. *Ethan Frome* – Edith Wharton
As bizarre a love story as you're ever likely to read.

5. *Catch-22* – Joseph Heller
Heller's darkly humorous take on war in Italy.

6. *The Good Soldier* – Ford Madox Ford
Ford takes his scalpel to the loves and lies of two Edwardian couples.

7. *Jude the Obscure* – Thomas Hardy
A sometimes harrowing account of Jude Fawley's dogged pursuit of his dreams.

8. *Disgrace* – J.M. Coetzee
Exquisite tension between Coetzee's spare prose and the book's massive themes.

9. *Victory* – Joseph Conrad
As ever with Conrad, Good and Evil do battle – on a small island in the Malay Archipelago this time.

10. *To Kill a Mocking Bird* – Harper Lee
Racial injustice in the Deep South as seen through the eyes of a child. Remarkably, the only novel she ever published.